FRANCINE PA

Château D'Amour
Collection

including

ONCE UPON A TIME
TO CATCH A THIEF
HAPPILY EVER AFTER

SWEET VALLEY HIGH
CHATEAU D'AMOUR COLLECTION
A BANTAM BOOK : 0 553 81279 3

Individual titles originally published in USA by Bantam Books
First published in Great Britain as individual titles in 1997
Collection first published in Great Britain

PRINTING HISTORY
Bantam Collection published 1999

Copyright © 1999 by Francine Pascal

including

ONCE UPON A TIME
First published in Great Britain, 1997
Copyright © 1996 by Francine Pascal

TO CATCH A THIEF
First published in Great Britain, 1997
Copyright © 1996 by Francine Pascal

HAPPILY EVER AFTER
First published in Great Britain, 1997
Copyright © 1996 by Francine Pascal

The trademarks "Sweet Valley" and "Sweet Valley High" are
owned by Francine Pascal and are used under license by
Bantam Books and Transworld Publishers Ltd.

Conceived by Francine Pascal

Produced by Daniel Weiss Associates, Inc,
33 West 17th Street, New York, NY 10011

All rights reserved.

Cover photo by Oliver Hunter
Cover photo of twins © 1994, 1995, 1996 Saban – All Rights Reserved.

Bantam Books are published by Transworld Publishers Ltd,
61–63 Uxbridge Road, Ealing, London W5 5SA,
in Australia by Transworld Publishers, c/o Random House
Australia Pty Ltd, 20 Alfred Street, Milsons Point, NSW 2061, Australia,
and in New Zealand by Transworld Publishers, c/o Random House
New Zealand, 18 Poland Road, Glenfield, Auckland, New Zealand.

Printed and bound in Great Britain by
Cox & Wyman Ltd, Reading, Berkshire.

ONCE UPON
A TIME

Written by
Kate William

Created by
FRANCINE PASCAL

BANTAM BOOKS
NEW YORK · TORONTO · LONDON · SYDNEY · AUCKLAND

To Chris Moustakis

Chapter 1

"Shampoo, conditioner, soap," sixteen-year-old Elizabeth Wakefield muttered to herself on Friday evening, throwing the last of her toiletries into her pink floral travel case.

She and her twin sister, Jessica, were leaving in the morning for the South of France, where they were spending the summer as au pairs for a royal European family. Jessica's best friend, Lila Fowler, was throwing a big going-away bash for the twins that evening, so they had to be ready to go before they left for the party.

Elizabeth put her hands on her hips and surveyed her bedroom. A large blue suitcase was packed and standing by the door, and her backpack was full to bursting. Her cream-colored room was neat and orderly. She had put away all her schoolbooks, and she had left a new message on her answering machine with her summer phone number. Everything seemed to be in order.

Elizabeth quickly performed a mental list, ticking off items in her mind. *Passport. Plane ticket. Traveler's checks. Journal.* Apparently she was all set to go. But still a nagging thought was bothering her. She felt as if she were forgetting something. What was it?

Then it hit her. *Todd.* She walked over to her dresser and tenderly picked up the framed photograph of her longtime boyfriend, Todd Wilkins.

Elizabeth gazed at the portrait of her handsome boyfriend. He was wearing his red Gladiators basketball jersey and a navy blue visor pulled low over his forehead. A few dark brown curls peeked out from underneath the cap, and his deep, coffee-colored brown eyes smiled at her warmly from the photo.

Elizabeth's heart fluttered as she read the words scrawled at the bottom. *To my good luck charm,* Todd had written. Elizabeth remembered exactly when she had taken the picture. It was the night of the championship basketball game in the fall, when Todd had scored the winning basket. "I couldn't have done it without you," he had whispered in her ear after the game. "You were my inspiration."

A sharp pang of regret hit Elizabeth. The thought of leaving Todd for so long was heartbreaking. They were going to be separated for a whole month, and it would be too expensive to make phone calls. And impossible to make weekend visits.

Elizabeth's chest tightened as she thought of

her upcoming separation from her boyfriend. She wondered if she'd have even a moment alone with Todd at Fowler Crest, Lila's father's mansion. She and Todd were sure to be surrounded by their friends all night.

Well, I'll just have to take him away from all that, Elizabeth decided as she slipped Todd's picture into the inside pocket of her shoulder bag. She resolved to leave Lila's party early and whisk Todd away to Miller's Point for a more private farewell. Miller's Point was a popular parking spot overlooking Sweet Valley, and it was Elizabeth and Todd's favorite place to go when they wanted to be alone.

Elizabeth sank down onto her bed. Tonight would be the last night that they would get to enjoy the beautiful view together. "It's going to be a long summer," she whispered wistfully.

Suddenly the door to the bathroom adjoining the twins' rooms flew open, and Jessica breezed in. Elizabeth looked up, startled.

Jessica bounded into the room, her whole body bursting with energy. She looked glamorous and sexy in a long, deep red cotton skirt with a cream-colored Lycra T-shirt. Her golden blond hair was swept up on her head, one long lock twisted into a curl over her forehead. Her blue-green eyes sparkled dramatically, and her cheeks were flushed pink with excitement.

Jessica put her hands on her hips. "Aren't you ready yet?" she demanded. "Lila said to come over around seven-thirty."

3

Elizabeth smiled wryly. Jessica was perpetually late, a quality that she tended to justify on the grounds that the party didn't start until she got there. "Since when are you concerned about the time?" Elizabeth asked.

"Since I'm the guest of honor—along with you, of course," Jessica replied. She picked up a compact disk from Elizabeth's bookshelf and spun it around on her index finger. "And if you don't hurry up, we're going to miss all the fun." The CD spun off Jessica's finger and sailed across the room. It hit the far wall and fell onto the bed.

"Jes-si-ca!" Elizabeth moaned, retrieving the CD and quickly putting it back in its case.

Now Jessica was rummaging around in Elizabeth's backpack. She pulled out a pair of rose-tinted sunglasses and pushed them up on her forehead. Then she began dancing around the room in an imitation of a waltz, singing an Edith Piaf song. Ever since Jessica had learned they were going to France, she had started to listen to French music obsessively even though she didn't understand the words.

"Quand il me prend dans ses bras, il me par-le tous bas, je vois la vie en ro-se," she crooned.

Elizabeth couldn't help laughing. "Hey, Jess, why don't you take some of that energy and use it to transport your hundred suitcases down the steps?"

"My bags! That's right!" Jessica ripped off the sunglasses and threw them back in Elizabeth's bag. Then she sped out the door.

4

Elizabeth shook her head as her hyperactive twin exited. Sometimes she couldn't believe she and Jessica were even related. Despite their identical appearance, from their sun-streaked blond hair to their aquamarine eyes to their slim, athletic figures, the girls couldn't be more different in character.

Jessica was thrilled to get away for the summer. There was nothing she liked better than change. Jessica went through boyfriends even faster than she went through social trends and clothing styles. If she sensed a moment of calm in Sweet Valley, Jessica was sure to stir things up. The cocaptain of the cheerleading squad and an active member of Pi Beta Alpha, the most exclusive sorority at Sweet Valley High, Jessica's energy was infectious. Whether on the sidelines of the football field, in the middle of the beach disco, or in the thick of the mall, Jessica always drew a crowd.

While Elizabeth had just as much energy as her sister, she directed it toward more internal pursuits. A staff writer for the *Oracle* and a straight-A student, Elizabeth had high aspirations to be a famous journalist one day. In her spare time she preferred quieter activities: taking a moonlight walk on the beach with Todd, going to a movie with her best friends, Enid Rollins and Maria Slater, or just sitting alone in the park, writing in her journal.

Unlike Jessica, Elizabeth hated it when her world was rocked. She had been looking forward to a peaceful, productive summer in which she could work on her writing and spend some quality time with Todd.

Elizabeth took one last look at the picture in her hand and her eyes narrowed in a scowl. "I can't believe I let Jessica talk me into taking this job," she grumbled to herself.

Recently their father had done some legal work for Children of the World, an international employment agency that specialized in educational and child care positions. One evening he had casually mentioned that an opening for an au pair position to the prince and princess de Sainte-Marie had suddenly become available. The royal family of a European principality was looking for somebody to take care of their children at their summer château on an island in the Mediterranean.

Jessica had nearly jumped out of her seat at the possibility of living with royalty, even though she didn't even know at the time what an au pair was.

"It's a fancy term for a live-in baby-sitter," Elizabeth had explained.

Her twin had remained undaunted. She had immediately put a plan into action with typical Jessica Wakefield energy and stubbornness. With lightning quick speed, she had gathered together an impressive portfolio, complete with a résumé, a cover letter, and letters of recommendation. A short time later she had been hired for the job. However, there had been one stipulation. Because Jessica was younger and less experienced than the family desired, the agency had to find a second girl to share the duties.

That's when Jessica began working on Elizabeth—begging, cajoling, and threatening to drive Elizabeth insane if she didn't agree to join her. "It'll be an adventure," Jessica had said. "We'll get to live in the South of France." "We'll be able to practice our French." "We'll learn all about a foreign culture."

After two weeks of nonstop pressure Elizabeth had finally given in. *I should have put my foot down from the start,* she told herself as she hugged Todd's photo to her chest. Not only would she be away from Todd and her friends for months, she would also be giving up a chance to work at *Flair* magazine over the summer. She had recently served as the assistant to the managing editor of the famous fashion magazine as part of a two-week internship program. The editorial board had been so impressed with her work that they had offered her a summer position.

Elizabeth heaved a sigh as she zipped her shoulder bag shut. Instead of working in the editorial department for a renowned magazine, she was going to spend the summer *baby-sitting* on some deserted island in a foreign country. *Why can't I ever say no to my twin?* she thought in disgust.

Frowning, Elizabeth hoisted her backpack over her shoulders and picked up her suitcase. After nudging open her bedroom door, she lugged her bag down the hall and carried it downstairs to the foyer.

Jessica was standing by the front door, jingling the keys to the Jeep. "It's about time!" she exclaimed.

Elizabeth stumbled over a duffel bag on the floor and quickly steadied herself. Her mouth dropped open as she took in Jessica's bags, which were stacked by the door. Jessica had filled up a five-piece floral set of luggage, plus a dress bag and an oversize backpack.

"You planning to move to France permanently?" Elizabeth asked.

"Sorry, no time for small talk," Jessica responded cheerfully, nudging the door open with her foot. "The party is about to begin!"

Elizabeth shook her head as Jessica took her firmly by the shoulders and steered her through the door.

"You and Liz certainly can draw a crowd," Amy Sutton remarked to Jessica at Fowler Crest later that evening. It was 10 P.M., and the party was in full motion. The Droids, a popular rock group from Sweet Valley High, were playing on a raised dais on the back patio. Everyone was dancing, laughing, eating, and obviously having a great time.

Jessica laughed. "That's nice of you to say, but I think we should give Lila credit for this fab turnout."

Lila *had* really outdone herself this time. Jessica's best friend was famous for throwing lavish parties, and this one was no exception. But then, any event at Fowler Crest was always magnificent. The white,

Spanish-style mansion was surrounded by plush, sculptured lawns with Olympic-size tennis courts and a sparkling fountain. The back patio, with its red clay tiles, hanging baskets of plants, and tall lemon trees, was the perfect example of California beauty.

But tonight Fowler Crest was even more extravagant than usual. The patio was decorated with fresh flowers, tropical plants, and citronella lanterns. An elegant buffet table was set up, and black-tailed waiters were walking around with platters of hors d'oeuvres. A big banner reading Bon Voyage, Jessica and Elizabeth! hung over the patio.

It looks like everybody *in the junior class showed up!* Jessica thought with satisfaction. Ronnie Edwards and Aaron Dallas were trying to throw Sandra Bacon and Jean West into the pool, and the girls were shouting with laughter. Maria Slater and Olivia Davidson were surrounded by a group of admiring guys by the refreshment table. And Penny Ayala, Enid Rollins, and Ken Matthews were doing a crazy line dance across the dance floor, which was drawing lots of laughs.

From the moment she had arrived, Jessica had barely been able to take a breath. Every time she turned, it seemed like somebody else wanted to wish her well.

Usually Jessica was thrilled with this kind of attention, but for some reason the party tonight left her flat. She shifted impatiently, wishing she were already on the plane to France.

9

"Ah! Jessica! *Zere* you are!" a familiar voice from behind her called.

Jessica turned to see Winston Egbert approaching.

"Oh, boy," Amy said with a groan. "Get a load of Winston."

Affectionately known as the class clown, Winston was looking particularly ridiculous that evening. He was wearing a French-cut tuxedo jacket with sleeves that were too short, revealing his knobby wrists. A black French beret was pulled low over Winston's left eye, and a baguette was tucked under his arm.

Winston made a low, sweeping bow when he reached them. *"Bonsoir,* mesdemoiselles," he greeted them in French.

Amy giggled. *"Bonsoir,* Winston."

"Monsieur Eg-berrrt, eef you pleez," Winston corrected her.

Jessica couldn't help laughing at Winston's exaggerated French accent. "Winston, you are such a geek," she said.

"I eve brought you end your lovely seester a pre-sent," Winston said. "Where eez your ozer alf?"

My other half? Jessica pondered. Now that she thought about it, she hadn't seen her twin for a while. She had noticed Elizabeth and Todd slip away from the crowd about an hour ago, and they hadn't reappeared since. "I think she and Todd snuck off together."

"Ahh, too bad!" Winston exclaimed. "Pleez give

10

Leez my best weeshes." He held out a small white box with a big red bow wrapped around it.

Jessica untied the bow and lifted off the lid. A tiny pin with a little green frog on it was nestled in a bed of tissue paper. She shook her head with a smile, holding up the pin for Amy to see. "Winston, you are too much."

"It eez a French frog," Winston explained in mock seriousness.

Jessica nodded. "Yeah, I got it," she said. "Thanks, Winston, it's lovely."

Just then Dana Larson, the lead singer of the Droids, spoke into the microphone. "Hey, everybody, I'd like to introduce a brand-new song. It's called 'Solid Ice.' We hope you like it!" The band broke into a funky blues beat, and the crowd roared enthusiastically.

"Hey, let's dance!" Winston exclaimed.

"You go ahead," Jessica said, waving him away.

Jessica watched pensively as Winston joined the crowd on the dance floor. She had been thrilled about this party, and it had turned out to be even better than she had imagined. But still, she felt somehow disappointed. She couldn't quite put her finger on the reason for it. After all, she was lucky. She had really great friends, and they had all turned out to say good-bye.

Jessica bit her lip. *Obviously I'm ready for a change*, she thought.

●   ●   ●

Elizabeth stood in Todd's arms on the Spanish-style veranda, gazing into the Fowlers' pool. The pool was filled with dozens of floating candles, which cast a melancholy yellow glow along the surface of the water. The tiny flickering lights seemed to reflect her somber mood.

Elizabeth leaned back against Todd's chest and pulled his arms tighter around her. "We won't get to spend much time at Baywater this summer," she said sadly. Baywater was a deserted strand of beach that had become Elizabeth and Todd's private haven. They often went there on summer nights for moonlight picnics.

"I know," Todd responded. "It's weird. In just twenty-four hours you're going to be staring out at the Mediterranean Sea."

Elizabeth sighed. The thought didn't excite her at all. Her chest felt tight, and she was on the verge of tears. She didn't know what had come over her, but ever since the au pair job had become a reality, all she could think about was Todd. *Maybe it takes a separation to make you realize how much you appreciate someone,* she thought.

"I wish I weren't going," Elizabeth declared.

Todd murmured in agreement.

Elizabeth turned and took both of Todd's hands in hers. She looked up into his familiar deep brown eyes, which gleamed warmly in the light of the candles, and her heart skipped a beat. "I love you, Todd," Elizabeth whispered in a throaty voice.

"I love you too," Todd said quickly.

"And I promise to write every single day," Elizabeth continued, feeling a tear come to her eye. "Maybe we can call each other a few times too."

Todd nodded, but his eyes darted away from her.

Elizabeth frowned and blinked back her tears. Todd seemed distinctly uncomfortable. In fact, he had been acting odd all evening. "Todd? Is something wrong?" she asked.

Todd coughed, but he shook his head quickly.

"OK, you don't have to write every day," Elizabeth joked. "You can write every *other* day." She laughed nervously, waiting for Todd to join in. But his expression remained serious.

Now Elizabeth was really concerned. "Todd, is there something you'd like to tell me?" Her breathing quickened.

Todd swallowed hard and glanced away. "Yeah," he muttered. "There is." He took a deep breath and stared at the ground.

After a moment's silence Todd cleared his throat. "Elizabeth, we need to talk."

"Having fun, Jess?" Lila asked, heading up to Jessica with a plate of appetizers in her hand. Lila looked particularly elegant in a loose-fitting black silk pantsuit. The jacket tapered in at the waist, and the pant legs flared out at the ankles. Her long brown hair was tied back at the nape of her neck with a wine-colored silk scarf.

Jessica shrugged. "The party is nice."

"*Nice?*" Lila echoed, obviously miffed at the bland praise.

"It's a fantastic party," Jessica amended.

"That's better." Lila sniffed. She picked up a cheese-filled pastry puff and popped it into her mouth. "Mmm," she murmured appreciatively. Then she held her plate out to Jessica. "Want one?" she offered.

Jessica shook her head. "No, I don't have much of an appetite."

Lila shrugged and jabbed her fork into a stuffed mushroom. "What's *with* you tonight?"

"I just can't wait to get out of Sweet Valley," Jessica explained. "I feel like I've been dancing with the same ten cute guys my whole life."

Lila sighed. "I know what you mean. Every year this school seems to get smaller and smaller." She lifted her fork and took a bite of the mushroom.

"That's exactly it!" Jessica agreed. "We've been around here for too long. It's time for a change." She smiled, feeling excited again. "I know France is going to be absolutely wonderful."

Lila shook her head. "I wouldn't get your hopes up, Jess. It may sound exotic, but Europe isn't that different from America. I've been to France a hundred times. Guys there are like guys everywhere— fun for a while, but ultimately disappointing."

Jessica knew that her friend's attitude had a lot to do with her frustration with her current

14

boyfriend, Bo Creighton, a guy she had met while she and Jessica had been junior counselors at Camp Echo Mountain, a performing arts camp in the mountains of Montana.

Bo was a cute guy from a wealthy D.C. family, and Lila had fallen head over heels in love with him. They had been inseparable at camp and had even managed to keep up a long-distance relationship for a few months. But Bo's calls and letters had started to drop off, and Lila was getting discouraged.

Jessica shrugged. "You can be as negative as you want," she replied. "But I plan to fall in love with a prince and have the time of my life."

"I hate to break it to you, but you won't be in much of a position to find a prince," Lila remarked. "You're going to be cooped up with a bunch of royal European brats." Lila brushed back an errant strand of hair with a carefully manicured nail. "Being an au pair is *not* glamorous."

Jessica smiled, but she didn't say anything. She wasn't about to let Lila spoil a single moment of her anticipation. This was going to be a summer she'd never forget. She could feel it in her bones.

Elizabeth's heart fluttered nervously as Todd led her to a bench under a huge oak tree on the Fowlers' landscaped grounds. A light wind whistled gently through the leaves, and she could hear the faint sounds of the party in the distance.

Todd sat down and faced her, his face pale.

"Well, I . . . *uh* . . ." He coughed. "I've been thinking. . . ." Todd's voice trailed off, and he stood up. Then he walked in a small circle and sat down again.

Elizabeth's heart began pounding in alarm. Obviously Todd had something important to tell her. And she had a feeling she wasn't going to like what she was about to hear.

"Yes?" Elizabeth prompted him.

"Well, it's just, it's just—I'm worried about this separation," Todd blurted suddenly. "We know from past experience that long-distance relationships are hard to maintain."

Elizabeth let out her breath in a rush, overcome with relief. She had been expecting some horrible news, but Todd was just nervous about being apart from her as well. And she knew to what he was referring. When Todd had moved away to Vermont temporarily, Elizabeth had gotten involved with his best friend, Ken Matthews. Elizabeth and Ken had kept their brief affair a secret for a long time, but eventually the truth had come out. Todd had been devastated. In time, though, he had forgiven her, and their relationship had grown even stronger after that.

Elizabeth weighed her words carefully. "I understand what you're worried about, but this isn't really a long-distance relationship," she said. "It's just for the summer."

"So was Camp Echo Mountain," Todd pointed out, reminding Elizabeth of the time she spent working as a junior counselor in the mountains of Montana. Elizabeth's face burned at the memory. Although neither one mentioned her brief fling with a senior counselor there, the name *Joey Mason* seemed to hang in the air between them.

"That was different," Elizabeth insisted quickly, but she stared down at the ground. That wasn't much of an argument.

"If anything, this is worse," Todd responded. "You're going to be practically on the other side of the world, meeting all kinds of exotic guys."

Elizabeth bit her lip. She had known that her affair with Joey Mason would come back to haunt her someday. Todd had claimed he'd forgiven her, but obviously that wasn't true. Elizabeth looked at him with imploring eyes. "Todd, I promise I would never cheat on you again," she said, her voice catching in her throat.

Todd nodded. "I know that," he said softly.

Elizabeth shook her head, feeling tears of frustration come to her eyes. "No, you don't," she insisted. Elizabeth kicked at a leaf on the ground. "You don't trust me anymore."

"It's not that," Todd responded. "I *do* trust you. I just don't think it's fair to you. You should be able to go out with anyone you want while you're in France."

Elizabeth frowned, suddenly suspicious of Todd's self-sacrificial air. Since when was her boyfriend concerned about *her* freedom to see other guys? "And what about you?" Elizabeth

17

threw back at him. "I suppose you're anxious to start dating other girls."

Todd shrugged. "I wouldn't exactly say *anxious*," he responded carefully. "But I do think we should let each other loose for the summer."

Todd's words hit her like a ton of bricks. Obviously he didn't care about her feelings at all. He just wanted his freedom. Elizabeth felt a tiny fist gripping her heart.

"Just for the summer, Todd?" she retorted.

Todd gently squeezed her hand. "I don't want to lose you, Elizabeth. I hope you'll come back to me. We could reevaluate our relationship at the end of the summer."

Elizabeth yanked her hand away. "And what if I don't *want* to come back to you?" she snapped.

Todd's jaw clenched, and he sighed. "I guess that's a chance I'll have to take," he replied.

Elizabeth could hardly believe what she was hearing. "You've already decided all this, haven't you?" she asked, her eyes flashing angrily.

Todd didn't respond, but the pained look in his brown eyes provided the answer. Elizabeth realized that he had already made his decision and that there was nothing she could do to change his mind.

Elizabeth stood up slowly, blinking back tears. "Well, don't worry," she said quietly. "You can have all the freedom you want. *Forever.*"

With that she turned and walked away with all the dignity she could muster.

"Elizabeth, wait!" Todd called from behind her.

Elizabeth could feel her eyes burning. "Leave me alone!" she yelled. She slipped off her sandals and grabbed the straps in one hand. Then she ran as if a demon were after her. Barely able to see through her tears, she crossed the manicured lawns, sprinted around a tennis court, and raced toward the circular front driveway.

As she was running toward the Jeep, parked in front of the mansion, she heard the sound of Todd's footsteps chasing her. "Liz, wait!" he shouted. "Liz! Come back!"

Panting, Elizabeth reached the Jeep and yanked open the driver's-side door. "Leave me alone!" she yelled over her shoulder to Todd. She jumped in the car and slammed the door shut. But Todd reached her just as she was revving the engine.

"Elizabeth, be reasonable," Todd pleaded through the open window. "Just because I think we should give each other freedom for a while doesn't mean that I don't love you."

"Yes, it does," Elizabeth replied hotly. "I never want to speak to you again."

She jerked the Jeep into gear and backed out of the Fowlers' driveway, tears streaming down her face.

Chapter 2

"Bonjour, je m'appelle Jessica," Jessica chanted into the mirror above her bureau on Saturday morning. *"Comment allez-vous? Je vais très bien."* She smiled charmingly into the mirror, letting the dimple in her left cheek deepen.

Jessica pranced around the room, her heart bursting with excitement. She'd been up since dawn, rushing around the house to get ready. But even though she had barely gotten any sleep, she was wide awake. Not only were she and Elizabeth really going to spend the summer in the South of France, but they were going to be living with royalty—a real prince and a princess.

The only problem was Elizabeth. She hadn't stopped crying for more than five minutes since the party the night before. Jessica had tried to comfort her when she had gotten home, but her sister had been inconsolable. She had finally fallen into a troubled sleep around two in the morning.

Jessica furrowed her brow worriedly. She hoped Elizabeth was feeling better this morning. She didn't want anything preventing their departure for France.

She walked through the bathroom adjoining their rooms and knocked lightly on the door. There was no answer. Jessica hesitated, then knocked again.

"Come in," her sister replied in a wooden voice.

Jessica pushed open the door. Elizabeth was sitting on the edge of the bed, still in her nightgown. She was staring into space with a hairbrush in her hand, and her eyes were red and swollen. A big box of blue tissues sat by her side. Jessica frowned. It wasn't like her sister to fall totally to pieces.

"Lizzie, we're going to *Europe* today!" Jessica exclaimed, trying to infuse some excitement into her twin. She plopped down next to Elizabeth on the bed.

Elizabeth just scowled.

"I know you like to dress casual, but don't you think the occasion calls for something a bit more formal?" Jessica piped up.

Elizabeth cracked a smile, then she burst into tears.

Jessica wrapped an arm around her sister, feeling a little desperate. "Elizabeth, if you keep this up, you're going to flood the room," she chided her gently.

Elizabeth nodded, but her sobs just increased. Jessica hugged her tightly and rocked her back and forth. Finally Elizabeth's sobs subsided. She hiccuped and reached for the box of tissues by her side.

"Our plane leaves in three hours, Liz," Jessica pointed out. Elizabeth nodded and wiped her damp cheeks with edge of her pillowcase. "It's just that . . . when Todd . . ." Her voice broke on a sob.

"Shhh, I know," Jessica said, rubbing her sister's back. "Try not to think about it for now." She paused, then she spoke softly. "We'd better go downstairs because Steven and Billie came home last night just to see us off. And Mom and Dad are downstairs cooking a special farewell breakfast."

Elizabeth cried even harder. She pulled out a tissue and blew her nose loudly. "I just *knew* this trip would be a big mistake," she said through her tears.

"What are you talking about?" Jessica protested. "You and I are going to have the best time ever."

Elizabeth scowled and twirled a finger in the air. "La-di-da," she said. She pulled her pillow into her lap and wrapped her arms around it. "I don't feel like ever leaving my room again." She sniffed.

Jessica sighed and stood up. Clearly she wasn't helping matters. "Listen, I think you need some time alone to get yourself together. I'll come back to check on you in a few minutes, OK?"

Elizabeth nodded, but she kept staring fixedly at the wall.

Jessica headed back to her room, feeling discouraged. She could cheerfully murder Todd for upsetting her twin right before their trip. Of course, Jessica personally thought it was a good idea for Elizabeth to have a little breathing room. She'd been dating Todd since the Stone Age, and he was even less interesting than a caveman.

Jessica checked her hair and makeup in the full-length mirror. She looked bright and lovely. She had been wearing a light cotton dress, but her mother had insisted she change. "It'll get cold on the plane," Alice Wakefield had said. So now Jessica had on a pair of chic beige linen pants and a black blazer. Her hair hung in loose golden waves around her face. Jessica paced around her empty room. Finally she crossed through the bathroom to her sister's room.

Elizabeth was still sitting on the bed, holding the hairbrush. "Uh-oh," Jessica muttered under her breath. "This is getting serious."

Jessica sat down beside her twin and gently squeezed her hands. "Elizabeth, you *have* to get yourself together," she insisted. At this rate she was worried that Elizabeth would back out of their trip completely.

"I know," Elizabeth replied tearfully.

Jessica decided to appeal to Elizabeth's intellectual interests. "Think of how much we're going to *learn* this summer. France is full of history and culture." *And cute guys,* she added silently.

Elizabeth shrugged. "I don't care," she said.

Finally Jessica lost her patience. "Elizabeth

24

Wakefield, what has gotten into you?" she scolded. "You've never been one to let a guy get in the way of your intellectual interests." Jessica stood up and crossed the carpet as she lectured her sister. "This is a chance in a million. We're going to be living in the midst of real culture, and we're going to learn a foreign language." Jessica paused for a moment. "You know, if Todd can't handle a one-month separation, then he isn't the person you thought he was."

Elizabeth sat up straighter. She seemed to be weighing Jessica's words. Finally she managed a smile. "You're right," she said firmly. "I'm going to use this summer to put Todd behind me—once and for all."

Jessica breathed a sigh of relief. She didn't know what exactly she had said to turn her sister around, but she was glad it had worked. "Now hurry up and get ready before Steven eats all the pancakes!"

Half an hour later Elizabeth dragged herself down the stairs. Despite her resolve, she couldn't stop thinking about Todd. Her legs felt as though they weighed two tons each. She had showered and put on a fresh pair of jeans, but she didn't feel any better. She could hear everybody laughing and chatting at the breakfast table, and the aroma of blueberry pancakes and fresh-roasted coffee wafted up the steps.

Elizabeth groaned. She didn't know how she

was going to face her family. She was tempted to head up the stairs and climb back into bed. The last thing she felt like doing was enduring a big Wakefield family farewell . . . or taking a long plane ride to meet some old-fashioned royalty . . . or spending a lonely summer in France. . . .

Sighing, Elizabeth turned the corner into the kitchen.

"There she is!" Steven cried. "Sleeping beauty!" Steven, the twins' older brother, was flipping pancakes at the stove, a white apron tied around his waist. Billie Winkler, his girlfriend from Sweet Valley University, was standing next to him, mixing batter. Billie looked fresh and beautiful as usual. She was wearing faded blue jeans and a teal-colored T-shirt, and her silky chestnut hair hung loose around her shoulders.

"We were worried you were going to sleep through your flight," Billie chimed in.

"I wish I had," Elizabeth muttered under her breath.

"Is something wrong, honey?" Mrs. Wakefield asked from the table.

Elizabeth shook her head and slipped into her seat. "Just tired," she mumbled, averting her gaze.

"The party went on until pretty late last night," Jessica piped up. "It was really great. The food was incredible, and almost *everybody* showed up. Winston Egbert was dressed like a typical French guy, with a tuxedo jacket and a beret. He gave us a

French frog as a gift." Jessica held up the tiny green pin, and everybody laughed.

Elizabeth gave her twin a small smile, grateful for her efforts to divert their parents' attention.

Steven came to the table with a plate of steaming pancakes and flipped a few onto Elizabeth's plate.

"Thanks, Steven," Elizabeth mumbled. She picked up her fork and obligatorily cut into a pancake. Blueberry pancakes were Steven's specialty, and these were done to perfection. But they tasted like sandpaper to Elizabeth. She forced herself to chew and swallow, and quickly gulped down some orange juice.

"When does our plane leave?" Jessica asked suddenly. "What time is it? Are we late? Are the bags in the car?"

"Whoa!" Ned Wakefield said with a smile, holding up a hand. "The car is all loaded up, and we've got plenty of time. Now eat your breakfast. You'll need all your strength for the trip."

Jessica made a face but picked up a piece of toast and bit into it.

Mrs. Wakefield shook her head. "Well, even if you two aren't sad to leave, we're going to miss you terribly this summer," she said.

Prince Albert, the Wakefields' golden retriever, came bounding to the table. "Arf! Arf! Arf!" he chimed in.

"Atta boy!" Steven said, patting him on the side.

While her family discussed the details of their

trip, Elizabeth's attention wandered to the phone. It was hanging innocently on the wall, mocking her with its silence. Despite the fact that she'd told Todd she never wanted to speak to him again, Elizabeth expected him to call this morning. She couldn't help hoping that he would admit that he'd made a terrible mistake and didn't want to break up with her for the summer.

Of course, Elizabeth thought stubbornly, *I would absolutely refuse to go out with him this summer. There's no way I'd forgive him for last night.*

Still, said a little voice in her head, *he could at least make an effort.*

But a half an hour later, when everybody was heading out the door, the phone still hadn't rung. Elizabeth was shocked. She had been sure Todd would call her to apologize, or at least to wish her well. Pain squeezed her heart.

Elizabeth was quiet on the way to the airport, feeling nostalgic as she watched the familiar winding streets of Sweet Valley go by. Fortunately nobody seemed to notice her mood. Jessica was cheerful and animated enough for both of them.

When her father turned onto the coastal highway, Elizabeth could see the foamy Pacific Ocean glittering green in the distance. Jumbled memories flooded into her mind: swimming with Todd in the ocean, playing volleyball with him on the beach, having a moonlight picnic at Baywater, walking barefoot hand in hand on the sand. . . .

Elizabeth felt a pang of sadness. Each sight they passed seemed to have sentimental value for her. And each step was taking her farther and farther away from Todd.

Even when the family was at the airport, waiting for the twins' flight to be announced, Elizabeth couldn't help scanning the crowd for Todd's face.

Her family was talking animatedly in the background; loud voices were announcing flights over the loudspeaker in different languages; well-dressed businessmen and businesswomen hurried by with briefcases tucked under their arms. But it was all a blur for Elizabeth. All she could think of was Todd.

"Flight 786, now boarding!" boomed an announcement.

Jessica squealed and jumped up and down. "That's our flight!" she exclaimed.

Mrs. Wakefield was teary eyed as she hugged them good-bye. "What will I do without you two for the whole summer?" she asked.

"You'll get some rest!" Jessica quipped.

"That's for sure!" Mr. Wakefield said with a grin. "You two are quite a handful!"

"Use the phone whenever you want!" Steven interjected jokingly.

Jessica made a face at him, then giggled.

"Girls, do you have your tickets?" Mrs. Wakefield asked nervously.

The twins nodded.

"And your passports?"

"Yes, Mom," they said in unison.

"Oh, dear, this is harder than I had thought," Mrs. Wakefield said, her eyes clouding over. "Remember, don't talk to any strangers. Write to us often! Make sure you eat properly! Look out for each other!"

"And have a good time!" Mr. Wakefield said with a wink.

Jessica giggled again, and the girls hugged him good-bye.

"Bon voyage!" Steven called.

"Have a wonderful time!" Billie added.

"C'mon, Liz!" Jessica exclaimed, grabbing her sister's hand.

Elizabeth followed her, her heart heavy. She turned back and looked at the crowd. Steven, Billie, and Mr. Wakefield waved, and Mrs. Wakefield blew her a kiss.

Elizabeth waved back, scanning the crowd quickly. But there was no sign of Todd.

Hours later Elizabeth gazed absently out the airplane window, still dwelling on Todd's hurtful words. She couldn't believe Todd wanted to date other girls. After all the time they'd been together, Todd wanted his freedom. He was sick of her.

Their final words from the night before echoed in her mind. *And what if I don't want to come back to you? That's a chance I'll have to take.* Elizabeth squeezed her eyes shut, fighting back tears. If

Todd was willing to risk losing her, one thing was crystal clear—he didn't love her anymore.

The plane was packed, but it was pretty calm. The flight attendants had served an early chicken dinner, and then the passengers had watched a movie. Now everybody was sleeping or reading quietly. The only lights on in the plane were tiny overhead beams. Next to her Jessica was curled up in a blanket, sound asleep. Even though she had slept fitfully the night before, Elizabeth was wide awake.

Elizabeth bit her lip, trying to make sense of her and Todd's breakup. Maybe it was really her fault. After all, she *had* cheated on Todd with Joey Mason. She had broken their trust. Elizabeth squinted, remembering a saying Maria had once recited to her: "Trust is like a crystal vase. Once it's shattered, it's broken forever."

But I really believed Todd had forgiven me, Elizabeth thought. She drew her knees up to her chest and wrapped her arms around them. Something just didn't make sense. It seemed like Todd was just searching for an excuse to break up with her. Was he interested in someone else? Was he just waiting for her to get on the plane so he could date another girl? If so, who was it?

No, Elizabeth thought with certainty. *This isn't an issue of trust. Or self-sacrifice.* Todd wasn't concerned about her feelings at all. He just wanted his freedom. It was as simple as that. *He probably has a date lined up for tonight already,* she thought.

Elizabeth sighed and leaned her head back against the headrest. She had been turning the same thoughts around in her mind for hours, and she wasn't getting anywhere. She had to focus on something else. She fumbled through her back-pack and took out *The Baby-sitter's Guide to Children*, a book she had bought as soon as she'd given in to Jessica's plan. Concentrating on her future charges would help take her mind off Todd. Besides, it never hurt to be prepared.

Elizabeth turned to the first page, but then she sighed again. Worrying about baby-sitting wasn't the best alternative to thinking about Todd. The thought of spending an entire summer as an au pair made her stomach turn.

Even though Elizabeth loved children, she'd had a bad experience with kids at Camp Echo Mountain. Her ten-year-old charges had hated her and had dubbed her "Dizzy Lizzie," a name that had caught on with the whole camp. Elizabeth's face burned at the humiliating memory.

Then Elizabeth shook her head hard. *This time will be different,* she decided. *This time I'll be ready.* She returned to her book with determination and opened to the table of contents. The twins would be taking care of three children, aged three, five, and six. Elizabeth flipped to the chapters that dealt with these ages specifically.

"Six-year-olds can be a handful," Elizabeth read. *"They are full of energy and surprises. . . ."*

But as she read, her eyes began to droop. Slowly she fell into a deep sleep.

Flowers . . . Elizabeth was surrounded by fields of wildflowers. As she walked, the fragrance enveloped her. The sun was warm on her skin. Spellbound, she drew in a deep breath. Southern France was almost as beautiful as her own Sweet Valley.

But suddenly she realized she was lost. The path she had followed had disappeared. For miles around her all she could see was acres of wildflowers—and the sky, which was rapidly turning gray. It would be dark soon. Elizabeth began to panic.

Then, out of nowhere, a gorgeous guy with jet-black hair and deep blue eyes rode up on a white stallion. In one smooth movement he leaned over and lifted her up onto his horse. Elizabeth wrapped her arms around his lean, muscular waist. Her heart beat wildly as they rode off into the sunset. . . .

Elizabeth woke up with a start.

"Sorry," Jessica said with a giggle. She was searching through Elizabeth's backpack. "I was looking for your French-English dictionary. I was trying to be very quiet."

"No problem," Elizabeth mumbled. *It was a ridiculous dream anyway*, she added silently. *I've already discovered that my prince is really a frog.*

Chapter 3

"This is a very famous café," Louis Landeau remarked on Sunday morning to his eighteen-year-old son, Jacques. He spoke in the slow, lilting French typical of natives of the South of France. Jacques and Louis were having a leisurely breakfast at Les Deux Magots, a well-known café on the Boulevard Saint-Germain in Paris.

Louis made a sweeping gesture with his hand, indicating the dark interior of the refined café. "Jean-Paul Sartre and Simone de Beauvoir used to be regulars here," he said. "Some of their most heated philosophical debates took placed in this very spot."

"Really?" Jacques asked, his interest piqued. "The existentialists?" His father was always full of little-known facts. No matter where they traveled, his father seemed to know something about the history or culture of the area.

Louis nodded. "And the existentialist slogan was 'existence precedes essence.'"

Jacques frowned. "What does that mean?" he asked. He picked up his coffee cup and took a sip of his café au lait.

"That means that we are the sum total of what we *do*," his father explained, a twinkle in his eyes. "In other words, 'to be is to act.'"

Jacques recognized the glint in his father's eyes. Louis Landeau was certainly a man of action. For him life had two purposes: finances and women. He spent most of his time chasing after one or the other.

Sure enough, his father leaned over to speak to a tall, well-dressed blond woman seated by the window. A cup of espresso sat in front of her and a newspaper was laid out on the table. She had a mildly bored expression on her pale face.

"Excuse me, but do you mind if I pose a slightly indiscreet question?" Louis asked.

The woman looked up, obviously grateful for the distraction. "That depends on the question," she responded with a slight smile.

Jacques Landeau stifled a grin as his father flirted with the young woman. Even though his father was in his fifties, he looked as elegant as ever. His dark hair was just graying around the temples, giving him a distinguished look, and his tanned face contrasted sharply with his light blue eyes. Despite the passage of time, his father still had an uncanny knack for charming females.

"You wouldn't by any chance be related to Catherine Deneuve?" Louis asked. "You have a striking resemblance to her."

The woman blushed, obviously flattered by the comparison to the beautiful French actress. Then she laughed and regained her self-composure. "I am related to Catherine Deneuve as much as you are related to President Chirac."

"Ah! Touché!" his father said, expressing his appreciation of her wit. He raised his glass to her. "I see I have met my equal."

The woman laughed, her slate gray eyes dancing. Then she waved him away with a flick of her wrist and went back to her paper.

Louis turned back to his son, his face full of good humor. "You're never too old for love," he said in a philosophical tone. He reached for another croissant from the bread basket in the middle of the table.

Jacques smiled in response, even though he knew that his father's attitude was mostly false bravado. His father certainly appreciated women, but inside he was lonely for one woman: his wife, who had left him years ago.

Jacques's mother had died when he was just a little boy, and he barely remembered her. He had a vague memory of a tall, graceful blond woman with a charming smile. Louis had never been able to replace her. Still, Jacques couldn't help hoping that his father would fall in love again and settle down with somebody else.

Louis sat back in his chair and bit into his croissant. Suddenly he was taken by a fit of coughing. Choking and sputtering, he leaned over and gasped for air. His breath came in short starts and his face turned bright red.

"Father, are you OK?" Jacques asked worriedly, leaning forward in concern.

His father nodded, but he continued to choke and cough.

"Here, have some water," Jacques said. He quickly poured a glass from the carafe in the middle of the table and handed it to him.

His father gave him a grateful smile and took a long gulp of water. His coughing eventually quieted down, and his face returned to its normal color. "Ahem!" Louis said, clearing his throat. "Too much rich living, eh, son?"

Jacques smiled and nodded, hiding his concern. He knew that his father was getting older and wouldn't be able to keep up their current lifestyle forever. The nonstop traveling wasn't good for him. They were constantly on the move—hopping a plane from one country to the next, shuffling from one hotel to another, dining in foreign restaurants and cafés. . . . Louis needed a place he could call home, and so did Jacques.

The winter before, Louis had suffered a bout of the flu that left him weak for nearly a month. The flu had turned into a serious case of pneumonia, and it had been touch and go for a while. After he had given him a clean bill of health, the doctor had warned Louis to take it easy. "If you don't settle down soon, your body is going to do it for you," the doctor warned him sternly.

"Of course, Doctor," his father had hastily agreed.

The next day they were back on the road.

Jacques sighed, remembering the promise he had made to himself back then. He had vowed to find a way to help his father establish a life that was better for his health. And he had to do it before the summer was over. His father couldn't handle another long European winter.

Jacques stirred his café au lait pensively. His father needed a house of his own, with a garden where he could sit on sunny days and a cook to prepare healthy meals. Their place would have to be close to the city so his father wouldn't be bored and restless.

Maybe we could get a dog to accompany father on his walks, Jacques reflected, *and a handyman to keep up the place.* After all, neither Jacques or Louis knew anything about plumbing or carpentry. . . .

Only one question remained. *How am I going to manage all that?* Jacques wondered.

"Attention! Nous vous prions de ne pas laisser vos bagages sans surveillance!" a female voice boomed over the loudspeaker system. *"Ne vous séparez pas de vos bagages!"*

"What'd she say?" Jessica asked Elizabeth as they

made their way through the crowded Paris train station early Sunday morning. Jessica's duffel bag slipped off her shoulder and she adjusted it, jumping to shift the weight of her backpack. Wringing out her aching hands, she picked up the straps of her three suitcases and tugged them forward.

"She said not to leave your bags unattended," Elizabeth translated, walking along lightly beside her. "I guess it's a precaution against terrorist bombs."

Jessica nodded, unconcerned. The last thing she was worried about was bombs. All she cared about for the moment was getting to the train and getting her bags on it.

They reached the end of the corridor and came to a series of flashing signs. Jessica blinked and tried to make out the directions. "Gare du Nord, Gare de l'Est, Gare d'Austerlitz, métro, RER, TGV . . ." Jessica racked her brains, trying to recall her French vocabulary. *Gare* meant train station, and the *métro* was the subway system. But what was an *RER?* And what was a *TGV?*

Jessica sighed in frustration. She felt completely and utterly helpless. Everything was in French: the loudspeaker announcements, the signs, the conversations swirling around her. . . . She felt as if she were swimming underwater in a surreal dream. Or a nightmare.

Jessica had traveled in the past, and she had even spent some time in England as an intern at the *London Times*. But still, it seemed strange to be in the midst of a non-English-speaking crowd. Now she wished she had paid more attention in Ms. Dalton's French class. Of course, Elizabeth had managed to use *her* French to get them a cab from the airport to the train station.

Jessica wriggled out of her backpack and let it drop to the ground with a thud. "What now?" she asked, stretching out her aching neck.

Elizabeth was busy consulting their tickets. "I think we should go that way, to track six," she said, pointing to an archway on the left. "We're taking the train to the South of France."

"The *TGV?*" Jessica inquired.

"No, that's the *train à grande vitesse*," Elizabeth explained. "It's superfast. I think we're taking a normal train."

Suddenly the loudspeaker crackled and a modulated female voice came over the system. "*Votre attention, s'il vous plaît. Il y a un changement de dernière minute. Le train numéro quatre-vingt dix-huit à destination de Nice partira de la voie trois. Attention au départ!*"

Jessica hoisted her backpack over her shoulders and turned in the direction of track 6. "Well, let's get going," she said.

"Wait!" Elizabeth cautioned, holding up an index finger. "I think she's talking about our train."

The message repeated itself. "*Voie trois— départ du train numéro quatre-vingt dix-huit.*"

"Ninety-eight," Elizabeth said. "That's our train."

"Ninety-eight?" Jessica repeated. "But she didn't say ninety-eight."

Elizabeth nodded impatiently. "Yes, she did. Four times twenty plus eighteen. Ninety-eight."

"The French don't know how to count," Jessica grumbled.

"Maybe you should have studied a little harder in Ms. Dalton's class," Elizabeth said pointedly.

Jessica made a face, but before she could retort, a little man in a suit shuffled up to them. He was wearing a toupee that was in disarray, revealing a bald spot on the top of his head.

"Excusez-moi," he said to Jessica, a frazzled look on his face. *"Est-ce que vous avez l'heure, s'il vous plaît?"*

Jessica looked back at him, trying to digest his words. *"Parlez-vous anglais?"* she asked finally, asking him if he spoke English.

"L'heure!" he repeated loudly, pointing at his wrist frantically. *"L'heure!"*

Elizabeth smiled graciously and glanced at her watch. *"Il est trois heures,"* she said.

"Merci, mademoiselle," the man thanked her with a little bow. Then he hurried off.

Elizabeth smiled a little self-satisfied smile. Jessica rolled her eyes, disgusted with her sister's preening attitude.

"Jess, c'mon," Elizabeth urged her. "We've got to go to track three now. We're going to miss our train at this rate." She rushed off to the archway to the right.

Jessica picked up her suitcase straps and hurried after her sister. She groaned as one of the straps slipped out of her sweaty hand. Suddenly the biggest suitcase toppled over and fell onto its side. A wheel popped off and rolled away.

Jessica put her hands to her head. Now she was going to have to carry the suitcase, and every part of her body was screaming out in pain. Her back was in knots, her shoulders ached, her neck was tight, and even her hands hurt.

Jessica clenched her jaw and picked up the suitcase, dragging the other two bags in her left hand. Suddenly both suitcases fell over with a clatter and her garment bag slid onto the floor on top of them.

"Liz, will you stop for a minute!" Jessica shouted.

Elizabeth turned around, obviously annoyed.

"It would be a lot easier if you would carry one of my suitcases," Jessica said. "Take the small one." After all, Elizabeth only had one suitcase and her backpack to carry.

"No way," Elizabeth responded, walking back in her direction.

"Elizabeth, *please*," Jessica whined. "I simply can't—"

But Elizabeth cut her off. "Absolutely not," she said in a firm voice. "You're the one who talked me into coming on this trip. You can carry your own bags." Elizabeth crossed her arms over her chest. "Besides, you shouldn't have brought so much stuff," she added.

Jessica uttered an exasperated sigh. Elizabeth was in her "Miss Perfect" mode. She was even wearing comfortable shoes. Jessica, on the other hand, had on her gorgeous new Italian sandals, which were pinching her toes and cutting off the circulation in her feet.

"Fine," Jessica retorted, gritting her teeth and picking up her bags.

But ten minutes later she stopped again. She simply could not carry her big suitcase one moment longer. Her arm muscles were aching, and she was beginning to get blisters on her palms. "Elizabeth, we're going to have to find a cart."

Elizabeth put her hands on her hips. "I told you that you shouldn't have packed for a year."

Jessica tapped a foot impatiently. "Look, there's nothing I can do about it now. Can you just find out where we can get a cart?"

"You know, I don't know why *I* should have to take care of everything," Elizabeth said huffily. "We both took the same French classes, and we're both going to spend the summer in France." Elizabeth flipped her ponytail in annoyance. "You're going to have to make an effort sooner or later."

Jessica exhaled loudly. Clearly Elizabeth wasn't going to be any help. Jessica was going to have to test out her rusty French. Sighing, she stopped a passing woman. She was young, with frizzy red hair and a pointed nose.

Jessica searched her mind for the translation of

"I'm looking for a cart." *"Pardonnez-moi. Je cherche une carte,"* she said hesitantly.

The woman narrowed her eyes. *"Une tarte?"* she asked.

Jessica felt like screaming in frustration. *"Des cartes,"* she repeated.

"Vous voulez jouer aux cartes?" the woman asked, looking surprised.

Elizabeth laughed out loud. "She thinks you want to play cards."

At this, Jessica practically exploded. "Liz, it's not funny. Can you *please* tell me how to say *cart* in French?"

Elizabeth shrugged. "I have no idea."

"Merci," Jessica said to the woman, beginning to despair.

The woman gave them an odd smile and walked away.

Elizabeth glanced at her watch. "Look, Jess, we've really got to hurry. If we see a cart, we'll grab one. But for now we've got to haul these ourselves."

Jessica sighed and picked up her suitcases again. As she started to lug her bags forward a cute young guy appeared at her side. He was slim, with dark brown hair and smooth almond-shaped brown eyes. He had a rakish look on his face, and a slight stubble darkened his jaw.

"Excuse me, mademoiselle," he said, smiling shyly.

A distinguished-looking older gentleman was

45

standing by the guy's side, and Jessica glanced at him. He gave her a slight bow.

"You speak English!" Jessica exclaimed, beaming. She quickly dropped all her bags and stretched out her shoulders.

"But of course!" responded the young man with a very sexy French accent.

Jessica breathed a sigh of relief. "Can you tell me how to say *cart* in French?" she asked.

The older man's brow furrowed quizzically. "Cart?" he repeated.

Jessica made a gesture with her arms, pretending to load her bags onto a cart and push it.

"Ah!" said the older gentleman with a charming smile. "She wants *un chariot*."

"But you do not need a *chariot!*" interrupted the young guy. He put out a gallant arm and picked up her bags. "Would you allow me to be your *chariot?*"

Jessica stared into his warm brown eyes, feeling as if she were going to melt in the liquid fire of his gaze. "Thanks, that would be great," she said gratefully.

Elizabeth stowed her bags on the overhead compartment of the train and glared at Jessica. "I can't believe you handed over your luggage to a complete stranger," she hissed sharply.

Jessica smiled innocently. "What's the problem? I thought it was very nice of him to help me out—especially when my own sister wouldn't," she added pointedly.

46

Elizabeth shook her head. Somehow Jessica managed to turn everything around. It wasn't *her* fault that Jessica insisted on bringing her entire wardrobe with her. Elizabeth was doing her a favor by coming with her on this trip in the first place. She shouldn't have to be her porter as well.

"Besides, he happened to be gorgeous," Jessica added with a grin.

Elizabeth clenched her jaw. Sometimes her sister's logic was mind-boggling. "You know, thieves can be just as gorgeous as anyone else," she pointed out. "What would you have done if he'd taken off with your luggage?"

Jessica laughed. "Well, I would have had a lot easier time carrying my bags."

Elizabeth rolled her eyes. "Very cute."

"Look, Liz, chill out," Jessica replied smoothly. "He didn't take my stuff, so what's the big deal?"

Elizabeth continued to grumble to herself as she and Jessica took their seats. True, the guy had carried her sister's luggage onto the train. But she was furious that Jessica had taken such a big risk in trusting him. After all, they'd come to France to take care of young children. Jessica certainly wasn't showing a high level of responsibility and maturity.

I have a feeling I'm going to have to keep my eye on her this summer, Elizabeth realized. *Otherwise we'll both end up in a heap of trouble.*

Elizabeth settled into her seat by the window and took in her surroundings. The train was sleek and modern, with lots of legroom and wide aisles. The beige seats were set up in groups of four, with wooden tables between them. Flashing red signs indicated the lavatories and a dining car.

Suddenly Elizabeth felt Jessica nudging her. "Hey, Liz, look who's coming," Jessica said with a wicked grin.

Elizabeth followed her gaze to see the older man and the guy who had helped Jessica making their way down the aisle. "I hope they don't hijack the train," Jessica whispered to her sister.

"Very funny," Elizabeth said, but this time she couldn't help smiling. *Maybe I did overreact a little bit,* she admitted to herself. After all, nothing had happened. She was just in a bad mood because she hadn't gotten any sleep.

"Are these seats free?" asked the older man.

"Of course," Jessica replied graciously, giving him a charming smile.

The younger man took the older man's luggage and stowed it above them. Then they settled down in the seats across from the twins.

"We meet again, mademoiselle," the younger one said to Jessica. "What an unexpected pleasure!"

He kissed her hand, and Jessica blushed in delight. Elizabeth narrowed her eyes in suspicion. The guy might have helped her sister out, but Elizabeth instinctively didn't trust him. He was too smooth for her liking.

"But, but! *Sacrebleu!*" the elderly man exclaimed.

He was gazing at them with a look of surprise. "You are *jumelles!*"

"*Jumelles?*" Jessica whispered to Elizabeth.

"Twins," Elizabeth supplied.

"*Quelle beauté extraordinaire!*" the man exclaimed in wonder. "Such beauty and freshness one might expect to find in a single rose. But in two flowers, it is unheard of!" He waved his hands around excitedly. "Never have I experienced such unique and matching loveliness."

Jessica giggled in delight. His flattery was so outrageous that even Elizabeth couldn't help chuckling.

The man bowed low. "Allow me to introduce myself. I am Louis Landeau, the duke of Norveaux. And this is my son and heir, Jacques," he added.

Jessica's eyes widened. Obviously she was very impressed. Elizabeth shook her head. She hoped her sister wouldn't spend the summer falling all over herself every time she met somebody with a title.

Jessica leaned forward eagerly. "I'm Jessica Wakefield," she said with a bright smile. "And this is my *jumelle* sister, Elizabeth."

"Charmed," the young man said, gazing into Jessica's eyes.

Elizabeth rolled her eyes and looked out the window. *Where's Norveaux?* she wondered, trying to place the area. She quickly went over her French geography in her mind. Forming a mental map, she pictured the country of France and its

49

various regions. There was Normandy in the north, and Bretagne in the west, the Loire Valley in the center. . . . But she couldn't visualize Norveaux.

Elizabeth turned back to the Landeaux. "Where exactly is—"

Her words were interrupted by a loud commotion in the next car.

Suddenly a hefty, red-haired woman came charging down the aisle. She was shrieking in French at a harried-looking conductor, who was bowing and apologizing meekly.

Elizabeth turned her attention to the exchange with interest. At last people were speaking French. Elizabeth squinted in concentration, trying to make out the words. To her delight, she found she was able to understand most of what was being said.

The woman stood up straight. "I am the Countess Doloria di Rimini," she announced haughtily. Her thick red hair was swept up on top of her head, and her cold green eyes glittered darkly, reflecting the chain of emeralds she wore around her fleshy neck. Her pale face was carefully made up, and her jowls sagged. She lifted her chin, as if expecting everyone in the vicinity to bow down in worship.

A tall girl came up behind her. She had a pointy, angular face and luminous green eyes, which contrasted with her short fiery hair. Elizabeth figured she must be the woman's daughter. They looked a lot alike, right down to the grumpy scowls on their faces.

"I demand that you correct this mistake," the woman barked. "My daughter, Antonia, and I should be in first class."

The conductor bowed his head. "I am so sorry, madame," he responded politely in French. "Please accept our greatest apologies. There appears to have been a mix-up. Er, hmmm . . ." His voice wandered off.

"Well, fix it," the countess demanded in an imperial tone. *"Now."*

The conductor seemed to shrink in her presence. "I'm afraid there are no more available seats in first class. Perhaps you'd care to wait for a later train," he sputtered.

"I will not be put off this train," the countess raged.

"Madame, what do you suggest I do?" the conductor asked with a sigh. He was clearly getting fed up with the woman's histrionic display.

The countess's imposing chest heaved. "I suggest that you and your *incompetent* coworkers remedy this *outlandish* situation immediately," she said in a low voice.

The conductor's eyes flashed at the insult. "Countess di Rimini, if you care to enjoy our service, then I am afraid you have no choice but to ride second class," he said. With that he turned and walked away.

"Humph!" the woman exclaimed, sitting down in a huff. "Of all things!"

Her daughter sat down next to her. "Humph!" she echoed.

Elizabeth shook her head. *I can't believe people like this exist!* she thought.

Chapter 4

Eighteen-year-old Prince Laurent paced back and forth across the ornate parlor of his family's château on the coast of France on Sunday afternoon, searching for the right words to say. His footsteps across the marble floor echoed lightly in the airy room. He had called a family conference this morning, and now his father and his stepmother were sitting on the eighteenth-century red velvet divan, watching him expectantly.

Prince Laurent looked at them warily. His father, Nicolas de Sainte-Marie, sat straight on the sofa, his dignified face wrinkled in concern. Catherine, his beautiful stepmother, wore a kind expression on her face as well. They were waiting patiently to hear him out. All he could hear was the crackling flames coming from the stone fireplace.

Prince Laurent groaned inwardly. It would be

easier if his father and stepmother weren't so considerate. The last thing in the world he wanted to do was insult them. But somehow he had to make them understand his point of view.

Finally he faced them, his hands spread wide open. "Well, the long and short of the matter is—I feel trapped," he declared in French.

His father nodded, slowly absorbing his words. "That's not unusual," he responded, speaking in the same cultured French as his son. "Every young man your age goes through this phase."

Laurent winced, biting back a sharp retort. This wasn't just some "adolescent phase" that he would grow out of in a few years. This was his *life*, and he was serious about it. "I don't believe it's just a phase," he said quietly.

His father's deep gray eyes twinkled wisely. He stood up to his full length and clapped Laurent on the shoulder. "Believe me, Laurent, I went through the same thing when I was your age."

"You did?" Laurent asked in surprise. He had never heard anything about this before.

His father nodded. "When I was eighteen, I was a bit of a renegade."

Laurent looked at the refined prince in amazement. He took in his father's silver gray hair, his distinguished bearing, his French-cut royal blue suit, his gold tie clip. His father—a renegade? "What—?" Laurent murmured.

"I think you've shocked him, Nicolas," his

stepmother said with a smile. She lifted up the silver teapot and refilled her china cup. Then she took a sip of tea and crossed her legs at the ankle, her wine-colored raw silk dress rustling. "When it was your father's time to take the throne, he refused it categorically," she said, a glimmer in her dark brown eyes.

At this Laurent sat hard down in a straight-backed gold-embroidered chair. His father had refused the throne? Was the world turning upside down?

His father chuckled. "Oh, they were just boyhood dreams—you know, everybody's fantasy of revolution and equality." He waved a dismissive hand and picked up his pipe.

Laurent sat up straight. "So what did you do?" he breathed, fascinated. He had never really considered his father a role model. Certainly he was noble and dignified, but Laurent had always found him a bit too conservative. But now his father was revealing a side of himself that Laurent had never known about. Or had dreamed could be possible.

His father leaned back on the divan and lit his pipe. "Oh, nothing much," he said modestly, taking a puff.

The princess rolled her eyes. "I'll tell you what he did," she said, leaning forward. "First he refused his title and created a big scandal," she said.

Laurent's eyes almost popped out of his head.

"Yes, and I organized, hmm, a bit of a revolution among the youth of the area," his father added. He smiled at the princess warmly. "Catherine and I were just friends at the time. And she was an active member of our youth group."

The princess stood up and crossed the marble floor. "You have to realize, this was in the seventies," she explained. "It was sort of the thing to do."

For a moment Laurent was speechless. Suddenly the past was being radically rewritten. "And what did grandfather do?" he asked.

His father chuckled. "Nothing. He did absolutely nothing. He told me to go right ahead and make a revolution."

Laurent sat forward eagerly. "And?"

His father shrugged and sat back in the divan, crossing one leg comfortably over the other. "And it was a complete failure," he said with an elegant wave of his hand. "We ended up with the same sort of unjust system as we'd had before, except that it was even more chaotic and less functional."

Catherine laughed softly. "Ah, the follies of youth."

"And so," concluded his father, "eventually I took my rightful place as the head of our principality."

"And married Marianne—your mother," Catherine added.

Laurent was silent for a moment. He stared into the flickering flames of the fire, deep in thought. Somehow he'd thought he was the first in his lineage to question the royal family, to fight against tradition. Maybe his father was more complicated than he'd realized. And maybe there was more to their traditions than Laurent understood.

Laurent turned back to his father. "Why didn't you ever tell me this before?" he asked softly.

His father smiled. "Because it's up to you to fight your own battles and make your own decisions. As the saying goes, the only real teacher is experience. You must forge your own path."

Laurent held his breath. Was his father giving him permission to go off on his own, to construct his own life outside of the royal family? Was his father actually giving him his blessing?

"But I know you will come to value your place in society and take up the responsibilities into which you were born," his father concluded, sounding like his old conservative self.

Laurent let out his breath in a rush. He stood up and walked to the window. Brushing back the heavy velvet curtains, he gazed out at the acres of open meadows. He wished for the millionth time that he hadn't been born into royalty. He was sick of hearing about his family obligations.

Laurent turned and faced his father and stepmother. "I *do* value our family traditions," he said. "It's just that I want my life to be my own."

Laurent's father stood and put a solid hand on his son's shoulder. "Give it time, son," he said. "Think about it."

The kindness in his dad's voice made Laurent feel even worse. *I can't put off my decision much longer,* he realized. But there didn't seem to be any

57

way to compromise. He had to decide whether to sacrifice his own freedom to the royal family or break out and make a life for himself. He had the choice between hurting himself—or hurting his father. And destroying a long legacy of tradition and honor as well.

Laurent bit his lip as he stared out at the endless stretch of land. It was an impossible choice.

"So we all decided to play a prank on the head schoolmistress and transport her *lit*, that is to say, her bed, into the main cafeteria," Jacques was saying.

The train was rolling along at a comfortable pace, and Jacques was telling Jessica a story about his early years at a boarding school in England. His father was sitting next to him, listening with an amused smile on his face. Elizabeth was curled up by the window at Jessica's side, engrossed in her baby-sitting book.

"You know how the English are," Jacques continued. "Boring and—how do you say—*stoufy?*"

"Stuffy," Jessica supplied with a grin.

"Right, stuffy. Well, obviously she was not very pleased. She found out I was one of the leaders and called me to the front of the cafeteria. She demanded that I return her bed immediately." Jacques pursed his lips and imitated the cultured English accent of his schoolmistress. "Mister Landeau, this is an outrage! Please restore the furniture at once! At once!" A small smile curled on

Jacques's lips. "Then she dumped a bowl of hot oatmeal right on my head."

Jessica burst out laughing. "Is that really true?" she asked.

Jacques nodded, a sheepish expression on his face. "I'm afraid so."

Louis shook his head. "Tsk, tsk," he said, chiding his son jokingly. "Jacques, that is no way to win the heart of a beautiful girl. You have to tell her stories of heroic deeds, not of embarrassing moments when you ended up with porridge on your head."

Jacques smacked his palm against his forehead. "You're right! What was I thinking?" He leaned in close to Jessica, his brown eyes dancing with laughter. "Actually, I was just being modest. What really happened is that no one had any food to eat due to a—" Jacques paused, searching for the word. "Due to a strike! Yes, a food strike! So I went off all alone to the next town in search of food. I had to walk for many days and many nights. Finally I found an old farmhouse and brought back buckets and buckets of porridge." Jacques smiled a self-satisfied smile. "And everybody was saved from starvation."

The new version of the tale made Jessica laugh even harder.

"It's no use," Louis declared, throwing his arms up in the air. "It's too late."

Jacques raised his eyebrows. "Is that true, Jessica?" he asked. "Have I totally ruined my chances to impress you?"

"Well . . . ," Jessica teased.

Jacques clutched at his heart dramatically.

"Not yet," she admitted.

"Phew!" Jacques exhaled deeply. *"Quel bonheur!"*

Jessica smiled at his exaggerated expression of happiness, and then they both cracked up.

"OK, enough of this fooling around," Louis said sternly, whipping out a deck of cards. "It is time for some serious business." He shuffled the cards expertly and tapped the deck on the table between them.

"Vous voulez jouer aux cartes?" Jessica asked, repeating the French sentence she had heard at the train station.

Jacques stared at her admiringly. "You can speak French as well!"

Jessica grinned. "Well, actually, that's about the only sentence I know."

"What?" Louis exclaimed. *"You* are modest as well?" He shook his head disapprovingly. "Both of you could use some lessons in seduction. I have had enough of this self-deprecating humor." He gave Jacques and Jessica a stern look. "Is that clear?" Jacques and Jessica both nodded, giggling.

"Good! Now watch carefully," Louis commanded. He fanned out the cards and held them up. "Pick a card."

Jessica reached for a card and glanced at it. It was the queen of hearts. "Now put it back in the deck," Louis ordered.

Jessica did as she was told, and Louis shuffled

the deck again. Then he spread out the cards on the table and told her to find the card. Jessica looked through all of them, but the queen of hearts was gone. "It's not there," she said.

"What?" Louis exclaimed in mock horror. "Not there?" He turned to his son. "Jacques, have you seen it?"

Jacques shook his head solemnly. But then Louis reached into Jacques's shirtsleeve and pulled out the card. "Tut, tut, tut," he said disapprovingly. "Jacques, I'm ashamed of you. What in the world are you trying to pull? Are you trying to steal her heart?"

Jacques nodded.

"Aha!" Louis said. "I thought so!" He gave Jessica a knowing wink. "Watch out for him. He's a foxy one."

A warm glow came over Jessica. Even though it was clear that Louis and Jacques had played this trick before, Jessica found them absolutely charming. She loved Jacques's French accent and the way his brown eyes twinkled with humor. It didn't hurt that he was also a duke-to-be.

Jacques smiled at her warmly, and an electric current raced down her spine. Jessica sighed contentedly. She had been sure this trip was going to be fantastic. And she had been absolutely right.

Is it really possible? she wondered. *My first day in France and already I seem to be falling in love. . . .*

*   *   *

As the train continued to speed toward the coast Elizabeth fidgeted in her seat. She was getting bored and restless. She stared out the window listlessly. Miles and miles of beautiful countryside stretched out before her, and the land was getting greener and hillier as they headed toward the South of France. It was beautiful, but Elizabeth's mood was so bleak, she might as well have been staring out at a barren gray landscape.

Elizabeth shifted in her seat and turned back to her book. She stared down at the page, trying to concentrate. *"Time-outs and loss of privileges are effective punishments, but the most efficient method of shaping a youngster's behavior is through the use of positive reinforcement— rewards, such as . . ."*

Elizabeth stopped reading and yawned. She realized she'd gone over the same passage three times already.

She put *The Baby-sitter's Guide* away and pulled out a novel by George Sand, called *La Petite Fadette*. Elizabeth had decided to read only French literature this summer, and George Sand was a heroic figure for her. She had been a feminist before her time. She had used a male pseudonym in order to get her writing published, and she had been one of the first women to wear pants in public. Elizabeth had always wanted to read her novels.

Elizabeth curled up in her seat and read the jacket copy. The story took place in *le Berry*, a small agricultural village in France. It was about an unattractive girl with a great mind and a spirit of independence. Elizabeth closed her eyes and tried to imagine the scene. She pictured rural France and a young, spirited girl. Then she turned back to the book and opened to the first page. But after she'd read a few lines, her mind started to wander again.

Elizabeth dropped the book in her lap and turned her attention to Jessica and Jacques's conversation. The two of them had been talking and laughing for hours.

"Well, he dumped an ice cream shake on me, not a bowl of porridge," Jessica was saying.

Jacques chuckled softly. "It was, how do you say, a sticky situation?"

Jessica laughed appreciatively. "Exactly!" she agreed.

"What are you guys talking about?" Elizabeth asked.

"Heroic deeds," Jessica said. At that, both Jacques and Jessica burst out laughing.

"Huh?" Elizabeth asked.

But Jessica just waved a hand in the air. "It's a long story," she said.

"And not a pretty one," Jacques added, a twinkle in his eye.

I know when three's a crowd, Elizabeth told herself silently, looking around for better company. Jacques's father was napping soundly. In the seats across the aisle the Countess di Rimini and her daughter still seemed to be sulking. The countess was knitting a piece of dark blue wool rapidly, a scowl on her face. Her daughter was staring out the window, a bored pout on her vapid features.

Elizabeth fished through her shoulder bag for something else to read. But she hadn't packed any more books in her carry-on luggage. All she had was a couple of magazines and a box of cream-colored stationery. Elizabeth pulled out the stationery, deciding to write a letter to Enid and Maria. But as she lifted the lid, what she saw made her suck in her breath. Sitting on top of the paper were several envelopes preaddressed to Todd.

A painful lump formed in her throat. *While I was getting organized to write to Todd every day, he was probably planning to dump me!* she thought in indignation.

Elizabeth ripped up the envelopes viciously and stuffed the pieces into the trash receptacle. *There!* she said to herself in satisfaction, wiping off her hands. *I'm rid of him forever!*

But despite her angry gesture, she couldn't help feeling an overwhelming sense of loss. *I wonder what Todd's doing right now?* Elizabeth thought. *I wonder what he's thinking. . . . Is he thinking about me?*

Elizabeth, stop it! she commanded herself. She looked around desperately for a distraction. Somehow she had to keep herself from thinking about Todd. But she was sick of reading, and now she didn't feel like writing any letters.

Elizabeth stood up and inched pass Jessica, who didn't even seem to be aware of her presence. Jacques was regaling Jessica with another story, and she was giggling happily.

Once in the aisle Elizabeth rubbed her eyes and stretched her arms above her head. Her stomach growled, and she decided to get something to eat. She walked down the aisle and headed for the dining car.

After pushing through the last set of double doors leading to the dining car, Elizabeth was surprised to find the car fashioned like a real restaurant. There were white lace curtains on the windows and elegant red tablecloths draped over the tables. A black-tailed waiter hurried about, serving warm meals. The crowd was somewhat raucous. A bunch of young people were sitting at a long wooden table playing poker, and the bar was filled with laughing voices. The rest of the tables were filled with attractive young couples and families. A couple of children were playing on the floor.

Elizabeth headed sadly to the food counter. *Todd would have loved this,* she thought despite herself. She and Todd had always talking about taking a long trip on a train. It was so romantic. She could just see them eating a fancy dinner and laughing as they tried to order in French. . . .

"Vous désirez?" a voice said, asking her what she wanted.

Elizabeth blinked and came out of her reverie.

The older man behind the counter was looking at her expectantly. "Uh," Elizabeth mumbled, scanning the order board on the wall quickly. The menu was written in French, and Elizabeth could only make out a couple of the items. *"Un sandwich au fromage, s'il vous plaît,"* she ordered finally.

"A votre service!" the man replied, reaching for a fresh baguette filled with Gruyère cheese, lettuce, and tomatoes. He handed the sandwich to her with a flourish. *"Vingt francs, s'il vous plaît."*

Elizabeth quickly translated in her head. *Twenty francs—that's about four dollars.* Fortunately the twins had already changed money at the airport. Elizabeth pulled out her purse and dumped the foreign coins into her palm. She fished through the change and picked out two ten-franc pieces.

"Merci!" the man said. *"Et bon appétit,* mademoiselle!"

Elizabeth gave him a small smile and headed back to her seat. She sighed as she threaded through the boisterous crowd. She felt more alone than ever.

On her way back Elizabeth decided to strike up a conversation with the Countess di Rimini and her daughter. *Maybe they're nicer than they seemed at first glance,* Elizabeth thought. *Maybe they were just cranky about the mix-up in their reservations.*

Elizabeth sat down in one of the empty seats

across from the di Riminis and gave them a friendly smile. "So what's your destination?" she asked brightly.

The countess dropped her sewing in her lap and fixed her with a cold glare. "Excuse me?" the woman drawled, responding in English.

Elizabeth swallowed hard. "I was just wondering where you were traveling," she replied lightly. "My sister and I have never been to France before."

"*American*, I presume?" the countess asked, making it sound like an insult.

Elizabeth tried not to feel defensive. "Yes, we're from southern California. We're famous for our lovely beaches, although I've heard the French Riviera is nice. Is that where you're going?" she asked.

The countess snorted. "My daughter and I are traveling on holiday to the summer château of the prince and princess de Sainte-Marie. We will be staying on a small island in the Mediterranean Sea." She stuck her prominent nose in the air. "I'm sure *you've* never heard of it."

Elizabeth took a deep breath and forced herself to let the insult go by. Maybe the countess would take a liking to them when she realized that they were staying in the château too. "That's really a co-incidence!" she exclaimed. "Jessica and I are going to the same place. We're going to be au pair girls for the de Sainte-Maries."

Antonia wrinkled her long nose. "Mother and I don't associate with servants."

Servants! Elizabeth could feel her face burning. She opened her mouth to reply, but Antonia got in the final word. "I would appreciate it if you would stop bothering us. Mummy and I have had a long voyage."

Elizabeth's jaw dropped. *Thank goodness I'm from America—where everyone is equal!* she thought, fuming.

"Excuse me," Elizabeth said quietly, standing up with as much dignity as she could manage. She walked quickly back to her seat, her whole body trembling with anger.

Elizabeth sat down hard in her seat and whipped out her sandwich, taking a furious bite. She only hoped the de Sainte-Maries were more enlightened than these two members of the so-called nobility. A whole summer with a bunch of rich snobs would be pure torture!

Chapter 5

"So what are you doing in France this summer besides stealing men's hearts?" Jacques asked Jessica early Sunday evening.

Jessica made a face, but she blushed despite herself. The train was moving along with a lulling, rocking motion. Most of the passengers were sleeping or reading quietly. Elizabeth and Louis were dozing. But Jacques and Jessica were still up. Jacques had made a trip to the dining car and had returned with beverages, a baguette, and a plate of cheese, along with a bunch of purple grapes.

Now they were sitting across from each other, talking quietly so as not to disturb the other passengers. Jacques was so close that Jessica could smell the faint musky odor of his cologne, and she could practically feel the heat emanating from his body. A delicious tingle crawled down her spine, and she felt her face flushing again.

"Well, you don't have to tell me what you're doing here," Jacques said, a comic look on his face.

Jessica laughed softly, relieved that he had broken the spell. "Elizabeth and I are going to be au pair girls for the de Sainte-Maries," she explained. "We're staying at their summer château." She ripped off a piece of bread and spread some soft Brie cheese on it with a plastic knife.

"Ah! Le Château d'Amour Inconnu!" Jacques said knowingly.

Jessica looked at him in surprise. "You've heard of it?"

Jacques nodded. "But of course!" he said. "It is well-known in France."

Jessica's eyes widened. "Well-known for what?" She took a bite out of her baguette, savoring the taste of the sharp French cheese.

"For tales of passion, what else?" Jacques said with a grin. "*Inconnu* means 'unknown' or 'unheard of.' And of course, the château is known for its strange and mysterious love stories. Its name comes from an old French legend." He reached for the grapes and popped a few in his mouth.

Jessica was enthralled. She pulled her blanket tightly around her shoulders and brought her knees up to her chest, curling up comfortably in her seat. "Tell me the story," she demanded breathlessly.

Jacques gave a half bow with his head. "At your

service, mademoiselle," he said with a rakish grin. Jessica couldn't help giggling.

Jacques put a mock-serious expression on his face and cleared his throat loudly. Then he leaned in close to Jessica, his voice barely a whisper. "Well, supposedly one summer long ago, Prince Frédéric the Third *est tombé amoureux,* that is, fell madly in love with a *jeune* handmaiden of eighteen. Her name was Isadora, and she was sweet and *belle,* with rosebud lips and hair like spun silk."

Jacques paused, and Jessica waited eagerly for him to continue.

"Isadora was just a domestic servant, but she had one extraordinary quality," Jacques recounted softly. "She had a voice of gold. Her voice was pure and sweet like that of a nightingale. When she sang, the canaries sang back. Of course, the union between the prince and Isadora was strictly forbidden."

"So they had a secret affair!" Jessica guessed. She picked up a cluster of grapes and bit off a few.

"That is correct," Jacques said with a nod. He brushed back a lock of hair that had fallen over his forehead. "All summer long they met in secret—in hidden verandas, in the woods, in all the underground passages. . . ."

"There are underground passages?" Jessica breathed, wiping her mouth on a napkin.

Jacques nodded. "What is a castle without an underground passage?" he asked, looking somewhat mischievous. "Now, where was I?"

71

"The love affair," Jessica reminded him. She picked up her can of lemonade and took a sip through the straw.

"Right, right," Jacques said. "So they had a passionate and tumultuous affair. And all summer long the handmaiden sang as she worked, a pure and beautiful sound that made even the doves sit still and listen."

Jessica held her breath, waiting for him to go on. She felt herself transported back to another world in another time, a magical place of romance and passion.

"But then one day Frédéric was to be wed to a young marquise," Jacques went on. "Torn between his love and his duty, Frédéric agonized day and night. But the preparations proceeded as planned."

Jessica shook her head in disappointment. "Too bad," she said.

"But wait." Jacques held up a hand. "There is more." He picked up his can of mineral water and took a gulp. "On the day of the wedding, which was held outside in the royal gardens, the handmaiden ran into the forest. From deep in the woods came the low, mournful crooning of a sorrowful bird. Tortured by the sound, Frédéric ran out of the chapel and into the woods after her."

"And so they lived happily ever after!" Jessica finished.

"Ah, no!" Jacques said, his face darkening dramatically. "This is a tragedy. Frédéric searched the woods inside and out, but the *belle* Isadora was nowhere to be seen. And so the marriage went through after all. But at the very moment Frédéric took his vows, a beautiful white dove appeared at the altar. It sang a low, sad song, and then it flew away. And it is said that even today on long summer nights, the sweet and sorrowful sound of a mournful dove can be heard."

Jessica sighed. "That's beautiful," she said. "Maybe I'll hear the dove when I'm there."

Jacques winked. "Maybe you will have a mysterious love affair."

Jessica's cheeks flushed at his insinuation.

Suddenly Monsieur Landeau awoke from his nap, mumbling in French. *"Mais qu'est-ce que c'est que ça?"* he grumbled under his breath. *"On est où, là?"* He coughed and muttered to himself. Then he cleared his throat loudly and sat up, glancing around with a disoriented look on his face.

Jacques's expression quickly turned serious. *"Papa, ça va?"* he asked worriedly, trying to find out if his father was all right.

"Eh? Quoi?" Louis muttered, squinting in the dim light.

"Papa? Ça va?" Jacques repeated.

Jessica looked at Louis in concern. Suddenly Monsieur Landeau looked twenty years older than he had before. His tanned face was drained of color and looked lifeless. Jessica wondered if he had some kind of illness. She bit her lip, debating whether or not to call the conductor.

But then Louis seemed to recover his bearings. He blinked a few times and focused on Jacques and Jessica. *"Pas de problème,"* he asserted with a dismissive wave of his hand. He coughed deeply, holding his hand over his chest. Then he drew a handkerchief out of his breast pocket and patted his face.

"Do you want some water?" Jacques asked, quickly filling a plastic cup.

"I'm fine," Louis insisted, the color beginning to return to his face. "Healthier than when I was your age." But he accepted the water gratefully and took a long drink. "The only thing wrong is this seat."

Jacques didn't look convinced, but he didn't say anything.

Suddenly Louis got a playful look on his face. "Mademoiselle Jessica, would you mind trading places with me?" he asked. "I'm an old man, and this seat is terribly uncomfortable."

"Uh, sure," Jessica agreed, standing up quickly.

After Jessica was settled next to Jacques, Louis grinned and winked at his son. Obviously he had just been trying to get Jacques and Jessica together. Jessica giggled at their antics.

"We're French, you see," Louis said with a shrug. "We cannot help it. Romance is in our hearts from the moment of our birth."

Jacques chuckled. "Papa, go back to sleep."

Louis folded up his overcoat like a pillow and

74

settled into his seat. "But remember, don't do anything I wouldn't do," he added.

"Don't worry," Jacques responded with a smile.

"Prochain arrêt, Marseille!" announced the conductor, walking down the aisle of the train. "Next stop, Marseille! Twenty minutes!"

The overhead lights flashed on, and the train came alive with movement. Passengers started talking and shuffling in their seats. Some of them began gathering their bags and reaching in the overhead bins.

Jacques looked at Jessica sadly. "My father and I are getting off at the next stop," he said.

Jessica felt an unexpected pang of loss. She stared into Jacques's liquid brown eyes, wondering what had come over her. She had just met this guy, and yet she felt as though she'd known him for years. And now she didn't know when she'd see him again. *Maybe he'll come visit me at the château,* she thought hopefully.

Jacques sighed deeply. "I wish I could stay on the train forever," he whispered in her ear. He brushed a feather-light kiss on her cheek, causing Jessica to shiver in delight.

Elizabeth opened her eyes slowly. She was wrapped up in a light brown blanket in the corner, and her blond hair was in a wild disarray. "Hey, are we here?" she mumbled sleepily, turning her head. She jumped with a start as she noticed Louis sitting next to her.

Louis was reading the paper, a cup of coffee in his hand. He grinned at Elizabeth mischievously. "Your sister insisted on sitting next to my son," he explained solemnly.

"Don't believe a word he says," Jessica said with a laugh.

Elizabeth pushed her hair out of her eyes. "Where are we?" she asked again. She pulled her blanket off her lap and began folding it up.

"We're just making a stop," Jessica said. "We've still got a few hours."

"Mmm," Elizabeth said, yawning and stretching her arms over her head. She looked around for a few minutes, watching passengers flurrying around. Then she seemed to get bored. She pulled a book out of her backpack and buried her nose in it.

Jacques squeezed Jessica's hand and tipped his head toward the aisle. "Let's go for a walk, Jessica," he suggested.

Jessica nodded and slipped out of her seat.

As she got up, Elizabeth shot her a stern look. "Where do you think you're going?" she demanded.

"Relax," Jessica told her. "I'll be right back."

"Now, now," Louis admonished Elizabeth gently. "Remember, this is France, my dear," he said. "The country of love."

Jessica giggled at Elizabeth's parting scowl.

Jacques and Jessica walked through the aisles hand in hand, looking for a place where they could be alone. Finally they found a deserted compartment, and they slipped inside.

Jessica stared out the compartment's window. It was twilight outside, making the sleepy French village look enchanted. Tiny pink houses jutted against one another, and the rich Mediterranean Sea glittered a deep blue in the distance.

"It's beautiful," Jessica said wistfully. "Is this where you live?"

"I live where my heart takes me," Jacques said enigmatically. He slipped an arm around her waist and gazed out the window with her. For a moment they stood in silence. Only the low hum of the passengers and the steady movement of the train could be heard.

An announcement for Marseille came over the loudspeaker, and Jessica turned toward Jacques. "You're going to have to go soon," she whispered.

Jacques moved closer, encircling her waist with his arms. Jessica tilted her face upward, wishing he would kiss her.

"Jessica," Jacques said softly. "You're the most fascinating girl I've ever met." He seemed to search in the air for the right words. "You have that certain *je ne sais quoi*."

Jessica repeated the words to herself silently, feeling a thrill go through her. When Lila had first met Bo, she had talked nonstop about how wonderful and cultured the French were. At the time Jessica had thought Lila was ridiculous. But now

Jessica decided her best friend was right. The French language was incredibly romantic—and so were French men.

But then a wave of disappointment came over her. This was just a brief romantic interlude. She might never see Jacques again.

Jacques brushed back a wisp of hair from Jessica's cheek. "Can I see you again?" he asked, as if he were reading her mind.

Jessica blinked in surprise. "I was just wondering the same thing," she said softly.

Jacques smiled in relief. "I'll come to see you at the château as soon as I can."

Jessica's heart soared. This summer was going to be even more exciting than she had expected. Not only was she going to be living with royalty, but she was going to receive a visit from the son of a duke.

The train slowed down, and people began moving down the aisle.

Jacques coughed and shuffled his feet uncomfortably. "Before I go, I'd like to give you something," he said, pulling a red box out of his pocket. He handed it to her and looked down at the ground.

Jessica took the box and opened it carefully, feeling nervous. Nestled in a midnight blue velvet case was a huge emerald pendant.

Jessica gasped. With shaking fingers she lifted the jewel out of the box, watching it glimmer iridescently in the dim light. "It's beautiful!"

she exclaimed finally. "But . . . but I can't. . . ." She quickly gave it back to him.

"Don't worry, the jewel isn't real," Jacques reassured her. "It's just a great copy." Then he looked at her earnestly. "But even though the stone isn't real, my feelings for you are."

Jessica's heart fluttered wildly.

Jacques pressed the pendant into her hand. "I'd like you to keep it to remember me until we meet again."

Jessica nodded, feeling tears come to her eyes. The sentiment was even more beautiful than the stone.

Then Jacques grinned disarmingly. "But someday I'll replace this fake jewel with the real thing," he assured her.

Jessica shook her head. "It wouldn't have as much meaning as this," she whispered.

"So you did feel something for me as well?" he asked softly, gazing into her eyes.

Jessica nodded.

Jacques put a hand behind her neck and brought his lips to hers, kissing her tenderly. Jessica returned the kiss, and soon they were kissing passionately, like Jessica had never kissed anyone before. Jessica closed her eyes, and the world seemed to melt away. All she could feel was the soft touch of Jacques's lips on hers and the steady beating of his heart. They were locked in a private universe.

But suddenly the train came to a grinding

halt, and Jessica was jolted back to reality.

Jacques touched her softly on the nose. "Until we meet again," he said. He kissed her tenderly one last time, and then he slipped away.

Jessica stayed in the compartment for a moment, savoring the kiss in her mind. She held up the stone to the light, and it glimmered like a secret promise. Jacques was a dream come true. She couldn't wait to see him again.

When Jessica returned to her seat, Jacques and his father were already gone.

Chapter 6

Duty . . . obligation . . . my place in society . . .
Prince Laurent's mind was spinning as he galloped
across his family's property on his white stallion
early Sunday evening. He had been riding madly
for the past few hours, trying to escape from his
troublesome thoughts.

Ever since his talk with his father and stepmother,
Laurent had been racked with anxiety. He had been
replaying the conversation over and over again in his
mind all day, trying to come to a decision.

It's up to you to forge your own path, he heard
his father's wise voice saying. *But I know you will
take up the responsibilities into which you were
born.*

Laurent clacked lightly on the horse's flanks.
"Go, Pardaillan!" he urged him. The horse whinnied and charged forward. A brisk wind whipped

through Laurent's hair, and the lush landscape rushed by in a blur.

Prince Laurent closed his eyes, trying to lose everything in the sensation of the stallion's steady strides. He recalled the wonderful sense of freedom he used to get from riding his horse. His family had come to the château every summer since he was a little boy, and Laurent had spent all his days out in the meadows, riding his horse and practicing his fencing.

Laurent remembered the thrill he used to feel each time he saw the château. With its spiked gables and tall red tower, the old stone castle seemed to be shrouded in mystery. It was the site of courageous deeds and passionate love affairs. The legend of the Château d'Amour Inconnu only added to the mysterious aura surrounding the castle.

Laurent used to ride like wildfire across the fields, dreaming of fashioning his own legend. Alone in the calm of the meadows, he dreamed of meeting a young girl with spun gold hair and the voice of a lark. But unlike Frédéric in the tale, Laurent wouldn't let her fly away.

But now Laurent's innocence was gone. No longer could he enjoy the simplicity of the rich landscape or the beauty of the family legends. His boyhood dreams were only dreams. It was time to face reality.

They reached the end of the meadow, and Laurent pulled Pardaillan's rein, guiding him into the dense forest. The horse slowed down and trotted at a brisk pace along the dirt path.

Laurent stopped near a pond and led his horse to the water. As far as the eye could see were acres and acres of land. The property had been in the de Sainte-Marie family for hundreds of years. Laurent felt overwhelmed with the burden of his heritage.

Laurent sighed. He almost wished that his father had been less understanding. Then Laurent could have gotten angry and self-righteous. It would have been easier to rebel. Now he just felt confused.

As his horse was drinking, Laurent lay down on a soft patch of clover and closed his eyes. He wished he could just stop time right now, that he could put off his decision forever. He envied his younger brother and sisters. They were free—free to live their own lives.

A light breeze caressed his face, and the scent of lilacs wafted in the air. The last rays of the setting sun shone warmly on him. Laurent could feel his tension slowing easing out of his body. He closed his eyes and fell into a deep sleep.

Dressed in his formal royal uniform, Laurent stood at the entrance of a huge ballroom. The music and dancing stopped. Everyone was staring at him as his name was announced.

Laurent walked down the majestic red carpet, and the music started up again. Although he'd attended countless balls like this one, he had a feeling

that something was different here. He was sup-
posed to find a treasure here tonight, but he didn't
know what it was. . . .

Suddenly his eyes met those of a girl across the
room. His heart melted as he watched her. She was
absolutely beautiful, with golden hair, ocean blue
eyes, and the sweetest smile he'd ever seen. He
didn't know who she was, but in his gut he was
certain she was The One.

He made his way to her. But just as he was
about to put his arms around her and lead her into
a dance, someone nudged him aside. And the girl
vanished. . . .

Laurent opened his eyes. His horse was standing
over him, pressing his nose against the prince's face.
"Pardaillan, stop!" He groaned, waving his arms.
The horse whinnied softly and nudged him again.

Laurent sat up and sighed in disappointment.
The beautiful girl was just a dream.

Jessica gazed out the train window dreamily,
her mind whirling with thoughts of Jacques. She
missed him already. He was funny and playful, but
romantic at the same time. It was an irresistible
combination.

The sun was just beginning to set in a luminescent red ball, enveloping the tranquil countryside
in a pink haze. They passed through one charming
town after another. Small red houses dotted the
hills, and sharp white cliffs jutted into sparkling

blue waters. In the distance a snow-capped mountain range could be seen.

Jessica gazed in wonder at the extraordinary beauty of the French seaside. Now she understand why the French had their reputation for passion. The South of France was clearly the perfect setting for romance. It was too bad that Jacques wouldn't be at the château with her.

Jessica curled up at the window, dreaming of their next encounter. She hoped Jacques would show up at the château soon. She imagined them frolicking on the beautiful white sand of the Riviera, far away from the countess and her daughter, far away from the little kids. . . .

Jessica glanced at her twin and grinned. *Thank goodness Liz is with me*, she thought. If Jessica were alone, it would be difficult to arrange time off from her baby-sitting duties. But she had complete confidence in her twin. She was sure Elizabeth could handle everything during Jacques's visit.

Jessica closed her eyes and imagined herself and Jacques standing on the shore of the Mediterranean Sea, the wind gently blowing. She could feel Jacques taking her hand. She saw them running across the white sand, hand in hand, stopping only to kiss passionately. . . .

Suddenly the Countess di Rimini started to shriek. Jessica's eyes popped open, her fantasy shattered. The countess was standing in the aisle, shouting in French and gesticulating wildly.

"Mais qu'est-ce qui se passe?" several passengers asked at the same time.

"What's going on?" Jessica asked Elizabeth, whose face was scrunched up in concentration.

Elizabeth raised a finger to her lips. "Shhh! I'm trying to figure it out!" she said.

A conductor rushed to the countess's side. "What seems to be the problem?" he asked.

The countess looked as if she were about to burst. Her face was bright red, and an angry vein popped out of her neck. She was flapping her thick arms around like a bird, and her chest heaved up and down in agitation. *"Mais ce n'est pas possible!"* she screeched. *"Ce n'est pas possible!"*

"What's not possible?" Jessica asked quickly.

Everybody had turned to listen, and a number of passengers from others cars were gathering around to see the commotion.

"J'ai perdu mes bijoux!" the countess was yelling, her voice high and shrill. *"On a volé mes bijoux de famille! C'est un désastre!"* She flung her arms out in a hysterical gesture. *"Quelle horreur!"* Then she swooned dramatically and fell into her seat in a faint.

Antonia shook her quickly. *"Maman, Maman,* wake up!" she said anxiously. She fanned her mother's face quickly. Then she pulled a packet of smelling salts out of her bag and wafted them under her mother's nose.

"Liz! What's going on?" Jessica insisted.

"She says she's been robbed," Elizabeth explained to Jessica quickly. "Her family jewel is missing."

Jessica's eyes lit up. "How exciting!" she breathed. Elizabeth looked at her as if she were insane.

"OK, make way, everybody! Everybody out!" the conductor ordered in English, trying to clear the aisle. "Everybody back to their seats." Eventually the disappointed crowd dispersed.

The countess quickly regained consciousness. Her eyes popped open, and she waved away the smelling salts. Soon she was up on her feet again, screaming in French.

"Now, ma'am, if you could just calm down," the conductor suggested, biting his lip nervously.

"Calm down! Calm down!" shrieked the countess in English, waving her arms around wildly. "I want the police! Immediately!"

The conductor nodded. "Yes, yes. We're going to contact the local police station as soon as possible."

"I should hope so!" huffed the countess.

"Now, when did you lose the jewel, Madame di Rimini?" the conductor asked.

"*Coun-tess!*" the countess barked.

The conductor blanched. "Excuse me, Countess."

"That's better." The countess sniffed.

The conductor shifted his feet impatiently. "Please, if you could just cooperate. We need to make a full report."

"Well, how should I know when I lost my

jewel?" she asked self-righteously. "I just noticed the gem was missing. I was checking the contents of my jewel box for a very important ball this evening. This is a family heirloom. . . ." She faced the conductor with a piercing gaze. "Do you understand the gravity of the situation?"

"Yes, Mad—er, Countess, yes, indeed. Now, when was the last time you checked your valuables?" the conductor asked.

"Well, er—," she stumbled. "I believe it was when my daughter and I left Italy."

The conductor looked visibly relieved. "So your jewel could have been stolen at any point along your voyage."

The countess's thin red lips formed a tight line. "Perhaps. But I just know they were taken on this train." Her eyes roamed the passengers' faces suspiciously.

"She's crazy," Jessica whispered to Elizabeth.

"A real nutcase," Elizabeth agreed.

The countess stood up and shook a finger in the air. "I demand that the doors be sealed tight and that every passenger be searched. Immediately!"

The conductor took a deep breath. "Er, madame, I'm afraid that isn't possible. We'd need a search warrant for that kind of thing."

"This is an *outrage!*" the countess shrieked. "Of all the trains I have ridden, I have never experienced such incompetence, such . . ." She seemed to run out of steam and fell in her seat in a huff, gasping for air.

"Shhh, it's OK, Mother," Antonia said, patting her hand.

"Don't worry," the conductor said, rubbing his nose nervously. "We'll do a full investigation."

The conductor circulated in the car, questioning passengers and taking notes. The whole car was buzzing with excitement, and most of the passengers were eager to be interviewed. Finally he got to the twins' seats. "Have you girls noticed anything suspicious?" he asked them.

Both Jessica and Elizabeth shook their heads. "Nothing at all," Jessica said, batting her eyelashes sweetly and innocently at the countess.

The countess pursed her lips, and Jessica smiled to herself.

Jessica was secretly pleased that the countess had been robbed. *Serves her right for being such a snob!* she thought. *I'm sure whoever has the heirloom deserves it a lot more than she does!*

"Finally," Elizabeth said with a groan as the train came to a full stop. She was beginning to think the ride would never end. Elizabeth stood up and stretched. Her whole body ached from sleeping in the chair.

Elizabeth pulled down her suitcase from the overhead bin and fastened her backpack on her back. Jessica joined her in the aisle and reached for her suitcases in the opposite bin.

"Yow!" Jessica exclaimed as she set an avalanche of suitcases in motion. She and Elizabeth quickly jumped out of the way. Jessica's dress bag slid onto the seat, and her three suitcases tumbled down quickly after it. Her duffel bag flew out of the bin and landed in the aisle.

"Jessica! Somebody could have gotten seriously injured!" Elizabeth reprimanded her.

"Not to mention my clothes," Jessica added, yanking out her dress bag from underneath the suitcases. "I hope they're not wrinkled."

Elizabeth shook her head. "Here, let me help you," she said, reaching for a suitcase.

"What?" Jessica asked in mock amazement. "Is my sister actually offering to help?"

"Don't push it," Elizabeth grumbled. She heaved the biggest suitcase off the seat and retrieved Jessica's duffel bag, slinging it over her shoulder. Then she joined the throng of passengers getting off the train.

Jessica squeezed in behind her, struggling with her remaining bags. Elizabeth didn't know how Jessica had managed at all at the airport in Paris. Now she wished she had helped her.

Maybe then she wouldn't have met Jacques Landeau, Elizabeth reflected as she and Jessica got off the train. The guy struck her as being too good to be true. But she knew better than to give Jessica her opinion. Any sign of opposition would only make Jacques seem more attractive.

But then, Elizabeth thought, *it doesn't really matter.* After all, Jacques and his father were long gone—and the twins would never see them again.

As soon as they were inside the train station both girls dropped their bags on the floor. "Now what?" Jessica asked, rubbing her neck with her hand.

Elizabeth peered at the signs. This train station was much smaller than the last one. There was just one main room and a cute little café with a coffee bar. Elizabeth spotted a sign that said *Sortie* and pointed toward it. "That's the exit," she said. "It must be that way."

"Aye, aye, Chief," Jessica said, bubbling over with good spirits.

Elizabeth picked up the straps of the two suit-cases and headed toward the sign. Suddenly Jessica's suitcase wobbled and fell onto its side.

"Hey, what's with this?" Elizabeth asked, picking it up. Then she dropped it quickly, shaking out her wrist. The suitcase felt like it weighed about two tons.

"It's missing a wheel," Jessica explained. "You've got to carry it."

Without giving her sister time to protest, Jessica picked up the straps of her remaining two suitcases and hurried off. "Hurry up, Liz!" she called over her shoulder.

Elizabeth took a deep breath and lifted the

suitcase with a groan. "Hey, Jess, what'd you pack in here? Lead weights?"

"Dumbbells," Jessica answered with a wry smile. Then she waved her sister on. "Liz! C'mon! The royal family is waiting for us!"

Elizabeth shook her head. Suddenly she wasn't so sorry she hadn't helped her sister at the airport in Paris.

Several uniformed drivers were standing near the exit, holding signs with the names of the passengers they were there to meet. Elizabeth scanned the crowd. Finally she caught sight of a sign that said Wakefield. A dignified-looking man in a red uniform was holding the sign.

"Look, Jess! There's our name," Elizabeth pointed out.

Jessica gave a little squeal of excitement, and the girls hurried up to the uniformed chauffeur. He bowed elegantly. "You must be the Wakefield twins," he said in English, a British accent to his voice. "I am Gaston. Delighted to meet you. This way, please." Gaston picked up two of the suitcases and led the twins out of the train station.

Jessica and Elizabeth followed the chauffeur to a light blue van parked at the curb. They stood aside as he loaded their suitcases in the back.

"Hey, look who's here," Jessica whispered in her ear. "The witch and her spawn."

Elizabeth turned to see the countess and her daughter approaching. The countess had her nose pointed up in the air, and Antonia followed behind her in exactly the same manner. A uniformed chauffeur was hurrying after them with their bags.

"Come along, Jeeves!" the countess ordered.

A sleek black stretch limousine was waiting at the curb, and the countess marched up to it. Her head swept the crowd imperiously, but she made no sign of having recognized the twins. "If you please," the chauffeur said, holding open the back door.

"Thank you," the countess responded as she and her daughter slid into the plush interior.

"That's not fair," Jessica pouted. "We should have gotten a limo too."

"What difference does it make?" Elizabeth replied. "A car is a car."

Jessica scowled. "We're already being treated like lowly servants."

Elizabeth watched the limousine drive smoothly away. She just hoped that Jessica was wrong. If everybody at the castle was like the di Riminis, Elizabeth would be on the next plane back to the States.

Chapter 7

Louis and Jacques were seated at an outdoor café overlooking the Mediterranean Sea in Marseille on Sunday evening. The evening was warm and mild, and the blue-gray ocean was calm. A shipyard stood to their right, cluttered with wooden piers and small fishing boats. A few men were still out on the docks, carrying heavy buckets of fish and lugging about huge coils of rope.

Jacques didn't respond. He looked out at the ocean and followed its contour directly south, where Jessica and Elizabeth would be staying. He wondered if they had already arrived. He could just imagine Jessica's reaction to the Château d'Amour Inconnu—she was sure to love it.

Jessica is sort of an enigma, Jacques thought, peering out to sea. *A puzzle.* She was full of energy and vitality but had a strange innocence as well.

She seemed worldly and naive at the same time.

Jacques's heart contracted, and he felt suddenly light-headed. *Is this what it feels like to fall in love?* he wondered.

"Jacques, you better eat up," Louis said. "We've got a long day ahead of us tomorrow."

Jacques blinked and looked up at his father.

"I must say, all that excitement has certainly given me an appetite," Louis said, taking a deep breath of the salty sea air. "Ah, nothing like the South of France to cleanse the soul." He picked up his fork and cut into his omelette with gusto.

Jacques took an obligatory bite of his steak, forcing himself to chew and swallow. The steak was done to perfection, but he didn't have much of an appetite. Every time he thought of Jessica, he felt his stomach turn. Jacques frowned and pushed his french fries around on his plate.

Louis looked at him carefully. "Something is troubling you?" he inquired, his brow furrowed. He wiped off the corner of his mouth with a cloth napkin.

Swallowing hard, Jacques looked up at his father, choosing his words carefully. "I'm not sure we did the right thing," he said finally.

But Louis waved a dismissive hand in the air. "Don't worry, son. It's completely harmless. You'll see. It'll all work out in the end."

Jacques sighed. He had a feeling his father would say that. "I know," he said. "It's just that I would have loved to stay on the train and talk to Jessica."

Louis chuckled. "I don't blame you. She's a lovely girl." Then he leaned forward and lowered his voice. "But you know we had very little choice in the matter," he reminded him. "We had to get off when we did."

Jacques nodded. He knew his father was right. They couldn't have stayed on the train one minute longer.

"Besides," Louis said, laughing, "I have a strong feeling you and Jessica will meet again." He sat back and picked up his glass of white wine, crossing one long leg over the other. "Jacques, my boy, we've outdone ourselves this time." He took a sip of his wine, his cheeks gleaming. "It was a stroke of genius—pure genius."

Jacques tried to laugh, but the laugh caught in his throat. A knot of anxiety twisted in his stomach, and his tongue went dry. Once again he felt he was in over his head. And this time his heart was involved as well. Jessica really meant something to him. He had felt a deep connection to her, unlike anything he'd experienced in the past.

"I'm not sure," Jacques ventured. "We could get the twins in trouble."

But Louis shook his head with assurance. "Not a chance," he said with certainty. "The plan is foolproof."

For once in his life, Jacques wanted to back out. He didn't want to go along with his father. He sighed, his heart heavy. He wished they could undo what they had done.

But when he looked up at his father, he noticed the signs of Louis's weakening health again. Despite his father's jovial air, his eyes were tired and his face was pale with fatigue. *He needs me,* Jacques reminded himself. He couldn't back out now.

"Completely foolproof," his father repeated.

"I know," Jacques replied softly.

Jacques picked up his hot chocolate and stared out at the tranquil sea. If everything went according to his father's plan, he'd see Jessica again. That was for sure.

But it won't be like it was on the train, he thought sadly. *She'll never have the same innocence again.*

"Here we are, girls," Gaston said, steering the car up a long, winding driveway on the de Sainte-Maries' property. They were on a completely private island connected to the mainland by a drawbridge. The property was covered with lush green meadows and tall flowering trees.

Jessica let out an excited squeal from the back of the car.

Elizabeth laughed. "Jess, control yourself," she whispered. "Remember, we're about to meet real royalty."

Gaston pulled the car to a stop at an elaborate wrought-iron gate. Two identical-looking guards in gold uniforms stood at attention in front of the gate.

The chauffeur got out of the car, and the girls followed.

"*Bonjour*, Gaston!" said one of the guards, greeting him politely.

"*Bonjour*, Émile!" Gaston responded.

The other guard opened the back of the car and began unloading the luggage.

Jessica stared at the castle in wonder. It was even more magnificent than she had imagined. It was a beautiful white stone fortress with a moat surrounding it. A number of charcoal gray gables poked out on the left and right, and a huge medieval clock with roman numerals was nestled between them. A tall round, red tower stood in the middle of the castle.

"This is incredible!" Jessica exclaimed.

Elizabeth looked equally impressed. She was staring openmouthed at the sight in front of them. "It's straight out of a fairy tale," she breathed.

"If this is their summer house, I can't imagine how amazing their year-round home is," Jessica whispered to Elizabeth.

Gaston chuckled at their reactions. "Come along, girls," he said to them in English. "You'll have plenty of time to get acquainted with the grounds during your stay." He grabbed a few of their bags, and the guards took the rest.

Jessica and Elizabeth followed them across the lovely grounds. They passed through a tiny gate leading into a well-kept French garden, which was crisscrossed by red cobblestone paths. The scent of lilacs and honeysuckle filled the balmy night air, and birds flew overhead. A tiny footbridge crossed the moat, and they walked across it single file.

Jessica felt her heart rate accelerate as they reached the front door. Long vines of English ivy climbed across the castle walls, and an arch-shaped rose-covered trellis surrounded the entranceway. Gaston unlatched the huge stone door and pushed it open, ushering Jessica and Elizabeth inside.

As they entered the castle Jessica gasped again. They were in a pink marble foyer, which was larger than the Wakefields' living room and dining room combined. Through a big archway to the left was a large salon with a polished floor and mint green velvet furniture. An imposing grand piano stood in the corner, and huge eighteenth-century gold-framed portraits hung on the walls.

Jessica bit her lip in excitement, wondering if this was what Jacques's home was like. *Obviously he and Louis must live in this kind of splendor,* she thought.

Jessica imagined herself as the duchess of Norveaux, residing in a romantic castle like this one in Norveaux. She pictured herself in a long, glittering golden gown, throwing a lavish dinner party for visiting royally and Hollywood celebrities. And of course, all her friends from Sweet Valley would be invited as well. Lila would be green with envy. . . .

Jessica's daydream was interrupted when an attractive young woman came into the front hall. She was slim, with big, wide-open brown eyes and straight long brown hair tied back in a red satin ribbon. A few dark freckles were scattered across her nose and cheeks.

"You must be the twins!" said the woman in English, giving them a wide, friendly smile. "I'm Anna." She had a low voice and spoke English with just a slight French accent.

"I'm Jessica," Jessica said. "And this is my sister, Elizabeth."

Anna blew a strand of hair off her forehead. "Boy, am I glad to see you!" she exclaimed with a laugh. "These kids are getting to be a handful. Now that they're on summer holiday, they're always afoot." She shook her head and whisked off her apron. "Follow me," she said. "The princess wishes to see you."

Jessica's throat contracted nervously as she and Elizabeth followed Anna down the elegant hall. She hadn't realized that she was nervous about meeting the prince and princess. But the castle was overwhelming and intimidating in its splendor. They passed through a magnificent dining room with a crystal chandelier and an ornate parlor with red velvet divans. All the rooms seemed to have old stone fireplaces in them.

Anna pulled open a door and led them into a small, sunny room with three huge bay windows looking out over the back of the castle. Through the window Jessica could see miles of rolling hills leading up to a dense green forest.

A tall, poised woman was seated at an ornate gilded desk. She looked up as they walked in. "Welcome, girls!" she said warmly, speaking English with a strong French accent. "Welcome to my home." Pushing back her chair, she stood up and walked over to them.

"Princess Catherine, this is Jessica," Anna began, pointing to Elizabeth. But then she furrowed her forehead. "Or are you Elizabeth?"

The girls laughed. "I'm Elizabeth," Elizabeth corrected her. "And this is Jessica."

The princess shook both their hands. "Well, I'm sure we'll be able to tell the difference eventually," she said with a gracious laugh.

Jessica watched the elegant woman in awe. She had never seen someone with so much self-possessed grace. The princess's dark, satiny hair was twisted into a tasteful bun at the nape of her neck, and small diamonds sparkled in her ears. She was wearing a wine-colored silk dress accentuated by a long strand of pearls. When the princess moved, she seemed to glide across the floor. And when she laughed, her voice sounded like the tinkling of a bell.

"Anna will show you to your rooms and explain your duties," the princess told the twins. "And after you've settled in a bit, I'll introduce you to the children. They're eager to meet you." Then she glanced at her watch. "On second thought, it's quite late. Perhaps we should postpone the explanation of your duties until *after* dinner."

"I thought I heard the sounds of young American voices," came a kind voice by the door.

Jessica turned to see a distinguished-looking man with silvery gray hair and a gold tie clip standing by the door. "You must be the au pairs," he said, coming forward to greet them. He spoke English as well, with a less marked accent than his wife. The prince smiled warmly, and tiny laugh lines appeared at the corner of his eyes.

"Jessica and Elizabeth, may I present Prince Nicolas de Sainte-Marie?" the princess asked.

Jessica fought back the urge to curtsy and nodded, unsure how to greet him. She glanced at Elizabeth quickly, but she just shrugged, obviously at a loss as well. The prince seemed to be aware of their confusion and chuckled.

"In France we kiss on both cheeks as a greeting," he said, giving the twins light pecks on the cheeks. Then he winked at them. "And sometimes we give four kisses."

The princess shook her head. "You can't imagine how tiresome the custom becomes when you throw a royal ball!"

The girls laughed, and Jessica felt herself relaxing. The prince and princess were warm and understated. They were nothing like the snobby countess and her daughter.

"Well," the princess said, clapping lightly. "The children will be served dinner in about twenty minutes. After you two have settled in, you may go to the kitchen and join them."

She smiled warmly. "Anna, would you please show the twins to their rooms?"

Anna nodded. "Of course, *Votre Altesse*," she said, employing the French term for "Your Majesty." Then she turned and headed out the door. "Right this way, girls."

Jessica frowned. She had hoped they would eat with the royal family at the regal dinner table that they had passed.

But as she and Elizabeth followed Anna up a long stone staircase, Jessica smiled. *Once the princess realizes that a duke's son is in love with me, I'm sure I'll be accepted as one of the family around here.*

"Imagine all the people who have stayed in this very room over the years," Elizabeth said as she and Jessica settled into their new quarters. She heaved her suitcase up on the bed, sending up a cloud of dust.

Jessica coughed and waved her arms wildly in the air. "I don't think anybody's been here for a long time," she disagreed, making a face.

Elizabeth smiled at her twin's grumbling. The girls had been assigned to two tiny, circular rooms at the top of the stone tower, and Jessica was miserable about it. "But this is the attic!" she had complained. The rooms were light and dusty, with wooden floors and long cracks in the yellowing walls. There were rectangular French windows all around with panoramic views of the island.

Jessica had immediately claimed the larger room, which was equipped with a chest of drawers and a tiny bureau with an antique mirror hanging over it. Elizabeth had happily agreed, preferring the cozy charm of the smaller room. Jessica didn't have a closet in her room, so Elizabeth had offered to share hers.

Elizabeth put her hands on her hips and surveyed the small space. A twin-size four-poster bed with a down quilt was pushed against the wall. An old rickety chest of drawers stood against the opposite wall next to a nonworking fireplace, and an antique cherry desk was in front of the window. In the corner was an old iron washstand with a dusty silver pitcher underneath it.

"This must have been an old *chambre de bonne*," Elizabeth remarked.

"Care to translate?" Jessica asked with a scowl, kneeling on the ground and unzipping her suitcase. She picked it up and turned it upside down, dumping the entire contents on Elizabeth's bed.

"A *chambre de bonne* is a maid's quarters," Elizabeth explained. "In France the domestic staff often lived in small attic rooms."

"Maid's quarters!" Jessica responded in disgust.

She fished through the pile of clothes, separating out skirts and dresses. "I can't believe we're living in a castle and we're staying in a dump," she grumbled. She turned the skeleton key in the latch of the solid oak armoire and pulled out a handful of wire hangers. "Gross!" she exclaimed, wiping dirt off the hangers with the back of her sleeve.

Elizabeth stared at her twin in amazement. "A dump? What are you talking about?" she asked incredulously. "This place is incredible, filled with history and culture. And the view is breathtaking."

Jessica exhaled wearily. "I'd gladly trade all that for some closet space," she complained. "And nicer furniture." She picked up a pile of dresses and began hanging them up in the closet.

Elizabeth shrugged. "It's cozy," she said.

"Which is another way of saying it's a *tiny* dump," Jessica retorted. After hanging up the last of her clothes, she let out a loud *hmmph* and walked out of the room.

Elizabeth shook her head and returned to her unpacking. She thought the room was absolutely perfect. It was old and romantic, with an almost magical feel to it.

Elizabeth imagined herself waking up in the morning with the sun streaming through all the windows. She would push back the lace curtains and gaze out at the extraordinary view. And then she would sit at the beautiful old desk and write in her journal. Elizabeth sighed. She felt like a girl in a fairy tale.

Ever since they had crossed the drawbridge leading to the island, Elizabeth had felt some of her old energy returning to her. It *was* exciting that they were spending the summer on a private island in the South of France. She was sure to learn more about French culture in one summer than she had learned in all her years in Ms. Dalton's class. And her French would improve immensely.

A beam of moonlight peeked through the window, and Elizabeth smiled. *Maybe it wasn't such a bad idea to come here after all,* she thought.

Elizabeth opened her suitcase and lifted out the dresses she had carefully placed on top. She slung them over one arm and opened the door of the armoire. But the closet was crammed full of Jessica's clothes. Elizabeth shook her head. Of course, Jessica hadn't even left her one inch of space. The closet was packed tight with Jessica's summer dresses, miniskirts, and silk T-shirts.

Oh, well, Elizabeth thought, lying out her dresses flat on the bed. *I'll have to negotiate with Jessica later.* For the moment she had to get settled in. Now that she had seen how warm and elegant the prince and princess were, she couldn't wait to meet the rest of the royal family.

Elizabeth hummed as she unpacked the contents of her travel case. She set out her toiletries on the bureau and placed her journal on the marble mantel. Outside, a wind picked up, and a gust of cool air shot through an open window. Elizabeth closed the window quickly, gazing out at the magnificent view. Tiny stars twinkled in the midnight blue sky, and the stormy ocean crashed from afar. The cawing of seagulls could be heard in the distance.

Elizabeth sucked in her breath. She couldn't wait to tell Todd all about the castle and the royal family. But then, words couldn't really capture the beauty of the island. She'd have to take pictures and send them to him.

Then she grabbed onto the mantel, feeling as if she'd been struck. She couldn't tell Todd about the château. She was never going to speak to him again. The sense of loss hit her so hard that she felt out of breath.

Almost against her will, Elizabeth unzipped the inside pocket of her shoulder bag and pulled out Todd's picture. Her hands trembled slightly as she picked up the frame and stared at Todd's familiar face. *Why did I bring this with me?* she reprimanded herself. Tears pooled in her eyes.

Finally Elizabeth wrenched away her gaze and forced herself to tuck the picture into a side pocket of her suitcase. Then she shoved the suitcase underneath the bed, pushing it against the wall with her toe.

I may be a damsel in distress, Elizabeth thought miserably, *but no Prince Charming is going to rescue me*.

As Elizabeth wiped a lone tear from her cheek there was a knock on the door.

Elizabeth blinked quickly and dabbed at her

eyes. She cleared her throat and tried to compose herself. "Come in," she called out, her voice shaky.

Anna poked in her head. "Time to meet the children!" she announced.

Elizabeth forced a smile on her face. Then she took a deep breath and followed Anna out the door.

"Children, I'd like you to meet your new au pairs, Jessica and Elizabeth," Anna said, kneeling down in front of the kids in the huge kitchen of the château.

Six saucerlike brown eyes stared at them solemnly. The children all had curly dark hair and big brown eyes. Manon, the three-year-old, was wearing a tiny pale yellow dress with a matching ribbon in her hair. She was holding on to her older sister's hand tightly. With her long brown curls and pink cheeks, Claudine looked surprisingly mature for a five-year-old. Pierre, the oldest child, was wearing a blue-and-white sailor suit. He stood huddled close to Anna, holding on to her leg.

They're adorable, Jessica thought, giving them a warm smile.

"Bonjour!" Manon piped up.

"Bonjour!" Jessica responded.

"Now, remember," Anna reproached the little girl lightly. "You have to speak English at all times with your new au pairs."

Manon nodded silently, her eyes wide.

Jessica breathed a sigh of relief. She had been a

little bit worried about dealing with the children in a foreign language.

Anna stood up straight and turned to the twins. "Make sure you're very strict about speaking only English with the children," she said. "One of the benefits they will get from your company is the chance to improve their English."

"Don't worry," Jessica reassured her with a grin.

Anna turned back to the kids. "Jessica and Elizabeth came all the way from America to be with you," she said.

Claudine's eyes grew wide. "America!" she breathed.

Anna smiled and patted her on the head.

"Did you take a *bot?*" Pierre ventured.

Jessica giggled. "No, we took a plane."

Pierre jumped up and down excitedly. "Vrroom!" he exclaimed, making a motion of a plane with his hand.

"Exactly!" Elizabeth said.

"OK, children, time for dinner," Anna said, leading the group to the other side of the kitchen. A big, round table covered with a beautiful pale blue tablecloth stood in the corner by a bay window.

"Up you go!" Anna said, lifting Manon into a high chair. The other children scampered to their seats.

They're little angels, Jessica thought in relief as she watched Anna interact with the children. They obeyed Anna just as if she were their own mother.

Anna gestured toward the stove across the

110

room, where several pots were simmering. "Help yourselves to a meal," she told the twins. "The cook has prepared bouillabaisse and steamed vegetables this evening."

"What's bouillabaisse?" Jessica whispered to Elizabeth as they headed across the enormous room.

"I think it's some kind of fish soup," Elizabeth said.

Jessica wrinkled her nose. "Gross!" she complained. "It's bad enough that we have to have dinner in the kitchen, but we have to eat fish soup as well."

"Doesn't bother me," Elizabeth said, glancing around the airy room. "This could easily be a ballroom."

Jessica had to admit her sister was right. The kitchen was enormous, with a red brick fireplace in the corner and a gigantic old-fashioned stove against the wall. Huge brass pots and pans hung down from hooks on the ceiling.

Jessica lifted the lid of the pot of soup and sniffed it. *It doesn't smell so bad,* she thought, remembering how hungry she was. She filled up two bowls while Elizabeth ladled out steamed vegetables onto their plates. Carrying their bowls of soup carefully, the girls joined the children at the table.

Anna adjusted Manon's bib and stood up. "It looks like you're all set," she said with a smile. "I'll check on you later to make sure everything's okay."

"See you later," Jessica said.

Anna waved and headed out the door.

111

Jessica was totally psyched to get to know the children. When she had been a junior counselor at Camp Echo Mountain, she had been a huge success with her little eight-year-old charges. The kids had adored her and had imitated her every word. At camp she had been solely responsible for eight little girls. Now she only had to worry about three children, and she was sharing the work with Elizabeth. Compared to her junior counselor duties, this job was going to be a snap.

"Hi, kids!" Jessica said, smiling brightly.

Pierre gave her a military salute with his spoon, then burst into giggles. Claudine eyed her warily, a slight pout on her full lips. Manon looked up from her high chair and grinned, food oozing from her teeth.

"Je n'aime pas le céleri!" Claudine grumbled, picking up a stalk of cooked celery with her fingers.

Jessica smiled encouragingly at Claudine. "Can you tell me what you just said in English?"

"This!" Claudine whined, hurling the piece of celery at Jessica. "I no like to taste it!"

Jessica recoiled as the stalk hit her in the chest and bounced onto the table. "Why, you little twerp!" she burst out, standing up angrily.

"Whee!" Manon laughed with glee, throwing a handful of peas into the air. The peas scattered in the air and landed all over the floor. Pierre tossed his bread at Claudine, knocking over her glass of milk. Claudine grinned devilishly as she watched the milk trickle across the table.

112

"Oh, great!" Elizabeth groaned, jumping up and righting the glass. She quickly grabbed some cloth napkins from the table and tried to soak up the milk.

"That's enough!" Jessica commanded, her hands on her hips.

The kids giggled, but they didn't say anything. Claudine looked at the twins innocently as she stabbed a forkful of vegetables. Then she held her fork back like a slingshot and shot them at Pierre. "Ping!" she yelled. Pierre ducked, and a shower of carrots and peas hit the wooden counter behind him. Grinning, Pierre grabbed a stalk of broccoli from his plate and readied his arm to retaliate.

"I said, stop this right now!" Jessica yelled.

Pierre made a face, reluctantly lowering his arm.

"Stop it! Stop it!" Claudine repeated, imitating her.

Well, at least she's speaking English, Jessica thought dryly, scooping up a handful of peas from the floor. Elizabeth returned to the table with a sponge and began wiping up the milk. Jessica quickly cleaned up the vegetables from the table. She headed to the sink and dumped the contents into the garbage can. Elizabeth followed her with a handful of wet napkins.

"I think these little monsters should be sent to bed right now, without finishing dinner," Jessica grumbled.

"Absolutely not," Elizabeth disagreed, wringing out the sponge in the sink.

"Well, do you have a better idea?" Jessica asked, her hands on her hips.

"According to my baby-sitting guide, children should be reasoned with—not punished," Elizabeth explained as they headed back to the table. "They're probably stressed out about meeting us," she added. "This is simply their way of sharing their feelings."

Jessica rolled her eyes and took her seat. Now Manon was banging her hands against her tray and Claudine was building a fort on her plate with her vegetables. Pierre was pretending to drive his beets around the fort. Jessica looked at her plate and realized that she'd lost her appetite.

Elizabeth moved her seat closer to Manon's chair and began a serious conversation with her. "Do you like to play outside? Maybe tomorrow you can show me your favorite place. . . ." She reeled back as Manon shot a handful of warm bouillabaisse into her face.

Just at the moment the kitchen door swung open. "Is everything OK?" Anna asked.

Elizabeth's face reddened, and she quickly wiped the dripping soup from her face. Jessica swallowed hard and looked down. From the way things were going, it looked like she and Elizabeth might not be working at the château for long.

Anna took one look at their horrified faces and laughed. "Don't worry, you'll get the hang of being au pairs in no time," she assured them. "It just takes practice."

Jessica was doubtful. It looked like these kids

would demand more attention than her eight campers combined.

Claudine banged her fork on the table. "I want to see Laurie!"

"Yeah, we want to see Laurie," Manon and Pierre joined in. Soon the three of them were clapping and chanting, "Laurie! Laurie! We want to see Laurie!"

Elizabeth gave Anna an inquiring glance. "Laurie?" she mouthed.

"'Laurie' is Prince Laurent, the children's older brother," Anna explained. "The children adore him."

A prince! Jessica thought excitedly.

"Excuse me, I'm just going to go wash up," Elizabeth said. "I'll be back in a minute." She threw her napkin on the table and hurried out of the kitchen.

Anna began clearing dishes, and Jessica stood up to help her. She stacked up the children's plates and carried them to the sink. "So when will we meet Prince Laurent?" Jessica asked Anna, trying to sound casual.

"I'm not sure about that," Anna said. "You probably won't see much of him while you're here."

Jessica's face fell, but she tried not to let her disappointment show. "Oh?" she asked.

"Prince Laurent is very reclusive," Anna explained. "He spends most of his time alone, reading and thinking." Then she chuckled softly. "Of course, all that might change now that Antonia di Rimini is visiting the château."

"What do you mean?" Jessica asked.

But Anna just shrugged, giving her a pointed look.

Prince Laurent and Antonia? Jessica thought, grimacing. She was totally bummed. A real live prince—and he was a dud.

Thank goodness I already met Jacques! she told herself.

Chapter 8

"Come, children," Anna said, as she pushed back her chair after breakfast on Monday morning. "Elizabeth and Jessica are going to play with you outside today."

Elizabeth took a last sip of her espresso, feeling relaxed after a refreshing night's sleep and a delicious breakfast. Elizabeth had woken to a blue sky and a sun-filled room. When she and Jessica had come downstairs, the table was already set with fresh croissants and bowls of yogurt and granola.

"Shall we clear the dishes?" Claudine asked, sitting straight in her chair. She looked darling in a white lace dress and matching boots. Her hair was pulled up in a thick barrette, and long brown ringlets streamed down her back.

Anna smiled. "That would be lovely."

Elizabeth watched the exchange with suspicion. The children had been startlingly well behaved at

117

breakfast, but Elizabeth had a feeling that this was because of Anna's presence.

Claudine scraped off the dishes and piled up the silverware on top of them. Then she stood up and carefully carried the pile to the sink. Pierre stacked up the breakfast bowls and followed her solemnly.

"I want to play!" whined Manon from her high chair, flailing her little dimpled arms about.

Elizabeth picked her up and swung her high in the air. Manon laughed with glee.

After the table was cleared, Anna led the twins outside. The children followed in a line like little angels.

Elizabeth sucked in her breath as they got outside. It was a beautiful, clear day. Lush green meadows stretched out for miles, meeting up with the dense forest. A sparkling lake could be seen through the trees, and a neat maze of square hedges stood off in the distance to the right. Directly in front of the castle was a wild rose garden, which perfumed the balmy summer air with its sweet scent.

Anna led them past a covered gazebo, where the countess and her daughter were having tea with the prince and princess. A silver teapot stood on a glass table, and china blue cups were set out.

The countess glanced at the twins as they passed and began to gesticulate wildly, speaking loudly in French. The scornfully pronounced words *"les Americaines"* reached Elizabeth's ears, but she couldn't catch anything else.

Oh, well, Elizabeth thought, shrugging. It was just as well that she couldn't hear what the witch was saying about them.

"Hey, is that a maze?" Jessica asked, pointing to the huge labyrinth of trees far to the right.

Anna nodded. "One of the biggest topiary mazes in France."

Elizabeth was enchanted. "Really? How long has it been here?"

"Supposedly it was constructed sometime in the twelfth century as an amusement," Anna responded. Manon jumped in front of her and stretched out her arms. Anna leaned down and picked her up.

"Let's take the kids into the maze!" Jessica suggested.

"No, that is something you absolutely must not do," Anna said, bouncing Manon on her hip. Her voice was stern and solemn. "The maze is more complicated than it looks," she warned. "You can get lost in it for days." Manon squirmed in her arms, and Anna set her down on the ground.

"Oh, come on," Jessica scoffed.

But Anna wasn't fooling around. "People have been known to go in the maze and never come out," she said.

A chill coursed down Elizabeth's spine. For a moment the girls were silent. Then Anna clapped. "Now, let me show you the children's play area."

Anna led the girls to a designated area that was bordered by low hedges. It was a paradise for children, with a deluxe swing set, a sandbox, and a huge wooden dollhouse in the shape of a castle. There was also a small shed full of toys and games.

"Dollhouse!" Manon exclaimed, clapping. She immediately fell onto all fours and crawled into the castle. She peeked at them from a window, her eyes big in her pale face.

"Well, I'll leave you girls for the day," Anna said. "Call me if you have any problems. I'll be with the prince and princess."

"Have a good day, Anna!" Claudine said sweetly. She and Pierre waved as she walked away.

As soon as Anna was out of sight Claudine flew into action. "I no want to play!" she yelled, her face scrunched up in determination. She balled her hands into fists and jumped up and down. Then she grabbed a doll and hurled it at the wall of Manon's castle.

Manon burst into tears and crawled out the back door of the dollhouse. Claudine ran after her and picked her up. Manon pulled at her sister's long curls, and Claudine started screaming. "She pulled my hair!" she wailed.

"OK, you two, break it up," Jessica said, running after the girls.

Pierre looked unconcerned. He was rolling a big plastic ball along the ground. Suddenly he gave it a solid kick with his foot, and it bounced away.

Then he plopped down on the ground and began digging in the dirt.

Elizabeth bit her lip and knelt down by his side, contemplating if this was OK or not. She remembered her book saying that children should be encouraged to play and express themselves freely. *Is this a creative activity?* Elizabeth wondered.

Suddenly Pierre leapt up and took off running.

Elizabeth stood up. "Pierre!" she called. "Stay in the playground."

But Pierre slipped through the hedges and disappeared.

"Pierre!" Elizabeth yelled, running out of the play area into the meadows. Pierre was sprinting across the field with a clear goal in mind. Elizabeth's face fell as she saw where he was headed—right for the gazebo.

"Darn!" Elizabeth muttered, chasing after him. She reached him just as he was hopping up the steps. Elizabeth bit her lip as Pierre dove across the countess's lap. The countess's teacup went flying out of her hand and crashed against the wall, splintering into bits. Warm tea spilled across her lap.

"Oh!" the countess cried in shock. Pierre slid off her lap and ran into the corner. Anna quickly began picking up the broken fragments of the teacup.

Elizabeth shrank back against the door, her face burning.

The countess jumped up, spluttering. The front of her flowing green dress was covered with a huge tea stain smeared with dirt. "Well, of all things!" she burst out in French, futilely rubbing at the stain with a napkin. "This is a brand-new dress, and now it is entirely ruined!" She pursed her lips, shaking her head angrily.

The prince and princess jumped up as well. "My dear, are you all right?" Prince Nicolas asked in French, taking the countess by the arm. "You haven't burned yourself, have you?"

"No, no, I'm fine," the countess responded in a martyred voice. "I've just experienced a slight discomfort, that's all."

"Oh, Countess, please do accept my apologies," Princess Catherine said graciously. She gave Pierre a stern look. "Pierre! What have I told you about staying in the playground?"

Pierre ducked his head and hid between his father's legs.

"You mustn't blame the boy," the countess said, glaring at Elizabeth. "It's not his fault at all. After all, children will be children." She snorted. "Those au pairs are obviously incapable of controlling the children."

Antonia cast Elizabeth a haughty sneer.

Elizabeth bristled with anger. *Who do they think they are?* she thought indignantly.

"Come along," Anna said, putting out a hand to Pierre. He grabbed onto his father's legs, and the prince picked him up with a chuckle. "You're a handful, aren't you?"

Pierre nodded, giggling in delight. When the prince put him down, Pierre ran to Anna. She took him by the hand and led him out of the gazebo. Elizabeth followed quickly, her face still hot with humiliation.

When they reached the play area, Anna gathered the three children together. "Now, remember," she told them, kneeling down to talk to them. "The twins are your baby-sitters now. You're to obey them completely. Is that clear?"

"Yep!" piped up Manon, an innocent look on her face.

Pierre nodded solemnly.

"All right," Anna said, standing up with an indulgent smile. "Now be good, OK?"

"We promise!" Claudine promised.

"I believe them, don't you?" Jessica muttered sarcastically to Elizabeth.

Elizabeth heaved a sigh. This job was turning out to be even worse than she had expected.

I'm definitely not cut out for baby-sitting, Jessica thought as she applied a second coat of crimson nail polish. She was sitting under a luxuriant weeping willow, watching Pierre and Claudine play catch out of the corner of her eye.

She and Elizabeth had tried to get the children to play as a group, but Manon had refused to give up the ball whenever she got hold of it. Then they had decided to teach the kids how to play softball.

123

The twins had found a plastic bat and a whiffle ball in the playroom and had explained the basics of the game. Claudine and Pierre had caught on, but the game was clearly too advanced for Manon. She was only interested in getting the bat in her hand and pounding it on the ground.

Finally Elizabeth had decided to play with Manon alone, leaving Jessica in charge of Pierre and Claudine. Elizabeth and Manon were across the lawn in the sandbox, and it looked like they were playing hide-and-seek. Elizabeth kept building sand dunes and ducking behind them. Manon was throwing fistfuls of sand in the air and squealing with glee.

At first Jessica had protested about being left alone with the two older monsters. After all, it was the twins' first day at the castle, and Jessica wanted to enjoy it. But now she was glad they had been left in her care. Manon was more work than the two of them combined.

Of course, watching the older kids is still work, Jessica thought with a sigh, waving her wet nails in the air. Out of the corner of her eye she could see Princess Catherine and the di Riminis by the in-ground swimming pool.

When Jessica hadn't seen the obnoxious noble pair the night before, she had entertained the hope that they weren't staying in the castle after all. But it turned out that they had attended some royal ball. They had arrived early in the morning, breezing into the castle with all the pomp of a pair of visiting celebrities.

The countess was stretched out on a chaise lounge, a glass of iced tea in her hand. She was wearing some sort of garish red-flowered silk kimono. Her legs were bent at the knees, and her dimpled elbows rested lazily on the arms of the chair. The princess was sitting on a lawn chair next to her, and Anna was setting out a platter of hors d'oeuvres on a small glass side table.

"Mummy, look!" Antonia called in a grating voice from the pool, speaking English with a cultured British accent. She stepped onto the diving board in a sleek white maillot. Jessica scrunched her nose in distaste as Antonia stood poised at the end of the board, obviously trying to draw everybody's attention. "Look what my swimming instructor taught me!"

"Go on, dear!" the countess cooed, responding in English as well.

Antonia held her arms above her head and dove into the air like a graceful swan. Then she crashed into the water flat on her belly, and Jessica burst out laughing.

Serves the royal snob right, she said to herself.

Antonia surfaced, spluttering. "Humph," she said with a scowl, swimming to the edge. She pulled herself out of the water and shook out her short red hair. "That board is too low," she declared in a petulant voice.

"Remember, dear, we're not at home anymore," the countess said in a comforting tone. "Even the swimming pools here are different."

Jessica shook her head in disgust as Antonia stretched her long white body out on the chaise lounge next to her mother. She had never seen a more spoiled girl in her whole life.

Jessica rolled her eyes and returned to her task at hand. She bent her fingers and inspected her nails. Satisfied with her work, she pulled off her leather sandals and stuck cotton balls in between her toes. Bending over, she carefully applied a coat of polish to her little toe.

"Pierre is throwing *la balle* too hard," Claudine whined suddenly.

"The ball," Jessica automatically corrected her without looking up.

Suddenly Elizabeth let out a shriek, and Jessica gave a start. She nearly spilled her nail polish all over her foot.

Jessica looked up in irritation. "What's wrong?" she grumbled.

"Pierre is running away again!" Elizabeth shouted, pointing across the lawn.

Jessica followed her gaze. Sure enough, Pierre was charging across the meadow as fast as his little legs could carry him. With his arms and legs straight out, he looked like some kind of toy robot.

"Pierre! Come back!" Elizabeth screamed, her hands on her hips. "Pierre! Come back this instant!"

126

"He doesn't seem to be listening," Jessica pointed out blandly. She wasn't too worried about him. After all, they were on a private island. He couldn't get very far. Jessica leaned down and began carefully painting her big toe.

"I'm going after him!" Elizabeth declared.

Jessica nodded, intent on her handiwork. "Gotcha," she said.

"Jessica, look at me!" Elizabeth commanded.

Jessica glanced up, annoyed. "What is it now?" she asked.

"Don't take your eyes off the girls," Elizabeth warned. Then she strode off after Pierre.

"All right, all right," Jessica muttered, bending down again. Sometimes Elizabeth could be such a pain.

"Pierre!" Elizabeth shouted as she jogged across the enormous expanse of lawn. She caught sight of him hiding behind a big oak tree. "Pierre! I see you!" she yelled, charging after him.

At the sound of her voice he darted out from behind the tree and sprinted across the clearing. Then he slipped into the huge topiary maze.

"Not in there." Elizabeth groaned, watching in dismay as he disappeared into the enormous tangle of trees.

Anna's warning came back to her, and Elizabeth shivered. *You can get lost in there for days*, she heard Anna's solemn voice saying. *People have been known to go in the maze and never come out. . . .*

Elizabeth put her hands to her head, feeling scared. She had to get Pierre out of there somehow. But Anna would be angry if she found out Elizabeth had disregarded her warning. And what if both she and Pierre disappeared in the twisting labyrinth?

Elizabeth thought quickly. She remembered a passage in her book regarding tone of voice. It had said that children respond instantly to authority. Elizabeth cleared her throat and put on her strictest voice. "Pierre de Sainte-Marie, I demand that you come back here this instant."

She held her breath, but he didn't reappear. All she could hear was the pitter-pattering of his little feet somewhere to the right of her.

"Pierre!" Elizabeth warned, starting to feel slightly hysterical. "If you don't come back this instant, you won't get any lunch!"

She heard him laugh in response. But this time he seemed to be to the left of her. Elizabeth's stomach coiled nervously. He was just a little boy. He could get lost all alone in the maze. Or he could get hurt. *What if he falls down?* Elizabeth worried. *Or what if he gets bitten by a poisonous snake?*

Panicked, Elizabeth rushed headlong into the maze. She found herself in a twisting tunnel of green. The hedges were several feet taller than she was, blocking her view on both sides. The path forked every few feet, and she hurried through it, turning randomly.

Suddenly she stood perfectly still and looked around her. All she saw was a tangle of trees. She was lost already.

"Pierre?" she called, her heart pounding frantically. She heard his laughter and stiffened, listening closely. Elizabeth gritted her teeth in frustration.

The laughter repeated itself, and Elizabeth chased after the sound. But the farther she ran, the more the giggles seemed to change direction. Elizabeth ran left and right along the dirt path. She took turn after turn. But the deeper into the maze she got, the more complicated it seemed to become.

Finally Elizabeth stopped, panting. She looked around, trying to get her bearings. But she was totally disoriented. She had no idea which way was north, and the sound of Pierre's laughter was totally gone.

Don't panic, Elizabeth told herself, trying to stay calm. She'd only been stuck in the maze for several minutes, although it seemed like hours. Obviously there was a way out of the labyrinth. She just had to figure out what it was.

Elizabeth closed her eyes and forced herself to take long, deep breaths. "You need a plan of action," she said to herself. Finally she decided to continue straight ahead, taking only left turns. That had to lead her out eventually.

She walked quickly through the maze, turning

left at every fork. The dirt path was soft underneath her feet, and the hot sun beat down on her back relentlessly. Elizabeth's throat felt parched, and beads of perspiration dripped down her face. But she trudged on with determination.

Suddenly she heard the sound of little footsteps. She stood perfectly still, holding her breath as she gazed around her. The sound of footsteps came again, closer to her.

Elizabeth tiptoed in the direction of the noise, keeping close to the bushes. Then she spied Pierre on his hands and knees, peeking through the hedges.

Elizabeth crept up to him silently, afraid he'd take off again.

"I've got you now," she said, springing on him. She knelt down and held him softly to her, her arm wrapped around his belly. Elizabeth trembled in relief. She would have never forgiven herself if something had happened to him.

Pierre giggled, leaning in closer to her. Elizabeth's anger dissipated immediately. The boy was adorable. "Pierre, you scared me," Elizabeth scolded him softly. "You shouldn't run away like that."

Pierre pressed his finger to his lips. "We mustn't disturb Laurie," he warned her.

Elizabeth peered through the hedges and saw that they were at the edge of a clearing. Obviously they were in the outermost tunnel of the maze. There was a small cottage up ahead. A young man with black hair was fencing with a jousting dummy in front of it. He seemed to be a skilled swordsman.

Elizabeth's entire body flushed at the sight of him, and a strange tingling sensation ran up and down her spine. For a moment Elizabeth felt as if time had stopped. She had the eerie sensation of arriving at the place she had been headed for her whole life.

Pierre grabbed her hand. "Elizabeth, let's go," he said.

But Elizabeth just gazed at the guy, spellbound.

"'Lizabeth!" Pierre repeated.

Elizabeth blinked. "That's your brother?" she asked.

"Yes," Pierre whispered. "But he likes to practice by himself."

Elizabeth silently watched Prince Laurent expertly thrust his sword at the dummy. There was something about him that seemed familiar—his stance, his muscular arms, the chiseled lines of his profile. . . . For some reason he reminded her of someone she knew.

Pierre pulled up a fistful of grass and sprinkled it on Elizabeth's head.

Elizabeth turned to Pierre, the spell broken. Then she shook her head hard and exhaled wearily. "Pi-erre," she said with a groan. "Now stop it!" She quickly wiped the remaining strands of grass from her hair.

Pierre giggled and did a little dance. Elizabeth couldn't help smiling at his antics. She realized that reading books didn't help much when it came to learning to take care of children. Of course, the job would be a lot easier if Jessica would do her share. It was their first day, and Jessica had already managed to let Pierre run off twice.

She'd better shape up immediately, or I'm going to slaughter her, Elizabeth thought.

"Come along, Pierre," she whispered. "Let's see if we can find our way back."

At that, Pierre's eyes lit up. "I know the way easily," he declared. He took Elizabeth's hand firmly in his and tugged her back into the maze.

But Elizabeth felt a strange pull on her heart and turned back to the clearing for a moment. Her breath caught in her throat again as she watched the beautiful guy fencing. He moved as easily and naturally as a wild animal.

I know you, she spoke to him in her mind. *But who are you?*

Prince Laurent leapt into the air and thrust his sword at his imaginary partner. His partner swung his sword forward, and Laurent ducked quickly.

"Attention, *chevalier!*" Laurent yelled, jumping up and lifting his sword in the air. He swiped gracefully at the dummy's sword, his wrist flipping nimbly with each movement. *Click! Clack! Click!*

Suddenly he heard a sound behind him and whirled around quickly. He stood perfectly still, his body coiled. But all he heard was the familiar sound of crickets chirping and birds tweeting high in the trees above him. Laurent shrugged and turned back to the dummy.

But then a dove cooed from a tree branch and flew past him, diverting his thoughts again. Laurent stopped in midair, his sword uplifted. As he followed the path of the lovely white bird, the famous legend of the Château d'Amour Inconnu came back to him.

Every time he heard the sweet sound of a dove, he couldn't help thinking of the romantic tale of Frédéric the Third and Isadora the hand-maiden. And he couldn't help dreaming of meeting his *own* fair-haired girl with a voice of gold someday.

Something rustled from the maze again. His sword in hand, Laurent turned quickly to the hedges. Then he sucked in his breath.

A vision appeared through the thick bushes—an angelic girl with golden blond hair and startling blue-green eyes. She was peeking through the hedges, and she seemed to be watching him. Enchanted, Laurent moved forward toward the maze.

For a moment their eyes met, and Laurent's breath caught in his throat. A liquid current seemed to unite them, and Laurent followed it slowly toward her. Time seemed suspended in the magic of the moment.

But then she disappeared.

Laurent blinked and stared at the hedges. "Was

she really there?" he whispered. There was no trace of her now.

Laurent shook his head and laughed at himself. *Now I'm dreaming awake as well as asleep.*

"OK, now it's Manon's turn," Jessica announced. She was playing hopscotch with the girls on the playground. They had drawn the borders of the game in blue chalk on the ground, and Manon stood on the home square.

Jessica placed a pebble in Manon's hand and helped her toss it onto the first square. Manon squealed with delight as the pebble landed in the middle of the square. She jumped up and down and clapped her plump little hands.

"OK, go get it," Jessica said. Manon did a two-legged jump with an extra bounce in between. Jessica giggled at her creative version of the move.

"I got it!" Manon exclaimed happily. She went to pick it up and lost her balance. Jessica grabbed her quickly and steadied her. Then she guided Manon's hand to help her pick up her rock.

"Here comes Mademoiselle Elizabeth *avec* Pierre," Claudine announced.

"English, Claudine," Jessica murmured.

"*Wiz* Pierre," Claudine corrected herself.

"Very good!" Jessica said. Claudine smiled proudly, flipping her curls over her shoulder.

Jessica looked up as Elizabeth approached. She was holding Pierre by the hand, and he was running

134

along happily beside her. As soon as they reached the playground Pierre flew across the ground and dove into the sandbox.

"Pierre, promise me you'll stay put for a while?" Elizabeth asked, eyeing him warily.

Pierre nodded, already engrossed in his new activity. He was on his hands and knees in the sand, drawing circles with a little stick.

"I want to play in the sand!" Claudine shouted. She pulled off her white boots and jumped into the sandbox with him.

"Me too!" chimed in Manon, slipping out of Jessica's arms and waddling after her sister. She promptly plopped down on her bottom, her legs stretched straight out. She dug her palms in the sand and flung handfuls of it into the air.

Pierre chucked his stick aside and flopped onto his back in the sand. "I'm making *un ange de neige!*" he said proudly, gliding his arms and legs back and forth to form the shape of an angel.

Claudine knelt down by his side. "A snow angel," she corrected him pertly.

"A sand angel!" Pierre yelled out. They both giggled.

Jessica sat down on a bench, relaxing for the first time in an hour. It looked like the kids were going to entertain themselves for a while.

"Did you two have a nice walk?" Jessica asked, turning toward her sister.

"Jessica, I've had it with you!" Elizabeth raged.

"I'm not going to put up with your selfish, lazy attitude this summer!"

Jessica reeled back, shocked. She had been playing all alone with the girls for the past hour while Elizabeth was off running around in the maze. And for the first time since they'd been there, the children were actually behaving. *Who does Elizabeth think she is?* she fumed.

Jessica stood up angrily. "Just because I'm not tripping over myself trying to be Miss Perfect all the time doesn't mean I'm lazy," she responded.

"Yes, it does!" Elizabeth retorted. "If you had been doing your job, then Pierre wouldn't have run off again."

Jessica tossed her hair. It wasn't *her* fault that Pierre had decided to run away. And besides, nothing had happened to him. "Oh, Liz, you're such a worrywart," she said in disgust.

"And you're such a prima donna!" Elizabeth returned.

"Well, at least *I'm* not the most boring au pair in the history of the world," Jessica shot back. "Maybe the kids would listen to you if you'd be a little more fun."

"*Fun?*" Elizabeth responded, her eyes flashing. "It's easy to have fun when you're totally irresponsible. I'm sick of being *your* baby-sitter."

Jessica planted her fists on her hips. "Well, I'm sick of it too! Why don't you leave me alone and stop being so bossy?"

"Me! *Bossy?*" Elizabeth yelped. "Who forced me to come here in the first place?"

"Well, if it weren't for me, you'd never do anything with your life," Jessica said in a huff. "You're the most boring person on this planet!"

Sparks shot from Elizabeth's eyes. "And you're the most selfish, unreliable sister imaginable!"

"Well, if that's the way you feel, why don't you go back home?" Jessica yelled.

"Maybe I will!" Elizabeth replied hotly.

"Good!" Jessica returned. Then she caught a glimpse of Anna out of the corner of her eye. She and the gardener were standing at the edge of the playground, staring at them. The kids were silent from the sandbox, watching the fight with interest.

Jessica turned red and lowered her eyes, her lips pursed.

Elizabeth stared at her feet, her arms folded across her chest.

Then Jessica glanced at her sister, wordlessly establishing a stony truce. Obviously they couldn't continue fighting in front of everybody.

But the truce is only temporary, Jessica thought stubbornly. *I'll never forgive Elizabeth for humiliating me like this.*

Chapter 9

Jessica sat outside on a stone bench in the rose garden on Tuesday afternoon, eating a picnic lunch by herself. It was another beautiful day. The sky was a clear, bright blue, and a light rose-scented breeze wafted through the air. Fernand, the cook, had gone out of his way to prepare a French specialty for Jessica called a *"croque monsieur."* It was the French version of a grilled cheese sandwich.

Jessica took a big bite out of her sandwich, catching some melted cheese on her index finger and licking it off. Despite the delicious lunch and the warm rays of sun beaming down on her shoulders, Jessica's spirits were low. She was still fuming about her fight with Elizabeth the day before.

Jessica couldn't believe the horrible things Elizabeth had said to her. Her sister had accused her of being selfish, lazy, and unreliable. *And* a prima donna! Jessica's face burned at the memory. It was so unfair. She hadn't done a thing to deserve her sister's insults.

In fact, Elizabeth's been nothing but unpleasant ever since we left Sweet Valley, Jessica thought angrily. Her sister was acting as if she were doing Jessica some huge favor by agreeing to spend the summer with her in a castle with royalty in France.

Jessica shook her head. She didn't know why she had wanted Elizabeth to come with her in the first place. Her sister was no fun at all. She was treating their au pair job like it was the most important position in the world, and she was treating Jessica like one of the children. Jessica puffed out her cheeks in frustration. She wished Elizabeth would chill out and relax a little. There was no way Jessica could enjoy their trip if her sister insisted on being the baby-sitting police.

After their fight the girls had barely spoken to each other. They had been virtually silent during dinner, only exchanging words when absolutely necessary. Even the kids had been well behaved at dinner, obviously sobered by the twins' solemn moods.

The evening had been endless. When the kids were finally tucked into bed, Jessica had exploded. "This is impossible!" she had exclaimed. "I can't go on like this!"

"Neither can I!" Elizabeth had agreed hotly.

But neither of them had budged. So finally the girls had agreed to split their duties. That way they would avoid spending more time together than was absolutely necessary and the work would be equally distributed. Jessica had taken the morning shift, and now it was Elizabeth's turn to take care of the children.

Jessica ate the last of her sandwich and wiped the crumbs off her hands. She picked up her orange soda and finished it off as well. Then she crumpled up her napkin and stuffed everything into the paper bag by her side.

Now what? Jessica thought gloomily. It was great that she had a break from the kids, but it wasn't so much fun being alone. She wished Jacques would come and visit her. Now that she and Elizabeth weren't speaking to each other, she wanted to see him more than ever. *I wonder what Jacques is doing right now?* she thought.

Jessica leaned back against the bench and drew her knees up to her chest, realizing that she didn't know anything about him at all. She tore absently at a hole in her faded blue jeans, deep in thought. Jacques looked like he was about her age, so he must be in high school. But she had no idea what a duke's son did over summer vacation. *Maybe he spends the break out on the beach, windsurfing and sailing,* Jessica pondered. *Or maybe he travels to exotic places all over the world with his father.*

Suddenly a white dove flew overhead, crooning softly. Jessica sucked in her breath, reminded of the legend of the Château d'Amour Inconnu. She

141

watched breathlessly as the beautiful bird fluttered around a rosebush. Then the bird let out a plaintive cry and flew away. Jessica exhaled sharply. She was sure it was a sign. Obviously she was meant to have a mysterious romance this summer. Fate had brought her and Jacques together.

Even though she had just seen Jacques two days ago, the train ride seemed like a distant memory now. Jessica closed her eyes, dreamily remembering Jacques's passionate kiss on the train and the intense look in his liquid brown eyes. She could feel his strong arms around her waist, and she could hear his soft voice whispering, *Until we meet again*.

"Mademoiselle, I have mail for you," Anna called, startling Jessica out of her daydream. Jessica open her eyes quickly, blinking in the sun.

Anna was approaching from the castle, waving a letter in her hand. *It must be from Jacques!* Jessica thought excitedly. A letter from home couldn't possibly have reached her so fast. *What a wild coincidence!* she thought. His letter had arrived at the exact moment she was thinking about him. They definitely had a cosmic connection.

"Looks like somebody has an admirer," Anna with a smile, her brown eyes sparkling.

Jessica jumped up, her cheeks flushing happily. "Thanks, Anna!" she said, taking the letter from her outstretched hand.

"My pleasure!" Anna responded with a wink. "I

always like to help out in affairs of the heart." She turned and headed for the gazebo.

As soon as Anna was out of sight Jessica turned the letter over, a small smile on her face. Then she jumped as if she had been burned. The letter was addressed to Elizabeth, and it was from Todd. It had been sent Express Mail. Jessica's heart sank to her feet.

"Express Mail," she grumbled in disgust. "I wonder what Mr. Boring as Toast has to say that's so important."

Jessica tapped the envelope on her palm, thinking of how sad Elizabeth was about Todd. After he had broken up with her for the summer, her sister had cried for about twenty-four hours straight. But now she seemed to be doing better. She hadn't mentioned his name for a few days. *Elizabeth is just starting to get over him,* Jessica told herself. *It's a shame that he's bothering her again.*

Jessica stood up and headed for the playground to deliver the letter. She sighed, feeling sorry for herself. *I'm the one who deserves a love letter,* Jessica thought. *Especially after the way Elizabeth abused me in public yesterday.*

Suddenly she stopped in her tracks. What was she doing, delivering Elizabeth's mail to her? Had she lost her mind? Once again, Elizabeth's mean words came back to her. *You're the most selfish, irresponsible sister imaginable!* she heard Elizabeth's sharp voice yelling. Jessica felt her blood boiling again.

You want to see selfish? Jessica responded in her mind. *Fine!*

Jessica did an about-face and headed directly to the château, stuffing the letter into the back pocket of her jeans. She breezed into the kitchen and dropped her lunch bag in the trash.

"How was your *déjeuner,* Mademoiselle Jessica?" Fernand asked. He was standing at the counter, chopping up fresh vegetables on a cutting board.

"It was *délicieux!*" Jessica responded.

Fernand beamed with pleasure. *"Tant mieux!"* he said. "So much the better!"

Jessica walked casually down the hall and tip-toed into the parlor. A fire was crackling in the hearth as usual, but the room was entirely deserted. Jessica looked around quickly. Then she held her breath, listening for voices. Nobody was in the vicinity.

Her pulse quickening, she pulled the letter out of her pocket. She hesitated for a moment, then she shoved it into the fireplace. The fire crackled loudly and the red flames licked hungrily at the sides of the envelope.

Sweet revenge! Jessica thought. Feeling guilty but happy, Jessica folded her arms and watched the letter disintegrate into nothing.

"Pierre, stop throwing the books," Elizabeth snapped.

Pierre turned to her guiltily, an oversize hardcover

book in his outstretched arm. Pouting, he slowly lowered his hand to his side.

It was late in the afternoon and Elizabeth was in the nursery with the children, trying to read a story to them. The children had a whole bookshelf full of English books, and this was their favorite. It was called *The Big Apple* and recounted the tale of a little French girl who took a trip to New York City. She befriended an elephant that had escaped from the Bronx Zoo and hid out with him in Central Park.

The girls were enthralled with the story. Curled up on either side of Elizabeth, they were taking in her every word. But Pierre wouldn't sit still. He was having more fun pulling books off the shelves and pitching them at the wall. A pile of children's books was already scattered all over the floor.

Where is Jessica? Elizabeth wondered, checking her watch. Her twin should have taken over two hours ago. Sighing, she turned back to the story.

"And so Susanna jumped up on Edward the Elephant's back," Elizabeth read aloud. "He lifted his big trunk in the air, and they galloped through the snowy woods in Central Park together."

"Is that Central Park?" Claudine asked, pointing to the picture.

"There's Edward!" Manon exclaimed.

Another book hit the wall with a loud thud. "That's it! I've had it," Elizabeth declared firmly, slamming the book shut.

"But we're not finished with the story!" Claudine protested.

"Book! More book!" Manon yelled out. She leapt to her feet and jumped up and down on the couch. Picking up a pillow, she flung it at Pierre.

Pierre ducked, and the pillow hit the wall. Pierre danced on his little feet, sticking out his tongue at Manon. Manon started to cry.

Elizabeth felt like pulling out her hair. Standing up, she placed her hands firmly on her hips. "Pierre, I want you to pick up every single book right now," she said in a quiet, authoritative tone.

Pierre looked at her with big round eyes. Then he turned his lips down and began picking up books.

"Claudine, will you please put the pillows back on the couch?" she asked with a sigh.

"OK, Elizabeth," Claudine agreed, obviously sensing her distress.

"And you," Elizabeth said, reaching for Manon and picking her up in the air. "You sit with me." Manon stopped crying and wrapped her arms around Elizabeth's neck. Elizabeth breathed a sigh of relief, sitting down with her on her lap.

Pierre glanced at her through lowered eyelids. "Everything's all cleaned up now, 'Lizabeth," he said.

"Great!" Elizabeth said with a smile. She patted the space by her side. "Now if you'll sit here quietly, I'll let you read out loud."

"I want to read too!" Claudine yelled.

Elizabeth nodded. "You'll both get your chance."

146

Elizabeth laid the book open on Pierre's lap and indicated where he should pick up with the story.

"All the zookeepers came, and Edward the Elephant hid behind a tree. But he was too big. . . ." Pierre read.

Elizabeth glanced at her watch again. She couldn't believe the audacity of her twin. Yesterday Jessica had spent the morning painting her nails instead of watching the kids, and today she wasn't even bothering to show up.

"What's a 'sleigh ride'?" Pierre asked, pointing to the page.

"It's a ride in the snow on *un traîneau,* a sled," Elizabeth explained.

Just then the door opened and Jessica breezed in, smiling. "Are we ready to have some real fun, kids?"

Manon hopped off Elizabeth's lap and ran to her sister. "Jessica! Can we go swimming again?" She held out her arms and Jessica picked her up, giving Elizabeth a triumphant smile.

Elizabeth glared at her sister. She was about to give her a piece of her mind, but then she bit her tongue. After all, the kids were there. And besides, it hardly seemed worth the trouble. *I should be thankful she bothered to show up at all,* Elizabeth thought.

Elizabeth stood up. "See you later, guys," she said, smiling at the children. Then she stuck her nose in the air and breezed by Jessica without a word.

Elizabeth walked quickly down the hall and headed for the back door, getting more and more furious by the minute. It was bad enough that Jessica had shown up almost three hours late, but now she was competing with Elizabeth for the children's affection as well. Elizabeth shook her head in disgust.

Once she was outside, Elizabeth took long, deep breaths to calm herself. What she needed was a long, quiet walk away from the kids and away from her sister. Elizabeth glanced warily at the sky. Despite the earlier sunshine, it looked like a storm was approaching. The air was cool and damp, and a wind seemed to be picking up. Big black clouds hung threateningly in the sky.

A cold wind whipped through the trees, and Elizabeth shivered. She was dressed for summer, in a long, wraparound Indian print cotton skirt and an ivory T-shirt. Elizabeth hesitated, wondering if she should run upstairs and grab a jacket. But she didn't want to go back inside and risk facing Jessica again. Then she shrugged. Dinner was in less than an hour, so she wouldn't have time for more than a short walk anyway.

Elizabeth ducked her head and walked rapidly toward the forest, her heart heavy. She didn't know when she'd been so unhappy. First Todd dumped her, and now Jessica was turning on her. Elizabeth sighed deeply. She felt all alone in the world.

A deep bolt of thunder rumbled in the distance, agreeing with Elizabeth's black mood. Elizabeth hurried into the woods, hoping the approaching storm would hold off for an hour. It was damp and calm in the dense forest, and the smell of wet pinecones filled the air. Elizabeth walked quickly along the winding dirt path, taking deep breaths of the cool, fresh air.

After many twisting turns the path led out of the forest, and she found herself at a new entrance to the topiary maze. Elizabeth peeked into the tunnel of trees, feeling an almost irresistible urge to go inside it. She was sure she could take it back to the other side, to the meadow leading to the Château d'Amour Inconnu. Elizabeth hesitated a moment, then pressed on. Now that she wasn't chasing Pierre, she'd be careful to remember which turns she had taken.

Elizabeth felt a twinge of excitement as she entered the thick labyrinth of trees. The hedges blanketed her against the wind, and it was strangely silent in the maze. Elizabeth imagined herself as a princess slipping away for a few stolen moments of solitude. *What would a princess be thinking about right now?* she wondered. "True love, of course," she murmured aloud, answering her own question.

Obviously I'm not a princess, Elizabeth thought with a scowl, taking a turn to the right.

As she followed the damp path her mind drifted to Todd. *What's he doing right now?* she asked herself. She pictured him at the beach, playing volleyball on the sand with the guys. Or maybe he was alone on the basketball court, practicing his layups. Or maybe he was out on a date with another girl. . . .

Elizabeth shook the thought away. *Think positively,* she commanded herself. For all she knew, Todd was sitting alone in the park, thinking about her.

Does he miss me? she wondered, tears coming to her eyes. *Is he sorry that we broke up?* A tear slipped down her cheek, and Elizabeth wiped it quickly away.

Drawing a shaky breath, Elizabeth blinked back her tears. She reached another fork in the path and turned to the right again. Then she hesitated. Was the château to the right or the left? She looked around in all directions, realizing that she was totally disoriented. She'd lost her way once again.

How could you be so stupid? she berated herself. As she tried to find her bearings a bolt of thunder rocked the sky, and raindrops began to fall.

"Oh, great!" she grumbled, hugging her arms around herself. Now she was wet *and* lost. And it was getting dark. Feeling nervous, Elizabeth ran quickly to the left. After all, she reassured herself, she didn't have to find the château exit. She just had to find a way out of the maze. Elizabeth ran faster and faster, getting more and more scared.

The rain fell harder, causing the path under her feet to turn to mud. Panicked, Elizabeth began running blindly, sloshing through the maze in her soggy sandals. After a few minutes her clothes were soaked and she found herself shivering uncontrollably.

I'll never find my way out of here, she thought anxiously. She heard a sharp crack of thunder, and a flash of lightning zipped through the sky. A cold wind whipped through the trees, shooting big drops of rain into her face. "This is a nightmare!" she whimpered to herself, wrapping her arms around her body again. She could catch pneumonia. Or get electrocuted. Now Elizabeth was truly terrified.

Another flash of lightning shot through the sky and lit up the area for a second. Through the hedges Elizabeth caught a quick glimpse of a small cottage. Her whole body trembled in relief. She charged directly through the hedges to the clearing, scratching her bare arms on the branches.

But Elizabeth was oblivious to the pain. Breathing hard, she flew across the wet grass and pounded on the door of the cottage. *Please, please, let someone be here,* she said to herself. Otherwise she was doomed.

"Are you still working, Jessica?" Princess Catherine asked, popping her head into the nursery on Tuesday evening.

Jessica looked up at the sound of the princess's voice. Jessica was kneeling on the floor, stacking up a pile of board games. "I was just cleaning," she explained. The nursery was almost all tidied up, and the children were bathed and tucked into their

151

beds. Getting them to bed had been a harrowing ordeal in itself.

The princess gave her a kind smile. "Well, everything looks perfect," she said. "Why don't you relax and enjoy yourself for the evening?"

Jessica flashed her a grateful smile, and the princess shut the door behind her.

"Finally!" Jessica muttered after the princess left the room. She carried the stack of games across the room and placed them carefully on the shelf. She was exhausted after playing with the children all evening, and she was starving as well. The kids had been so boisterous at dinner that Jessica had barely been able to take a bite.

Jessica leaned her head against the wall and closed her eyes. All she wanted to do was crawl into her bed and fall into a deep sleep. For once her tiny attic room seemed appealing. But her stomach was growling insistently. Jessica forced her eyes open and dragged herself to the kitchen.

The head chef was busy at the stove. A couple of steak filets were sizzling in a pan, and the rich smells of a chocolate cake came from the oven. Obviously he was preparing a gourmet dinner for the royal couple and their guests.

Jessica wandered over to him. "Is there anything left to eat?" she asked him.

The cook looked annoyed at being interrupted and snapped at her in French.

Jessica bit her lip. "Um, *répétez, s'il vous plaît?*"

she said, asking him to repeat what he had said.

The chef pointed to a covered pot on the stove and grumbled, "Beef."

Jessica smiled and lifted the lid. *Ah!* she thought, recognizing the dish as beef bourguignon. She ladled out a heaping plateful. Then she grabbed a bottle of soda from the refrigerator and carried everything to the table.

Jessica took a hungry bite out of her meal. "Mmm," she murmured appreciatively. This was much better than the pasta the children had eaten earlier.

Just then Anna breezed into the kitchen, a blouse and sewing supplies in her hand. She said something to the cook in French, then she joined Jessica at the table. "The job—it goes well?" she asked Jessica.

Jessica rolled her eyes dramatically. "I'm learning," she admitted. She wiped her mouth with her napkin and took a sip of her soda.

Anna smiled and patted her hand. "The children are very spirited, but they're loving and kind. They will respond to you soon enough."

"I hope so," Jessica said. "They're sweet, but they're exhausting." She dipped her fork into her food and blew on it.

Anna laid the blouse on the table. Then she ripped off a piece of thread and knotted it adeptly. "Is it difficult being so far from home?" she asked.

Jessica shrugged. "No, it's OK," she said

thoughtfully. "I miss my friends and my family, but it's nice to get away for a change." She brought her fork to her lips and took a big bite.

"So you did not leave a handsome boyfriend behind?" Anna asked. Her round brown eyes twinkled mischievously.

Jessica swallowed and shook her head. "No. I was dating a guy named Cameron, but it didn't work out." Jessica had met Cameron Smith during her internship as an assistant to the head photographer at *Flair* magazine. They had gone out for a while, but eventually the relationship had fizzled out. Cameron had to travel all the time on business, and they rarely got to see each other.

"Oh, that is too bad," Anna said. She opened her sewing kit and picked out a small blue button. Then she sewed it on the shirt with nimble fingers.

"Well, I did meet a fascinating guy on the train," Jessica ventured.

Anna dropped the shirt on the table. "You don't waste any time, do you?"

Jessica shook her head with a laugh. Then she leaned in close to Anna. "What do you know about the son of the duke of Norveaux?" she asked.

Anna tipped her head, visibly confused. "There is no duke of Norveaux," she said.

Jessica frowned. "What do you mean?"

Anna shrugged. "Well, as far as I know, Norveaux doesn't exist."

"Maybe you've just never heard of it?" Jessica suggested.

But Anna shook her head firmly. "I'm afraid not. France isn't a very big country, and the regions have been established for a long time." Then she laughed. "Poor Jessica. You've obviously run into a dashing French rogue with a silver tongue."

Jessica's stomach dropped to her feet. *Is it possible that Jacques lied to me?* she wondered. She thought of his flirtatious lines, his smooth jokes, his seductive accent. . . . *It's more than possible,* she realized finally.

"Don't be sad," Anna told her. "In France everything is forgiven if it is for love. Maybe this young fellow wanted badly to impress you."

"For love," Jessica muttered, lowering her eyes.

Jessica pushed her food around on her plate with her fork, angry with herself for being so stupid. She didn't think Jacques had lied to her for love. He was probably just looking for a fun time on the train. After all, the jewel he gave her was just a cheap piece of junk. Suddenly she felt sick to her stomach.

"I'm too tired to eat anymore," Jessica said, quickly pushing her chair back and standing up. "If you'll excuse me."

Anna followed her with worried eyes. "Good night, Jessica," she said softly.

Jessica climbed the long, winding steps to her tiny attic room and pushed open the door. Without bothering to turn on the light, she threw herself across her bed. She felt totally dejected. Nothing was working out right.

I'm treated like a servant around here, Jessica thought. *Elizabeth hates me. I burned an important letter. I'm a terrible baby-sitter. And Jacques turns out to be a jerk!*

Jessica sat up and folded her arms, tears stinging in her eyes. "Life is so unfair!"

Chapter 10

Prince Laurent opened the door of his cottage, and an electric current coursed through his body. Standing before him was the blond girl from his dream. Startled, he stood rooted to the spot, his heart pounding.

"Can I please come in?" she demanded in English, trembling.

Suddenly Laurent realized that the girl was soaked to the skin and shivering violently. Obviously she was very real—and in distress.

"Oh, excuse me!" Laurent exclaimed, responding in English as well. He held open the door and ushered her inside, kicking himself for thinking she was a mirage. *She must be one of the au pairs,* he realized suddenly. *Otherwise she wouldn't be speaking English.*

"Please, follow me," he said, leading her to a

small, rustic den. A thick red throw rug covered the wooden floor, and a bright fire crackled in the hearth.

"Why don't you warm up by the fire?" he suggested. She smiled at him gratefully and sank down on the rug in front of the fire. Laurent glanced at her in wonder, then he rushed off to find some towels.

When he returned, the sight of her startled him all over again. Framed by the fire's glow, she was kneeling with her hands outstretched. Her heart-shaped face was flushed pink and her lips curled in a soft smile. Something in Laurent's heart stirred, as if warmed by the same fire.

She turned to him at that moment, and Laurent felt his heart melt completely.

"Um, are those for me?" she asked with a small grin.

"Oh, right! Yes!" he said, hurrying toward her and handing her a stack of fluffy blue towels. He didn't know what had come over him. Usually he was calm and in control, and now he was falling to pieces.

"Thank you," she said, accepting them gratefully. She wiped off her arms and rubbed a towel briskly through her wet hair. Laurent sat down in an armchair by the corner of the rug, trying not to stare at her.

The girl wrapped the towel turban style around her head, and Laurent glanced at her admiringly. Now she looked even more like a princess than ever. Her eyes glittered like sapphires, and her wide cheekbones stood out in her luminescent face. Laurent's stomach fluttered strangely.

"I'm Elizabeth Wakefield," she said with a smile. "I'm working at the château as an au pair for the summer."

Laurent nodded and smiled back. "That is what I guessed," he said. "Most French girls don't speak perfect English." He pushed a lock of dark hair off his forehead. "I'm Laurent, the oldest de Sainte-Marie."

"I know," the girl admitted, a sheepish grin on her face. "I saw you yesterday when you were practicing with your sword." She blushed suddenly and looked down. "Pierre is a bit devilish at times," she explained. "He ran into the maze, and I had to go in after him. I finally found him by the hedges in front of the cottage."

So I didn't imagine her after all, Prince Laurent realized, somewhat relieved. *She really did disappear into the maze.*

Elizabeth shivered, and Laurent jumped up quickly. "You're still cold," he said. He grabbed a thick red blanket from the sofa and knelt down next to her. "Here," he said, handing her the blanket. "Try to warm up a bit."

Elizabeth wrapped the blanket tightly around her shoulders and smiled at him gratefully.

Laurent smiled back and stood up. "Uh, I'll go make you a pot of tea," he said, backing out of the room awkwardly.

Laurent rushed to the kitchen and quickly put on a kettle of water. He was completely shaken up.

Even if he hadn't imagined Elizabeth in the maze, he *had* dreamed about her. He was sure of it. She had the same golden blond hair and the same ocean blue eyes as the mysterious girl in his dream. It was uncanny.

A few minutes later Laurent returned to the den with a steaming pot of tea and two china cups. He quickly poured Elizabeth a cup and sat down opposite her.

Elizabeth took a sip of hot tea and set down the cup. Her hair hung loose around her shoulders now, and her face was glowing. "What a relief!" she exclaimed. "I feel a hundred times better." She shook her head. "I was worried I would never get out of the maze."

"It's a lot more complicated than it looks," Laurent said. "I used to play in it for hours and hours as a little boy."

Elizabeth grinned. "Just like Pierre!" she said.

Laurent nodded. "But *my* nannies never found me!" he said with a wink.

After Elizabeth had finished her cup of tea, she stood up. "I should be getting back to the château," she said. "I'm already late for dinner."

At that moment a bolt of thunder crashed through the sky, followed by a streak of lightning. Elizabeth bit her lip, going to the window and pulling back the curtain. Laurent got up and joined her. It was dark outside, and a steady stream of rain was pouring down. "I hope there's an easier route than the maze," Elizabeth said.

Laurent shook his head. "There's a dirt road that loops around the estate, but it's probably flooded. And the maze is out of the question. Even *I* couldn't find my way through it in this weather."

Elizabeth looked at him, worry in her clear blue-green eyes. "What am I going to do?" she asked softly.

"You'll have to stay here with me tonight," Laurent decided.

And let me take care of you, Laurent added to himself. He only wished the rain would never stop.

Hours later Elizabeth was curled up in a heavy blanket on the couch, sipping hot cider. She and Laurent were in a small sitting room with big bay windows and wooden ceiling beams. A warm fire burned in the hearth, casting an orange glow about the cozy room.

Prince Laurent was telling her about some of the childhood pranks he had pulled on his baby-sitters. He spoke almost perfect English, with just the slightest French accent. With his smooth, chiseled features and jet-black hair, he looked every bit the refined noble. But when he talked, everything about him changed. His deep blue eyes crinkled and his face lit up, giving him a warm, mischievous air. Elizabeth found herself completely entranced by him.

"One summer I had a young British girl as an au pair," he said. "She was very polite and very timid. I made up a legend about a headless horseman, and then one night I rode in front of her window on my horse. I was wearing a sheet and carrying a dummy's head in my hand. I've never heard anybody scream so loud." He grinned sheepishly. "She left the next day."

"That's despicable," Elizabeth said, laughing. "Compared to you, Pierre, Claudine, and Manon are perfect angels!" Elizabeth took a sip of cider, shaking her head. "In fact, I'm surprised you're even related."

A shadow crossed Laurent's face suddenly, and his expression turned serious. "Well, they're only my half siblings," he said.

Elizabeth looked at him quizzically.

"My mother died when I was ten," Laurent said quietly. "She drowned in a boat accident on the Mediterranean Sea."

Elizabeth gasped. "How horrible!" she exclaimed sympathetically.

Laurent nodded. "I know," he said. He picked up his mug of cider and took a sip, a pensive look on his face. "But you know, somehow it was comforting to me that she died at sea." Laurent was quiet for a moment. Then he stood up and walked to the window, pulling back the curtain and gazing out the window. "My mother was a creature of the water. She grew up on the coast of France and spend her childhood sailing and waterskiing." Laurent walked across the room, deep in thought.

"It was like she returned to her natural habitat." Then he looked embarrassed and scuffed his foot along the floor. "I've never told anybody that before," he said.

"Was she your father's first love?" Elizabeth asked softly.

Laurent frowned. "I think so, or at least I *thought* so," he corrected himself. He shook his head and walked to the fire, picking up an iron poker. "It's the strangest thing. I just found out that my father and Catherine were friends before he married my mother." Laurent shrugged and stoked the fire. "Who knows? Maybe they were in love way back then."

Elizabeth was quiet, caught up in Laurent's tale. But suddenly Laurent turned around and faced her, a small smile on his lips. "And do you know what's even stranger?"

Elizabeth shook her head. "What?"

"When my father was my age, he refused the throne and tried to establish a more equitable political system. He was a sort of revolutionary."

Elizabeth's mouth dropped open. "Prince Nicolas? A revolutionary?"

"I didn't believe it myself," Laurent said with a laugh.

Elizabeth was pensive. "You know, that's funny. My mother was exactly the same in the seventies. She was a bit of a radical herself. She organized peace marches and political rallies—"

"And she had long hair and wore colored beads around her neck," Laurent finished for her.

Elizabeth laughed along with him. "Exactly!" she said.

Laurent's expression softened, and he caught her eyes in his. Elizabeth felt suddenly light-headed, as if she were flying.

Laurent sat down across from her on the couch. "You know, Elizabeth, I feel like I've known you forever," he said quietly.

Elizabeth nodded. "I feel the same way," she whispered.

Suddenly a bird tweeted and a faint golden light shone through the white lace curtains. Laurent went to the window and pulled them open. The sun was just appearing over the horizon. Elizabeth stared at it in disbelief. They'd been up all night, talking and laughing.

"Good morning," Laurent said, facing her with a smile. "It looks like it's going to be a beautiful day."

"It does," Elizabeth agreed. The sky was bright and clear, and there wasn't a cloud in sight.

"I know you're anxious to get back to my angelic siblings," Laurent joked, "but what about breakfast first? I make a very terrific cheese omelette."

Elizabeth raised her eyebrows. "I've been rescued by a prince who can cook?" she declared. "I am one lucky damsel in distress."

"Does that mean you accept my offer?" Laurent asked.

164

Elizabeth nodded with a laugh.

"Right this way, my damsel in distress," Laurent said, leading her down the hall.

The kitchen was small and cozy, just like the rest of the wooden cottage. The floor was covered in faded red tiles, and the walls were painted a pale green. Potted plants lined the windowsill.

"Let me help you," Elizabeth said.

"Absolutely not," Laurent refused with a shake of his head. "Today is your day off." He pointed to a chair sternly.

Elizabeth smiled and sat down at the round wooden table in the corner. She rested her chin on her hand and watched him prepare breakfast. Laurent tied a white apron around his waist and plopped a big white chef's cap on his head. Then he gave Elizabeth a deep bow. "Chef Laurent, at your service!"

Elizabeth couldn't help chuckling. Grabbing a handful of eggs from the refrigerator, Laurent proceeded to juggle them in the air. He flipped an egg behind his back and caught it in one hand. "That's to impress the visiting au pair," he said with a wink. Then he cracked the eggs against a bowl and mixed them with a fork.

A few minutes later a big Spanish omelette was sizzling in a frying pan. "Now we are going to fleep zee omelette," Laurent said, exaggerating his own accent. "Just like they do in the movies." With that he whisked the pan off the stove and flipped the omelette into the air, catching it smoothly on a big plate. He set the plate in front of Elizabeth with a flourish. "At your service, my princess." He bowed low again.

Elizabeth giggled as he joined her at the table. *Laurent keeps showing me new sides of himself,* she thought. He was obviously quite complex. He was serious, deep, funny, and silly all at the same time. *He's a lot like me,* Elizabeth realized with a start.

Laurent cut the omelette in half and served her. *"Bon appétit!"* he said.

"Bon appétit!" Elizabeth responded, cutting into the omelette and taking a bite.

Elizabeth sat back and took a sip of fresh-roasted coffee, feeling at peace for the first time since she'd arrived on the island. She'd never met a boy she felt so comfortable with. *Except Todd,* she silently reminded herself. But she pushed the thought out of her mind. *He hasn't tried to get in touch with me,* she thought. *Todd is history.*

Besides, she and Laurent were just friends. Obviously that was why she felt so comfortable with him. But she looked into his dark blue eyes, and her heart fluttered.

We are just friends, she told herself. *Aren't we?*

Where are you, Liz? Jessica worried on Wednesday morning, her heart in her throat. *Where are you?* She had been repeating the words all morning.

166

She was trying to supervise the kids at breakfast, but her mind was a blur of panic. She didn't have any idea where Elizabeth had gone. And she had no idea how long she'd been missing. Jessica had only noticed her disappearance this morning.

When she told the prince and princess de Sainte-Marie about her sister's absence, they assured her that Elizabeth was OK. "She probably took shelter from the storm in one of the cottages or huts on the estate," the princess had said. They promised to send some workers to look for her if she didn't return by midmorning.

But that could be too late, Jessica thought worriedly. *Elizabeth could be lying in a ditch, hurt and bleeding, right now.* Her tongue went dry at the thought.

"Jessica, can I have another croissant?" Claudine asked.

Jessica nodded and handed her the bread basket absently. She pushed back her chair and went to the window, willing her sister to appear. But all that greeted her eyes were long, clear stretches of meadow. Elizabeth was nowhere to be seen.

Elizabeth, please be OK, Jessica pleaded silently to the empty fields. She only hoped that Elizabeth hadn't gotten lost in the storm the night before. *Maybe she fell down in the forest and hurt herself,* Jessica thought. *Or maybe she was attacked by a wild animal.* Then a horrible thought struck her. What if Elizabeth had gone into the ocean by herself?

167

Jessica bit her lip, tears coming to her eyes. If anything had happened to her sister, it would be all her fault. After all, Jessica was the one who had upset her yesterday. If Elizabeth had taken off in the storm, it was because of Jessica.

Finally Jessica decided she couldn't stand it any longer. She had to go out and look for her sister. She would just have to bring the children with her.

"C'mon, kids," Jessica said, clapping sharply. "Let's get the table cleaned up. Pronto!"

"Pronto!" Pierre said with a giggle, imitating the new word.

After the table was cleared, Jessica mopped up the children's hands and faces and herded them outdoors. The day was calm and clear, and everything was fresh and glistening from the rain. But the ground was still damp, and all three kids promptly ran for the muddy puddles. Pierre splashed about wildly, kicking dirty water at Claudine. Claudine shouted in pleasure, jumping up and down in a puddle.

"Chil-dren!" Jessica called, running after them. Just as she reached the puddle, the Countess di Rimini and Antonia walked by. The countess lifted her waxed-thin eyebrows as she took in the sight of the children playing in the mud. Then she pursed her lips, muttering something in French to Antonia.

Jessica had no idea what she had said, but she flashed her a wry smile. "The same to you," she replied.

The countess gasped and rushed off in a huff with her daughter. Jessica made a face behind their backs.

Claudine and Pierre snickered, making nasty faces at the di Riminis as well. The children tried to outdo each other, sticking their tongues out and putting their thumbs in their ears.

Jessica rolled her eyes. "You kids are too much."

"Mademoiselle Elizabeth!" Manon cried suddenly, pointing across the yard.

Jessica whirled around and saw her twin sauntering toward them. Elizabeth looked relaxed and happy, whistling as she headed across the meadow. Jessica's whole body trembled with relief, and she flew across the lawn to meet her.

"What in the world happened?" Jessica demanded when she reached her. "I was worried sick about you!"

"I got lost in the maze, trying to find my way back to the castle, and then the storm started," Elizabeth explained. "Fortunately I stumbled on Prince Laurent's cottage, and he let me stay there for the night."

Jessica's eyes widened, her curiosity piqued. "The prince? What's he like?"

Elizabeth shrugged. "He's nice," she replied evasively.

Jessica raised an eyebrow, wondering if there was more to the story than Elizabeth was letting on. But she'd have to press her for details later. "Well, all that matters is that you're all right,"

Jessica said. She hugged her sister close, tears coming to her eyes. "I was so scared, Liz," she said in a throaty voice. "You're the only twin I've got." Jessica pulled back, sniffing. "Promise me you won't run off again without letting me know first?"

Elizabeth nodded, her eyes glistening with tears as well. "I promise." Then she smiled. "Hey, does this mean we're talking to each other again?"

Jessica nodded. She had been so worried that she had completely forgotten about their fight. And now she realized how stupid it was. She also recognized how selfish she had been. Elizabeth was going through a really hard time. The least Jessica could do was support her. "Let's stop being mad at each other, Liz," Jessica said. "Our fight was totally idiotic."

"I couldn't agree more," Elizabeth replied.

Jessica looked down at the ground. "Elizabeth, I'm sorry. I guess I *was* sort of shirking my duties."

"Well, now I've made up for it, right?" Elizabeth said.

Jessica grinned. "That's right! You missed breakfast duty!"

Elizabeth leaned back and looked into Jessica's eyes. "Friends?" she asked.

"Friends," Jessica murmured.

Jessica felt like a weight had been lifted from her. Linking arms with her sister, she walked with her toward the garden, where the children were playing.

But on their way back to the castle Jessica was

struck with a horrible thought—Elizabeth's letter! *What was I thinking?* Jessica berated herself. *Now the letter is gone, and there's no way to get it back.*

Now that she and Elizabeth had made up, Jessica felt terribly guilty. Elizabeth was miserable about Todd. Nothing would make her happier than to receive a letter from him.

Jessica bit her lip and turned to her sister. She had to tell her about the letter from Todd. At least Elizabeth would know that Todd was thinking about her. Elizabeth smiled warmly at Jessica and slung an arm around her shoulders.

Jessica turned away. She just couldn't bring herself to confess. If Elizabeth knew what she had done, she might never forgive her.

He'll write again, Jessica assured herself.

Chapter 11

Elizabeth hummed to herself as she wandered through the wild English garden behind the château on Friday evening. It was a warm, balmy evening, and the sun was setting over the horizon, casting a pink glow over the meadows. Red and yellow tulips lined the white stone path, and beds of miniature pink roses were clustered on either side.

The prince and princess were hosting a formal dinner party that evening at the château, and the entire household was involved in a flurry of preparations. Elizabeth was glad to escape from the chaos during her break from the children. Although the twins had made up, they had decided to keep up their system of trading off shifts. Elizabeth was scheduled to take over shortly, and she'd have the kids until bedtime.

Swinging her arms, Elizabeth strolled along the

stone path. She came upon a narrow, gurgling brook surrounded by fields of red and blue wildflowers. She stopped in awe, marveling at the natural beauty of the landscape. It seemed as if every day she discovered something new on the property. Bending down, Elizabeth picked a tiny bunch of red wildflowers.

Elizabeth whistled as she continued along the path, her spirits high. She had been at the château for almost a week now, and she was beginning to get accustomed to the lifestyle. In fact, ever since she had met Laurent, she felt at peace with the world. She and Jessica were getting along, and even the kids were behaving better. The summer was turning out to be more fun than she had expected.

Elizabeth heard a man's voice humming softly, and her heart leapt. She hadn't seen Laurent since Tuesday night, but she knew he'd be coming to the château for the royal dinner.

She hesitated for a moment. Then she headed in the direction of the sound, her heart beating faster in her chest.

She turned the corner and peeked around it. Henri, the gardener, was crouched among the flowering bushes, shearing the plants and pulling weeds. He was humming a soft tune as he worked. Elizabeth shook her head, laughing at herself for her false hopes.

"*Bonsoir*, mademoiselle," Henri said, wishing her a good evening.

"*Bonsoir*, Henri," Elizabeth responded politely.

Then he pointed to her bouquet of flowers, a glint in his light brown eyes. "You have picked those for me?" he asked in broken English.

Elizabeth nodded and handed them to him. "I picked them just for you," she said.

Henri put a hand to his heart. "Mademoiselle, I am touched," he said.

Elizabeth laughed as she walked away, but she couldn't help feeling disappointed. Then she shook her head hard. *I'm not hoping to run into Prince Laurent*, she told herself. *Not at all*. Her decision to take a walk had *nothing* to do with the fact that Laurent was expected at the château that evening.

Although she'd had a wonderful time with him the other night, she didn't think anything would come of it. Why would Laurent want to get involved with an American girl who lived all the way across the sea? And why should she think he was interested in her anyway? Just because he took care of her the other night didn't mean anything. After all, it was the gentlemanly thing to do. And Laurent was certainly a gentleman.

It's a good thing I'm not interested in him, Elizabeth thought firmly. The path forked and she turned to the right, coming upon a fallen tree. Elizabeth grabbed onto a branch and climbed over the tree trunk. *Besides*, she thought, *it's too soon to go out with somebody else*. She needed time to heal after her breakup with Todd.

Elizabeth followed the path out of the garden, recalling their last moments together at Lila's party. She thought of Todd's discomfort, of his cold words, of the pain in her heart. . . . . But somehow the memory didn't hurt very much now, Elizabeth realized with surprise. It seemed as if it had all happened ages ago, in another lifetime. Sweet Valley felt very far away.

Elizabeth ducked under a low tree branch and walked out into the meadow. Then she froze in her tracks. Prince Laurent was headed straight toward her, trotting on a beautiful white stallion. Next to him was a black mare, which he was leading by the reins. Laurent looked more handsome than ever on the majestic animal.

Elizabeth gazed at him, breathless. "A prince on a white horse," she whispered to herself. For a moment she felt as if she'd slipped into a romantic fairy tale.

Get real! she ordered herself with a swift mental kick. She clenched her hands together behind her back and ordered herself to stop acting like a fool.

Laurent pulled at the reins and brought the horses to a stop by her side.

"*Bonsoir,* Laurent," Elizabeth said, forcing her voice to sound casual.

Laurent looked into her eyes. "You're not surprised to see me," he remarked.

Elizabeth tipped her head, bemused. "I figured you'd be coming to the château for your parents' party."

He stared at her blankly for a moment, then groaned. "The party!" he said, hitting himself on the side of the head. "I'd forgotten all about it!"

"Well, aren't you glad that I reminded you, then?" Elizabeth asked.

Laurent shook his head with a smile. "Actually it doesn't matter, because I've already made other plans—and they're much too important to cancel for a formal dinner party."

Elizabeth eyed him suspiciously. "What sort of plans?" she asked.

"Would you like to take a ride with me and find out?" he challenged.

Elizabeth hesitated. It was her turn to take the kids, and her shift would be starting shortly. Jessica would kill her if she didn't show up for dinner. On the other hand, Elizabeth thought, she loved horseback riding. And a handsome prince on a white horse was inviting her to go for a ride.

Elizabeth grinned to herself. Obviously no decision was necessary. Jessica could definitely handle the kids for a few more hours. Nothing was going to keep her from hanging out with Laurent.

"I think I'd like that very much," she said quickly. She put a foot into the saddle and climbed onto the black mare.

"Follow me!" Laurent said, turning his horse around and kicking his flanks lightly. The horse burst into a gallop and sped across the fields. "Whoa, Pardaillan!" Laurent exclaimed, bringing the horse to a stop and twisting around in his saddle.

Her heart beating in excitement, Elizabeth tapped lightly on her horse's sides. The black mare broke into a steady trot and Elizabeth tightened her grip on the reins, getting accustomed to the horse's movement.

"You ready to go?" he asked when she joined him.

Elizabeth smiled, her cheeks flushed. "Ready," she said.

And they were off.

"Pierre, stop playing with your food!" Jessica ordered as Pierre juggled a warm roll at the kitchen table on Friday evening. The roll flew out of his little hands and bounced across the table, falling onto the floor. "You see?" she said. "Now you can't eat it."

Pierre shrugged. "I'm not hungry anyway," he said.

"Well, then, why don't you play with your new toy set?" Jessica suggested, leaning over to retrieve the roll. The prince and princess had given Pierre a set of miniature plastic soldiers, and he had been playing with them all day.

Elizabeth, where are *you?* Jessica muttered to herself as she set the roll on the table. Elizabeth hadn't shown up for her shift yet, so Jessica was taking her sister's dinner duty. The children were having spaghetti and meatballs, but they were more interested in playing with their food than eating it. They were in a particularly rambunctious mood this evening, obviously wound up by the excitement in the air.

Pierre set two little toy soldiers on the table. "Bam, bam, bam!" he yelled out, marching one of them across the table.

Claudine scooped up the other soldier and positioned it behind Pierre's bowl. "Pow!" she returned.

"This is war!" Pierre yelled, picking up his soldier and making it leap into his bowl of spaghetti. Claudine quickly followed suit, stationing her soldier on a meatball. The children burst out into hysterical laughter as their soldiers fought in the field of pasta.

Jessica clapped sharply. "OK, that's enough!" she said.

"But you said I could play—" Pierre whined, crossing his arms over his chest.

"Well, I didn't mean in your food," Jessica interrupted. She grabbed the soldiers and wiped them off with her napkin. "You can play when you've finished eating."

Pierre stuck out his lower lip and stared down at his food. Pouting, he wound up a forkful of spaghetti and brought it to his mouth. Then he picked up a long strand with his fingers and pasted it above his lip, curling it into a mustache.

Claudine burst out laughing.

"Pi-erre!" Jessica groaned.

Pierre looked at her innocently, sucking the pasta into his mouth. "You don't like my mustache?" he asked.

Jessica shook her head, hiding a grin. "Well, you're a little bit young," she said.

"I almost have six years!" Pierre shouted out.

"I *am* almost six years old," Jessica corrected him.

Manon banged her hands on her tray. Then she picked up one of the toy soldiers and brought it to her mouth.

"Manon! That's for playing, not eating," Jessica said, gently disengaging the soldier from her mouth.

Jessica sighed and glanced at the antique clock on the kitchen wall. Elizabeth was over an hour late, and Jessica was beginning to get worried.

She had tried to find out if anyone had seen her sister, but everybody was preoccupied with the preparations for the royal dinner party. The entire kitchen staff was in a frenzy, as if they were getting ready to launch a space rocket instead of a dinner party. The head chef was in the kitchen barking out orders to the other cooks, and caterers were bustling around with platters of food.

Even Anna didn't have a moment for her. She was whirling around the house like a tornado, frantically taking care of last-minute details. Every time she passed through the kitchen, she had something else in her hand. On her last trip she had swept through the room carrying a long, unrolled scroll with the guest list on it. Jessica had tried to grab her, but Anna hadn't even stopped to look at her. "I'll be with you in a minute, Jessica!" she had promised on her way out the door. That was half an hour ago.

Jessica sighed and slumped down in her seat, feeling completely helpless. Nobody would talk to her, and she couldn't go out to look for Elizabeth herself because of the children. Jessica puffed her cheeks out in frustration.

The back door slammed shut suddenly, and Jessica sat up quickly. She listened for the sound of her sister's voice, but she couldn't make anything out over the buzz of the kitchen staff.

Jessica pushed back her chair and jumped up, grabbing the soldiers in her hand. "You guys, make sure Manon doesn't put anything else in her mouth, OK?" she said.

The kids nodded, and Jessica hurried across the room. She really hoped it was her twin because she didn't think she could handle one more minute of the children.

The entire household staff was in a frenzy in the kitchen. The head chef was preparing oysters at the stove, and Fernand was at the counter, rolling dough on a cutting board. Caterers were hurrying to and fro, carrying trays of exotic-looking hors d'oeuvres. The sweet smell of an apple tart wafted from the oven. Jessica inched her way through the kitchen, trying not to disturb the staff.

Suddenly she collided with a big platter of hors d'oeuvres lifted in the air.

"Excusez-moi," Jessica exclaimed, jumping back.

The caterer lowered her arm and looked at Jessica with pursed lips. "Tut-tut-tut," she clicked.

The head chef muttered something under his breath in French, and the woman agreed.

"Sorry," Jessica said, backing up a few feet.

The woman lifted the tray high above her head and swept away.

Just then Henri walked into the room, wearing a light blue jacket. He was carrying a pair of garden shears and a small bouquet of red wildflowers.

Jessica's face fell when she saw him. Obviously he had just come in from outside.

"Good evening, Mademoiselle Jessica," he said, bowing his head politely. "You look sad. Perhaps you were expecting someone else?"

"Actually, I was," Jessica replied. "I was hoping you were my sister. I'm afraid she might have gotten lost again."

Henri smiled broadly. "If she is lost, then she is not lost alone."

"Huh?" Jessica asked.

"I saw Elizabeth ride off with Prince Laurent on a horse," he informed her.

Jessica's jaw dropped. "Are you sure?" she asked.

"It is not possible," Fernand put in from the stove in English, where he was stirring a rich-smelling cream sauce. "Prince Laurent is expected for dinner, and the first course will be served in less than an hour." He dipped a wooden spoon into his sauce and sniffed at it. "Prince Laurent will certainly not miss such an affair."

Henri shrugged. "I do not know about that. He

had a basket with him." He reached up into a cabinet for a vase. "It seems he has already taken care of their dinner."

"Mais, ce n'est pas possible!" the head chef burst out, waving his arms around in an agitated manner. Then he spoke in rapid-fire French to Fernand.

Fernand shook his head in disapproval and stirred his sauce harder. Henri shrugged and filled the vase with water.

How could she do this to me? Jessica fumed silently.

When she returned to the table, she found the kids were building a model village across the table with their food. They had fashioned little round huts out of mounds of spaghetti, with chimneys made out of meatballs. Now they were constructing a forest out of broccoli stalks and carrots.

Elizabeth, I'm going to strangle you, Jessica vowed.

Pierre looked up, beaming proudly. "Do you like it?"

"Love it," Jessica grumbled. "Now let's clean this mess up or there won't be any dessert for you guys."

Giggling, the children scooped up the clumps of food with their hands.

Jessica started to protest, but then she stopped herself. At least the children were cleaning up. She just hoped they would raze their city before the royal couple arrived. She headed for the pantry to find something for dessert.

A number of caterers were in the pantry, preparing trays and speaking a mile a minute in French. Jessica pushed through the door and glanced at the shelves.

"Out, out!" one of the caterers yelled in English, shooing her away as if she were a fly.

"You again!" said the woman whom she had collided with earlier.

"But I promised the kids dessert," Jessica protested.

The woman grabbed a silver tray and shoved it at Jessica. The tray was filled with chocolate- and cheese-filled croissants that were left over from breakfast. "Stay out, mademoiselle," she ordered tersely.

Jessica scowled as she carried the croissants back to the children's table. It was bad enough that she wasn't invited to the party, but she was being completely abused by the staff as well. Plus she was stuck having to cover the evening shift with the royal monsters because her sister had ridden off with a prince.

"Here's dessert," Jessica announced, setting the tray on the table with a loud thud. The kids dove for the croissants, and Jessica barely batted an eye. Sighing, she sank down into her seat.

"Will Mademoiselle Elizabeth read the elephant book to us again tonight?" Pierre asked, stuffing a flaky chocolate-filled croissant in his mouth.

Jessica flashed him a brittle smile. "Who knows what she'll do?" she replied tightly. "Elizabeth is full of surprises."

"Surprises?" Claudine echoed cheerfully. "We love surprises."

Manon bounced in her seat, her face smeared with chocolate. "Surprises, surprises," she chanted happily.

I will strangle Elizabeth, Jessica thought hotly.

"This is wonderful, Laurent," Elizabeth declared as she ripped off another chunk of sourdough bread.

They were sitting on a blanket on the beach, sharing a picnic dinner. Laurent had prepared a gourmet meal with a selection of cold cuts, French cheeses, duck pâté, and fresh bread. He had also brought a jug of apple cider and two wineglasses.

"Even better than my omelette specialty?" Laurent asked with a grin.

Elizabeth nodded. "Well, it's a close second," she said. Then she gestured toward the ocean. "Actually, I was talking about the view." She spread some pâté on the bread and took a bite.

Stars were twinkling in the midnight sky, and the full moon was shining brightly above the eastern horizon. A short distance away the waves of the Mediterranean splashed rhythmically against the rocky shore.

"I thought you would be the sort of girl who would enjoy dining under the stars," Laurent said. He picked up her glass and refilled it.

Elizabeth smiled. "You thought right." She

185

gazed at the sea and sighed in contentment. "This is all so beautiful."

"Does it remind you of your home?" he asked.

Elizabeth thought for a moment, then shrugged. "In some ways it does," she admitted. "We come from southern California and live close to the beach. I'm used to warm summer nights and the smell of the sea in the air." She paused, deep in thought. "But you know, there's something different about the Mediterranean. It's more savage, somehow."

Laurent looked at her with interest. "Savage? What do you mean?"

"Well, there seems to be more of a contrast here," Elizabeth explained. "In California we have sand dunes and beaches on the ocean." She gestured out to sea. "But here there are huge white cliffs jutting into the water and giant mountain ranges in the distance." Elizabeth scooped up a handful of white pebbles and let them sift through her fingers. "And the beaches are covered with tiny stones." Elizabeth took a sip of her cider. "The island is more—" She paused as she searched for the right word. "Passionate," she said finally.

"Ah! Passion! Of course!" Laurent said with a grin. "That is because the island is French."

Elizabeth rolled her eyes. "And the moon? Is that French too?"

"Yes, of course," Laurent said. "Here in France we have our own moon." He looked at her with a matter-of-fact expression on his face.

186

Elizabeth shook her head, laughing.

"But it is true!" Laurent claimed, waving his arms around dramatically. "In France everything is unique—the cheese, the wine, the men, the moon!"

"Laurent, stop it!" Elizabeth said, laughing in earnest. He joined in with her, and soon they were laughing uproariously. After a few minutes she sat back, wiping tears out of her eyes. She realized she hadn't felt this relaxed in ages.

"I have never known anyone like you before," Laurent said quietly. He reached for her hand. For a moment they were silent, listening together to the lulling rhythm of the waves beating against the shore.

Then he gazed into her eyes and spoke in a whisper. "Elizabeth, there are things you don't know about me—things you *should* know."

But Elizabeth shook her head. She didn't want to spoil the mood. She curled her fingers around his and looked into his eyes. "I know everything I need to know—at least for this moment," she told him.

Laurent smiled and brushed her hair back from her face, his eyes intent and serious.

With a start she realized why he looked familiar when she first saw him. *The dream on the airplane,* she thought. She closed her eyes, remembering the details—how she'd been lost in a field of wildflowers until a handsome guy on a white horse had rescued her, a guy with jet-black hair and deep blue eyes. . . .

Laurent was the guy in my dream! Elizabeth

marveled. A thrilling sensation tingled up and down her spine. *Is Prince Laurent my destiny?* she wondered.

Late that evening Jessica dragged her body up the long, winding staircase to her room. She was exhausted after an entire day with the kids, and her legs felt like they weighed two tons each. Sounds of the party wafted up the steps from the salon. Classical music was playing, and guests were laughing quietly.

Jessica scowled fiercely. Not only was she tired, but she was furious. Everybody was having fun but her. She couldn't believe Elizabeth had skipped out on her duties for the entire evening. She deeply resented having had to cover her sister's shift. She had been hoping to go for a late night swim while the prince and princess entertained their guests.

Jessica grabbed onto the wooden banister and pulled herself around another turn. Breathing deeply, she plodded up the stone steps. "I'll never forgive her for this," she muttered through clenched teeth.

Of course, a nagging voice told her, *I often dump my work on Elizabeth.* In fact, she had shown up three hours late for her shift on Tuesday afternoon.

Then Jessica shrugged. *Elizabeth is supposed to be the responsible twin,* she reasoned. And Jessica hoped she would start acting like her old reliable self soon. The summer would be unbearable if her sister didn't shape up quickly.

Jessica reached her room and pushed open the door. It was pitch-dark inside and smelled damp and musty. Jessica felt along the dusty wall for the light switch, shivering unexpectedly. "This place gives me the creeps," she grumbled.

Suddenly a large hand gripped hers on the wall. Jessica gasped and let forth a scream. But then another hand covered her mouth, blanketing the sound.

Jessica felt as if her heart had stopped. Then it began to pound fiercely, sounding a drumroll in her chest. She reached for the door, trying to pull free, but a solid arm locked itself around her and pulled her farther into the room.

Don't panic, Jessica said to herself, her stomach coiling in fear. *Don't panic*. She forced herself to stand perfectly still. Then she gathered all her forces together and struggled wildly with her captor. But the arms were like a vise around her, and they kept tightening. Soon she couldn't move at all.

Jessica gasped for air, feeling as if she were suffocating. Her eyes wide with terror, she opened her mouth and screamed. But like in a nightmare, no sound came out.

I'm going to die, she thought.

Chapter 12

"There's a special place I want to show you," Laurent told Elizabeth as they were riding through the forest back to the château. The path narrowed, and Laurent guided his horse between the thick trees.

"This way, Cendrillon," Elizabeth directed, pulling lightly at the reins and directing her horse along the path.

Elizabeth sat back comfortably in the saddle, enjoying the steady movement of the mare's trot. It was peaceful and serene in the forest. The night air was cool and crisp, and fresh pine needles scented the air. She didn't know when she'd ever felt happier.

Elizabeth felt a twinge of guilt as she noticed the full moon above them. It was very late already. She had been gone for hours. Jessica was going to kill her. Elizabeth knew she really should be getting back soon.

Then Elizabeth shrugged. *You only live once,* she thought. Jessica was always telling her to loosen up, and now she was going to do it. For once she was going to choose the dream over reality. *Besides,* Elizabeth thought, *there's really no reason to go back now anyway.* The kids would already be in bed.

A small pond glimmered in the moonlight through the trees, and Laurent headed toward it. Elizabeth rode up next to him, pulling Cendrillon to a stop.

She caught her breath at the loveliness of the golden pond. Water lilies covered the surface, and huge weeping willows dipped into the edges. The moon beamed down on the water, making the surface glisten like a gold coin.

Laurent dismounted his horse and turned to her, his arms outstretched. Elizabeth put a foot in the stirrup and swung her leg over the horse's body. Taking her lightly by the waist, Laurent lifted her to the ground. Elizabeth shivered in delight at the feel of his strong hands on her body.

"You handle Cendrillon as if you've been riding horses forever," Laurent said admiringly.

Elizabeth flushed in pleasure. "I've actually been going horseback riding since I was a little girl. It's sort of in my blood."

Laurent lifted an eyebrow. "In your blood?" he questioned.

Elizabeth blushed slightly. "Well, my distant relatives

were, um, acrobats in the circus," she admitted.

Laurent laughed. "That I would have never guessed!" He studied her face carefully. "I might have thought you came from a family of actresses, or dancers, or movie stars—"

"Laurent, stop it!" Elizabeth cut him off. "Flattery will get you nowhere."

Laurent looked at her intensely. "Elizabeth, I am not flattering you."

Elizabeth swallowed hard, feeling her chest tighten suddenly. Laurent already had a dangerously strong hold on her emotions. She stepped away quickly, walking closer to the pond.

Laurent joined her at the edge of the water. For a moment they were silent as they gazed together at the peaceful water.

"This is incredible!" Elizabeth breathed finally. The sky was a deep blue, and the woods were full of night sounds. Crickets were chirping, and leaves were rustling. Elizabeth felt as if she were in a glorious, romantic dream.

Laurent reached for her hand. "This is where I first saw you," he whispered.

Elizabeth frowned. "But I've never seen this pond before," she said. "I'm sure I didn't wander off this far from the château when I got lost."

Laurent chuckled softly. "That's because you weren't here."

"Huh?" Elizabeth asked, turning to him with a puzzled expression.

"I saw you in a dream," he explained softly, giving her hand a squeeze.

Elizabeth's heart skipped a beat. Was it possible? Had Laurent dreamed of her as well?

Laurent let go of her hand and sat down on the bank of the pond. "I fell asleep right on that spot last Sunday," he said, pointing to a clover patch on the bank.

"And what did you dream?" Elizabeth asked softly. She sat down next to him, curling her legs underneath her.

Laurent looked pensive for a moment. "I dreamed I was at some sort of royal ball. From across the room I saw a beautiful girl with golden hair and ocean blue eyes."

Laurent looked at Elizabeth intently, his eyes searching her face. Elizabeth's heart fluttered under the intensity of his gaze, and she looked down quickly.

"I went to her, and I put my arms around her to dance," Laurent continued. Then he sighed. "But then she disappeared."

Elizabeth turned to look at him, smiling slightly.

Laurent gently touched her face. "I never thought I would be lucky enough to meet the beautiful girl who appeared to me that day. But now the dream has come true."

Elizabeth felt a rush of happiness sweep over her body. *Is this really happening?* she asked herself, awed.

For a moment Elizabeth was tempted to tell him about her dream, but then she stopped herself. *For now,* she decided, *I'll keep that secret to myself.* After all, she and Laurent had all summer to discover each other.

Laurent took her chin and lifted her face to his. Then he kissed her softly—a long, sweet, tender kiss. He tangled a hand in her silky hair, and his other hand reached out for hers. At the feel of his strong hand over hers, Elizabeth felt her whole body melt.

Maybe fairy tales can come true, she thought. And then she returned his kiss with a passion so strong, it surprised even her.

"Let me go!" Jessica muttered through clenched teeth, trying to bite at her captor's hand. Her heart pounded like a jackhammer as she tried to pull herself free.

A beam of moonlight peeked through the lace curtains, suddenly illuminating the room. Jessica blinked, trying to make out her surroundings. Then her blood froze in her veins. Her three bureau drawers were open and had been rifled through. *A robbery?* she thought. *Does the thief have a knife? Or a gun?* A bolt of fear shot through her.

Summoning all her energy, she yanked an arm free and elbowed her captor.

A male voice groaned, and two strong arms enfolded her. Jessica struggled wildly, but to no avail.

Her captor's arms felt like solid lead around her. She couldn't move at all. Jessica whimpered in fear.

But then the grip loosened and a voice whispered in her ear, "Jessica, please be still."

A jolt of recognition shot through her at the sound of the sexy voice. Jessica nodded, holding her breath.

The guy turned her around, took his hand away from her mouth, and flicked on the light. It was Jacques, and he looked cuter than ever. His hair was in disarray, and his jaw was covered in a thick stubble. His eyes were wide with worry.

"Jacques!" Jessica uttered breathlessly.

"Jessica," Jacques said softly. "I've found you at last."

Jessica's whole body trembled in relief. She felt suddenly weak and grabbed onto the bureau for support. Then she stared at him in shock, her mind racing. *How did he get in? What is he doing here? Why did he scare me like that?* "Jacques . . . I . . . why—" she began.

But Jacques cut her off. He crossed the room swiftly and grabbed her in his arms. "Jessica," he whispered. Then he pressed his lips against hers. For a moment she resisted, but then she felt herself melting at the sensation of his delicious kiss.

Jacques wrapped his arms tight around her, and his mouth devoured hers hungrily, as if he couldn't get enough. Jessica closed her eyes and returned his embrace with the same ardor.

Finally Jacques pulled back, out of breath. Then he stared at her intensely, his liquid brown eyes on fire. He ran a finger along her cheekbone, a tender look on his face. "I've missed you so," he whispered.

Jessica looked up at him, amazed. She still couldn't quite believe he was here. "But . . . but what are you doing in here?" she stuttered.

Jacques paced across the wooden floor. "I couldn't wait to see you again," he explained. "Ever since I met you, I haven't stopped thinking about you. You're in all my thoughts, in my dreams—"

Jessica's heart fluttered at his words.

"I took the first train I could," he continued. "And as soon as I arrived at the château, I had to find you." He leaned against the bureau. "I didn't want the de Sainte-Maries to know I was here because they'd never let us be alone together." Jacques gave her an intense look and spread his hands out in a wide gesture. "I . . . I desperately wanted to steal a few minutes alone with you."

Jessica sat down on the edge of the bed, trying to make sense of what he was telling her. "But how did you get in?" She gestured toward the stairs. "In case you haven't noticed, there's a major dinner party going on."

Jacques smiled, the familiar rakish look in his eyes. "I have my ways," he said mysteriously.

"The underground passageways?" Jessica guessed.

Jacques nodded. "There's an old, unused dumbwaiter that connects all the floors. I got into the castle through one of the underground routes and then took the dumbwaiter," he explained.

Jessica silently digested the information. But then she frowned. "But why were you going through my bureau?" she asked.

Jacques averted his eyes. "I'm sorry for invading your privacy like that," he said, looking abashed. "But I didn't know if I was in the right room." He paused. "I was looking for something that would indicate this one is yours." He flashed her a sexy smile. "And then you came in."

Jessica nodded. His story made sense, but still, something was bothering her. For a moment she thought about Anna's claim that there was no duke of Norveaux. *Poor Jessica,* she heard Anna's laughing voice saying. *You've run into a dashing French rogue with a silver tongue.*

Jessica squinted, looking at Jacques carefully. His head was lowered, and he looked slightly embarrassed. He returned her gaze, searching her face quickly with wide, sincere eyes.

Anna can't be right, Jessica decided. Obviously Jacques wasn't a rogue like she'd thought. He had come all this way to see her, just as he had promised he would. And that was all that mattered.

"Jessica?" Jacques asked, a question in his voice. "Is something wrong?"

Jessica shook her head, giving him a tiny smile. "No, nothing's wrong," she whispered. "Nothing at all."

Then she slipped back into his arms and stared into his warm eyes. With the moonlight shining on his strong jaw, Jacques bent his face to hers. As their lips met, the whole world seemed to disappear.

This is all that matters, Jessica thought again, and then she lost herself in the searing heat of his kiss.

TO CATCH
A THIEF

Written by
Kate William

Created by
FRANCINE PASCAL

BANTAM BOOKS
NEW YORK · TORONTO · LONDON · SYDNEY · AUCKLAND

To Jordan Silverman

Chapter 1

Elizabeth Wakefield felt as if she'd drifted into a fairy tale. *Where else would I be riding on horseback in the moonlight alongside a handsome prince?* she wondered. The cool night air was scented by salty breezes blowing off the Mediterranean Sea, with a whiff of the lavender that grew abundantly all over the island.

Can all this really be happening? Elizabeth asked herself. She glanced at Prince Laurent de Sainte-Marie, riding beside her on his white stallion. Tall and lean, with broad shoulders and sharp features, Laurent was incredibly handsome—the very image of a regal hero. He was the oldest son of a royal European family and the heir to the de Sainte-Marie fortune. He was also a wonderful person, warm and down-to-earth.

1

Elizabeth and her twin sister, Jessica, were working as au pair girls for the summer, taking care of Laurent's three young siblings. The job had been Jessica's idea. She'd jumped at the chance to spend her vacation on a private island off the coast of southern France. But the de Sainte-Maries had wanted an older girl with more experience. They'd agreed to hire Jessica only if they could also find a second girl to share the job. Immediately she'd starting working on Elizabeth, trying to convince her to take the second au pair position.

Elizabeth had balked at her twin's plan. The idea of spending the entire summer so far away from her home in Sweet Valley, California, hadn't appealed to her at all. But Jessica had worn her down—as usual.

She had regretted caving in to Jessica when she'd had to say good-bye to her longtime boyfriend, Todd Wilkins. The thought of having to spend months away from him had hurt deeply. But apparently Todd hadn't felt the same way.

Elizabeth felt a pang of regret as she recalled their last time together, the evening before she'd left for France. Todd had broken up with her, claiming that long-distance relationships were too difficult to maintain. She'd felt terribly wounded and had thought the pain would never end.

She certainly hadn't planned to get involved

2

with anyone else for some time. But then a handsome prince had come into her life. . . .

"Here we are," Laurent said, slowing his horse to a trot as they came over a hill.

Elizabeth brought her black mare to a stop, shifting her weight as the horse sidestepped a few paces. "I can't get over how beautiful this place is," she murmured as she gazed down at the Château d'Amour Inconnu, the summer home of the de Sainte-Marie family. The château looked like a fairy-tale castle, its white stone walls glimmering in the moonlight. Several spiked gables jutted up from the roof around the main tower, which was covered with red stone shingles.

Laurent helped Elizabeth down from the mare. "I think Cendrillon likes you," he said. He pronounced his words with a melodic French accent that Elizabeth thought was delightful.

Elizabeth stroked the animal's glossy black fur. "I like her too," she replied.

She watched as Laurent looped the horses' reins around a tree trunk.

"Cendrillon means Cinderella, doesn't it?" Elizabeth asked as she and Laurent hiked down the hill, hand in hand.

Laurent nodded. "The mare's name used to be Noir because her color is like the night," he told her. "But the first time we were outfitting her for the horseshoes, she pulled the cross-tie out of the wall and escaped with only three of the shoes attached to her

3

hooves. After that everyone called her Cendrillon."

Elizabeth laughed. "How disappointing," she said wryly. "I was expecting a much more romantic explanation."

Laurent chuckled. "The blacksmith was also disappointed."

As they drew closer to the château Elizabeth noticed that the de Sainte-Maries' dinner party was still going on, even though it was after midnight. The French doors to the formal parlor were open, and several guests were congregated on the stone veranda. The soft strains of a flute and piano duet seemed to float on the breeze.

Elizabeth grimaced as she caught sight of the countess di Rimini and her daughter, Antonia, who were vacationing with the de Sainte-Maries for the summer. They had traveled to the château on the same train as the twins and were two of the biggest snobs Elizabeth had ever met. On the train the countess had created a big scene about having to ride in the second-class car. Then she had created an even bigger scene by accusing everyone in the train of having stolen a precious heirloom from her suitcase.

"I think we should avoid the main entrances," Laurent suggested.

Elizabeth nodded. Laurent had skipped the party to be with her, and she understood why he might want to avoid being seen. "Are you going to be in big trouble with your parents?" she asked.

4

Laurent gently pulled her into his arms. "No matter the cost, I wouldn't have missed this time with you," he said.

Elizabeth smiled up at him. In the moonlight his dark blue eyes shimmered with emotion. "I'm glad," she replied. "But—"

He lowered his lips to hers, pushing her words right out of her mind with a deep, searing kiss. Elizabeth wrapped her arms around his neck and held on tightly, as if she might melt into the ground without his support.

"Oh, Laurent," she murmured. "This is all so . . ." She breathed deeply and rested her forehead against his chest. "I can't even describe how I feel right now."

"Neither can I," he whispered.

A sudden burst of laughter on the veranda broke the spell. Elizabeth sighed in disappointment. "I can go the rest of the way by myself," she offered. Laurent was staying in a small private cottage on the north side of the island, some distance from the château.

He squeezed her hand. "What kind of a prince would I be if I didn't see my lovely damsel safely to her door?" he chided her jokingly. "But don't worry. I have an idea."

He steered Elizabeth away from the château. "Have you discovered the secret tunnels yet?"

Elizabeth raised her eyebrows. "Secret tunnels?"

"But of course," he replied with a laugh. "They are a standard feature in old European castles."

"Sounds interesting," Elizabeth said. "Lead the way. The last thing I feel like tonight is another run-in with the di Rimini duo. Sometimes I get the impression that they don't consider Jessica and me worthy of breathing the same air. We are such *lowly* servants, after all," she added sarcastically.

Laurent cleared his throat and chuckled nervously without comment. Elizabeth narrowed her eyes, wondering about his strange reaction. *Maybe he feels embarrassed about his family's friendship with such horrid snobs,* she thought. She decided to drop the subject. The di Riminis were nothing to her and Laurent, especially on such a glorious evening.

"Where are we going?" Elizabeth asked as they crept into a small, enclosed garden. Its high stone walls were covered with dark climbing vines. Just inside the iron gate a pair of stone lions flanked the entrance. A grassy path curved into a shadowy jungle of flowering bushes.

"Trust me," Laurent said reassuringly.

Elizabeth felt giddy with a sense of adventure as Laurent led her farther into the garden. The air was perfumed with honeysuckle and rose, and the wind whispered through the tangled dark foliage.

They came to a white stone shed that seemed to glow like a ghost in the moonlit night. Laurent reached for the latch on the wrought iron door and pushed it open. It swung inward with an ominous-sounding creak.

Elizabeth gulped. "We have to go in *there?*" she asked nervously as she peered into the black interior.

Laurent rubbed the back of her neck. "It's perfectly safe," he assured her. "I've been sneaking through these tunnels since I was a child."

"I'm glad I wasn't *your* au pair," Elizabeth muttered dryly. Steeling her courage, she followed him through the doorway.

Elizabeth was immediately engulfed in blackness. She felt her way along a cold, damp wall, skimming her fingers over the bumpy ridges in the stones. With her sight disabled, her remaining senses grew sharper. The echo of their voices and footsteps into the distance told her they were in a cavernous tunnel of some sort. She sniffed the air and noticed it smelled like wet dirt and chalk.

"These tunnels were built in the twelfth century," Laurent explained. "They were used by the royal family to escape the invasions of their enemies In the time of the French Revolution noble families hid down here from the mobs, and during World War II the Jews found refuge from the Nazis."

"Wow!" Elizabeth exclaimed. "There's so much history in here. I wish these walls could tell us everything."

"I'm sure there is more than anyone knows,"

7

Laurent said. "Imagine all the *rendezvous en se-cret*—secret meetings—that have taken place over the years." He chuckled. "These walls could tell better stories than the American soap operas."

Elizabeth laughed. "As long as they don't tell on *us*." She flinched as her fingers slipped across a patch of slime on the wall.

The tunnel gradually widened enough for her and Laurent to walk side by side. "How did the Château d'Amour Inconnu get its name?" Elizabeth asked. "It means unfamiliar or unknown love, doesn't it?"

"Yes," Laurent replied. "There is a legend of sorts."

"Well—," Elizabeth prompted, gently squeezing his hand. "I hope it's more exciting than the one about how Cendrillon got *her* name," she added jokingly.

Laurent said nothing for several seconds. "Long ago a prince fell in love with a young maiden," he began at last. "But their love was doomed. And things for them ended badly."

"What happened?" Elizabeth asked, intrigued.

Laurent cleared his throat. "The prince married another; the maiden turned into a bird."

"That's it?" Elizabeth protested, laughing.

"It's a worn-out story and not so interesting to me. I prefer modern times." He lifted their entwined hands to his lips and placed a soft kiss on her wrist. "And modern love stories."

Chuckling, Elizabeth made a mental note to ask

8

about the legend at the château. One of the servants could probably fill her in on the missing details.

The passageway narrowed again. "We're almost at the end," Laurent told her.

Elizabeth sensed the floor rising at a steep incline, forcing her leg muscles to work much harder. She also noticed faint, luminescent patterns on the walls. "I can actually see something," she said.

"There are open panels near the ceiling in this part, which allow in the moonlight," Laurent explained.

He reached for her hand and guided her around a corner. "Here we are," he said.

Straining her eyes, Elizabeth noticed the faint outline of a small door several feet from the ground.

"That's strange," he suddenly murmured. "It's not locked. This entrance is usually kept bolted shut. Someone must have used it recently."

As Laurent opened the door a wedge of light filtered into the darkness. Elizabeth breathed a sigh of relief.

Laurent glanced at her over his shoulder, his eyebrows raised. "You doubted me?" he teased.

"Not for a minute!" she countered. "But I'm not cut out to be a mole. I'm from southern California—born in sunlight."

He laughed at that, then poked his head through the doorway. "All clear," he whispered.

Bracing his arms on the ledge, Laurent hoisted himself up through the opening, then reached down to help Elizabeth.

She crawled through the doorway and found herself crouched beneath a dusty staircase. She noticed the familiar brown-and-tan tiles that covered the floor. "This is the servants' wing," she whispered. The rooms she and her twin had been assigned were just up the stairs. Elizabeth flashed a broad smile at Laurent. "I'm truly amazed."

"I'm amazed also," he said, his voice low and sexy. "By you, Elizabeth."

She saw the passionate look in his eyes. Her mouth went dry. Laurent moved closer and slowly pulled her into his arms. "This night with you has been so special," he said. "If only . . ."

Holding her breath, Elizabeth waited for him to continue. Instead he lowered his lips to hers for a deep, powerful kiss that seemed to go on and on. Elizabeth felt as if their hearts were beating together, as if their souls were entwined. *I'm really and truly in love,* she thought. *With a prince!*

In her small room in the servants' wing of the Château d'Amour Inconnu, Jessica Wakefield snuggled closer to Jacques Landeau. Although they'd been apart for nearly a week, it seemed she'd been waiting for him forever.

Jacques shifted slightly, squeaking the rusty springs of her narrow bed. "I have missed you so, *mon ange,*" he whispered into her ear, his sexy French accent melting her heart.

Jessica had known that coming to France for

the summer would turn out to be a fabulous, romantic adventure. But falling in love with Jacques was even more wonderful than she'd imagined. Not only was he gorgeous, with warm brown eyes and curly dark hair, but he also happened to be from a royal family. His father, Louis Landeau, was the duke of Norveaux.

Jessica had met Jacques and his father a week earlier, at the train station in Paris. She had been struggling with her luggage and had begged her twin for help. In response Elizabeth had spouted off a litany of I-told-you-so's in an annoying, bossy-older-sister tone of voice and had marched off without a backward glance. Of course, *Elizabeth* had managed to pack all her things into two bags and had worn sensible shoes.

Jessica's arms, back, and shoulders had been throbbing painfully under the heavy load of her many bags, and her new leather sandals had blistered her feet. Suddenly the hottest guy she'd ever seen and a distinguished-looking gentleman had appeared at her side. After introducing himself and his father, Jacques had offered to carry Jessica's luggage. Then the Landeaus had boarded the same train as the twins. Jacques and Jessica had sat side by side, talking and laughing for hours . . . and somewhere along the way Jessica had fallen totally in love.

Jessica sighed deeply and wrapped her arms

11

around Jacques's neck. "I missed you too," she said. "This week has been miserable without you."

He gently ran his fingers up and down her arm, setting off a cascade of tingles all through her body. "You and I, Jessica, we share something that is so . . . *magnifique*. With you I feel like I am at home in my heart. You inspire me to many dreams."

Jessica snuggled closer. "What kind of dreams?"

Jacques's brown eyes glimmered. "I dare to see in my mind a future with you," he whispered. "I imagine new things we shall discover together. I wish to show you the many wonderful places I have traveled. You are so full of life . . . all the days with you become a beautiful adventure."

Jessica basked with pleasure. "I like your dreams."

Jacques leaned over her, bracing himself with his elbow. "Two years ago my father and I made a trip to Morocco. We stayed in a white palace that dazzled the eyes in the bright desert sun. And the sounds in the village, the people and the animals, the markets . . . they were like a strange, exotic song."

Jessica closed her eyes, letting his words paint a picture in her mind. She imagined herself draped in silk and jewels, riding with Jacques on a camel across the sandy desert. . . .

"Another time we joined with a safari in central Africa," Jacques continued.

Jessica wrinkled her nose. "Did you have to

12

sleep in tents and fight off giant killer mosquitoes?"

Jacques grinned sheepishly. "The tents, they were appointed as lavishly as a luxury hotel, with soft beds and elegant furniture. But the mosquitoes, they are pesky like everywhere."

"What about the wild lions and rhinoceroses?" Jessica asked. "Wasn't it dangerous?"

"It was not," Jacques replied. "We don't go too near the wild animals. We shoot them only with the cameras, with the lenses that are, how you say . . . long-range. But of course, my father would advise I tell of my courage in facing a hundred fierce lions, so as to impress you," he added with a laugh.

Jessica grinned, recalling Louis Landeau's blatant matchmaking efforts and indiscreet romantic advice to both her and Jacques during the train ride from Paris. "Your father is too much," she said jokingly.

Jacques rolled his eyes. "*That* he is. When we went to Saint-Tropez last month, he fell in love with three different women in only one day."

Jessica laughed, then put on a mock-fierce expression. "I hope you're not planning to follow his example!"

"Not me." He cupped her jaw in his hand and gazed into her eyes. "My heart is taken," he breathed. "It belongs to you."

Tears of joy pooled in Jessica's eyes. "You're crying?" Jacques said, his voice filled with concern.

13

Jessica flashed him a watery smile. "I'm happy."

"I am also," he told her. "Happier than ever in my life." He brushed his fingertip over her lips. "I love you, Jessica."

Jacques kissed her then, a deep, passionate kiss that went on and on. A million emotions swirled through Jessica, all of them wonderful. It was as if she and Jacques were sealing an unspoken promise to each other that would last forever.

When the kiss ended, Jacques brushed a lock of hair behind her ear. "I only wish I could stay longer. But I must go."

Jessica frowned. "Why?" she demanded. "You just got here."

Jacques sat up and turned to her. "My father is waiting for me," he replied.

"I'm sure he won't mind if you're a little late," she insisted, reaching for him again.

"Believe me, I'd stay longer if I could," Jacques told her.

Jessica scooted back against the headboard and crossed her arms. It seemed Jacques was already taking her for granted, even though their relationship was barely a week old. "Maybe you're not as excited to see me as you say you are?"

"This is not true," Jacques argued. He pushed his hand through his hair and exhaled sharply. "I wish I could explain. . . . But I really must go."

Jessica felt a quick flare of irritation. She raised her chin and gave Jacques a cold look. "So, go," she said tersely.

Groaning, Jacques pulled her into his arms and hugged her tightly. "Don't be angry with me, please." He leaned back and framed her face with his hands. "You torture my soul, Jessica."

Seeing the anguish in his eyes, Jessica softened. "OK, I won't be angry, but only if you promise to come back tomorrow."

Jacques took her hand and raised it to his lips. "But of course, *mon ange.* Nothing can keep me away."

That's better, Jessica thought, grinning.

Jacques kissed her palm, then held it against his cheek. "I'll be counting the moments until I see you again."

Jessica sighed. She couldn't help being charmed by his romantic words and his irresistible French accent. "I'll be counting the moments too," she whispered.

Huddled under the staircase in Laurent's arms, Elizabeth heard a sound at the top of the stairs. She froze. "I think someone's coming," she whispered. Laurent pulled her farther into the shadows and kissed her again.

Elizabeth laughed softly against his lips. "How are we going to explain ourselves if we get caught?" she murmured.

Laurent sighed and lowered his arms. "You're right,

15

of course. Maybe I will see you tomorrow?" he asked.

"I'd like that," Elizabeth replied. "I have to take care of the children in the morning, but I'll be free after lunch."

Laurent touched his lips to her forehead in a kiss that was as soft as a feather. "I'd better go and let you get your rest," he said. "You'll need your energy; I know what my little brother and sisters are like when they first wake up."

"I'll be fine," Elizabeth assured him, even though she had her doubts. Taking care of the three young de Sainte-Marie children was quite a challenge, even with a good night's sleep.

Laurent touched the side of her face, then pushed a lock of her hair behind her ear. "*Bonsoir,* Elizabeth."

"Good night," she whispered.

Gingerly picking her steps, she crept up the long, winding staircase to her room. She felt a twinge of guilt as she walked past Jessica's closed door. Elizabeth had shirked her au pair responsibilities that evening, forcing her sister to pick up the slack. *I'll have to make it up to her somehow,* she decided as she entered her own room.

The twins had gotten into a huge fight when they'd first started working at the château. Jessica hadn't taken her duties as an au pair very seriously, and Elizabeth had been furious with her. They hadn't spoken for days and had

16

worked alternating shifts to avoid spending time together.

Although they'd patched up their differences since then, they had agreed to continue working in shifts so that they could each enjoy some time off. Elizabeth was supposed to have worked that evening, but then Prince Laurent had come along on his horse. . . . *Jessica of all people should understand why I ditched her and the children tonight*, Elizabeth thought with a laugh.

Younger by four minutes, Jessica lived her life as if it were one big adventure. She rarely stopped to consider her actions, always jumping blindly into any situation that promised fun and excitement. She had a knack for getting herself into trouble—and more often than not, the trouble had to do with a guy. It was Elizabeth who usually got her out of the mess. Jessica was extremely intelligent, but somehow the idea of learning from her past mistakes seemed to be beyond her comprehension.

Though the twins were identical, with shoulder-length blond hair, blue-green eyes, and lean, athletic figures, the similarities stopped at the surface. The differences in their personalities were as vast as the ocean. Unlike Jessica, Elizabeth planned her actions carefully. She was known as the serious twin, and in most instances the label fit. Her ambition was to become a professional writer someday,

17

and she took pride in the column she wrote for Sweet Valley High's student newspaper, the *Oracle*.

Elizabeth sometimes felt as if she were *Jessica's* baby-sitter, which had caused problems between them when they tried to take care of the de Sainte-Marie children together. But even before they had arrived at the Château d'Amour Inconnu, Elizabeth had sensed that her younger twin was going to get herself into mischief that summer.

Of course, Jessica's attitude that she was coming to France for a "romantic adventure" was a sure sign of trouble. She was hard enough to manage in her usual fun-loving state of mind, but Jessica Wakefield in *love* was an unstoppable force. Even in the train station in Paris she'd attracted a too-smooth guy to sweep her off her feet!

Elizabeth rolled her eyes at the memory of Jacques Landeau and his father, Louis, who was supposed to be a duke. Jessica had been thoroughly enchanted by them, especially Jacques. But there had been something strange about them. They were friendly enough . . . a little *too* friendly, in Elizabeth's opinion. She had breathed a deep sigh of relief when the Landeaus had finally gotten off the train. After all, the twins would probably never see Jacques Landeau again, and even Jessica couldn't get into much trouble on a small, private island.

Elizabeth turned on the lamp on her dresser and removed a neatly folded nightshirt from the top drawer. She liked to have fun as much as her twin did, but to her, fun meant losing herself in a great novel or watching old movies with her best friends in Sweet Valley, Enid Rollins and Maria Slater. *And spending quiet moments alone with Todd,* she added wistfully to herself.

"No!" Elizabeth spat, slamming her drawer shut. "I'm *not* going to think about Todd!"

She kicked off her shoes, then placed them in front of the nonworking fireplace next to the dresser. "Todd is history," she declared, forcing herself not to wince at the sound of the words. *He* had broken up with *her.* It wasn't her fault that their relationship had ended, and she refused to spend another minute wallowing in misery.

Besides, she had Laurent in her life now, a real Prince Charming.

Elizabeth turned off the lamp and plopped down across her narrow, four-poster bed. Moonlight shone through the windows, bathing everything in pale blue light. An image of Laurent's handsome face floated into her mind. *What an awesome, phenomenal, incredible night,* she thought, reliving the way it felt to be in Laurent's arms . . . to kiss him. . . .

During the airplane flight to France a week

earlier, Elizabeth had fallen asleep and dreamed that she was lost in a field of wildflowers during a storm. A young man on a white horse had rescued her, and together they'd galloped away.

At the time Elizabeth had dismissed the dream as ridiculous nonsense. But on her first day as an au pair, she'd gotten lost in the winding topiary maze on the grounds of the de Sainte-Marie estate while chasing after six-year-old Pierre. When she'd finally caught up with him, he was crouched behind a tall bush, watching Laurent practice his fencing in front of his small cottage. Something about him had stirred Elizabeth's memory, but she hadn't been able to figure out why.

The following evening she had gotten lost in the topiary maze again. The sky had suddenly turned dark. Lightning had flashed, and rain had begun to pour. Cold, wet, and shivering, Elizabeth had panicked. Finally she'd found her way to the prince's private cottage—his hideaway from the pressures of royal life.

Laurent had seemed shocked to see her standing there when he'd opened the door. But he'd quickly recovered and had led her inside, where a cozy fire was burning in the hearth.

Elizabeth sighed deeply, remembering how great it had felt to come in from the cold. Curled up in a wool blanket, sipping hot tea, she had spent the entire night talking and laughing with Laurent.

Elizabeth had been surprised to discover how much they had in common despite their very different backgrounds. Laurent was serious-minded, deep, and silly all at the same time. But as much as she'd enjoyed his company, she hadn't expected anything more than a casual friendship.

Elizabeth certainly hadn't expected him to show up at the château that evening with two horses and a picnic basket. Then later Laurent had surprised her even more when he'd told her about a dream *he'd* had, in which a beautiful blond girl had appeared in the middle of a huge ball. In the dream, he had made his way over to the mysterious stranger, but just as he was about to lead her to a dance, she vanished.

"But now the dream has come true," he had said to Elizabeth. Then Elizabeth had suddenly realized why he had seemed familiar to her. Laurent was the guy who had rescued her in her dream.

Thinking about it now, Elizabeth shivered. The logical part of her mind insisted that it must be just a coincidence that she and Laurent had dreamed about each other before they'd met. But her heart felt differently.

Elizabeth snuggled under her blanket and closed her eyes. *Are Laurent and I destined to be together?* she wondered.

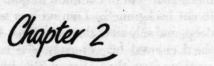

Chapter 2

Jessica opened her eyes slowly and smiled, her whole body tingling with excitement as she awoke to another beautiful day at the Château d'Amour Inconnu. Sunlight streamed through the open windows. A soft gust of tangy sea air blew into the room, fluttering the sheer lace curtains. On the horizon the Mediterranean shimmered in the early morning light. Even her tiny room seemed less shabby, though the walls were still a ghastly shade of dirty yellow and the chest of drawers and bureau on the other side of the room were still old and rickety. But thanks to Jacques, the world seemed brighter.

Jessica stretched out her arms, yawning, and exhaled with a deep, satisfied sigh. "I *knew* I was going to fall in love this summer," she murmured.

She reached under her pillow and pulled out the red velvet jewelry case she'd put there for safekeeping. Her heart fluttered as she opened the lid and lifted a beautiful emerald pendant by its delicate gold chain. The stone dazzled her eyes.

Jacques had given it to her the day they'd met, just before they'd parted. He'd taken her to a private compartment on the train for a special goodbye. Jessica had gasped when she'd seen the huge stone, but Jacques had admitted that it was a fake. "Someday I'll replace it with the real thing," he'd declared. Then they'd shared their first kiss. . . .

Jessica felt warm tingles dancing up and down her spine at the memory. Meeting Jacques was a dream come true, although she was sure her twin wouldn't agree. For some reason Elizabeth had seemed totally against Jacques from the start. *What a spoilsport!* Jessica thought, giggling.

She raised the pendant, watching the sunlight filter through the beautiful stone. *I don't care if it is a fake; I think it's beautiful!* she decided.

She slipped the jewel into the case and tucked it back under her pillow. "I have a feeling my life is about to get very exciting," she whispered into the empty room.

Before arriving at the Château d'Amour Inconnu a week ago, Jessica had imagined herself living in luxury, attending lavish dinner parties, and hobnobbing with the rich and famous. But she'd quickly realized that *au pair* was just a fancy name for *baby-sitter* and that *working* for royalty didn't mean she'd be *treated* royally.

The de Sainte-Maries weren't harsh or rude, but they didn't go out of their way to make the twins feel comfortable either. Despite the number of elegant, *vacant* suites in the château, she and Elizabeth had been assigned two cramped, ugly rooms in the servants' wing. Jessica had been forced to store most of her clothes in Elizabeth's closet because the one in her own room was too small.

Instead of sitting in the posh dining room and eating from priceless heirloom china, the twins had to eat their meals in the kitchen with the children and servants. They hadn't been invited to socialize with any of the important guests who visited the château either.

But Jessica was sure all that was about to change—thanks to Jacques. When the de Sainte-Maries found out that she was dating a duke's son, they would surely start treating her much better.

Suddenly Jessica heard a soft tapping at the door. Even though it was barely six o'clock in the morning, instinctively she knew it was Jacques. *He really is eager to see me again,* she thought. *How romantic!* Grabbing her short, blue silk robe off the floor, she jumped out of bed.

But before she reached the door, it opened. Jacques gasped, obviously shocked to see Jessica. "I—I did not expect . . . that is, I w-was hoping to . . . surprise you while you slept," he stammered.

Jessica smiled tenderly. "That's so sweet." She moved closer and wrapped her arms around his neck. "I couldn't sleep, thinking about you. . . ."

Jacques swept her off her feet in a passionate embrace and carried her back to her bed. Bracing his hands on either side of her face, he leaned over her and kissed her deeply.

Jessica let herself get caught up in the delightful sensation. But after a few seconds she pushed him away and sat up. She didn't want him to get overly confident about their relationship. She knew how important it was to keep guys hanging and wanting more.

"What's wrong?" he asked.

Jessica tossed back her hair and flashed him a flirty grin. "Nothing. I just need a few minutes by myself," she replied.

When he made no move to get up, Jessica walked to the door and opened it for him. She stared at him expectantly. "See you later, Jacques."

He responded with a smooth, challenging grin. "I'm not ready to go."

Hearing the arrogant tone in his voice, Jessica felt her temper flaring. "This is *my* room, and *I* say you're leaving."

"But I have only just arrived," he pleaded.

"And now you're *leaving*," she repeated.

Jacques exhaled loudly and slowly rose to his feet. He crossed the room and took Jessica into his arms again. "You are a very stubborn girl."

Jessica smiled up at him. "You're very stubborn yourself. And if you don't get out of here in three seconds . . ." She shot him a wide-eyed, threatening look.

He kissed her forehead. "What will you do?" he whispered teasingly.

"Out!" Jessica instructed with a laugh. She placed her hands flat against his chest and shoved him hard, pushing him through the open doorway. Before he could react, she stepped back and slammed the door shut.

"Wait!" he called to her through the door. "I must speak to you about—"

"*Later*, Jacques," Jessica replied. She leaned against the door, waiting until she heard his footsteps walking away.

Now what am I going to wear today? she asked herself. She wanted to look spectacular when she waltzed into Princess de Sainte-Marie's sitting room with Jacques at her side.

My days as a nobody around here are about to end, Jessica thought.

"Pierre, stop playing with your food," Elizabeth scolded, trying to inject a forceful tone into her voice. She and the children were having breakfast in the nursery because the kitchen was being scrubbed and polished. Apparently it was a monthly ritual at the château, overseen by the de Sainte-Maries' head chef himself.

In contrast to the heavy antique furniture in the other rooms of the château, the decor in the nursery was strictly modern. The walls were covered with cartoon wallpaper. The colorful pattern was repeated in the curtains that hung on the wide bay window. Ceiling-high, wooden bookcases stood on either side, one filled entirely with English books. A bright orange play unit with a slide, stairs, tunnel, and pull-up bar stood in one corner of the room. Along the wall blue-and-yellow built-in cubby boxes held building blocks, games, and stuffed animals.

The de Sainte-Marie children were adorable, with dark curly hair and big dark eyes, but they were also incredibly rambunctious and exhausting. They had enthusiastically helped Elizabeth wash and set the table in the nursery.

Now, as they shared the fresh croissants, fruit, and milk the kitchen staff had sent up, Elizabeth tried to maintain order. Six-year-old Pierre, the oldest of the three, had a sharp mind and inquisitive nature. He was also boisterous, impulsive, and often very silly.

Ignoring Elizabeth, he continued buzzing an apple slice through the air like an airplane. "How big the plane was that brings you and Mademoiselle Jessica from America?" he asked.

"*Pierre,*" Elizabeth said, making it sound like a warning. He looked at her with a wide-eyed, innocent expression that didn't fool her for an instant. "Put the apple on your plate or in your mouth," she told him.

His five-year-old sister Claudine pushed back

her long brown curls and held a banana up to her eye like a telescope. *"L'aéroplane est très grand, n'est pas?"*

"Can you ask me if the plane was very large in English?" Elizabeth asked. The children were supposed to practice their English by speaking it with Elizabeth and Jessica at all times. "And please take the banana out of your eye," Elizabeth ordered.

Claudine giggled and shifted the banana to her nose. "Maybe your airplane, it is so grand like an elephant?"

The youngest, three-year-old Manon, began to clap and bounce in her seat. "I want the book of the elephant!" she cried, referring to the story Elizabeth had read to them at least a thousand times already that week.

Elizabeth sighed wearily. "There will be no elephant book, or any other story, until you three learn not to play with your food during meals," she told them.

According to *The Baby-sitters' Guide*, which she'd recently read, the best way to teach children how to behave properly was to take away privileges. So far the book's advice hadn't proved to be much help, but to Elizabeth's amazement, Pierre and Claudine immediately put their fruit back down on their plates. "That's better," Elizabeth praised them.

"But when the meal is finished, then we can play with our food, yes?" Claudine asked.

"No, you may not," Elizabeth replied, exasperated. From the corner of her eye she noticed Manon beginning to raise a croissant in the air. Elizabeth glared at her, and Manon bit into the pastry instead, dripping strawberry filling down her chin.

How am I going to last until noon? Elizabeth wondered.

Brigitte, one of the maids, came into the nursery. Tall, with short dark hair and a friendly smile, she appeared to be only a few years older than the twins. *"Bonjour,"* she said cheerfully, greeting them with the French version of "good morning." "I come to clear the dishes, but everyone still eats?"

"Just give us a few more minutes," Elizabeth said.

"I shall wait," Brigitte replied. "I must apologize for the rude way I addressed you yesterday, Elizabeth. With the preparation for the party and so many people in the kitchen . . ." She shuddered.

Elizabeth frowned. "I don't know what you're talking about."

"When you were feeding the children their dinner," Brigitte said.

Elizabeth shook her head. "It wasn't me. Jessica had the children last night." She smiled to herself, recalling where *she* had been during that time . . . and with *whom*.

"Then I will apologize to Jessica." Brigitte plunked herself down on the couch and crossed her legs. "Later I will apologize. For now I sit too comfortable. Don't hurry your breakfast," she added with a laugh.

Elizabeth was pleased to have some grown-up company. "Do you work for the de Sainte-Maries all year round?" she asked.

"No, only during my holidays from university," Brigitte replied. "This is my second summer here at Château d'Amour Inconnu."

Elizabeth stopped Pierre from grabbing the heavy ceramic milk pitcher. "I'll pour it," she told him. After she'd refilled his glass, the girls demanded more milk too.

"Your job, it is much harder than mine," Brigitte remarked.

Elizabeth rolled her eyes. "You have *no* idea," she said, fluffing Manon's mop of brown curls. "These guys keep me hopping, running, jumping, and completely twisted in knots."

"Twisted in knots?" Claudine piped up excitedly. "Is it a new game?"

Elizabeth and Brigitte laughed. Suddenly Brigitte's jaw dropped and the color drained from her face as she stared at something across the room.

Startled by the maid's reaction, Elizabeth turned around, half expecting to see a ghost hovering in the doorway. But instead she saw that Laurent had entered the nursery and was creeping up to the table, his eyes wide with mischief, his finger pressed against his lips for silence.

"Laurie!" the children yelled wildly, scrambling to get out of their chairs and run to him. It was obvious they adored their older half brother.

30

"I wanted to surprise you," Laurent said to the children, laughing as he hugged all three of them at once.

Brigitte, who had jumped to her feet, bowed her head and curtsied, then scrambled out of the room.

How ridiculous! Elizabeth thought. The servants seemed to view Laurent and his family as being on a par with minor deities. That attitude might have been understandable a thousand years ago, when a prince or princess could have had a person's head chopped off, but it seemed terribly silly in modern times . . . especially for a college student like Brigitte.

Haven't these people ever heard of social equality? Elizabeth wondered hotly. *What was the French Revolution all about anyway?*

But the instant Laurent's eyes met hers, Elizabeth's heart leaped, her throat went dry, and all thoughts of history and social studies flew out of her mind.

Laurent shifted uncomfortably, embarrassed by the maid's reaction and quick departure. *I'm a human being!* he had wanted to scream at her. Sometimes he felt as if his parents and their household were stuck in the Middle Ages. And it bothered him.

But Elizabeth's beautiful smile immediately lightened his mood. It hardly seemed possible that a girl so lovely could exist outside of his dreams. *"Bonjour,* Elizabeth," he said softly.

"Bonjour, Laurent," she replied.

31

"Are you going to eat with us?" Claudine asked, jumping up and down at his side with Pierre and Manon.

Laurent gently tweaked her nose, then scooped Manon up into his arms. "If my three little pigs haven't gobbled down every last crumb, I will."

Pierre and Claudine cheered. Manon threw her arms around his neck and gave him a sticky strawberry kiss on the side of his face. Elizabeth pulled up a chair for him.

When the children were settled back into their seats, Claudine turned to him with a serious expression. "Laurie, you can't play with your food until after you finish your breakfast," she warned him.

Laurent narrowed his eyes, bemused.

"It's Mademoiselle Elizabeth's *rule*," Pierre explained, shrugging with his hands palm up at his sides. "We don't understand it either!"

"Well, if it's her rule, I will try to resist the temptation," Laurent said, grinning at her. "We should all do whatever we can to make Elizabeth happy."

Elizabeth blushed a delightful shade of rose. "Thanks," she replied.

Laurent couldn't stop looking at her. Her eyes were the color of the Mediterranean, and her lips looked as soft as the skin of a ripe peach. But Elizabeth was more than beautiful. Sharing breakfast with her felt perfectly natural, as if they'd known each other for *years*.

"Later we will play a game to twist Elizabeth *en*

knots!" Claudine interjected. "She told us."

Elizabeth laughed. "I certainly did not," she countered. "And I never said you could play with your food after breakfast."

The children responded with a chorus of groans. Chuckling, Laurent sat back and watched Elizabeth's interaction with his siblings. Her kindness and warmth radiated outward and shone in the way she treated the little ones. She was firm with them but gentle at the same time. And it was obvious to him that they adored her.

Suddenly Manon reached for another croissant and accidentally knocked a glass off the table. Laurent reached down to pick it up, thankful that it had been empty and that it was made of plastic.

"Welcome to the nursery, Laurent," Elizabeth said wryly. "Where life is never boring."

"And rarely it is sane," Laurent added jokingly. "I have an idea, kids. Let's pretend we are all grown-up and have perfect table manners."

Claudine shook her head, pursing her lips. "We're not allowed to play at breakfast."

Laurent and Elizabeth turned to each other and burst out laughing. At that moment he realized that he felt closer to her than to any other girl he'd known. None of the daughters of the nobility that his parents considered suitable for him could melt his heart the way Elizabeth did.

If only I were free, Laurent thought wistfully.

* * *

Standing in front of the antique mirror that hung above her bureau, Jessica placed her hand on her hip and raised her chin, striking a pose. *Perfect*, she thought, pleased with her reflection. After having tried on dozens of outfits, she'd finally settled on a short blue skirt, topped with a flowing, multicolored silk tunic. For an extra touch of elegance she had put on the diamond earrings her grandmother had given her.

Jessica felt an odd shiver as she watched them sparkling in her ears. Earlier that year she had lost one of the earrings. Then, a few nights later, it had mysteriously reappeared on her windowsill. Painful, frightening memories of that time hovered in the back of Jessica's mind.

"No!" she said, squeezing her eyes shut as she forced the images away. Back then her life had been filled with death and obsession. But she'd survived.

Jessica gripped the edges of the tiny bureau and drew in a deep gulp of air. She refused to let the past spoil the romantic adventure she was having with Jacques. With fierce determination she turned her attention back to the present.

Her hands trembled only slightly as she rummaged through the odds and ends strewn across her dresser, picking through her selection of cosmetics. "Mauve Madness?" she wondered as she uncapped a tube of lipstick. Grimacing, she closed it and tossed it aside.

"I must have been crazy to buy such an ugly

34

shade," she muttered. She found another more to her liking called Strawberry Sundae and smoothed a generous layer across her lips.

Finally Jessica was ready. "This is it," she whispered to her reflection, her eyes shimmering with excitement. She couldn't wait to see everyone's reaction when she introduced her new boyfriend, the duke-to-be of Norveaux. *Things are going to change around here,* she thought. *Good-bye, "Jessica, the lowly servant." Hello, "Miss Wakefield, the honored guest."*

Giggling, she made her way to the door, absently stepping over piles of discarded clothing on the floor.

In the hallway Jacques was leaning against the wall with his arms folded. "At last," he muttered.

Jessica's eyes narrowed slightly at the petulant tone in his voice. "Aren't I worth waiting for?" she asked sharply.

Jacques rushed over to her and enveloped her in a huge hug. "Of course you are, *mon ange,*" he told her. "It's just that I care for you so deeply . . . I lose all my patience when we are apart." He touched his lips to hers and whispered, *"Je t'aime."*

Jessica sighed contentedly. She'd picked up enough French in her classes at Sweet Valley High and around the château to understand those words. "I love you too," she replied.

He kissed her fully, and Jessica felt as if a million sparks of brilliant light were cascading over her and Jacques.

35

Afterward she leaned back and smiled up at him. "I suppose I should touch up my lipstick before we go downstairs to breakfast."

Jacques's eyes became clouded. Jessica giggled, presuming the reason for his troubled look. "I won't take more than ten seconds this time. I promise," she assured him.

"We need to talk," he said flatly.

Jessica shrugged out of his arms and opened the door to her room. "In ten seconds we'll talk. First I have to put on more lipstick."

"No, Jessica." He followed her into the room and shut the door behind him. "*First* we will talk."

Hands on her hips, Jessica glared at him. She didn't care how gorgeous and sexy he was—he didn't have the right to order her around. "I don't remember inviting you in here," she said.

"You must hear me out," Jacques pleaded.

"You're in no position to tell me what I *must* do," she retorted hotly. "Now if you don't mind . . ."

Jacques rubbed his hand over his face and exhaled loudly. "You're absolutely right," he admitted. "I don't know what gets into me sometimes. But the thing is . . . I can't be seen here with you."

"What?" Jessica gasped incredulously. How was she going to show off her royal boyfriend to the de Sainte-Maries if he refused to be seen with her? All her plans for the summer would be ruined!

A cold suspicion began to take shape in her gut. "Why, Jacques?" she demanded. "Because you're a

36

noble heir and I'm not? Is that what this is about?"

Jacques shook his head emphatically. "No, of course not. That would never stand in the way of my feelings for you. But there is another reason."

Jessica tapped her foot impatiently. "I'd love to hear it."

"It's about the family . . . ," he said, hesitating.

"Whose family—yours or mine?" she asked tersely.

Jacques pushed his hand through his hair and rocked back on his heels. "The others . . . the other family."

Jessica frowned, confused. "The de Sainte-Maries?"

Jacques nodded. "That's correct," he replied. "The de Sainte-Maries. I can't be seen with you because of the de Sainte-Maries. . . . I can't allow them to see *me*."

Jessica sat down on the edge of her bed. "You don't think the prince and princess would welcome you?"

"Welcome me?" Jacques choked out an incredulous laugh. "They would sic their wild dogs on me and allow my body to be torn to shreds!"

Jessica stared at him for a long moment, wondering whether or not to believe him. She hadn't seen any wild dogs on the de Sainte-Maries' property. But the vulnerable look in Jacques's eyes tugged at her heart.

Jacques lowered himself on one knee before her, as if he were proposing marriage in one of those sappy old black-and-white movies her twin loved to watch. "*Ma chérie*, will you at least listen to me before you cast me aside?" he begged.

Jessica pressed her lips together tightly to keep from giggling at his melodramatic action.

"The de Sainte-Marie family and mine are sworn enemies," he explained. "They've been locked in a feud with each other over a land dispute since the fourteenth century. You would lose your job if they found out about me." He reached up and squeezed her hand. "I wish I might make the peace with *les* de Sainte-Maries. But if I even try, my father, he would, how you say, *disown* me."

Crestfallen, Jessica sighed. "We can't have your father disowning you," she said. "And I don't want to be shipped back to Sweet Valley just yet." She smiled sadly. "It seems we'll have to keep our relationship a secret."

Jacques got off his knees and sat down beside her. "It's the only way," he agreed.

Jessica rested her head on his shoulder. "It's sort of romantic," she said, trying to get used to the idea. She wasn't going to spend the rest of her summer as a pampered guest of the royal family. *But I'll be sneaking off to meet the hottest-looking guy in France*, she reminded herself. *And someday Jacques will become the duke of Norveaux. . . .*

As he kissed her again, Jessica imagined herself as the duchess of Norveaux, living in a place even more spectacular than the Château d'Amour Inconnu. *Meeting Jacques was a dream come true*, she thought.

"I'm thankful that you understand," Jacques whispered.

Jessica recalled the story Jacques had told her about the secret lovers who'd lived on the island hundreds of years ago and whose tale had given the Château d'Amour Inconnu its name.

According to the legend, Prince Frédéric the Third had fallen hopelessly in love with Isadora, a pretty young maiden with a beautiful voice. But because she wasn't a member of the nobility, they'd had to keep their love a secret.

Jessica crossed her wrists behind Jacques's neck. "We'll be just like Prince Frédéric and Isadora," she said.

Jacques chuckled. "I only hope our story will finish differently."

The legend had a very unhappy ending. Prince Frédéric had been forced to marry another woman of his class. And poor, brokenhearted Isadora had turned into a white dove whose sad song lived forever.

Jessica smiled. "I hope so too," she replied with a giggle. "I can't sing."

Jacques tipped back his head and laughed. *"Tu es comme un rayon de soleil,"* he said.

Before Jessica had a chance to ask him what that meant, he lowered his lips to hers for another incredible, sizzling kiss.

Chapter 3

Jessica hummed to herself as she headed toward the children's outdoor play area later that morning. There was a joyful bounce in her step, and she couldn't stop smiling. Seeing Jacques again had energized her completely, and she was ready for anything—even three rambunctious, pint-size royal terrors.

Elizabeth was pushing Claudine on a deluxe swing set while Pierre and Manon were digging in the sandbox. The children's area was also equipped with a huge, wooden dollhouse in the shape of a castle, a jungle gym, slides, and seesaws. There was also a small shed full of toys and games.

"Mademoiselle Jessica!" the children called, waving to her. Pierre and Manon threw their pails and shovels aside and came running toward her.

Jessica felt a rush of delight at their enthusiastic welcome. They really were three of the cutest little kids she'd ever known. "Hello, *mes amis!*" she sang out cheerfully, greeting everyone as "her friends."

Claudine clamored to get down from the swing, then joined her brother and sister, who were jumping around Jessica like happy puppies. "Will you let us play with our food after lunch?" Pierre asked.

Jessica laughed and turned to Elizabeth. "What's he talking about?" she mouthed.

"Don't ask," Elizabeth quipped, watching her with a narrow-eyed, suspicious look. "What's going on, Jess?"

"Whatever do you mean?" Jessica drawled.

"You're *early*," Elizabeth replied dryly. "That always means something." Jessica's chronic lateness was legendary. She never wore a watch since she held the belief that nothing important would start until she had arrived anyway. "I have a feeling you're up to no good," Elizabeth added.

Jessica crossed her arms and sniffed, trying to appear insulted. "Thanks a lot," she retorted indignantly. Then she burst out giggling.

"Tell me!" Elizabeth demanded.

Jessica grinned and clapped. "Hey, kids, let's see who can swing the highest!" She wasn't sure if they were old enough to understand what she was about to say, but she didn't want to take any chances.

The children immediately scrambled for the swings, squealing enthusiastically. Jessica lifted Manon into a safety swing and fastened the seat belt.

As the twins stood side by side, pushing the

kids on the swings, Jessica shared her fabulous news. "Jacques has come to see me!"

Elizabeth stared at her blankly.

"Don't tell me you've forgotten him?" Jessica said. "We met him and his father on the train. . . . Jacques is the guy who helped me with my baggage—"

"Yes, I know who you mean," Elizabeth interrupted flatly.

"I knew he would come and see me," Jessica gushed. "He's such a fabulous guy. . . ." She smiled brightly. "I love him so much, Liz. I really think he's The One."

"Is he staying here at the château?" Elizabeth asked.

"I wish." Jessica pushed Pierre's swing, then stepped over to Manon's. "It would be so fabulous if Jacques could stay here. But he can't because of a problem between his family and the de Sainte-Maries. Some old feud that's been going on for hundreds of years."

"Who's the highest?" Claudine yelled, interrupting the twins' conversation.

"It's a tie," Elizabeth answered blandly.

"Push me the hardest!" Pierre shouted.

"No, me!" Claudine responded. "Push me up to the sun!"

"Up to the sun!" Manon echoed, kicking her legs wildly. Jessica absently noticed that Manon had flung off one of her blue sneakers.

"Jacques told me he'd be in big trouble if the

prince and princess catch him on their property," Jessica continued. "But he came to see me in spite of the risk. . . . Isn't that so romantic?"

"I don't know, Jess," Elizabeth replied carefully. "It doesn't seem right to go against the de Sainte-Maries on this issue. After all, the château *is* their home."

Jessica reeled back as if she'd been slapped. "How can you say that?" she snapped hotly. "Is it right for them to keep two people who love each other apart because of some ridiculous old feud?"

Elizabeth turned and gave her a gentle, big-sister smile. "I just don't want to see you hurt," she explained.

Jessica's expression softened. "I know." But she wasn't ready to let her twin off the hook completely. Elizabeth had been acting like a bossy know-it-all ever since they'd left Sweet Valley, and Jessica was tired of it.

She raised her eyebrows and gave Elizabeth a pointed look. "But it goes both ways," Jessica said. "I don't want to see *you* hurt either. Remember, even a prince can turn into a frog if you kiss him too much—and he can be a very bad influence on you."

Elizabeth's cheeks turned bright red. "I'm sorry about last night," she muttered.

"You should be!" Jessica replied. Then she threw Elizabeth's own words back at her. "Didn't I already tell you once that I wasn't going to put up with your *selfish, lazy attitude* this summer?" Jessica tilted her head and pursed her lips, as if she were struggling to remember something important. Then she abruptly widened her eyes with mock astonishment and snapped her fingers. "That's what *you* told *me*. Ironic, huh?"

"OK, I get your point," Elizabeth conceded. "It was totally irresponsible of me to ditch you last night and to force you to cover for me."

Jessica savored the victory over her twin. "Don't worry, I'll let you make it up to me, Liz. You can work my shift when Jacques comes back."

"Great," Elizabeth responded flatly. "I'll see you later . . . at five o'clock sharp."

Jessica smiled. "Say hello to Prince Laurent for me."

"What makes you think I'm going to see him this afternoon?" Elizabeth asked.

Jessica flashed her a knowing grin. "Aren't you?"

Elizabeth shrugged. "We haven't made any plans."

"Who's the highest now?" Pierre shouted.

"I think you're all the highest," Jessica responded breezily. Apparently satisfied with that, the children cheered.

Elizabeth chuckled. "I'll see you guys later," she said as she turned to go.

"Don't be late again," Jessica called after her.

Elizabeth glanced over her shoulder. "I won't," she promised.

Jacques Landeau, Elizabeth groaned to herself as she walked back to the château. *I thought we*

44

were rid of that fake charmer. But she knew it would be dangerous to let out her true feelings about Jacques. Any opposition would only make him seem more attractive to Jessica.

Elizabeth felt suddenly exhausted . . . and *hungry.* She realized she hadn't eaten much at breakfast, first because the kids had been behaving so outrageously. Then Laurent had arrived, and she'd totally forgotten about food. Elizabeth sighed, remembering how thrilled she'd felt sitting with him at the table. . . . *But even girls in love have to eat,* she reminded herself.

The kitchen was in the final stages of its Saturday scrub down when Elizabeth entered. At the table where the children usually took their meals, three maids were polishing silverware. Other workers were wiping down the appliances, hanging clean curtains, or replacing the newly washed glass fixtures on the lights around the room.

Fernand, the head cook, eyed Elizabeth sharply. *"Il n'est pas l'heure du repas,"* he grumbled, telling her it wasn't mealtime.

"Yes, I know," Elizabeth replied. "I thought I might make myself a sandwich or something if it's OK."

The chef let out a stream of French words, this time too rapidly for Elizabeth to understand. She suspected what he said wasn't complimentary, especially when several people turned to her and sniggered.

One of the maids polishing the silver apparently took pity on her. "The prince and princess have taken their guests to a restaurant off the island," she explained. "The children will have . . . how do you say? *Old* things."

"You mean leftovers?" Elizabeth asked.

"*Oui* . . . yes. Leftovers," the maid said, smiling brightly as she wiped her hands on a towel. "Because you help me with my English, I will assist you now."

A short time later Elizabeth left the kitchen loaded down with a basket of chicken sandwiches, red plums, green grapes, assorted pastries, and a large bottle of orange seltzer. *I'll never be able to finish all this*, she thought. She'd tried telling that to the maid, but the woman had replied that taking care of the de Sainte-Marie children required lots of strength. "You eat to keep the energy up," she had insisted.

Chuckling to herself, Elizabeth went outdoors to find a quiet, shady spot where she could enjoy her lunch in peace. The grounds around the château were covered with lush green lawns and patches of brightly colored flowers, and the day was just too perfect to stay inside.

Elizabeth meandered into the wild English garden. Clusters of red and yellow tulips lined the sides of the white stone path. When she came to a fork in the path, Elizabeth turned right. After a few minutes she realized she was heading toward the stables. *I wonder if anyone would mind if I took Cendrillon out for a ride*, she thought. She decided to find one of the workers and ask.

Elizabeth approached the largest of three white

barns and pushed open the door. Just then she heard her name called from behind. She whirled around and saw Laurent coming from one of the other barns. Watching him walk toward her, Elizabeth felt a warm sensation of pleasure. He was wearing faded blue jeans and a black T-shirt that showed off his lean, rugged build. *He's totally gorgeous!* Elizabeth thought.

"You're here," Laurent said, obviously surprised to see her.

Elizabeth lowered her gaze, suddenly self-conscious. *What if he thinks I'm chasing him too much?* she worried. "I just came to see if I could . . . if Cendrillon . . ." Elizabeth swallowed hard. "If this is a bad time . . ."

He drew her into his arms. "It's *perfect*."

"You're sure?" Elizabeth glanced up at him hopefully.

Laurent's deep blue eyes shimmered with a look of happiness as he gazed at her. "I've just instructed my groom to saddle up Pardaillan and Cendrillon," he explained. "In a few minutes I would have been on my way to find *you*." He gently touched the side of her face. "But what else could I expect from the girl of my dreams?"

A sweet, warm glow spread through Elizabeth's body. "Um . . . how about lunch?" she replied, holding up the wicker basket. "I probably have enough here to feed us *and* the horses."

Laurent chuckled. "Wonderful!"

47

Just then the groom brought out the white stallion and the black mare. "Are you happy to see me?" Elizabeth cooed to Cendrillon as she stroked the horse's neck. The animal whinnied and tapped its hoof.

Laurent laughed. "I didn't know she understood English."

The air was rich with the scent of damp earth and leaves as Elizabeth followed Laurent along a trail that meandered through the de Sainte-Marie forest. Sunbeams cut through openings between the trees, shimmering on a bubbling brook that ran parallel to the trail. *I'm riding through the enchanted forest,* Elizabeth marveled.

They came to a clearing and stopped for lunch. The area was dotted with bushes of lavender, and a natural dam had created a pond of crystal clear water. "This is beautiful!" Elizabeth exclaimed as she dismounted.

Laurent grinned. "I'm glad you like it," he replied.

As he led the horses over to the water for a cooling drink Elizabeth looked around for a good picnic spot. She noticed a wide, rectangular stone protruding from the ground near the pool. She draped her jacket over the stone for a tablecloth and set out the contents of her basket. On impulse she gathered a fragrant cluster of lavender blossoms for a centerpiece. Everything was ready by the time Laurent finished watering the horses.

"I didn't know we were dining formally this

afternoon," Laurent teased as he sat down across from her.

"That's all right," Elizabeth responded with a smile. "Just be sure to leave the waitress a big tip."

Bracing his hands on the edge of the rock, Laurent leaned toward her until his lips hovered close to hers. "Of course," he whispered. "The service here"—he kissed her softly—"is excellent."

Elizabeth kissed him back. "I'm glad you like it, Your Highness."

He chuckled at that. "I do."

They devoured the chicken sandwiches—which were delicious—then moved on to the assorted pastries. Elizabeth selected an éclair and nearly swooned at the first bite. She closed her eyes and chewed slowly to savor the rich, creamy flavor.

When she opened her eyes again, Laurent was watching her with an amused expression. "I take it you like that?"

Elizabeth laughed. "How could you tell?"

"*J'ai deviné* . . . a lucky guess," he replied jokingly.

After lunch they packed up the debris in the wicker basket. A cool breeze rustled through the trees. Elizabeth shook out her jacket and draped it around her shoulders. "Do you come to this spot often?" she asked Laurent as they sat side by side on the rock.

"I did when I was a child," he told her. "I used to play here by myself for hours."

"Was it lonely?" Elizabeth asked softly.

Laurent chuckled. "It was great fun," he countered. "I would pretend I was an American cowboy, and this rock where we sit now was a stagecoach. It was my job to shoot all the robbers that came near it. My parents would allow no toy guns, so I had to use a twig."

Elizabeth smiled. The image of Laurent as a little boy tugged at her heart. She could picture him playing, his blue eyes wild with excitement, wielding his "weapon" with fierce determination. "Did you also make those funny sound effects when you took your shots at the robbers?" she teased.

Laurent raised his eyebrows. "Of course." Elizabeth laughed as he demonstrated his skill at making the sound of a gunshot. "I also had an imaginary sidekick named François," he added. "François was supposed to cover me, but I usually wound up saving him."

Elizabeth playfully tugged the collar of his T-shirt. "What a hero!"

Laurent gave her a crooked smile. "I can't believe I'm telling you all this. I've never told anyone."

"I'm honored," Elizabeth responded, hugging his arm.

"What about you?" he asked. "Did you have the imaginary friends when you were growing up?"

Elizabeth thought back to her childhood. "No, I just had Jessica," she replied. "She was enough!"

They laughed. Laurent reached for her hand and laced his fingers through hers. "You're more than a dream come true, Elizabeth. You're a miracle."

Elizabeth rested her head on his shoulder. She felt totally at peace, yet excited and alive. *If only this moment could last forever,* she wished. But she realized it wasn't just that one moment that was so spectacular; *every* moment with Laurent was special. Elizabeth could almost imagine a future with him. . . .

"So deep in thought," Laurent remarked. He gently brushed his lips across her forehead.

Elizabeth sighed dreamily. "What's it like, being a prince?"

"My life is like anyone's—some parts of it are good, and some are not so good," he told her.

Elizabeth absently ran her finger over the rough surface of the stone as she considered his response. "Tell me about it," she said.

"Let's see. . . ." Laurent wrapped his arm around her, drawing her closer to his side. "The thing that is worse about being a member of a royal family is that people consider me often as an *institution* rather than a human being. They fawn all over me or jump around nervously . . . without ever looking me in the eye."

"That would be difficult for me to deal with," Elizabeth replied.

"You never treated me like a royal," he said. "I love that most about you, Elizabeth."

"You never treated me like a peon," she remarked.

Laurent nodded smugly. "That's right. Our first meal together, I cooked. And if you have time now,

I'll serve you a cup of the very best coffee in the world. My cottage is only a short distance from here."

Elizabeth glanced at her watch. She had nearly an hour before she had to take over from Jessica. "I'd love coffee," she said.

Hand in hand, they walked over to the shady spot near the pool where the horses were standing. "There are advantages to being a prince," he said, grinning. "I have an awesome horse."

Pardaillan raised his head and flicked his tail, as if in response to Laurent's compliment.

Elizabeth chuckled. "Cendrillon is just as awesome," she said, patting the mare.

"Oh, close, maybe," Laurent joked.

"What else is good about being a prince?" Elizabeth asked Laurent as they rode along the trail at a leisurely pace.

Laurent turned to her and laughed. "Isn't Pardaillan enough?"

Elizabeth scowled in response.

"OK, OK, let's see. . . . For one thing, my family's power and prestige makes it possible for me to influence social changes . . . and to help others on a grand scale," Laurent continued. "I uphold the traditions and dignity of my people."

"I'm sure you're a wonderful leader," Elizabeth responded, smiling broadly. She leaned over and kissed him. "You're a wonderful *person.*"

Laurent's mood seemed to darken suddenly, and a brooding look came into eyes. "I wonder if you'd still think that if you knew . . ." His voice trailed off.

Elizabeth shifted uneasily. "What do you mean? If I knew *what?*"

Laurent glanced away. Then, just as suddenly, he flashed her a huge smile. "Enough of this serious talk," he said. "I'll race you to the cottage!"

"You're on!" Elizabeth replied, urging Cendrillon to gallop. They rode like the wind, through the forest and across a wide meadow. From the corner of her eye she saw Laurent pulling ahead of her. "We can't let them beat us, Cendrillon!" she shouted.

Elizabeth laughed joyfully as the world seemed to rush by her in a streak of bright colors. She felt as if her heart were pounding as fast and as hard as Cendrillon's hooves. Finally Laurent's cottage appeared in the distance. The horses were side by side until the very end, when Cendrillon inched ahead. Elizabeth won the race by a nose.

She climbed off the mare and, whooping victoriously, jumped up and down. Laurent sauntered over to her with a wry grin on his face. "Congratulations," he muttered.

"Thanks, I deserve it!" she replied smugly. "Cendrillon and I were great, weren't we?"

"And you are so modest," he teased.

Elizabeth's stomach fluttered as Laurent took her into his arms. He kissed her slowly and deeply, as if they had all the time in the world to be together. Elizabeth's heart melted. Losing herself in the glorious sensations swirling through her, she clung to Laurent.

When the kiss ended, Elizabeth drew in a shaky breath. "Mmm, was that for winning the race?" she whispered, her arms still wrapped around his neck.

Laurent touched his forehead to hers and smiled. "No, that's my consolation prize for losing. This one is yours for winning. . . ." Then he lowered his lips to hers for another searing, passionate kiss.

Wonderful tingles coursed through Elizabeth's body. After a moment she broke off the kiss and pressed her lips against Laurent's neck, breathing in his delicious, masculine scent. She hadn't felt such strong emotions for a guy since . . . *Todd.*

A strong pang of guilt shot through Elizabeth, and she squeezed her eyes shut tightly for a moment, willing herself not to think about Todd. There was no reason she should feel guilty for kissing Laurent. Todd had broken up with *her.*

Still, Elizabeth thought, resting her head on Laurent's shoulder, *Todd could've at least written me a letter. Maybe there'll be a letter waiting when I get back to the château—*

With a wince Elizabeth forcibly derailed that train of thought. Laurent was here with her now, and *he* was the one who was making her heart sing.

Elizabeth gave Laurent a squeeze, and he gently hugged her back. Then he planted a soft kiss on the top of her head.

Todd is history, Elizabeth thought solemnly.

Chapter 4

I can't believe she's doing this to me again! Jessica raged silently as she glanced at the wall clock in the nursery. Elizabeth was nearly two hours late, the children had grown tired and cranky, and Jessica's nerves were stretched to the limit.

Pierre dropped a book on her lap. "Read it to us," he demanded.

"No," Claudine shrieked, running toward Jessica with another book. She pushed Pierre aside. He shoved her back, knocking her to the floor. Claudine let out a loud wail and threw her book at his head. Then Pierre starting crying too.

Jessica cast a stern look at Pierre and Claudine. "Sit on the couch and be quiet," she ordered. Suddenly a wooden block came whizzing by, narrowly missing Jessica's head. "What the—" She whipped her head around just in time to see

Manon ducking behind a huge stuffed rabbit.

I'm going to kill *Elizabeth,* Jessica fumed.

Just then she heard footsteps approaching from the hall. "Prepare to die, Liz!" Jessica grumbled under her breath, presuming it was her wayward twin.

But it was Anna, the housekeeper, who appeared at the door. In her midthirties, she was tall and slim, with brown eyes and long brown hair she wore tied back at the nape of her neck. A few dark freckles were scattered across her nose and cheeks. "I've brought your mail," she said, handing two envelopes to Jessica.

They were both addressed to her twin, one from Enid Rollins and one from Maria Slater. Smirking, Jessica tossed them on the table. *Of course Elizabeth's boring friends would have plenty of time to write to her,* she thought.

"Are the children behaving today?" Anna asked.

"Oui!" they answered in unison. "We're being very nice." As if to demonstrate, they all ran over to the doll corner and began playing quietly.

Suddenly Elizabeth burst in, red faced and breathless. "I am *so* sorry I'm late. I lost track of time. . . . Hi, Anna," she said, glancing at the housekeeper. Then she turned to Jessica with a pleading look in her eyes. "I ran all the way back from the stables. I hope you're not mad, Jess."

Jessica clenched her teeth, anxious to tell her sister exactly *how* mad she was. But she didn't want to do it in front of Anna.

"Is this today's mail?" Elizabeth inquired as she went over to the table.

"Yes, I just brought it up," Anna replied, turning to leave. "And now I must go check on the evening's meal. You may bring the children down to the kitchen in twenty minutes."

After Anna left, Jessica took a deep breath and prepared to pounce. "Elizabeth—," she began, her voice as cold as steel.

Her twin looked up with a sad, confused expression on her face. "Is this all there was for us? Nothing else?"

Jessica glared at her, seething. "Who cares about the mail?"

Elizabeth shrugged. "I just thought maybe Todd . . ." She pressed her bottom lip between her teeth, and a wistful look flickered in her eyes. Then Elizabeth shook her head, as if to clear it. "Oh, it doesn't matter," she said.

She was hoping to hear from Todd, Jessica realized. The harsh words she'd been gathering died in her throat, and her gut twisted with guilt. The truth was, Todd *had* sent Elizabeth a letter the previous week, which Jessica had intercepted. It had arrived in the aftermath of the twins' huge fight, when they still weren't speaking to each other. Furious at Elizabeth, Jessica had secretly destroyed Todd's letter.

But isn't Elizabeth better off without him? Jessica reasoned. After all, Laurent was a thousand times better. Then another pesky twinge nagged her. *What if it doesn't work out with Laurent either?*

Jessica had heard a rumor that Laurent and the countess's daughter, Antonia, were supposed to be getting together that summer. She hadn't mentioned it to Elizabeth at the time because it hadn't seemed important. But now that her sister seemed to be falling for the prince . . .

Jessica absently stared into space, trying to sort out the pieces. *Just the idea of stealing another girl's boyfriend would horrify Elizabeth, so I can't tell her about Laurent and Antonia,* she decided. Her twin would give up without a fight and let that nasty little witch take the prince.

Maybe I should just tell her about Todd's letter, Jessica thought. *Elizabeth will be angry about it, but she'll forgive me like she always does . . . won't she?*

Jessica nervously chewed the inside of her bottom lip as she hesitated. She didn't want to get into another fight, especially now that she was counting on her twin to cover for her when Jacques was around. *Besides, Todd will probably write again,* she assured herself.

"I really am sorry about being late," Elizabeth said, cutting into Jessica's thoughts.

Jessica shrugged and put on a cheerful grin. "No problem," she responded, trying to soothe her own guilty conscience. "But you're awfully sweaty." She sniffed loudly and wrinkled her nose. "And you smell horsey."

Elizabeth nodded. "We went riding."

"I'll stay here and watch the kids if you want to run upstairs for a quick shower," Jessica offered.

"Are you sure?" Elizabeth asked warily.

Jessica shrugged. "Of course, or I wouldn't have said it. But you'd better be back before it's time to take them to dinner," she added.

"I will," Elizabeth replied, bolting for the door. "Thanks, Jess. You're the best."

Again Jessica felt a pang of guilt for not being totally honest with Elizabeth. *It's for her own good,* Jessica reassured herself. *Besides, Todd Wilkins is a total drip. Elizabeth doesn't need him—she has a bona fide prince in her life now. And I know she can win him away from Antonia!*

Elizabeth wiped her hand across her sweaty forehead as she hurried toward the back staircase that led to her room in the servants' wing. She appreciated her twin's offer to watch the kids for a few more minutes while she showered and changed, although she was a bit concerned about the reason for Jessica's sudden generosity. *She's either going to try to manipulate me into doing something I don't want to do, or she's hiding something,* Elizabeth thought.

As she crossed the wide corridor at the end of the hall Elizabeth caught sight of Countess di Rimini and her daughter, Antonia, in the formal parlor. The countess was a tall, striking woman with bright red hair, piercing green eyes, and a

59

permanent scowl on her face. Antonia was a younger copy of her mother, with fewer wrinkles around her mouth. Both women were perched side by side on an eighteenth-century red velvet divan, sipping tea from dainty china cups.

"Those American girls are never working," Elizabeth overheard the countess hiss in a stage whisper.

"What do you expect from common servants?" Antonia responded.

Elizabeth's blood boiled, but she walked by with her head held high. *Why don't they mind their own business?* she thought. Clenching her fists at her side, Elizabeth headed quickly for the staircase. But she wasn't fast enough.

She heard the click-clacking sound of high-heeled footsteps on the polished wood floor behind her. "Now what?" Elizabeth muttered to herself as she turned around.

Antonia stood there, with her arms folded and her nose in the air, glaring at Elizabeth.

"Is there something you wanted?" Elizabeth asked, forcing an even, neutral tone into her voice.

"You are a servant to the de Sainte-Maries, so don't think you can charm your way out of your work here," Antonia warned.

Elizabeth blinked, taken aback by her rudeness. "I don't know what you're talking about. I take my duties as an au pair *very* seriously."

"Where are the children now?" Antonia

snapped. "You haven't left them alone, have you?"

Elizabeth gripped the ornately carved post on the banister and exhaled slowly, fighting to maintain control. "They're in the nursery, with my sister," she explained tightly. "Now if you'll excuse me, I'm in a bit of a rush—"

"Not so fast!" Antonia's lips twisted into a cruel, haughty smile. "Let me give you some advice. Perhaps in America family honor isn't important, but here in Europe it's *crucial*. And you must face it—you don't have the noble breeding necessary to rise above your station."

Something inside Elizabeth snapped. "You're right, Antonia. In America all of us are equal. We only keep breeding records for *animals*." With that she whirled around and rushed up the stairs.

"I would be careful if I were you!" Antonia called after her. "It's when you're standing next to nobility that you look your shabbiest!"

Elizabeth cringed but continued on her way without a backward glance. *I despise that girl!* she raged silently as she stormed into her room. She slapped her fist against her palm, wishing she could do the same to Antonia's face. *And I despise her mother too!*

"But I can't let them get to me," Elizabeth grumbled as she paced the length of her room. Fuming about the di Riminis was a total waste of energy and time. She reminded herself that she had a job to do, and if she didn't hurry up and get in the shower, she'd be late—*again*. Then Jessica's unexpected generosity would vanish as mysteriously as it had appeared

Elizabeth went over to her dresser and took out a clean outfit: blue jeans and a soft-green cotton sweater. She had exactly twelve minutes left to shower, change, and report to the nursery.

The di Riminis' narrow-minded view of the world was their own problem. *Thank goodness Laurent doesn't share their attitude,* Elizabeth thought.

Jessica was thrilled when Jacques came to see her again the following evening. It was just after sunset, and the sky was streaked with purple and red as they took a romantic stroll in the rose garden. The gardeners and servants didn't work on Sundays, for which Jessica was thankful. The last thing she'd need was to be spotted with Jacques by one of the de Sainte-Maries' faithful staff. She was equally glad that Prince Nicolas and Princess Catherine were out for the evening, having taken the countess di Rimini and Antonia to the opera.

Jacques picked a white blossom and gently traced a line across Jessica's chin with its soft, fragrant petals. "You are so beautiful, more than this flower," he whispered in a deep, husky voice.

Jessica almost swooned as a warm flush of pleasure rose to her cheeks. "I'm so glad you're here, Jacques."

They sat down on a wrought iron bench under an arbor of crimson roses and snuggled close together. Jacques brushed a gentle kiss across Jessica's lips. *"Je t'aime de tout mon cœur,"* he whispered.

Jessica murmured a sigh. She didn't know what he'd just told her, but she was sure it was something wonderfully romantic.

"Tu es si belle." Jacques kissed her again. *"Tu es aussi delicate qu'une fleur. Tu es aussi jolie qu'un ange."* He leaned back and gazed at her directly, his brown eyes dancing with amusement. "You understand these words I say, yes?"

Jessica smiled dreamily. "Not a clue."

"I teach you, then," Jacques offered.

"Later." Jessica boldly kissed him again.

Jacques chuckled against her lips, then pulled her closer and deepened the kiss. She felt his fingers brushing through her hair, caressing the back of her neck. Jessica shivered with delight.

Suddenly Jacques leaned back. "Are you cold, *ma chérie?*"

Jessica smiled. "Not in the least."

"Ma chérie means 'my dear,'" he explained.

"I actually know that," Jessica replied. "I did sit through several semesters of French class."

Jacques pushed a lock of her hair behind her ear and gazed into her eyes. "And *je t'aime de tout mon cœur* means 'I love you with all my heart.' *Tu es si belle,* this means 'you are so beautiful.' *Tu es aussi delicate qu'une fleur*—you are as delicate as a flower. *Tu es aussi jolie qu'un ange*—you are as lovely as an angel."

Jessica hesitatingly repeated each phrase after Jacques.

"Try rolling your *r*'s a bit more," he instructed. "Last night I told you this—*tu es comme un rayon de soleil*. It means you are like a ray of sunshine."

Jessica leaned closer to him and gazed into his warm brown eyes. "I remember."

Jacques placed a feather-soft kiss on her eyebrow. "Now, I say to you the words in English; you translate into *français*."

Jessica pursed her lips. "Are we really going to have a French quiz right *now*?" she asked. "Don't we have better things to do?"

Jacques shifted away from her. Facing forward, he rested his arms along the back of the bench. "French, it is a beautiful, romantic language," he said.

"No argument there," Jessica responded, bemused—and irritated—by the sudden chill in his mood. "What's wrong, Jacques?"

He turned to her and smiled. "I wish you could say these words to me in my own language," he whispered.

Jessica narrowed her eyes. "What?"

Jacques ducked his head sheepishly. "It is a foolish whim, I know. But for me it is important that we . . . how you say . . . *communicate* the feelings we have to each other with French words."

"Seems we were communicating just fine a minute ago," Jessica responded sharply. "Without any words at all."

"I have caused you to be angry, haven't I?" Jacques said, his voice filled with concern. "Do you want me to go?"

"No, of course not." Jessica exhaled loudly and reached for his hand. "If it means that much to you . . . OK, I'll memorize your sentences."

Jacques immediately enveloped her in a big hug. "Let's go quickly to your room and get a notebook and pen so you can learn better these words," he suggested.

"What if you get caught?" Jessica argued.

"You said the prince and princess are out for the evening, yes?"

"One of the servants might see us and tell the de Sainte-Maries," Jessica said. She snuggled closer to him on the bench. "Besides, it's nice and cozy here."

Jacques kissed her briefly. "We'll come right back." He stood up and held out his hand to her.

Jessica rolled her eyes. *Obviously I'm not going to talk him out of this,* she realized. Giving in, she placed her hand in his and allowed Jacques to lead her toward the château.

"And when the maiden woke up, she found the bluebird sitting on the highest branch of the weeping tree," Elizabeth read aloud. She sat wedged between Claudine and Pierre on the couch in the nursery, with Manon on her lap.

"The bluebird began to sing a sweet melody," Elizabeth continued. "It was so lovely that all the creatures of the forest came to listen."

Pierre pointed to a squirrel in the corner of the illustration. "Is that the bluebird's friend?"

"It could be," Elizabeth replied as she turned the page. "Suddenly the wicked spell was broken, and the bluebird turned into a handsome prince. The very next day he and the maiden were married. The bells of the palace rang joyfully for all to hear . . . and the prince and princess lived happily ever after."

Elizabeth sighed contentedly. "Happily ever after," she breathed. She couldn't help picturing herself as the princess and Laurent as her handsome prince. *Will our story end happily ever after?* she wondered.

Then she laughed at herself. *Get real!* she thought. She'd known Laurent for only a short time. It was a bit early for wedding plans! Elizabeth closed the book firmly.

"Read it again," Manon protested.

"It's time for bed now," Elizabeth replied. "We can read it again tomorrow. Let's have one big, group hug, and then it's off to dreamland for you three."

They snuggled together noisily for a few seconds, then the children scampered off to the adjoining bedroom. Elizabeth followed to tuck them in. Their mother usually did the honors, but the princess had gone out that evening.

"Good night," Elizabeth whispered after the children had settled down. "Sweet dreams."

"You look like the princess in the book," Claudine said sleepily.

Elizabeth smiled as she turned off the light and slipped out of the room. *Crazy as it seems, I feel like the princess in the book,* she thought.

She'd always imagined that she'd live an ordinary life, in or near Sweet Valley. She'd graduate from Sweet Valley University, then work as a journalist or freelance writer. . . .

Is it possible that I'm destined for another kind of life entirely? Elizabeth wondered. *Could my fairy-tale dreams really come true?*

"Jacques, stop pulling me!" Jessica hissed as they scurried up a rarely used stone staircase in the château. She'd had to run all the way from the rose garden to keep pace with him, but she drew the line at being dragged up the stairs.

"I'm sorry," he said, slowing down a bit. "I just don't want to waste a single minute of our time together."

Jessica sniffed indignantly. "So we're going to spend it on a French lesson?" she grumbled.

When they reached the landing, Jacques flashed her a sexy grin that made her heart turn somersaults. "I love the way you look at this very moment," he declared. "Your face is glowing, and your eyes are shooting silver sparks."

Jessica giggled. "I might shoot *you* if you don't stop acting like we're on our way to an emergency," she teased. "We're here to get a notebook and pen, for Pete's sake."

I don't know if I even have *a notebook,* Jessica thought wryly. But she knew Elizabeth probably had a ton of them.

Moving silently, Jessica and Jacques crept into

the servants' wing and up the stairs to the top floor. "Wait here," Jessica whispered when they reached the door to her twin's room. "I'll just be a minute."

Jacques gripped her elbow and gaped at her with a look of alarm. "This isn't your room," he pointed out urgently.

"It's my sister's," Jessica responded. "Elizabeth is the writer in the family." She slipped through the door, giggling at Jacques's strange reaction. *That guy should learn to relax,* she thought.

Sure enough, Elizabeth had an ample supply of yellow writing pads and sharpened pencils on her desk. Jessica grabbed what she needed and rushed out of the room. But Jacques was nowhere in sight. Then she heard sounds coming from her own room across the hall.

Jessica opened her door, and her jaw dropped. Jacques was on his knees in the middle of her floor, rummaging through a pile of discarded clothing. "What do you think you're doing in here?" she demanded.

Jacques looked up, obviously startled. "I heard someone coming up the stairs, so I ducked in here."

Tucking the notebook under her arm, Jessica pressed her fists against her hips. "And why are you playing with my laundry?"

"I was just going to . . . um . . ." He pushed his fingers through his hair and bit down on his bottom lip. "I want to make a surprise for you, so I was going to fold your clothes."

Jessica stared at him incredulously. "What?"

"I—I wish to prove that I'm a modern guy . . . that I am n-not . . . how you say . . . *male chauvinist,*" he stammered.

Jessica studied him for a long moment, noting the sheepish look on his face, the hopeful plea in his eyes. Finally she burst out laughing. "Oh, Jacques! You don't have to clean up after me. Believe me, I'm already impressed—beyond my wildest dreams."

"But I don't mind doing nice things for you," he countered, picking up a black sweater and shaking it out. "You're the kind of girl who deserves to be waited on hand and foot."

Jessica leaned back against her closed door. "I agree with you there, Jacques. And I'm sure someday I'll have lots of servants of my own." *Especially if I become the duchess of Norveaux*, she added to herself.

"Yes, of course you will," he replied. "But for now, why don't we tidy up a bit." He went over to her dresser and began lining up her makeup containers.

"Jacques, you really don't have to do that," Jessica protested.

"I don't mind," he told her.

"Well, I do," she insisted.

"It'll just take a minute. . . . I'll have this whole room in perfect order." He glanced at her. "You can wait for me in the rose garden if you like."

Jessica marched over to him and grabbed his elbows, effectively pulling him away from her dresser. "Come on, Jacques!"

69

Jacques ducked his head sheepishly. "As you wish," he said. "All I want is to make you happy." He kissed her briefly and smiled. "To the rose garden."

"That's better," Jessica mumbled.

Jacques moved toward the door, then stopped and glanced around the room. "By the way, Jessica, do you still have that piece of costume jewelry I gave you on the train?" He chuckled. "Although I wouldn't blame you if you'd thrown it away. It really wasn't much of a gift."

"Of course I still have it!" Jessica replied emphatically. She went over to her bed and pulled back the pillow to show him. "It gives me sweet dreams."

"Give it back to me," Jacques said.

Jessica replaced the pillow. "No way!"

"Please," he begged. "I'm embarrassed at the cheapness of it. A girl as special and precious as you are deserves a *real* gemstone—not a fake."

"I don't care if it's fake or not," Jessica insisted. "I treasure it because it's from you."

A confused, faraway expression flittered across Jacques's face. "You deserve better," he said softly, his voice heavy with regret.

Deeply touched, Jessica blinked back a sudden tear. "That is so sweet, Jacques." She sighed. "Now let's get out of here."

Monday morning Laurent headed over to the château, a feeling of happiness rising inside him. He couldn't wait to see Elizabeth again. Presuming he'd find her in the nursery with the children, he rushed upstairs. But as he passed the open doorway of his stepmother's sitting room, his father's voice called out to him. *"Entrez, s'il vous plaît,"* Prince Nicolas said, asking Laurent to come in.

Laurent stopped in his tracks and sighed wearily.

Princess Catherine and his father were seated side by side on a green velvet divan near the fireplace. By the serious looks on their faces, Laurent had a pretty good idea of what was about to be discussed. His heart sank as he entered the room and closed the heavy double doors.

Chapter 5

Laurent felt as if the walls of Princess Catherine's sitting room were closing in on him as he paced back and forth like a caged animal. "Father, I have *never* shirked my responsibility to the de Sainte-Marie name," he argued, speaking his words in French. "But you're asking me to give up my entire future. . . ."

Prince Nicolas's expression remained stern. "True, Laurent," he replied, also speaking French. "You've been a blessing to me ever since the day you were born, but you're not a child anymore. The time has come for you to take on a *man's* responsibilities. You are my heir and will one day assume my place as the leader of our people. The name de Sainte-Marie carries both privileges *and* burdens."

"But I'm not ready," Laurent said.

Prince Nicolas waved his hand as if to erase

Laurent's words. "There will be no more discussion. Catherine and I will be hosting an official ball this weekend, and I expect your decision before then."

Laurent inhaled sharply. "This weekend?" he asked incredulously.

"Marriage won't end your life, Laurent," Princess Catherine interjected, favoring her husband with a warm smile. She spoke with the same refined, cultured accent as her husband. "There are those who believe marriage and fatherhood are life's highest blessings."

Laurent gazed beyond them to the three bay windows that looked out over the back of the château. In the distance he could see the edge of the forest where he had taken Elizabeth horseback riding. "Isn't love one of life's blessings?" he asked.

"Duty and love are two sides of the same coin," his father retorted. "A man's honor stems from the love of his family and his people. And in doing his duty, he gives an outward symbol of what is in his heart."

Laurent threw up his hands. "I do honor my family and my heritage," he insisted. "But why must I sacrifice my happiness? What benefit will that bring to the name of de Sainte-Marie?"

His father and stepmother exchanged meaningful looks. "Is there something you aren't revealing?" Prince Nicolas inquired pointedly.

"I've met someone . . . a beautiful girl, with a sharp mind and a kind heart." Laurent took a deep

73

breath, bracing himself. "Her name is Elizabeth Wakefield."

"You can't be serious!" his stepmother uttered.

Prince Nicolas frowned. "Who is she?" he asked his wife. "The name is familiar."

"She's one of my au pair girls, the American twins," Princess Catherine answered.

Prince Nicolas nodded. "Yes, now I remember. They are very lovely girls."

"But they're hardly of a class for Laurent," Princess Catherine countered.

"I love Elizabeth for the person she is," Laurent told them. He turned to his father in desperation.

Prince Nicolas shook his head. "Tradition is wiser than any one man or woman," he said. "Always remember that. You are in a position to secure us a valuable political alliance. There is so much at stake here."

Laurent clenched his fists at his side, frustrated and angry at the situation. He wanted to scream, to pick up one of the priceless figurines on the window shelf and hurl it across the room. But temper tantrums had never been Laurent's style, even when he was a boy.

He looked at the deep lines in his father's face, the love and pride that shone from Prince Nicolas's eyes despite the harshness of his expression. *How can I turn away from my family?* Laurent asked himself. *But how can I live the life that's been chosen for me—a life without Elizabeth?*

Seated at an outdoor table in a seaside café, Jacques scanned the crowd walking by, hoping to catch a glimpse of his father. The old man was more than an hour late, and as the minutes ticked by, a cold panic squeezed Jacques's gut. *Where could he be?* he worried.

He'd nervously shredded his paper napkin and was moving on to the scalloped-edge place mat when he finally spotted his father crossing the street toward the café—with a bikini-clad, blond-haired woman on either arm. Jacques exhaled sharply and rolled his eyes. *When will that man learn to act his age?* he thought hotly.

Jacques rose to his feet as his father led his group over to the table.

"Mesdemoiselles, may I present to you my son, Jacques Landeau," Louis said, opening his arms with a flourish. "These lovely angels are Monique and Carlotta." He spoke in the slow, lilting French typical of natives of the South of France.

Jacques nodded politely, trying to hide his irritation. What he had to say to his father was going to be difficult, and he wanted to get it over with as quickly as possible.

"Enchanté," one of the girls said in a soft, breathy voice, holding out her hand. Jacques wasn't sure if she was Monique or Carlotta—and he didn't care. He absently noticed the bracelet she wore around her narrow wrist. It was made of pearls, not

valuable but with an unusual rosette motif. Jacques reluctantly kissed her hand, then repeated the gesture for her friend.

"Now it's time for me and my son to consult on business," Louis announced cheerfully. "Run along, my beauties."

The girls scampered away, giggling and blowing kisses over their shoulders.

Jacques watched them go, then turned to his father. The smug smile on his tired, wrinkled face tugged at Jacques's heart. Despite his failing health, Louis would always be a rogue.

"You are something else, old man!" Jacques muttered.

Louis Landeau snapped his fingers to signal for a waiter. "I may be old, Jacques—but I'm not *dead*."

"You will be soon if you don't slow down and start taking care of yourself," Jacques said. "Where do you *find* all these women anyway?"

Louis shrugged. "They find *me*."

Jacques laughed aloud, despite the worry and dread weighing heavily on his mind. His father's bouts of coughing and fever had grown much too frequent lately; he'd nearly died of pneumonia the previous winter.

Jacques knew that their current lifestyle, spending their days on the road, had to end soon—before it killed his father. *The old man needs rest and stability, a real home*, he thought. Jacques had made a vow to himself some time ago to provide that home for his father, even though he had no idea how he was going to do it.

"Monique and Carlotta insist on entertaining us for the day on their yacht," Louis said casually after he'd ordered coffee and croissants.

Jacques groaned to himself but said nothing.

His father shot him a pointed look. "What is the matter with you, boy? I find the prettiest girls on the beach and bring them right to you. And this is the thanks I get—nothing but a sour face?" Louis leaned closer and flicked his eyebrows. "Which one is your favorite? I'm partial to Carlotta, but you may have first choice."

"I'm not interested," Jacques replied, silently adding, *because I'm too much in love with Jessica Wakefield.*

Louis threw up his hands. "I will never understand the young!"

"And it seems I'll never understand *you*," Jacques returned.

"*Touché*, my son." Louis slowly stirred sugar into his espresso and raised the demitasse to his lips. "So, how was your weekend?" he asked, eyeing him over the rim.

Jacques cringed. He knew what his father was asking—and he wasn't going to like the answer. "I'm sorry," he replied. "I failed to get the emerald from Jessica."

"What?" Louis lowered the demitasse to the saucer with a loud clink. "Do you mean to say you've spent all this time doing nothing but flirting with the girl?"

"No, of course not," Jacques protested weakly. "I tried to get it, but . . . I just couldn't."

"Try harder!" Louis snapped. "I promised that emerald to one of our best clients. And he's not the kind of man to whom one brings bad news." He pinned Jacques with a sharp look. "Do you understand?"

"Yes," Jacques replied, lowering his eyes.

"This is serious business," his father said. "You can't lose your head over a pretty face right now—especially not *that* one. Trust me, other girls will come along, and soon you won't even remember Jessica's name."

I'll never *forget Jessica,* Jacques silently protested.

Louis smiled gently, all traces of his anger gone. "I'm counting on you, son."

Jacques nodded. "I know. And I won't let you down," he promised. "I'll get that stone one way or another." *Even if it breaks my heart to hurt Jessica.*

"Pierre, it's not polite to speak with your mouth full," Elizabeth told him. Immediately all three children began making singsong, babbling noises while they chewed their lunch. A thick blob of mashed chicken dribbled down Manon's chin and landed on the tray of her high chair.

Elizabeth sighed wearily. They were seated at

the table in a corner of the château's enormous kitchen. The room was pleasantly noisy as the staff prepared the meal that would be served that evening. Pots simmered on the old-fashioned stove, and something that smelled delicious was baking in the oven.

Elizabeth heard someone enter through the back door. Presuming it was Laurent, her heart leaped. She'd kept an eye out for him all morning, almost certain he'd drop in to see her. She turned around expectantly . . . but it was only Anna, the housekeeper, who was coming over to the table.

Elizabeth swallowed her sharp disappointment and smiled politely.

"Good afternoon," Anna said cheerfully.

"We're being very good today," Claudine told her. Pierre and Manon nodded their agreement. Elizabeth rolled her eyes.

"I have good news," Anna announced. "The prince and princess have decided to allow the children to attend the ball on Saturday."

"Hourra!" they cheered. Then Claudine ducked her head and giggled. "I mean, *yippee!*" she said, apparently remembering the rule about speaking only English.

"You and your sister will attend also, of course," Anna told Elizabeth.

"Really?" Elizabeth breathed as a quick image of herself dancing with Laurent flashed in her mind's eye. The two of them were swirling gracefully around the ballroom while everyone watched . . . he, handsomely dressed in an official uniform with lots of medals, and she, wearing . . . *jeans*?

Elizabeth blinked, frowning at the ridiculous picture. "I didn't bring anything dressy enough for a formal ball," she admitted.

Anna flicked her hand in a dismissive gesture. "That is nothing," she replied. "In the wardrobe room there are hundreds of gowns. We'll find something suitable, I know."

After the housekeeper left, the children were more rambunctious than ever. Pierre and Manon got into a fight over who could drink the most milk, which resulted in them knocking over their glasses.

"Now you've done it!" Elizabeth snapped, reaching for the dishrag at her side. Experience had taught her always to keep one on hand during meals. *After this summer I'll probably be able to write my own baby-sitting guide,* she thought.

"Aren't you happy about going to the ball?" Claudine asked—with her mouth full, of course.

"Sure, I am," Elizabeth replied. "I'm just sad about having to see your food while you're chewing!"

"Sorry," Claudine murmured. She clamped her mouth shut. Pierre and Manon did the same, and for several minutes the children entertained themselves by making silly humming sounds at each other.

The door opened and shut again. Elizabeth

glanced anxiously over her shoulder. This time it was Brigitte the maid who had entered the kitchen.

Elizabeth sighed, her hopes deflating like a brightly colored balloon with a slow leak. *Where are you, Laurent?* she wondered.

I never knew how boring France could be! Jessica complained to herself as she stretched out across her bed that night and stared at the swirled pattern in the ceiling. She'd been moping in her room for hours, disappointed that Jacques hadn't bothered to come see her that day. "He'd better have a good excuse," she muttered through clenched teeth.

To make matters worse, the children had been overly excited at dinner, bouncing in their seats like Ping-Pong balls. The entire château was in a frenzy over the upcoming formal ball. "Big deal," Jessica whined.

She flipped over onto her stomach. Bracing her elbows on the mattress, she propped her head up with her fists tucked under her chin. *It stinks that I can't invite Jacques to the ball because of that stupid feud,* she thought.

Just then Jessica's stomach growled hungrily. She and the children had eaten cold sandwiches for dinner while the prince and princess had entertained their guests with a gourmet feast in the dining room.

Jessica smiled slowly. *I'll bet there's lots of*

yummy leftovers, she realized, bolting off her bed. She stuck her bare feet into a pair of sandals and crept downstairs.

The kitchen was deserted at that time of night—and spotless. Jessica padded across the polished floor to the refrigerator and pulled it open. *I was right!* she silently cheered as she examined the contents.

The choice of leftovers was superb. There was baked salmon in what looked like dill sauce, green beans with cream and almonds, artichoke canapés, stuffed olives, black caviar, a huge platter of pâté and cheeses, assorted French pastries. . . . "Now *this* is what I call dinner!" Jessica declared, giggling.

She helped herself to a bit of everything, ending with a rich, custard-filled chocolate éclair. Feeling thoroughly satisfied, she rinsed off her plate and turned off the kitchen light.

Jessica tiptoed up the front staircase, then wished she'd taken another route back to her room when she saw the countess di Rimini in the corridor, heading her way. The scowling woman was wrapped in a yellow chiffon robe trimmed with black feathers.

Maybe if I ignore her, she'll return the favor, Jessica thought. But as they drew closer she saw the dirty look on the countess's face and realized it wasn't going to be a peaceful encounter.

"Just getting in?" the witch inquired coldly. "I would think you'd be ashamed to come in here at all hours, treating your employers' home like a hotel."

Jessica was stunned by the accusation, but she refused to defend herself. She didn't care what the nosy snob thought of her. "My personal life is really none of your business," Jessica retorted.

The countess raised her hand to her chest, her bony white fingers disappearing in the black feathery trim of her robe. "Your manners are deplorable, young lady. But I'm not surprised, considering." She gave Jessica a rude up-and-down glare, then stalked past her toward the stairs.

Jessica's blood was boiling by the time she reached the servants' quarters. She noticed the light shining from under the door of her sister's room and barged in without bothering to knock. "I absolutely can't stand that witch!" Jessica raged.

Elizabeth was sitting up in bed, writing something. "What happened?" she asked.

"That countess *creature!*" Jessica plunked herself down on the bed and drew her knees up to her chin. She recounted what had happened on the stairs. "If I wasn't so afraid of waking everyone up and causing a scene, I would've happily told that ugly witch what I thought of her so-called noble breeding!"

"They certainly are something else. The countess and Antonia make *Bruce Patman* seem humble and down-to-earth," Elizabeth said, comparing the di Riminis to the richest and most arrogant student at Sweet Valley High.

"Jacques isn't like that at all," Jessica pointed out.

Elizabeth lowered her eyes. "Neither is Laurent."

"Speaking of our favorite prince," Jessica began, "what did you guys do this evening while I was stuck feeding sandwiches to the little monsters?"

"I didn't see Laurent today," Elizabeth replied. "I thought I would, but . . ." She shrugged.

Jessica saw the dejected look on her sister's face. "I know how you feel, Liz," she empathized. "Jacques didn't show up today either. Maybe we need to teach these royal blockheads that they can't take the Wakefield twins for granted!"

Elizabeth smiled weakly.

"At least you'll get to be with Laurent at the ball this weekend," Jessica grumbled. "I'll probably have a miserable time, watching everyone else dancing. . . ."

Elizabeth rolled her eyes. "You mean because you're so *shy*?" she responded sarcastically. They both burst out laughing.

"OK, so I might have fun even without Jacques there," Jessica conceded. "But I still wish he were going."

Tuesday afternoon Elizabeth jumped to her feet the instant Jessica walked into the nursery for her shift with the children. "I'm in a bit of a hurry," Elizabeth explained.

"I can see that," Jessica said, smirking. "But don't you understand that it's best to keep the guy waiting?"

"Some other time, Jess," Elizabeth replied tersely. Waving good-bye to the children, she rushed out of the room. After waiting yesterday and all that morning for Laurent to show up, Elizabeth had finally decided to go see him. *I may be living in an old French château for the summer, but I'm still a modern, American girl,* she reminded herself pointedly.

Elizabeth slipped into the bathroom across the hall and checked her appearance in the beveled mirror above the sink. *I guess I'm not too modern to worry about my looks,* she thought wryly.

The glossy, pale rose lipstick Elizabeth had applied that morning was long gone, and her soft dusting of taupe eye shadow was hardly visible. "Maybe I should wear more makeup," she whispered, turning her head from side to side to study the various angles of her face. "How would I look with a more dramatic style, like Jessica's?"

Elizabeth pursed her lips, then wrinkled her nose. *I don't want anyone's style but my own,* she decided.

Laurent would have to accept her as she was— or not at all. But a small, frightened voice in the back of Elizabeth's mind piped up with nagging self-doubts. *What if I really am shabby looking and just don't know it? Maybe that's why Laurent hasn't come to see me for two days. . . .*

"Maybe I should quit letting that nasty Antonia poison my mind with her ridiculous insults!" Elizabeth said under her breath.

85

She focused her thoughts on seeing Laurent again, and a lush, happy feeling rose in her heart. There was a bounce in her step as she went downstairs.

The household was bustling in preparation for the ball. Extra staff had been hired for the occasion, and workers were dusting and polishing, moving furniture around, steam cleaning the curtains. . . . Elizabeth did her best to sidestep the commotion.

Anna called to her on her way out the back door. "If you plan to go outside, it's better you should bring this," the housekeeper advised, handing Elizabeth a large black umbrella. "It looks like the rain comes soon."

"Thanks," Elizabeth said, tucking the umbrella under her arm.

Anna smiled. "We cannot have you getting soaked and catching the cold just before the big ball. It promises to be one of Château d'Amour Inconnu's most magnificent affairs."

Elizabeth responded with an automatic smile, but all her insecurities suddenly rose up again. She knew it was silly, but she couldn't help the feeling of dread that surrounded her thoughts about the ball. *What if I stand out as a commoner among Laurent's noble friends?* she worried.

Elizabeth's stomach fluttered as if it were filled with nervous butterflies. She was in way over her head, trying to find her way through the strange culture of the nobility without a single clue. *What am I doing, having a romance with a prince?* she wondered.

"You give up, maybe?" Anna asked, cutting through the mental chatter in Elizabeth's head.

"Give up?" Elizabeth echoed, nonplussed.

"Do you decide to stay indoors today?" Anna clarified.

Elizabeth thought for a moment, then gripped the umbrella tightly, steeling her courage. She raised her head high and replied, "Not a chance."

I don't give up easily, Elizabeth added silently.

Chapter 6

Elizabeth felt a rush of pleasure as she approached Laurent's cottage. The rustic scene before her was like an illustration in one of the children's storybooks. Clusters of lavender lined the white stone path to the front door. Daisies and tiger lilies dotted the lawn. To the side of the cottage, a wrought iron bench was nestled under a rose arbor. Elizabeth couldn't imagine a more idyllic and romantic setting.

She was eager to see Laurent again. Being with him made her feel excited, happy, and comfortable all at the same time.

Elizabeth stepped up to the door and knocked firmly. At that very instant a large, cold raindrop splashed down on her wrist. She glanced up at the gray sky. "I guess Anna was right," she said.

When there was no answer, Elizabeth knocked

again. A few more raindrops fell on her. She was just about to open her umbrella when the door finally opened. "Hello, Laurent. It seems I always end up here when it rains," Elizabeth joked.

Laurent hesitated for an instant, as if he might turn her away. Then he flashed her a tight smile. "Come in," he said.

Elizabeth's spirits sagged at his less-than-enthusiastic greeting. Still clutching the umbrella, she nervously rubbed her thumb over the brass handle as she followed Laurent into the sitting room.

A warm, cozy fire blazed in the hearth, but Elizabeth felt chilled. "Did I come at a bad time?" she asked cautiously.

Laurent's gaze shifted away from hers. "I was just going through my mail in the study," he said. "Do you mind if I continue? I'm almost finished."

"I don't mind," Elizabeth replied automatically. "Can I make some coffee?"

"Help yourself," Laurent offered.

Elizabeth chewed her bottom lip as she watched him go. *He doesn't seem too happy to see me today,* she thought. But she refused to let her own insecurities cloud her judgment. *Everyone gets busy and preoccupied once in a while,* she reassured herself. *Even if they're royalty!*

Humming optimistically, Elizabeth went to make the coffee.

The kitchen was small and comfortable, just like the rest of the cottage. The floor was covered in red stone tiles, and the walls were painted a pale green. Potted plants lined the windowsill. Elizabeth recalled the first time she'd been there, the night she'd gotten caught in the storm. Laurent had prepared omelets in the morning. Wearing a white chef's hat, he'd juggled the raw eggs in the air and behind his back. "That's to impress the visiting au pair," he'd said with a wink.

Elizabeth chuckled at the memory as she poured a scoopful of coffee beans into the grinder. It took her a while to figure out how to work the complicated electric coffeemaker, but she finally had two demitasses of steaming, dark espresso prepared. She placed them on a tray that she'd found in a bottom cupboard, then added two linen napkins, the crystal sugar bowl, and two spoons.

Carrying the tray out of the kitchen, Elizabeth called out to Laurent.

"I'm in here," he answered.

She followed his voice to a small study at the end of the hall, where she found him working at a computer. The walls were lined with shelves of books, and the floor was covered with a braided wool rug. There was a comfortable-looking couch in a corner of the room that seemed perfect for curling up with a book.

A photograph of a woman hung on the wall near the door. The woman's smile, her eyes, and the shape of her chin were identical to Laurent's. Elizabeth assumed it was his mother, the late

Princess Marianne, who'd died when Laurent was ten years old.

On the other side of the room, in front of the window, an oak desk was piled high with papers and envelopes. "My goodness! Is all that your mail?" Elizabeth asked in amazement.

"Yes, it is," Laurent answered without looking up.

Elizabeth flinched at the dismissive tone in his voice. "You seem really busy."

"I am," he said.

Elizabeth shifted uneasily. She glanced down at the tray, suddenly feeling very foolish. "I thought you'd like some coffee, but . . ."

"Yes, thank you. Just set it down anywhere," he told her, obviously preoccupied.

Elizabeth set the tray on the desk next to the pile of mail, then took her own cup over to the couch. "I didn't know princes got so much mail," she remarked, trying to sound cheerful.

Laurent murmured something incoherent in response.

Elizabeth pressed her bottom lip between her teeth and slowly ran her finger around the rip of her cup. Apparently she'd picked a *terrible* time to drop in on him. "Laurent, I can see you're busy," she said. "Maybe I should come back later? I'll be free this evening after the children go to bed," she added hopefully.

Laurent turned to her, his expression masked. "No, I can finish this later." He stood up and

91

stretched his arms over his head, then helped himself to the coffee she'd brought for him.

"I don't think it tastes as good as yours," Elizabeth said as she watched Laurent raise the cup to his lips.

"It's fine." He sat down on the couch with Elizabeth, leaving several feet between them. "How have you been?" he asked blandly.

Elizabeth put on a bright smile. "It's been very hectic at the château. Everyone is in a frenzy about the upcoming ball this weekend—even the children."

A sharp look flickered in his eyes. "Yes . . . the ball. It's very important to my family."

"I know," Elizabeth replied. "I'm a little nervous about it. All the fancy preparations and royal protocol . . . it seems overwhelming." She lowered her eyes and stared absently at the gold pattern on her cup. "I have this terrible fear that I'll embarrass myself among those noble types."

Elizabeth turned to Laurent, looking for reassurance.

"I can see how you would feel that way, not having been brought up in the culture," he said.

That wasn't what Elizabeth had wanted to hear him say. "Like you?" she asked, feeling stung.

"Like me." Laurent glanced at her, then stared out the window. "I'm a product of heritage, Elizabeth. We all are."

"But people are people, right?" Elizabeth countered, her voice tight and high-pitched. "How much difference can there be between your people and mine?"

"An entire world," Laurent replied.

Elizabeth's heart sank. *What happened to the sweet, romantic guy who used to make me feel like a princess?* she sadly wondered. A long, tense silence filled the small room like a suffocating cloud. Elizabeth swallowed against the thickening lump in her throat. *Something is definitely wrong here,* she admitted to herself. She couldn't fool herself into believing that Laurent was simply preoccupied. The close bond they'd shared had been broken. A gulf of cold distance now stood between them, and Elizabeth didn't know how to reach him.

She exhaled a shaky breath. Her eyes stung, and she felt as though she might start sobbing any second. "My shift with the children starts in a few minutes, so I'd better get going," Elizabeth lied, rising to her feet and setting her empty cup back on the tray.

Laurent started to follow her, but she waved him back. "I can see myself out," she told him. He walked her to the front door anyway.

Elizabeth picked up the umbrella she'd left on a side table in the sitting room. "Thanks for the coffee," she said over her shoulder.

"Thank *you*, Elizabeth," he replied softly.

That sounds like a final good-bye, Elizabeth realized, hot tears streaming from her eyes as she rushed out of the cottage and into the pouring rain. *What did I do wrong?*

"This is so wonderful," Jessica whispered into Jacques's ear as they snuggled together on the beach Wednesday night. They had discovered the secluded spot tucked behind a ridge of high boulders earlier that evening and had immediately claimed it for themselves.

Now, as a silvery crescent moon shone like a jewel in the dark sky, Jessica and Jacques shared the chocolate-covered strawberries and sparkling cider he'd brought for her. Jessica felt as though she were being hypnotized by the crashing of the waves on the shore—and by the sexy glimmer in Jacques's brown eyes.

"Yes, wonderful," Jacques replied, punctuating his sentence with a gentle kiss.

Jessica felt a glorious sensation of pure happiness flowing through her heart. And although she and Jacques were a safe distance away from the château—and well hidden—the risk of being caught with the de Sainte-Maries' archenemy added to the excitement and romance.

"Tell me about Norveaux," Jessica said dreamily. "Is it beautiful?"

Jacques brushed his lips across her chin. "When I'm with you, *mon ange*, it is as if Norveaux doesn't exist."

Jessica's eyes narrowed. His words reminded

her of what the de Sainte-Maries' housekeeper had said about there being no Norveaux. "What do you mean?" she asked warily.

"No other world exists when I'm with you, Jessica. You are like everything to me. *Je t'aime de tout mon cœur.*"

"Oh," Jessica said with a laugh, pushing away her troublesome doubts. "And before we turn this into another French quiz—I also 'love you with all my heart.'"

Jacques flashed her a sexy grin. *"Tu es si belle."*

"You are so beautiful," Jessica translated, pleased with herself.

"Very good, mademoiselle," Jacques said. He picked up a fat strawberry and took a bite, then raised it to Jessica's lips. Giggling, she closed her teeth around it and took it from his fingers.

Jacques brushed a lock of her hair back from her face. "You are so special. . . ." He kissed her passionately.

Jessica shivered with delight as a million wonderful sensations danced up and down her spine.

Jacques abruptly ended the kiss. "But you are trembling?"

Jessica shot him a saucy grin. "I know."

"You're cold," he said.

"No, I'm not," she argued.

Jacques began rubbing his arms. "But I am. And the night air, it gives a chill. Let's go to the château, where it is warm."

Jessica leaned back and glared at him. "What about the feud? Aren't you concerned about being seen by the de Sainte-Maries?"

Jacques gave her a wicked, sexy grin. "We shall hide in your room."

Jessica laughed at his bold arrogance. "And what if I don't feel like inviting you up to my room?" she asked pointedly.

"I will beg, perhaps?" he replied sheepishly.

Jessica rolled her eyes. "Sometimes, Jacques . . . ," she said, her voice trailing off as she shook her head. "Are all French guys so strange?"

"Strange?" Jacques clutched his chest as if the word had stabbed his heart.

Jessica giggled. "How else could I describe a guy who'd rather be cooped up in a tiny room in the servants' quarters rather than lie here on this glorious beach?" She scooped up a handful of sand and let it sift through her fingers.

Jacques turned away and cleared his throat. "I must confess. You see, I feel . . . ill."

Jessica raised her eyebrows. "What?"

"I'm afraid the . . ." He raised his fist to his mouth and began coughing.

"What's wrong?" Jessica asked, suddenly concerned.

Jacques drew in a gasping breath and exhaled loudly. "I'm afraid the scratchy feeling I had in my throat this morning has become worse. And my head, it is pounding. If only I could rest for a few moments inside . . ."

Jessica eyed him suspiciously. She wasn't sure she believed him. After all, he'd seemed perfectly healthy a minute ago. But even if he were telling the truth, Jessica didn't want to risk being caught with him in the château—especially after her run-in with the countess the other night.

Jacques reached for her hand. "Come, Jessica. Let's go to your room." He started to get up, but she pulled him back down.

"I don't know if that's such a good idea," Jessica said. "There's a nasty witch and her spawn staying at the château for the summer. I met her in the hall late one night as I was going up to my room, and she freaked out. She accused me of abusing the Sainte-Maries' hospitality by running wild and dragging myself home at all hours. The scene got very ugly." Jessica sniffed indignantly. "I was afraid she'd pull out her evil wand and turn me into a toad."

Jacques tipped back his head and laughed. "I can't imagine you being afraid of anything," he remarked.

Jessica shrugged. "I'm usually not. But I'd hate to be sent back to Sweet Valley at this point. I'm sure they would if they caught me sneaking you up to my room."

"It is not so fair for you to be treated that way," Jacques said.

Jessica raised her knees to her chin and wrapped her arms around her legs. "I know," she replied. She gazed out at the darkened sea and exhaled a deep sigh. *This is going to be a legend someday,* she thought. *The romantic tale of the beautiful young maiden from Sweet Valley, California, who became the duchess of Norveaux after she'd captured the heart of a handsome—*

"You shouldn't let anyone push you around, *mon ange*," Jacques said, interrupting her fantasy.

Jessica lifted an eyebrow. "Not even you?" she asked.

"Not even me," Jacques echoed softly.

Elizabeth pushed open the heavy iron gate at the entrance of the enclosed garden. She needed a quiet place to think, to sort out her confused feelings. Ever since she'd left Laurent's cottage the day before, she'd been trying to make sense of his sudden coldness.

Elizabeth moved slowly along the grassy path through the dense bushes and vines. She could barely distinguish between the foliage and shadows, but the darkness felt comforting and safe.

She passed the white stone shed that hid the entrance to the secret tunnels. Memories rushed through her mind as she recalled the night Laurent had brought her there after their moonlight picnic on the beach. "I *know* he cared for me," she whispered.

Elizabeth was surprised when she came to a wide clearing in the middle of the garden. Dark, leafy vines cascaded over the marble ledge that bordered the perimeter. A flowering tree grew in the center, its branches thickly covered with pale blossoms. Fallen petals were scattered around the base of the trunk like a circle of lace.

Elizabeth walked over to the iron bench on the other side of the clearing and sat down wearily. The children had been particularly trying that evening. She'd had to read the story about the bluebird prince six times to calm them down. Elizabeth had been tempted to rip the book to shreds by the time Princess Catherine had come in to tuck the children into their beds.

"I'm sick of fairy tales!" Elizabeth hissed. Her fantasies of living happily ever after with a handsome prince seemed utterly ridiculous. She must have been carried away by the splendor of the Château d'Amour Inconnu. Elizabeth vowed never to make that mistake again. *From now on I'll stick to reality,* she swore.

Elizabeth draped her arm along the back of the bench and absently traced a swirl in the wrought iron design. *But what Laurent and I had together was real,* her mind argued.

Elizabeth thought back to the time they'd spent riding through the forest, the things they'd said to each other . . . the flutter in her heart just before his lips would touch hers. . . .

A feeling of sadness welled up in Elizabeth's throat. Tears streamed down her cheeks.

Planting her feet on the bench, she wrapped her arms around her legs and rested her forehead on her raised knees. "What happened?" she asked herself, sobbing. First Todd had broken her heart and now Laurent. *Is there something wrong with me?* she wondered.

Antonia's cruel, taunting words echoed in her mind: *"It's when you're standing next to nobility that you look your shabbiest."* Elizabeth shook her head, firmly dismissing the ridiculous insult from her mind. Just because she wasn't born into nobility didn't make her inferior. A person would have to be very narrow-minded and backward to hold such an old-fashioned attitude. *Laurent isn't like that*, she thought.

But a strong feeling of doubt hovered in her mind like a dark, heavy storm cloud. *Did Laurent decide to end our relationship because I'm not high-class enough for him and his royal family?* she wondered.

Elizabeth drew in a shaky breath and swiped her hand across her damp cheeks. If Laurent wasn't interested in her because she was a commoner, then it was his problem—not hers. She was proud to be an American, where everybody was considered equal. And she was also extremely proud to be a *Wakefield*. Her parents worked hard to provide for her, Jessica, and Steven, and that meant more to Elizabeth than all the vast holdings and power of the de Sainte-Marie family.

A sudden scraping noise startled her. Elizabeth whirled around and saw Laurent walking along the marble ledge toward her. Her whole body stiffened, all of her senses on alert.

"Elizabeth . . . ," he whispered. "I've been searching for you everywhere."

She cast him a scathing look and turned away.

"May I sit down?" he asked.

Elizabeth squeezed her eyes shut and rested her forehead on her knees again. *Leave me alone!* she silently pleaded. Her heart had suffered enough.

After a few seconds she felt his hand on her back. "Please, Elizabeth. Look at me."

She raised her head and glared at him. "What do you want?" she snapped.

Laurent sat down beside her and leaned forward, bracing his elbows on his knees. "I suppose I deserve that."

A sensation of cold anger shivered through her, numbing her pain. "I don't know what you think you deserve, *Prince* Laurent . . . and I don't care. If you're too proud to associate with an American, that's your loss!"

Laurent bolted upright and turned to her with a wide-eyed, astonished look on his face. "But you are wrong about me!"

"Am I?" Elizabeth asked bitingly. "Ever since I arrived at Château d'Amour Inconnu, I've been treated like an inferior being because my family doesn't have a pedigree."

Laurent reeled back as if she'd slapped him. "I

101

never treated you like that," he whispered. "To me, you're perfect as you are."

Elizabeth clenched her jaw, steeling her heart against him. "Those are nice words," she retorted. "But I'm not a fool, Laurent. I know when I'm being pushed out of someone's life."

"No, it is not that way!" Laurent shook his head. "I never meant to give you such an impression."

"What about yesterday at the cottage?" Elizabeth swallowed against the thickening lump in her throat. "You totally ignored me, as if I were an unwelcome pest."

Laurent uttered a sorrowful groan. "Never! You are always welcome to me," he said. He shifted so that he was facing her and draped his arm along the back of the bench. "I'm sorry for the way I acted. It is why this evening I had to see you—to apologize."

Elizabeth felt her anger beginning to thaw, but the hurt and confusion were still there. "I need an explanation," she told him. "I want to understand what was going on between us yesterday."

Laurent's gaze moved over her face, as if he were memorizing her. "I was so happy to see you, Elizabeth," he said at last. "But there was something on my mind. I've been troubled lately . . . things I have to work out for myself." He paused. "Can you forgive me?" he asked.

Elizabeth lowered her eyes. "I want to believe you, Laurent. But—"

Laurent curved his arm around her shoulders and gently pulled her toward him. "Be patient with me," he pleaded.

Elizabeth felt the protective wall she'd built around her heart tumbling down. She couldn't ignore the love that shone from the depths of Laurent's blue eyes. "I do forgive you," she breathed.

Laurent smiled tenderly. Then he kissed her, melting her heart completely.

Elizabeth felt tears of happiness spring into her eyes. "This is like a dream," she whispered.

Laurent held her close. "This isn't a dream, Elizabeth. I love you forever." She could feel his heart pounding as rapidly as her own.

"I love you too," she whispered.

Laurent kissed her again, and Elizabeth allowed herself to be swept up in the passion. She became aware of the beauty of the night, the bright crescent moon that shone in the black sky, the sweet lavender fragrance on the night breezes, and the glorious sensation of being in Laurent's arms again.

"I can't believe I let you talk me into this," Jessica complained to Jacques as they crept up the stone staircase to her room. "If we get caught, I'll be on the next plane back to Sweet Valley for sure!"

When they reached her door, Jacques pulled her close and touched his lips to hers. Jessica swayed against him and laced her fingers behind his neck.

Suddenly a burst of female chatter on the stairs brought Jessica back to her senses. Snapping to attention, she grabbed Jacques by the sleeve of his shirt and dragged him into her room. Peeking from behind the door, Jessica watched as two maids appeared on the landing.

She pushed the door closed all the way and leaned back against it. "That was close," she breathed.

Jacques was stretched out on her bed, his arms tucked under her pillow. He raised his head slightly and groaned.

Jessica crossed her arms and eyed him narrowly. *He seemed fine all the way up here,* she realized. "Jacques, what's going on?" she asked. "You're not really sick, are you?"

He began coughing violently. "Water," he gasped.

Jessica rolled her eyes. But she decided to play along just in case he wasn't faking. "I'll be back in a minute," she told him. "Stay in here."

Still coughing, Jacques nodded. Jessica opened the door slightly and checked to see if anyone was coming.

"All clear," she whispered to Jacques over her shoulder.

He sucked in a gasping breath, clutching his throat, and nodded again. But the instant she stepped out into the hall, the sound of his coughing abruptly stopped.

Jessica's brow furrowed and she pursed her lips. *A miraculous recovery?* she thought doubtfully. Now she was more than suspicious—she was absolutely certain he was up to something.

Jessica felt a surge of annoyance. Obviously he'd staged the whole sickness routine and desperate plea for water so that he could be alone in her room. *To do what?* she wondered. Determined to find out, she inched open the door and spied on Jacques through the crack.

He was sitting hunched over on the edge of the bed, his elbows resting on his knees. His gaze was fixed on something he held in his hands. At first Jessica thought he was reading. Bemused, she opened the door a little wider to get a better look.

Jessica's jaw dropped as she recognized the object in his hands. It was the red jewelry case she kept under her pillow. For a moment she was too stunned to move or to utter a sound. *Who does he think he is, going through my personal things?* she fumed silently.

She saw him slip the case into his pocket, and her blood began to boil. *He* knows *how much that pendant means to me!* she thought.

Jessica stiffened her spine, pulled back her shoulders, and took a deep breath. Primed for battle, she burst into the room.

Royal duke or not, Jacques Landeau needed to learn a few things about respect.

Chapter 7

Jessica lunged at Jacques, toppling him sideways on the bed before he had a chance to react. With a swift movement she grabbed the jewelry case out of his shirt pocket and whipped it behind her back. "This is mine!" she hissed in his face.

Jacques recovered instantly and sprang toward her. His arms shot out, capturing her in a tight embrace as he reached behind her. Giggling hysterically, Jessica struggled against him, twisting and buckling to loosen his hold. She managed to roll onto her back, her hands and the jewelry case tucked safely underneath her.

Jacques leaned over her, his face looming inches above hers, his lips curled in a challenging grin. A thrilling combination of fear and excitement shivered up and down Jessica's spine.

"You are a very stubborn girl," he whispered.

"Me?" Jessica replied breathlessly. "What about *you*?" Suddenly she felt his hand slip under her back, groping for the case.

Jessica shrieked. Digging her heels into the mattress, she scrambled away from him. Jacques made a grab for her, but Jessica jerked out of his grasp. Laughing excitedly, she rolled off the bed and scurried halfway across the room.

The air crackled with electricity as she and Jacques glared at each other, their eyes locked in a heated battle of wills.

Finally Jacques uttered an exasperated sound and shook his head. "Jessica, sometimes this *vigueur* you have . . . it is like the *énergie atomique*."

Jessica flashed him a saucy grin. "*Atomic energy*—I like that," she replied. "But flattery isn't going to save you now, Your *Royalness*. If I don't hear an extremely sincere apology from you in the next five seconds, I'll blow up like an atomic *bomb!*"

Laughing, Jacques raised his hands in surrender. "I wanted to make a surprise for you. That is why I pretended an illness."

Jessica snorted. "You should take acting lessons. I wasn't fooled at all."

Jacques clutched his heart and twisted his face into an exaggerated mask of pain. Jessica pressed her lips together to keep from laughing. She refused to let down her guard until things between her and Jacques were resolved—to *her* satisfaction.

Jacques dropped the silly charade and eyed

Jessica with a deep, soulful look. "Come here," he said softly, beckoning to her with his arms.

Jessica remained seated on the floor. "I can hear your apology just fine from right here," she told him.

Jacques threw up his hands and muttered some French words under his breath. "But it is *your* surprise to find," he insisted, gesturing toward the pillow on her bed.

Jessica's eyes narrowed, her curiosity piqued. "You brought me a present?" she asked, rising to her feet.

"Oui." Jacques lifted a corner of the pillow and picked up a small package wrapped in newspaper. "Voilà," he said, holding it out toward Jessica. "But to surprise you is most difficult," he added dryly.

Jessica grinned, beaming with delight as she accepted the gift. She tucked her red jewelry case under her pillow, then sat down beside Jacques and began unwrapping her new gift.

"It's beautiful!" Jessica exclaimed as she lifted the delicate pearl bracelet from its nest of old newspaper. The pearls were sewn in flower patterns, with seed pearl clusters surrounding a larger, center pearl, creating little flowers that were strung at regular intervals between gold and pearl links. Jessica draped it over her wrist, admiring the way the snowy white pearls contrasted against her tanned skin.

"You like it?" Jacques asked.

Jessica turned to him and smiled. "I *love* it," she

replied. She leaned over and kissed him. "Thank you, Jacques."

"The pearls are genuine," he said as he fastened the gold clasp for her. "Now I can take back that ghastly fake stone I gave you on the train."

Jessica sprang forward and grabbed the case from under the pillow. "I *told* you, I don't care if it's a fake," she said, holding it away from him. "This pendant is very special to me."

"But Jessica, *mon ange* . . . ," he pleaded. "I only gave it to you because I had nothing better at the time. It is . . . *junk*. The bracelet is for you."

Jessica glanced down at her wrist. "And I'll treasure it forever," she vowed. "But the pendant means a lot to me."

Jacques pushed his hand through his hair. "Jessica, remember on the train . . . when I gave you that stone. I promised I would replace it someday. And now I have."

Jessica tightened her hold around the case. "What are you going to do with it?" Then a suspicious thought popped into her head, responding to her own question. "Are you going to keep it handy in case another pretty girl happens to come along?" she asked bitingly.

Jacques shook his head, laughing. "When I first saw you, I——" He abruptly fell silent as footsteps sounded on the stairs.

Jacques and Jessica exchanged alarmed looks, their skirmish overshadowed by the present emergency.

Jessica glanced toward the door and noticed that she'd left it wide open. Cursing under her breath, she rushed over and shut it firmly.

Her heart beating furiously, Jessica pressed her ear against the door to listen. She held her breath as the footsteps came closer . . . and stopped. Then someone knocked on the door. Jessica jumped, her heart in her throat.

"Jessica, are you in there?" Anna's voice called through the door.

Now what? Jessica wondered, her body gripped with panic. She glanced at Jacques over her shoulder.

His face was pale, his deep brown eyes wide and luminous. "Answer her," he mouthed.

Jessica nodded. She tried to speak, but only a strange gasping sound came out. Jessica swallowed, drew in a strangled breath, and tried again. "Yes, Anna?"

"May I come in?" Anna asked.

"Um . . . just a minute," Jessica muttered, her whole body trembling.

Jacques gave her a reassuring wink and crept under the bed. Jessica noticed her blue silk robe on the floor in front of her bureau. With a sudden flash of inspiration she grabbed it and hastily slipped it on over her clothes.

Jessica inched open the door. Anna was standing in the hall, her eyes lowered to the clipboard in her hands.

"Um . . . A-Anna . . . ," Jessica stammered.

110

Anna looked up and smiled briskly. "We have details to talk over for the ball that concern the children."

Jessica clutched the front edges of her robe at her throat. "I was just getting ready for bed," she lied.

Anna nodded. "It's good I arrive now, before you are asleep." Suddenly someone hollered to the housekeeper from the staircase. Anna exhaled sharply and grumbled in French. "I'll be just a moment, Jessica," she said. "The ball this weekend makes everything in a chaos."

Thank you, lucky stars! Jessica thought as she quickly shut the door. She slumped back against it and exhaled a sigh of relief. Jacques squirmed out of his hiding place.

"That was way too close," Jessica said to him.

Jacques sat down on the bed and buried his face in his hands. "This is a disaster. Never I wished to cause you such trouble, *mon ange*." She could see how concerned he was for her, and it warmed her heart.

Jessica smiled tenderly and went over to sit beside him. "It's not *that* big a deal," she said, slipping her arms around his waist. "No one ever came out and directly said that I'm not allowed to have a guy in my room."

Jacques raised his head and gave her a small, grateful smile. "But if they see *me* . . ."

"So what?" Jessica countered. "This feud between your families is totally ridiculous. And anyway, it probably won't last much longer. I'm sure things will improve drastically when you and Laurent are in charge." *And when I'm the duchess of Norveaux and my very own twin sister is the princess de Sainte-Marie,* Jessica added silently.

Jacques framed her face with his hands and gently stroked her chin with his thumb. "Sometimes I feel the things in my life will never improve," he said in a soft, faraway voice. "I wanted so much more for you . . . for *us.*"

Jessica's heart melted. "This is more than enough for now," she said. She flashed him a wide, flirty smile. "I think it's *incredibly* romantic to sneak around with you."

Jacques curved his hand around the back of her neck, sending tingles up and down her spine. She closed her eyes as his lips touched hers. Jacques kissed her gently at first, then deeper, until Jessica felt as if she were drowning in a sweet, warm pool of honey.

Enveloped in such luscious, swirling sensations, she almost missed the slight tug on her hand. In a heartbeat a warning flashed through her mind. Still locked in the kiss, Jessica snapped to attention. She realized Jacques had one arm behind her back and was trying to pry the jewelry case out of her hand.

This guy doesn't know when to give up! she thought. Giggling against his lips, she swung her hand behind her own back. Jacques started laughing too. They kept the kiss going as another playful tug-of-war for the pendant broke out between them.

Suddenly a door slammed somewhere nearby and female chatter erupted in the hallway. Jessica and Jacques broke apart and froze.

"We must be crazy!" Jessica muttered. "Anna will be back any minute. You have to get out of here!"

Jacques nodded and slowly dragged himself up to his feet.

"Hurry!" Jessica urged.

Jacques walked over to the door, opened it a crack, and peered out. Then he looked back over his shoulder and blew Jessica a kiss. "I love you," he whispered.

Jessica gave him a dazzling smile. *"Je t'aime,"* she echoed in French.

Jacques crept down the stairs, his fists clenched in frustration. Once again he'd failed miserably. Jacques thought the pearl bracelet he'd lifted from Carlotta when he'd gone sailing with her, Monica, and his father a few days ago would do the trick. Carlotta had carelessly tossed it on a deck chair when she'd taken a swim and had forgotten all about it by the time she'd dried off.

But Jacques hadn't realized how attached Jessica had grown to the emerald. *Her heart is sentimental,* he reminded himself. It was one of the things he loved about her—but it was causing him such trouble.

His father's warning about their client came back to him, stopping him cold. *He's not the kind of man to whom one brings bad news,* Louis had warned. Jacques knew exactly what his father had meant. He'd grown up with people who lusted after treasures and who would do *anything* to satisfy their desires. They weren't very forgiving when they didn't get what they'd been promised.

An icy shiver of fear sliced through Jacques's gut. The stakes were too high for him to quit now. He couldn't return to his father empty-handed.

Elizabeth felt as though she were gliding on a dreamy cloud when she returned to the château that evening. Although she was realistic enough to know that she and Laurent had many things to work out, Elizabeth clung to the fact that they loved each other deeply. They would have to deal with the future one step at a time.

As she walked toward the stairs she heard voices coming from the kitchen. Preparations for the weekend ball had been going on night and day, so Elizabeth wasn't surprised. She was just about to poke her head in the open doorway and wave good night when suddenly she heard her name mentioned.

Elizabeth stopped in her tracks and pressed her back against the wall next to the door. She recognized Brigitte's voice, speaking rapidly in French. Elizabeth was able to figure out only some of what the maid was saying.

"Suddenly he appeared . . . his face aglow . . .

his eyes only for her . . . ," Brigitte said.

Elizabeth's eyes widened. She realized Brigitte was talking about the morning Laurent had surprised her and the children in the nursery. Then she heard Henri the gardener's deep, melodic voice recounting the evening he'd seen her and Laurent riding away on horseback.

Elizabeth's cheeks burned with indignation. *They're gossiping about us!* she fumed. Suddenly she heard the word *"fiançailles,"* and an alarm went off in her head. "A *betrothal?*" she translated under her breath.

A female voice Elizabeth didn't recognize chimed into the conversation. The woman spoke with a slightly different accent than the others. "I'm certain the engagement will be announced this weekend. Though I never thought the prince would go through with it."

Elizabeth pressed her fingers against her lips as she continued to eavesdrop.

"The marriage will benefit the royal family," a different maid remarked.

"But what about Elizabeth?" Brigitte asked.

"In time . . . ," Henri began in a low, pensive voice, "the American girl will realize the ways of the nobility and find her happiness."

Elizabeth's jaw dropped, her heart in her throat. She was totally stunned and a bit horrified. *Laurent is planning to marry me?* she thought. *They'll announce our engagement this weekend . . .*

and I'm just supposed to adjust *to everything?*
She'd assumed that she and Laurent would be able
to take their relationship one step at a time, but
apparently she'd been wrong.

Elizabeth darted past the doorway and raced
up to her room. She headed straight for her antique desk, plunked herself down in the chair, and
whipped open her journal. Her hand shook as she
picked up her pen.

Writing usually helped her make sense of things,
and at that moment Elizabeth needed it more than
ever. She was desperate to impose order on her
dizzying confusion. Thoughts and emotions were
thrashing through her mind, totally out of control.

Jessica lay sprawled across her bed, her head
bursting with romantic dreams as she gazed at her
bracelet. She imagined herself and Jacques, standing in the balcony of a glorious palace, waving to
the cheering crowds below. Jessica sighed. *I'll bet
Norveaux is the most awesome place in the world,*
she thought.

She rubbed her fingertip over one of the pearls.
The surface felt warm and smooth. Jessica decided
it was the most beautiful bracelet she'd ever seen.
Maybe when Elizabeth saw it, she'd finally realize
what a sweet, considerate guy Jacques really was.

Jessica grinned slyly. She'd heard her twin return and go into her room a short time earlier.
There's no time like the present, she reasoned.

She padded across the hall barefooted and knocked on her sister's door. Not bothering to wait for an answer, Jessica breezed into the room.

Elizabeth was sitting at her desk, writing furiously. "Do you mind, Jess?" she grumbled without looking up.

Jessica plopped down on the bed, undaunted by her twin's response. Elizabeth was always cranky at first when anyone disturbed her writing. "Notice anything different about me?" Jessica asked with an exaggerated, teasing drawl.

Elizabeth snapped her diary shut and twisted around in the chair. "Can't you see I'm busy?"

Jessica giggled and draped her arm gracefully over the side of the bed. "I think my wrist looks especially awesome this evening, don't you?"

Elizabeth sighed wearily. "I give up. What's on your mind?"

Jessica snorted. "Not my mind, silly." She stretched her arm out in front of her, the circle of pearls gleaming on her wrist. "Jacques gave it to me this evening," she said proudly.

Elizabeth barely glanced at it. "It's nice," she said flatly.

Jessica bolted upright and glared at her sister. "*Nice* is when a guy gives you flowers or a CD. This bracelet is totally awesome."

Elizabeth gave her a contrite smile. "I'm just a bit preoccupied tonight," she said, pushing back the

117

chair. She came over and sat down beside Jessica.

Jessica held up the bracelet, allowing her twin to admire it properly. "What do you think?" she asked, fishing for praise.

Elizabeth nodded. "It's breathtaking, Jess."

"That's much better," Jessica replied with a laugh. She lowered her arm and sighed dreamily. "I've decided that Lila was right all along—France is the most romantic place in the world."

All of a sudden, without any warning, Elizabeth burst into tears.

Jessica gasped a quick, startled breath. "What's wrong?" she asked, putting her arms around her twin.

"Laurent," Elizabeth sobbed.

Jessica felt her heart sink. She assumed Elizabeth was crying because she'd found out that Laurent was betrothed to Antonia. *I can't believe he'd prefer that sickly-looking snob over Liz!* Jessica thought hotly.

"I'm confused," Elizabeth wailed. "France is nice . . . but *forever?* Besides, I'm way too young to get"—she hiccuped loudly—"married."

Totally baffled by what she was hearing, Jessica leaned back and looked her sister in the eye. "What are you talking about?" she asked.

Elizabeth shook her head. "He's going to ask me to marry him."

Yes! Jessica mentally cheered. *Thank goodness I didn't tell Liz about Laurent and Antonia!*

"Everything is happening so fast." Elizabeth

sniffed noisily. "I need a tissue," she muttered, scooting off the bed.

Jessica's gaze followed her across the room. *If Elizabeth and Laurent get married, I'll have a bona fide prince for a brother-in-law,* she realized excitedly. Everything was turning out even better than Jessica had dared to hope.

Elizabeth took the tissue box from the desk and brought it back to the bed. "Laurent is a wonderful guy," she said pensively. "And what we have is very special. We like a lot of the same things, and we care about each other as friends."

"So what's the problem?" Jessica asked.

Elizabeth sighed. "I'm too young! And I'm not ready to get married. I mean, I love Laurent . . . at least I *think* I love him." She shrugged. "I really haven't known him that long. Maybe it's just that I *want* to be in love with him."

Jessica rolled her eyes. "Or maybe it's just that you think too much!"

Elizabeth cracked a smile. "You would say that."

"Because it's true!" Jessica insisted. "Now promise me you won't make any major decisions without talking to me first."

Elizabeth laughed at that. "That's just about the most ridiculous advice I've ever gotten. Anyway, as I was walking by the kitchen a few minutes ago, I overheard—"

She was interrupted by a knock on the door. "That's probably Anna," Jessica said, getting up to answer it. "She said she'd be back in one minute— ages ago." Jessica giggled to herself. *If I'd known how long one of Anna's minutes really was, I wouldn't have hurried Jacques out of my room so quickly.*

Jessica opened the door, and Anna breezed into the room, clutching her clipboard to her chest. "It is good you're both here," she said.

Elizabeth pulled the chair out from under her desk. "Please sit down, Anna," she offered politely.

Jessica smiled to herself. *When Liz becomes the princess around here, I hope these people realize how lucky they are to have her instead of Antonia,* she thought.

Anna glanced at Jessica. "You are no longer dressed with your, how you say . . . *par-jee-mas?*"

"You mean *pajamas?*" Elizabeth asked.

Jessica looked down at her black jeans and gulped, remembering her charade with the blue robe earlier.

"Pajamas," Anna repeated slowly. "I learn better my English with you, like the children."

"I changed," Jessica blurted. "I decided it was much too early to go to bed. I've been getting way too much sleep lately."

Elizabeth shot her a suspicious look, which Jessica ignored.

"Now, for the tableau," Anna began, glancing down at her clipboard. "It will be played before the ball on Saturday evening, and the princess leaves the children's part to you."

"Tableau?" Jessica questioned, looking to her twin for a translation.

Elizabeth's eyes narrowed. "Tableau? That means blackboard, doesn't it?"

Anna smiled. "That's one translation, yes. *Tableau* means also painting or scene. For the game each team chooses a scene from a story, then conveys it on the stage by posing as the characters," she explained.

"Sort of like charades?" Elizabeth asked.

Anna nodded. "But in tableau you must remain totally still for five minutes. Everyone dresses with the fancy costumes, and then the group freezes into a paintinglike scene. The audience must guess what story the scene is from. It is much fun."

Elizabeth chuckled. "Sounds interesting, but I don't know how we're going to get the kids to go along with it. It'll be torture for them to keep still for longer than two seconds."

"They'll love it," Jessica countered. "We'll find ourselves some fantastic costumes to wear. . . ." She pictured herself decked out in a fabulous gown, looking breathtakingly awesome. She'd finally have a chance to show that old countess a taste of real glamour.

Jessica caught herself staring at her pearl bracelet. *Too bad Jacques won't be there to see me,* she thought sadly.

Chapter 8

Sitting beside Jacques in the elegant throne room of their huge castle in Norveaux, Jessica opened the sealed message one of the butlers had just handed her on a gold tray. She smiled as she read the note. "My dearest friend from Sweet Valley, Lila Fowler, has just arrived for a visit," Jessica told her husband, the duke. She turned to the team of servants in fancy dress uniform who stood at attention beside her throne, waiting to jump at her slightest command. "Please show Miss Fowler in," Jessica requested in a cultured, regal tone of voice.

"As you wish, Your Highness," they answered, bowing respectfully.

A moment later the huge double doors were opened, and there was Lila, her eyes popping in awe and her complexion turning green with envy. . . .

Suddenly a loud, angry screech outside her

bedroom knocked Jessica right out of her glorious dream. She awoke with a start, a corner of the sheet clenched in her fist. *How is a person supposed to get any sleep around here?* she fumed. Doors were slamming up and down the hall, heavy footsteps pounding on the stairs. Voices were shouting in rapid-fire French.

Knowing she wouldn't be able to go back to her dream, Jessica threw off the bedcovers and swung her legs over the edge of the mattress. "This better be an emergency," she grumbled as she pushed her fists into the sleeves of her robe. She stepped into the hall and was nearly knocked to the floor by a rushing stampede of bodies.

Flattened against the wall, Jessica gaped at the strange scene. Servants ran around hysterically. The countess stormed through the hall in a bright blue filmy chiffon robe, with a white turban wrapped around her head, screaming, *"Au secours! Au secours!"* Antonia, wearing green silk pajamas, trailed her mother, clutching a shawl around her shoulders and sobbing hysterically.

Jessica covered her mouth and smirked discreetly. She presumed the di Riminis were hysterical over Laurent's having chosen Elizabeth over Antonia. *Seems those hags are extremely poor losers!* she thought snidely.

Then Anna made her way through the crowd, her face pale and her expression grave. Princess Catherine was right behind her. Jessica began to suspect that something worse than Antonia's broken engagement had happened. But even though her French had improved since she'd arrived at the château, she couldn't understand much of what was being shouted.

Jessica saw Elizabeth standing in the doorway of her room, watching the commotion with a look of astonishment. "What's going on?" Jessica mouthed.

Elizabeth inched her way over to Jessica. "I don't know exactly. Something terrible, I think."

"What's that the witch keeps yelling?" Jessica asked. "*Oh* something or other?"

"*Au secours,*" Elizabeth said. "It means *help.*"

Jessica waved over a maid who was standing near the stairs. "Do you know what this is all about?" she asked.

The girl stepped closer to the twins and shook her head, babbling something incoherent. "She doesn't speak English," Elizabeth explained. She began talking to the maid in French.

"What is she saying?" Jessica demanded impatiently, nudging her twin's shoulder. Elizabeth shrugged Jessica's hand away.

"Antonia's diamond necklace is missing," Elizabeth said at last.

Jessica sniggered. "Serves them right."

"The countess insists that one of the servants must've stolen it," Elizabeth added.

"That's ridiculous!" Jessica spat. "Antonia is such a ditz, she probably misplaced it."

Suddenly the countess's eyes locked on Jessica's, and her mouth twisted with rage. "Them!" she bellowed in English as she came over to the twins.

Jessica winced and touched her hand to her ear. The woman could probably outyell the entire Sweet Valley High cheerleading squad.

The countess glared at them, her massive chest heaving. The loose flesh around her jaw flapped and jiggled. "I demand these two be strip-searched at once!"

Jessica heard Elizabeth gasp, and a sudden, hot flame of defiant anger flared in her gut. *Who does that ugly hag think she is, trying to intimidate us like that!* she raged inwardly.

Jessica raised her head high, her fists clenched at her sides. She was sick of being treated like a lowly, scum-of-the-earth peon, but to see her sister being treated as one was more than she could stand. She met the witch's glare straight on. "I'd like to see you *try*," Jessica retorted.

The woman sputtered indignantly, obviously shocked that anyone would dare stand up to her. *Get used to it, Your Evilness,* Jessica thought, relishing the small victory.

Princess Catherine came up behind the countess, her complexion starkly pale. She patted the angry woman's shoulders and spoke to her in French in a soothing tone of voice. Jessica guessed the princess was telling the old witch to calm down.

Princess Catherine glanced at Jessica and

Elizabeth. "It is all a simple mistake, I am certain," she added with a thick French accent.

Jessica assumed the princess had switched to English for her and Elizabeth's benefit, and she was touched by the gesture. *She obviously doesn't believe the countess's ravings either,* Jessica thought.

"A simple mistake?" the countess raged. "A thief crept into my daughter's room in the middle of the night and stole the diamond necklace that had been her grandmother's." She threw her arms around Antonia and began sobbing hysterically. "What if my poor little girl had been murdered in her sleep?"

"The world would be a better place," Jessica muttered sarcastically under her breath. She didn't think she'd spoken loud enough to be heard . . . until she felt Elizabeth pinch her elbow.

"Ouch!" Jessica hissed, rubbing the painful spot and trying not to laugh.

Prince Nicolas appeared at the top of the stairs, and everyone fell silent. "The guards have been notified and the police are on their way," he announced.

"Those girls are the culprits, I am certain!" the countess insisted, pointing an accusing finger at Jessica and Elizabeth. "I want the police to arrest them."

"Let's go have some nice hot tea," Princess Catherine suggested, leading her hysterical guest toward the stairs. She gave the twins a quick smile over her shoulder, as if to reassure them that everything would be OK.

After they left, Anna clapped for attention and spoke sharply to everyone in French. "What is she saying?" Jessica asked Elizabeth.

"She's ordering everyone to go to work immediately," Elizabeth replied. "I suppose I should get ready to meet the kids for breakfast."

Jessica lifted her hand and gave a little wave. "My shift doesn't begin until noon. If all the fun is over for now, I'm going back to bed."

Elizabeth rolled her eyes. "Jessica, only *you* would consider a jewel theft and the threat of a strip search *fun*."

"No, the hands on the head!" Claudine hollered at Elizabeth, shaking her head vigorously. The children had wanted to teach Elizabeth the movements to one of their singing games, but her concentration skills that day were totally dismal. Pierre and Manon had already given up and were now rolling on the nursery floor, laughing at her.

Elizabeth put her hands on her hips and shot them all a playful snarl.

Suddenly the door opened and Jessica breezed into the nursery. "Hi, guys," she called cheerfully.

Elizabeth sagged melodramatically with relief. "I'm saved from further humiliation," she declared.

Jessica giggled. "I would have been earlier, but I heard the storm troopers coming down the hall, and I had to duck into the bathroom until they passed."

Elizabeth frowned, bemused. "Storm troopers?"

Jessica nodded. "The countess is marching the police through the château, screaming at them in French. Antonia is with them too, sobbing her eyes out," she added with a grin.

Elizabeth shuddered, remembering the countess's expression when she'd demanded that she and Jessica be strip-searched. "I just hope they find that necklace," she said.

"Isn't it cool?" Jessica asked excitedly.

Elizabeth blinked. "Cool?"

"Yeah!" Jessica exclaimed. She turned to the children. "Why don't you kids go play with your blocks," she suggested. "Let's see who can make the best tower."

The children squealed with delight and scampered off to get their blocks. Elizabeth laughed as she watched them go, then sent her twin a wry look. "Jess, explain to me again how we're going to get them to stay perfectly still for the tableau."

"They'll be fine," Jessica replied hastily as she led Elizabeth to the couch and sat her down. "Anyway, I've been thinking." She lowered her voice. "Maybe if we keep our eyes open, we'll be the ones to catch the jewel thief."

Elizabeth snorted. "Come on, this is real life. If the diamond necklace was stolen, the thief would be long gone by now. I think you've seen too many spy movies," she teased.

"But don't you think it's weird that there have

128

been two thefts since we've been on this trip?" Jessica persisted.

"It is kind of a strange coincidence," Elizabeth agreed. She thought about it for a moment, considering the possibilities. "Do you think the thief is someone here at the château?"

Jessica nodded. "I'm sure of it," she declared. "I have a pretty good idea who it is."

"Who?" Elizabeth asked.

"The countess!" Jessica replied emphatically.

Elizabeth rolled her eyes. "Jessica, just because she's a mean witch doesn't automatically mean she's a thief. Besides, why would she steal her own family heirloom and her daughter's diamond necklace?"

Jessica leaned closer, her eyes flashing excitedly. "Insurance!"

"Insurance for what?" Elizabeth questioned.

"The insurance *money*," Jessica clarified. "Rich people always take out huge insurance policies on their jewelry so that if they lose them, they can collect the money. Lila even suggested that we get insurance for the earrings Grandma sent us."

Elizabeth automatically fingered one of the diamond posts in her ear. "Insurance fraud is a major crime," she reflected. "Do you really think the countess is capable of something so serious?"

Jessica snorted. "Don't you?"

"I'm not sure," Elizabeth responded, her mind clicking. Her reporter instincts shifted into gear. "But I'd sure love to get to the bottom of this."

Later that day Elizabeth sat in her room, looking over her notes. She'd already filled seven pages of a yellow legal pad with her ideas and observations about the thefts. "Both items belonged to the di Riminis . . . one missing from the train . . . one from the château . . . ," she read. "The diamond necklace was stolen from Antonia's room in the château, and the di Riminis' family heirloom was stolen from the countess's luggage."

Elizabeth circled the word *heirloom* and drew a big question mark next to it. She didn't know what the heirloom object was exactly and made a mental note to find out.

Elizabeth realized that she and Jessica were the most obvious suspects. They were the only people who had been on the train *and* who were staying at the château.

Except for the countess and Antonia, of course, Elizabeth reflected. The more she considered the possibilities, the more convinced she was of the countess's guilt. All her bluster and rage in the servants' wing that morning might have been nothing more than an attempt to divert suspicion from herself.

Suddenly the door burst open and Jessica rushed in. "Come on, Liz, let's go!"

Elizabeth jumped up, responding to the urgency in her twin's voice. "Go where?" she asked, following Jessica to the stairs. "And where are the kids?"

"They're having their picture taken," Jessica

130

replied over her shoulders. "A hot-looking photographer is here to do a formal portrait of the royal family. The witches too, lucky for us. But I don't know how much time that gives us. . . ."

Elizabeth stopped her on the second-floor landing. "Time for what?" she demanded.

"To find the jewel," Jessica hissed.

Elizabeth's mouth snapped shut, and she shivered with excitement. *We just might crack this case*, she thought.

"I'm pretty sure the countess's suite is in the east wing," Jessica whispered when they reached the bottom floor. "I overheard some of the maids complaining about her constant demands for room service."

"Figures," Elizabeth said wryly.

A few minutes later they crept into the east wing. The hallway was softly illuminated by huge crystal chandeliers in the ceiling. Framed paintings and tapestries hung on the walls, and a plush red carpet runner covered the floor. Settees with red velvet cushions, marble-topped tables, and gleaming suits of armor stood at intervals between the closed doors along the length of the hall. Dozens of potted plants added a softening touch to the formal decor.

"I wish we were staying here," Jessica complained.

"Do you know which room is the countess's?" Elizabeth asked. Jessica shook her head.

Elizabeth tiptoed to the first door and pressed her ear against it. Holding her breath, she listened for any noise that might indicate someone was inside the room. But all she heard was the heavy pounding of her heart. Steeling her fluttering nerves, Elizabeth twisted the knob and slowly opened the door.

"This is the countess's room," Jessica whispered right behind her.

Elizabeth hesitated. "Are you sure?"

"Of course." Jessica waltzed into the huge sitting room and pointed to a filmy yellow chiffon gown with black feathery trim that was draped over the arm of an ornate antique couch. "I'd recognize those ostrich feathers anywhere," Jessica said.

Elizabeth chuckled nervously under her breath.

There were two bedrooms in the suite and three bathrooms. French doors in the sitting room and each bedroom opened up to a wide balcony overlooking the east gardens. "What a waste!" Jessica remarked as they made a brief investigation of the suite. "All this for those two . . . we should have had a suite like this!" Then she grinned. "But I suppose we'll be living in this kind of luxury soon enough, when you're the princess de Sainte-Marie and I'm the duchess of Norveaux."

Elizabeth flinched. She wasn't sure she wanted to be a French princess. *We have a job to do here,* she reminded herself firmly, dragging herself back to the reality of the moment. "Where would the countess have hidden her diamond necklace?" Elizabeth wondered aloud.

"It could be here anywhere," Jessica replied. She pushed up the sleeves of her sweater. "Let's get started."

They checked out the sitting room first, from top to bottom and corner to corner. Elizabeth crawled out onto the balcony on her hands and knees to avoid the possibility of being seen from the garden. Straining her muscles to lift the heavy potted plants, she looked under each one, then dug through the damp potting soil with her fingers. All she "discovered" were roots.

Next she scooted over to the white wicker seating arrangement at the opposite end of the balcony. Lying on her back, she slipped under the table and chair, checking to see if the elusive necklace had been taped to the underside of the furniture. That also proved fruitless. Elizabeth swiped her hand across her sweaty forehead. *It must be inside the suite,* she thought.

Her twin was groping through crevices between the couch cushions when Elizabeth stepped back into the sitting room. Suddenly Jessica jerked back her hand and twisted her face into a sour expression. "Yuck, how disgusting!"

"What?" Elizabeth asked.

"Old chewing gum!" Jessica answered. "Can you believe it? This couch is probably worth more than our entire house, and it's loaded with chewing gum!"

"I'm surprised the countess hasn't issued a written complaint," Elizabeth said.

Jessica smirked. "It's probably her gum." She stared at Elizabeth narrowly. "What happened to you?" she asked. "Your face is all muddy."

Elizabeth glanced at her dirty hands and realized she must've smeared herself with potting soil. "The necklace isn't buried in the plants," she remarked dryly.

"You'd better wash that off, or you'll leave dirty fingerprints all over the place," Jessica warned.

Elizabeth nodded and followed her twin into the bathroom that was off the sitting room. "This is really nice," Jessica said wistfully as Elizabeth washed her hands. "It's so unfair that they have *three* bathrooms while we have to share one!"

Next they searched through one of the bedrooms, which was obviously Antonia's. "She certainly is a sicko neat freak," Jessica remarked as she pulled open the top dresser drawer. "Worse than you, Liz."

Curious, Elizabeth peered over Jessica's shoulder and chuckled. Antonia's socks and underwear were folded and lined up in neat, color-coordinated rows. "You're right," Elizabeth remarked.

After they'd made a thorough sweep of Antonia's room, they checked out the countess's. Elizabeth searched through the clothes in the freestanding oak wardrobe, slipping her hand into each pocket. All she found was a used handkerchief and a roll of mints.

Elizabeth heard her twin gasp. Jessica was

kneeling on the floor in front of an open metal box. "Look what I found, Liz!"

"A diamond necklace?" Elizabeth asked hopefully, rushing to her side. She saw what was inside the box and slumped disappointedly. It was filled with candy bars, some of them partially eaten.

"I'll bet it's the countess's personal, secret stash," Jessica remarked with a giggle. "She's a closet junk-food addict. Now we can blackmail her."

Elizabeth glared at her twin mildly. "That's a *great* idea, Jessica," she muttered sarcastically.

Suddenly Jessica's face turned pale. "What was that?" she whispered.

Elizabeth perked her ears and heard it too—the sound of footsteps approaching the suite. Then the outer door opened, and someone entered the sitting room. Elizabeth's heart stopped, frozen. The twins exchanged wide-eyed looks of alarm.

Jessica soundlessly eased the metal box shut and slipped it into the bottom dresser drawer. "Let's hide!" she breathed.

Forcing back a feeling of cold panic, Elizabeth flattened herself on the floor and shimmied faceup under the bed with Jessica. An instant later the bedroom door burst open and someone entered. Elizabeth turned her head slightly and saw two feet in white leather pumps standing next to the bed. She recognized those shoes immediately.

Elizabeth's heart stopped. *It's the countess!* she realized. *We're trapped!*

Chapter 9

Elizabeth felt as if her heart were lodged in her throat as she and Jessica lay motionless in their hiding place under the countess's bed. The bed sagged closer to their faces, indicating that the countess had plunked herself down on the mattress. Then Elizabeth heard the phone handset being picked up, followed by the countess's haughty voice.

"Yes, the arrangements have been made for a smooth transaction," she said firmly. "But I suggest we move quickly. There may be complications . . . outside elements. . . ."

Jessica squeezed Elizabeth's hand.

"This has been planned carefully to the very last detail," the countess continued. "I won't tolerate any intervention at this point." With that she hung up and marched out of the suite, slamming the door behind her.

Elizabeth closed her eyes and took a deep breath. "That was way too close," she whispered shakily.

The twins squirmed out from under the bed and brushed themselves off. "What did you think about that phone call?" Jessica said. "I'll bet she was making arrangements to fence the stolen necklace and the heirloom she claims to have lost on the train too. By the way, do you know what the heirloom is? I couldn't understand what everyone was saying on the train."

Elizabeth shook her head. "I don't think anyone on the train mentioned what sort of an object it was." She gazed around the room and frowned. "But let's face it, Jess, the countess hasn't hidden the diamond necklace in this suite. It could be anywhere. We may never find it."

"We'll just have to keep looking," Jessica insisted.

Elizabeth sighed wearily. "This castle is bigger than the Sweet Valley Mall," she pointed out discouragingly. "And that's not including the miles of secret passageways under the château."

Jessica's face lit up. "Of course, the secret passageways! Let's get Jacques to help us. He knows them very well." She grinned mischievously. "That's how he sneaks in to see me."

Elizabeth shook her head. "I've been down there with Laurent," she said. "It's totally dark, and there must be trillions of nooks and crannies where a person could hide a necklace. We'd never be able to search every inch of the

137

passageways even if we spent the entire summer down there."

"We'll just have to stay close to the countess and wait for her to lead us to the treasure," Jessica suggested as they crept out of the suite.

"I'm sure she'll love that," Elizabeth replied sarcastically.

Jessica snickered. "I still think we should ask Jacques to help us," she said. "He's very resourceful."

Elizabeth grimaced inwardly. She didn't care how resourceful Jacques Landeau might be or how much Jessica gushed about him and the bracelet he'd given her. Something about the guy made Elizabeth uneasy.

Jacques uttered a low, sleepy groan as he opened his eyes Friday morning. He found himself twisted uncomfortably in a tight, dark space, and for one frightening moment he couldn't remember how he'd gotten there. When he tried to move, a quick, hot pain shot up and down his left leg, shocking him fully awake. Suddenly it all came back to him.

Le Château d'Amour Inconnu, he realized. He'd fallen asleep in the linen closet near Jessica's room. He had no idea what time it was. There was a shaft of light shining under the closet door, so it was probably well after daybreak. That meant he'd spent the entire night there. *I must be getting soft in the head*, Jacques chided himself.

138

He flexed his left foot and winced at the sudden burst of pins and needles. He reached down and rubbed it vigorously to get the blood circulating, then stretched his neck from side to side to ease the stiffness.

His father had been pleased when Jacques had presented him with the diamond necklace. "This fine bonus will set us up for the entire winter," Louis had said proudly. Then he had asked for the emerald.

Jacques cringed with remorse as he recalled his father's expression when he'd told him that he didn't have it. It was as if Louis Landeau had aged years in a matter of seconds—his eyes had turned glassy, and the worry lines on his face had deepened. Jacques had promised to bring him the emerald that weekend—without fail.

He had sneaked into the château the previous evening and had been about to enter Jessica's room when a flock of servants had come running up the stairs. That's when Jacques had ducked into the linen closet. By the time the corridor cleared, Jessica had gone to her room. Jacques had decided to wait until she was asleep. He'd peeked out from the linen closet every few minutes to see if she'd turned off her light. But apparently she'd outlasted him, and he'd fallen asleep without getting the emerald.

I won't let it happen again, Jacques resolved firmly. Taking a deep breath, he shifted onto his hands and knees and crawled out of his hiding spot behind a stack of folded sheets. He eased the door open slightly and peered through the crack. Several maids were set up with ladders and buckets at both ends of the corridor, washing the tall windows.

Frustrated, Jacques cursed under his breath as he closed the door. The windows were large, with dozens of wood-framed panes in each, all of which had to be washed individually. The job could take hours.

Jacques grabbed a stack of towels and made himself a cushioned seat on the floor. *I might as well make myself comfortable,* he thought wryly.

"The costumes are supposed to be grouped by size, but things have become disorganized in here," Anna explained as she ushered Jessica, Elizabeth, and the children into the wardrobe room after breakfast.

Jessica looked around, impressed. More than a dozen wardrobes were lined up along the walls. The large bay window at the far end of the room was flanked on either side by makeup tables with lighted mirrors. *I'd like a closet like this someday,* she thought.

"This room, it is used often during the summer," Anna commented. "The princess enjoys hosting lavish costume parties impromptu. On several occasions more than thirty guests are in here at once, scrambling to find the most outlandish outfit of all. Sometimes the parties never leave this room, and we end up serving the buffet on the makeup tables."

"Sounds wild," Jessica muttered.

Anna pointed out the wardrobes where they might find costumes for the children. "The ball gowns are in here," she said, indicating the wardrobe nearest the door. "Help yourself to something nice to wear after the tableau. The dressing rooms are through there." She pointed to a door on the right.

"This is going to be such fun!" Jessica exclaimed.

"I hope so," Anna replied. "Though I'll be glad when it's all over and I can soak for an entire day in a hot bath." Anna turned to the children. "You will behave nicely and do what you're told, yes?"

"Yes!" they shouted enthusiastically.

Elizabeth and Jessica looked at each other and laughed. "Promises, promises," Jessica muttered.

"I want to wear a costume like a tree," Pierre announced. "Or a tiger."

Claudine had already opened one of the wardrobes and was fondling the corner of a green velvet gown. "I want this one," she said. "I want to look like the beautiful girl in the bluebird story."

Manon jumped up and raised her hands in the air. "I want to look like a grand elephant!"

"Let's pick the story theme for our tableau," Elizabeth suggested.

"I want the bluebird story," Claudine announced.

Jessica shrugged. "It's not a very well-known story," she pointed out. "We should probably pick something that would be easier to guess. We do want our team to win, right?"

The children cheered excitedly.

"OK, so what about *Sleeping Beauty* or *Cinderella*?" Elizabeth suggested.

Claudine's eyes widened. "*Cinderella!* I love *Cinderella.*"

"Me too!" Manon said.

Pierre rolled his eyes dramatically. "Girls!" he grumbled.

Jessica and Elizabeth cracked up at his expression. "I think you'd be perfect as the prince's footman," Elizabeth said.

"What's that?" he asked.

"He's the guy who tries the magic slipper on the feet of all the maidens in the kingdom," Elizabeth answered.

Pierre didn't seem too impressed. Jessica ruffled his curly hair. "Come on, it's a fun job, Pierre. You get to shove that glass slipper on all those ugly feet. . . ."

Pierre sighed melodramatically. "All right," he agreed. "Let's do *Cinderella.*"

"Claudine can be Cinderella," Elizabeth said. "Jess, would you rather be the wicked stepmother or the fairy godmother?"

"The fairy godmother, of course," Jessica replied.

"Could I be *l'éléphant*?" Manon pleaded.

"Elephant?" Jessica asked, glancing at her twin for verification.

Elizabeth nodded and squatted down to Manon's eye level. "I'm afraid there aren't any

142

elephants in *Cinderella*. You could be a wicked stepsister," she offered.

Manon tipped her head from side to side, chanting, "Wicked stepsister," over and over.

"I think that's a yes," Jessica said cheerfully. "Now that we've got our theme, let's have some fun!"

They decided to create the scene where Prince Charming's footman was slipping the glass slipper onto Cinderella's foot. For the next hour they flitted around the room excitedly, poking through all the wardrobes and trying on item after item.

After some digging Jessica found a clear plastic sandal in a box of odds and ends. "I found our glass slipper," she announced proudly. "There's only one in here, though, and it's way too big for Claudine, but that shouldn't matter for the tableau."

"It's perfect," Elizabeth agreed. "What do you think of this dress?" She held up a full-length beaded shift in a severe shade of mustard brown. It was chic, elegant, glamorous, and yet matronly drab at the same time.

"It's awesome!" Jessica exclaimed. "*Exactly* what a wicked stepmother would wear."

Jessica tried on several potential outfits that would suit a fairy godmother. She finally spotted a pale green silk gown with silver threads woven through the fabric. "This is the one," she whispered excitedly as she took it off its hanger.

"That's beautiful," Elizabeth said when Jessica walked out of the dressing room wearing the gown.

"And I found a lace shawl we can use to make your veil." She sat Jessica down at one of the makeup stools. "Let me try something."

Jessica watched in the mirror as Elizabeth twisted her hair into a topknot. She anchored the veil with some hairpins, draping it across the lower half of her face.

"What do you think?" Elizabeth asked.

Jessica narrowed her eyes and turned from side to side as she studied her reflection. "Needs height," she said.

Elizabeth pursed her lips. "You're right. Hold on, I've got an idea. . . ."

Claudine skipped over to the makeup table, holding up the hem of the long pink dress she was wearing. "You're beautiful, Mademoiselle Jessica," she murmured.

Jessica grinned. "Thanks." She looked over Claudine's outfit and nodded. The dress had lots of lace trim, a high waist, and puffy sleeves. "You look very pretty yourself, kid," she said.

Elizabeth returned a moment later with a roll of toilet paper in her hand. Jessica glared at her. "What are you planning to do with that?"

"Put it on your head," she answered. She stuck her fingers into the hollow center of the roll and rotated it around her opposite hand, wrapping the tissue around her wrist.

Jessica snorted. "I don't know how to break it to you, Liz. But I'm not the sort of person who wears *toilet paper* as a fashion accessory."

"Trust me," Elizabeth insisted. "And sit still."
She gathered the entire length of toilet paper
around her hand and set it aside. Then she redid
Jessica's hair, using the empty cardboard roll as a
frame. Then she arranged the lace veil over her
creation, and the effect was totally stunning.

Jessica smiled broadly. "Liz, you're a genius!" The
delicate veil seemed to float down the sides of her
face like a pale green cloud. Jessica knew she looked
lovely, but not quite as glamorous as she'd hoped.
She frowned. *It needs . . . something,* she decided.

"What's wrong?" Elizabeth asked.

"I don't know." Jessica shrugged. "It seems
rather . . . *plain.*" Suddenly a brilliant idea popped
into her head. "I have the perfect solution!" she
cried, bolting from the chair.

"Where are you going?" Elizabeth asked.

"I have to get something from my room," she
replied over her shoulder. "I'll be right back."

Finally! Jacques mumbled to himself as he
slipped out of the linen closet into the deserted
hallway. He'd feared that those maids would never
leave. At one point he'd overheard them complaining that all the servants' rooms were going to be
searched by the police later that day.

*Thank goodness the emerald will be long gone
from the château before* that *happens,* he thought.
Otherwise Jessica would be blamed for its theft.

145

Jacques crept into her room and made his way over to her bed, stepping over the junk strewn across her floor. A gentle smile tugged at the corners of his lips. She was even messier than he was!

Jacques tried not to think about Jessica . . . but her face floated into his mind's eye. She would hate him forever when she discovered the emerald missing. *If only* . . . Jacques shook his head to clear it. Their love had been doomed from the moment he'd stepped off the train. Wishing that they might have a future would only cause him more pain. His father needed him, and Jacques would never let him down . . . even if it meant giving up the most wonderful girl in the entire world.

Jacques raised a corner of her pillow and grabbed the red velvet case underneath it. His hands trembled as he raised the lid. The emerald pendant was inside, glimmering in the bright sunlight that filtered into the room. Sighing with relief, Jacques snapped the lid shut and slipped it into the pocket of his jeans.

Suddenly the door opened. He jerked his head around and gasped, his heart stuck in his throat. "Jessica!" he uttered breathlessly.

Chapter 10

"Jacques!" Jessica gasped in pleased surprise. She quickly shut her bedroom door, then whirled around to face him. He was wearing a black shirt that accentuated his dark eyes and broad shoulders—and he looked absolutely gorgeous. Jessica's heart skipped a beat, and her mouth went dry.

Jacques appeared equally shaken at the sight of her, his brown eyes wide and luminous. His face was flushed, and his hands were trembling.

"You're here!" Jessica exclaimed breathlessly as she rushed to him.

But Jacques kept her at arm's distance with his hands on her shoulders. He stared at her in awe, his gaze moving slowly from her head down to her feet, then up to her eyes. "You appear like *un ange!*"

"This is my costume for the tableau," Jessica replied with a giggle. "I almost forgot I was wearing it."

"It is very beautiful," he whispered reverently. *"You're* beautiful."

Beaming proudly, Jessica turned from side to side. "I'm supposed to be the fairy godmother in *Cinderella.*"

He reached for her hand and brought it to his lips. "I love you, Jessica."

Jessica gave him a tender smile. "I love you too, Jacques."

Jacques kissed the back of her hand, then clasped it between both of his. A sad, wistful look came into his eyes. "Please, in the future days . . . ," he began, "know that it is forever I love you."

Jessica's heart instantly melted. Tears spilled down her cheeks. "Me too," she replied. *"Forever."* She leaned toward him and slipped her arms around his waist. Jacques hugged her tightly, whispering French words into her ear.

Suddenly, behind his back, Jessica felt a box-shaped object sticking out of his pocket. An alarm went off in her head. She wondered if Jacques had made another attempt to take back the emerald pendant. *No, he wouldn't do that,* she thought. *Would he?* She had to know for sure.

If this is my jewelry case, Jacques is dead! she fumed as she yanked the suspicious rectangle out of his pocket.

In the span of a heartbeat Jessica jumped away from Jacques and glanced at what she'd taken. As she'd feared, it was her red jewelry case. She raised the lid and saw that the pendant was inside.

Jessica snapped the case shut. Anger and confusion coursed through her as she faced Jacques. "Why don't you want me to have this?" she asked him.

Jacques lowered his eyes, his expression heavy with guilt. "You deserve only the real gems, not an inexpensive fake like that one."

Jessica gritted her teeth. "How many times do I have to tell you that I don't care about that? Fake or not, I love this pendant because it was a gift from you."

Jacques faced her squarely. "I'm ashamed to have given you such a cheap gift."

"Get over it!" she spat.

Jacques sighed wearily and lowered himself to the edge of the bed. "I don't understand how could a sophisticated, elegant girl as you become so attached to such a garish piece of junk."

Jessica opened the case and gazed at the pendant. "I think it's lovely," she argued.

Jacques uttered a derisive sound. "It is worthless."

Jessica shut the jewelry case and glared at him. "I think it's precious."

Jacques shook his head. "You are wrong!" he cried vehemently. "That is a thing for the garbage."

Jessica squared her shoulders and raised her chin. "Well, I feel differently," she said. "And if you can't respect my feelings, then there's nothing more for us to say to each other."

Jacques moved toward her, his arms open and

his eyes pleading. "Jessica, *mon ange* . . . it is only because you are ignorant that you treasure this meaningless scrap."

Jessica's temper exploded like an angry volcano. "*Ignorant?* How *dare* you!" she raged at him. "I never want to see you again."

Not bothering to wait for Jacques's reaction, she rushed out of her room, tears streaming down her face.

"Maybe you should tell the de Sainte-Maries about Jacques's visits," Elizabeth advised Jessica as they headed toward their rooms that evening. "With everything that's going on, it might be best if they knew."

Jessica sniffed. "I couldn't," she replied glumly. "As mad as I am at him, I still don't want to cause a major problem for his family."

Elizabeth glanced at her twin, noting the dark red circles around her eyes. Jessica had hardly stopped crying for more than five minutes since her blowup with Jacques.

I'd love to wring his neck! Elizabeth thought fiercely, clenching her fists at her side. She'd known all along that he would eventually hurt Jessica.

"I'm not going to let him ruin the weekend for me," Jessica declared. "Our tableau is going to be fantastic. And who knows . . . maybe I'll snag a handsome prince at the ball."

Elizabeth smiled. "You're something else, Jess," she teased gently.

Jessica looped her arm around Elizabeth's neck. "If my own sister is dating a prince, why should I settle for a duke?"

Elizabeth rolled her eyes, amazed at her twin's bizarre logic. "Things aren't exactly settled between Laurent and me," she pointed out cautiously. "I haven't even seen him since Wednesday."

"I have," Jessica replied.

Elizabeth raised her eyebrows at that. "When?"

"Yesterday," Jessica answered breezily. "He came to the château for the family photograph. I only caught a glimpse of him. He was wearing a fancy dark blue uniform with all sorts of medals on the jacket." She shot Elizabeth a sly grin and added, "He looked totally *hot!*"

Elizabeth felt a warm rush of emotion. "I wish I'd seen him," she murmured.

"You will at the ball," Jessica pointed out excitedly. "And I expect you to make him introduce me to all his royal buddies . . . the good-looking ones anyway."

Elizabeth laughed. "I'll see what I can do." But her smile instantly faded as they entered the servants' wing.

Maids were scurrying through the first-floor corridor, obviously upset, slamming doors, uttering protests about the way they were being treated. Some were even threatening to quit their jobs.

Elizabeth felt a sinking sensation in her gut. "I wonder what's going on now."

Jessica snorted. "Whatever it is, I'll bet the countess had something to do with it."

Elizabeth caught sight of Brigitte, the maid who worked in the kitchen. "What's wrong?" she asked.

Brigitte threw up her hands and shrieked, *"Une disgrâce!"*

Elizabeth frowned. "What's a disgrace?"

"They search our rooms!" Brigitte replied in English. "The police!"

"That's outrageous!" Elizabeth said. She and Jessica ran upstairs to check their own rooms.

Elizabeth opened her door and her heart plummeted. All her drawers were open, her clothes in disarray. Her blanket and sheets had been pushed to the foot of the bed. The pillow was on the floor. The contents of her canvas bag had been dumped out and strewn across the dresser top. "I can't believe this!" Elizabeth fumed. The very idea of strangers going through her personal belongings made her sick.

She went across the hall and knocked on her twin's door. Jessica opened it and waved her in. "I'm so mad I could scream," Elizabeth muttered through clenched teeth.

Then she looked around and uttered a horrified gasp. "Oh, Jessica . . . how terrible!" she cried. "They really tore up your room!"

Jessica shrugged. "Actually I'm not even sure if

anyone's been in here. No, wait . . ." She walked over to the dresser and picked up a bottle of nail polish. "They were here, all right. I haven't seen Malibu Mauve since the bottle fell behind the dresser three days ago."

Elizabeth sat down on the corner of Jessica's bed and folded her arms tightly. "I agree that this is probably all the countess's doing. I just wish the de Sainte-Maries would send her and her nasty daughter packing!"

"Don't worry," Jessica replied. "When we find the di Riminis' missing jewels and bust that witch for insurance fraud . . . we'll have our sweet revenge!"

The following morning Jessica sensed a strange atmosphere brewing in the château as she and Elizabeth supervised the children's breakfast in the kitchen. Although the entire staff was busy working on the final preparations for the evening's festivities, the household seemed unnaturally calm. It was as if a temporary cease-fire had been declared in honor of the royal ball.

After breakfast the twins brought the children back to the wardrobe room for a dress rehearsal of their tableau. "Manon, sit still," Jessica ordered as she drew a big, ugly mole on the little girl's chin.

"But it tickles," Manon complained.

Jessica stepped back and admired her work. With bright red lipstick and her eyes circled in heavy brown eye shadow, Manon looked almost frightening. "You're a perfect wicked stepsister," she pronounced, turning the chair so that Manon could see herself in the mirror.

Manon's jaw dropped. Then she raised her hands, her fingers curled like claws, and growled at her reflection. "I'm like a monster!"

Jessica laughed. "Only when you miss your afternoon nap," she replied jokingly. She uncapped the eyebrow pencil again. "I think you need one more black mole, right on your nose. . . ."

Claudine came barreling out of the dressing room with Pierre right behind her, both of them in full costume. "Give it back!" he was hollering.

Jessica's hand slipped. Instead of a mole Manon now had a jagged black line on her nose. "What's going on!" Jessica demanded.

"Claudine took the glass slipper," Pierre cried. "But *I* am the foot guy."

"We don't have time to fool around, guys," she warned. "Claudine, give him back the shoe, and why isn't your hair done yet?"

Jessica glanced over at her twin. Elizabeth was sitting at the makeup table, staring absently at nothing.

Jessica exhaled an exasperated sigh. "Earth to Liz!" she called tauntingly. "We have a tableau to win—*remember?*"

Elizabeth blinked. "Oh, right," she mumbled. "Come here, Claudine." Reaching for a comb, she knocked over an open jar of hairpins, scattering them across the table.

Jessica rolled her eyes. She knew exactly why her sister had suddenly turned into a scatter-brained ditz. Falling in love with Laurent had shaken Elizabeth's neat, orderly, *dull* world. *Thank goodness I talked her into coming to Château d'Amour Inconnu,* Jessica thought. *If it weren't for me, Liz would probably live her entire life in a permanent rut!*

When the children were finally ready, the twins slipped into their costumes. Jessica stood before a three-sided full-length mirror, admiring herself from different angles. The emerald pendant was the crowning touch—literally. She'd looped the chain around the tall chignon on top of her head, with the shimmering green stone adorning her forehead. *I look absolutely amazing,* she decided. She felt a sudden, sad twinge as she remembered how awed Jacques had been at seeing her in costume—just before she'd discovered her jewelry case in his pocket.

Jessica clenched her jaw as a wave of fresh pain crashed over her. *I'm sure he'll be back,* she thought. *And maybe he'll have finally learned that he can't dictate my feelings and opinions!*

"Let's get in position," Elizabeth called for attention.

They practiced holding the scene over and over, gradually working up to the five minutes that would be required during the actual game. Jessica was amazed by the children's serious attitude and excellent behavior.

After the rehearsal the twins turned their attention to what everyone would wear to the ball. They decided Pierre and Claudine could wear their costumes to the ball, but Manon's drab gray shift wouldn't do at all. Jessica found her a pink party dress, with flounces and satin bows along the hem. Manon was thrilled.

For herself Jessica selected a sleeveless lavender gown with delicate lace trim on the shoulder straps. Standing in front of the mirror in the dressing room, Jessica held the emerald pendant up to her neck to study the effect.

Jacques had called his gift "cheap" and "garish." *Will everyone at the ball think I'm cheap and garish if I wear this?* Jessica worried.

Just then she heard the sound of fluttering fabric coming from one of the dressing stalls, followed by her twin's muffled curse. Jessica frowned. *What is Elizabeth doing in there?* she wondered as she went to investigate.

She found Elizabeth struggling with a monstrous red velvet gown heavily trimmed with gold piping. Her hair was in wild disarray, and beads of perspiration dripped down the sides of her face. "Who's winning?" Jessica asked dryly. "My bet's on the dress."

Elizabeth shot her a withering glare. "Very funny!"

Jessica turned her sister around and saw a hidden row of buttons at the waist. "No wonder," she said as she began unfastening them. "Elizabeth, you're going to have to get ahold of yourself. You're acting like a total airhead, and it's driving me crazy."

"I know," Elizabeth breathed. "But I'm so nervous about everything . . . the ball tonight . . . Laurent. . . . Everything is so complicated all of a sudden. Plus I keeping thinking back to what happened between Todd and me. . . ."

How can she even remember boring-as-cold-toast Todd Wilkins when she has Laurent? Jessica wondered incredulously. She finished unbuttoning the gown, turned her sister around, and looked her in the eye. "Liz, you love Laurent, and he loves you, right? That doesn't sound too complicated to me at all."

Elizabeth chewed her bottom lip. "Maybe it would help if I could talk things over with him before the ball."

"That's a great idea!" Jessica replied enthusiastically.

Elizabeth glanced at her watch. "Laurent is probably at the cottage right now."

"Go see him," Jessica insisted. "We're pretty much finished here, and the kids will be taking a nap soon."

"You sure you don't mind?" Elizabeth asked.

Jessica rolled her eyes. "What I *mind* is having an air-brain twin who can't concentrate on anything for more than two seconds! And if you don't do something to put your mind at rest, I'm going to strangle you before the day is over."

Elizabeth smiled tremulously. "When you put it

that way, I don't seem to have much choice."

Jessica grinned. "None at all," she replied. "Now let's get you out of that ridiculous gown. It makes you look like a couch!"

Laurent cringed at the sound of Antonia's horsey giggle as they sat side by side in the garden behind his cottage. *Is that what I have to put up with for the rest of my life?* he wondered. Sitting directly across from him in a patio chair, the countess di Rimini shot daggers at him with her burning green eyes, as if she'd read his mind.

"You're not offended that I chose Giaccomo Monattini to design the bridal gowns, are you, Laurent?" Antonia was asking. She spoke French, overpronouncing each word as if she were onstage.

Laurent blinked, nonplussed. He didn't have a clue as to what she was saying. Last he knew, she'd been describing the quirky habits of her grandmother . . . or cousin. Apparently he'd lost track of the conversation.

Antonia whinnied again, setting his teeth on edge. "You are offended, aren't you!" she said teasingly. "Just because he's not French. Aren't you the stubborn one!" Her clammy fingers gripped his palm. "The honeymoon will be in France, of course. I flatly turned down the invitation to Laestra, not that I wouldn't have loved to go. It's so beautiful this time of year. But I absolutely loathe Princess Charlotte. . . ."

Laurent's eyes narrowed at the mention of his childhood friend. Princess Charlotte of Laestra was one of the nicest, kindest, and most intelligent people he knew. In many ways she reminded him of Elizabeth.

". . . And furthermore, she is one girl who should never wear red. She looked absolutely hideous. I told her that, but of course she wouldn't listen." Antonia grinned nastily. "I'm not one to listen to gossip, but I heard Princess Charlotte was recently seen in a Paris nightclub with a gang of American college students!"

The countess shuddered dramatically. "Americans are notorious for trying to wedge their way into noble society."

"Apparently Princess Charlotte met those lowlifes during her recent visit to New York City." Antonia sniffed loudly. "And she had the nerve to snub *me* in Monte Carlo last month! I wish we didn't have to invite her to the wedding, Mummy," she pouted.

"King Josef of Laestra is a dear friend of your father's," the countess said.

Laurent caught himself staring at a white dove that had touched down on the rose arbor. It brought to his mind the legend of the Château d'Amour Inconnu and the brokenhearted lovers who'd lost each other forever. For as long as he could remember, the story had symbolized for him the aura of mystery and romance surrounding the château.

But now the legend filled him with resentment. It had come to represent the traditions and heritage Laurent had been born into, which now demanded that he follow in the footsteps of Prince Frédéric the Third and give up his true love for the sake of duty and honor. *I'm doomed to live the legend—no, the* curse—*of the Château d'Amour Inconnu,* Laurent thought, his heart sinking with despair.

Antonia elbowed him in the side, startling him. Laurent stared at her blankly.

"I said a ski honeymoon will be such fun, don't you agree?" Antonia asked. "My uncle's chalet in Chamonix will be ours for as long as we care to stay. I just love skiing in the Alps. . . ."

Laurent's mind wandered off again. *I wonder if Elizabeth likes to ski. . . .*

A firm tap on his shoulder jolted him back to the present. He realized the countess had smacked him with her fan.

"You look tired, dear," she said to him. "Shall I go inside and fix some tea?"

"No!" Laurent blurted. He exhaled deeply and pushed his fingers through his hair. "What I mean is . . . it's very kind of you to offer, but no, thank you."

"It would help you stay awake," the countess persisted.

Laurent cringed at the thought of that woman in his cottage, rummaging around in his kitchen . . . where Elizabeth had prepared coffee for him only a few days earlier. . . .

A dull ache squeezed his heart. *There's no way I'll let them inside!* he vowed silently. He knew it was ridiculous, but he felt that if he opened up his cottage to the countess and Antonia, it would somehow diminish the memories he cherished of Elizabeth's visits.

"Don't worry, I'll stay awake," Laurent assured them, silently adding, *no matter what.*

Elizabeth hurried through the topiary maze toward Laurent's cottage. Created during the twelfth century, the huge labyrinth was one of the largest in Europe. Elizabeth had gotten lost in it on previous occasions—and had ended up at Laurent's cottage each time.

Maybe he really is my destiny, Elizabeth thought. *But am I ready for a relationship that will change my entire life?* She thought back to the conversation she'd overheard between Henri and the maids on Wednesday night. They'd said Laurent's engagement would be announced at the ball.

Elizabeth shook her head. *I must have misunderstood,* she decided. *Laurent wouldn't ask me to marry him in front of hundreds of strangers. He's much too considerate to turn such a private moment into a public spectacle.* But she knew she wouldn't have a moment of peace until she talked everything over with him.

Elizabeth was surprised—and disappointed—to hear voices as she drew nearer to the cottage. She had counted on Laurent's being alone. For a moment she considered turning around. *Oh, well, I've come this far,* she thought, pushing herself forward.

Elizabeth stepped out of the maze . . . and her heart plummeted.

Laurent was sitting in the garden, holding Antonia's hand.

162

Chapter 11

Elizabeth's jaw dropped. Time seemed to stand still, freezing the scene in the cottage garden into a horrible tableau. In the span of a heartbeat a myriad of impressions flooded her brain.

Laurent and Antonia were seated side by side under the rose arbor, holding hands. He had on a dark pin-striped suit, with a pale blue shirt and gray tie.

Antonia was wearing a blue dress, pearl necklace, and black pumps. Her red hair had been arranged in a tight French braid. A few rose petals and dry leaves were scattered on the ground by their feet. The countess was there too, watching the couple with a smug, calculating look on her face. Her hands were clasped on her lap, the deep ruffles of her pink blouse falling across her knuckles.

Elizabeth shook her head, trying to understand what her eyes were seeing. *Laurent loves* me . . . *but he's holding* Antonia's *hand.* . . .

Suddenly the truth hit Elizabeth like a splash of ice water in her face. *Antonia is his fiancée,* she realized. It was *their* engagement that would be announced at the ball that evening.

What a fool I was to think he was going to propose to me! she thought, giving herself a firm mental kick. Her gaze zeroed in on Laurent's and Antonia's clasped hands resting on the bench between them.

A sharp pain stabbed Elizabeth's heart. She couldn't believe Laurent had deceived her so cruelly. *And with Antonia of all people!* she fumed as she yanked a green bud off the hedges and threw it on the ground. *Was I nothing more than a fun pastime for him while he waited for his engagement to be announced?*

Her anger at its boiling point, Elizabeth strode forward with her hands clenched at her sides. "Did it occur to you even *once* that maybe you should let me *know* you're engaged?" she raged at Laurent.

Everyone turned to her with startled looks on their faces. Laurent immediately dropped Antonia's hand and jumped to his feet. "Elizabeth."

The countess glared at him. "Obviously your family's little au pair girl has taken your attentions toward her too seriously, Your Highness," she said in French. Elizabeth understood every word.

Antonia moved to stand beside Laurent. Looping her arm through his, she gave Elizabeth an insulting

164

up-and-down stare, then turned to her mother. *"Americans,"* she remarked, rolling her eyes.

"I'm proud of what I am," Elizabeth shot back.

The countess laughed coldly and addressed her in English. "Pride won't change your place in society. Only an American could fail to notice the difference between royalty and commoners," she said. "Imagine a prince, a man of worth, taking someone like you seriously."

Elizabeth's temper flashed dangerously. Spots of red seemed to glitter before her eyes, and her nerves were pumped for battle. "How dare you!" she spat furiously.

She glanced at Laurent and realized he wasn't going to say a single word in her defense. He wouldn't even look at her. *Isn't what we shared worth fighting for?* she silently fumed.

Her heart pounded as she waited for him to say or do something to let the di Rimini hags know that he wasn't one of them . . . that he loved and respected Elizabeth even though she wasn't of noble birth.

The seconds ticked by, and still Laurent hadn't made a move. Elizabeth crumpled inwardly as all the fight seeped out of her. She felt abandoned and defeated. *Laurent isn't on my side,* she thought, her heart shattering to pieces. Choking back a sob, she turned and ran out of the garden.

Laurent stared after Elizabeth, panic mounting

inside him. *Don't let her go!* his mind screamed.

Unable to stop himself, he freed his arm from Antonia's tight grip and took off running. "Elizabeth, wait!" he called urgently.

He caught up to her just before she reached the maze. "I love you, Elizabeth," he swore as he swept her up in his arms. "You have to believe me."

"Why, Laurent?" she sobbed. "Why should I believe anything you say?"

Laurent wove his fingers through her silky blond hair and gently tilted her head back so that they were gazing at each other directly. "Because it's the truth," he declared simply.

"Laurent—" Elizabeth pressed a corner of her bottom lip between her teeth. "At the Château d'Amour Inconnu, I'm considered an inferior being, along with my sister and the rest of the servants. *That's* the truth. And it'll never change."

"Neither will the way I feel about you." He pressed his lips against hers and put his whole heart into a deep, searing kiss.

Laurent heard the countess's shrill voice calling him. *My duty,* he groaned to himself. He remembered how much was at stake—the honor of his family and his future as a leader. But giving up his own happiness seemed too high a price.

Elizabeth abruptly ended the kiss. As if she sensed the conflict inside him, she gazed up at him with a question in her eyes.

Laurent felt as though a jagged blade were

bisecting his heart. He longed to put Elizabeth's mind to rest and reassure her that they could have a future together. But that would mean turning his back on his father—which Laurent wasn't willing to do. Elizabeth exhaled shakily. Tears filled her eyes, spilling in streams down her face. She jerked away from him and turned to go.

Laurent watched her disappear into the maze. A cold, empty sensation enveloped him. *I've just lost the only girl I've ever loved,* he realized sadly.

"Laurent!" the countess bellowed impatiently.

Laurent closed his eyes and clenched his jaw. "Duty and honor," he reminded himself under his breath as he headed back to the garden. *No matter how painful,* he added silently.

I never meant for this to happen, Jessica thought as her twin sobbed in her arms that evening. They were sitting on the couch in the nursery, away from the guests and servants buzzing around in the main areas of the château. Jessica had brought up the costumes from the wardrobe room and had laid out everything they would need for the tableau. They had less than an hour to get ready, but Elizabeth's tears showed no sign of easing up anytime soon.

Jessica swallowed against the thickening lump in her throat. She felt as if she were being choked by her own guilt and remorse. If she had told Elizabeth about Antonia and Laurent's engagement from the very start, her twin wouldn't be suffering a broken heart. *But Elizabeth and Laurent were supposed to get together and live happily ever after,* Jessica argued silently in her own defense.

Claudine came over to the couch, waving her pink sash like a banner. "I can't tie this to me," she said.

"I'll help you in minute," Jessica whispered. She glanced over at the other two children. Manon huddled in a corner, sucking her thumb, with a sad look on her face. Pierre was sitting at the table, playing with his plastic miniature soldiers. Jessica had managed to get the children changed into their costumes, but they still had to have their makeup and hair done. They would need to hurry to be ready on time.

"Elizabeth, listen to me," Jessica began in a gentle but firm tone. "The tableau starts in less than an hour." She leaned back and looked her twin in the eye. "Are we going to drop out of the game?" Jessica asked.

Elizabeth's eyes were puffy and red from crying. She drew in a shuddering breath, her chin quivering. "I can't believe what a fool I was," she sobbed.

Jessica gave her shoulders a brief shake. "Don't think about that right now. We have to get ready for the tableau."

"They were holding hands!" Elizabeth wailed. Fresh tears cascaded down her cheeks. "Why wasn't he honest with me from the beginning?"

Jessica flinched. *Why wasn't I honest with her from the beginning?*

Elizabeth hiccuped sharply. "I just want to go back to Sweet Valley."

"No, you don't," Jessica countered gently.

"I do," Elizabeth said with a shuddering gasp.

Jessica shook her head. "Elizabeth, if we win the tableau, we'll be beating all those royals and nobles at their own game."

Elizabeth sniffed loudly and reached for the tissue box on the side table. "I just can't do it, Jess. I can't face all those people . . . like this."

"Sure, you can," Jessica replied encouragingly.

Elizabeth shook her head and blew her nose. "I just want to stay in my room."

Jessica pressed her bottom lip between her teeth and let out a sharp breath. *I could just punch those di Rimini hags for doing this to Elizabeth,* she thought angrily. *Laurent too, that spineless prince!*

Elizabeth exhaled a shaky breath. "I feel absolutely miserable."

"Think how miserable you'll feel if you let those hags win the tableau," Jessica suggested.

Elizabeth pulled out another tissue and wiped her eyes. "I don't know, Jess. . . ."

Jessica gulped. She hated the idea of forfeiting their chance to win the tableau. But it didn't seem as if she was getting very far with Elizabeth. Jessica decided to appeal to her twin's higher instincts.

"Think of the kids," Jessica said. "They worked

169

so hard during the rehearsal, and they're so excited. Imagine how crushed they would be if we dropped out."

Elizabeth lowered her eyes and began fiddling with a loose string in her jeans. "I didn't believe they could keep still for minutes at a time."

Jessica felt a small flutter of hope. It was the first nonmiserable thing her twin had said since she'd returned from Laurent's cottage. Maybe her pep talk was working its way through Elizabeth's muddled brain.

"We need you," Jessica pleaded. "You're the only one who knows how to turn a toilet paper roll into an elegant hairstyle," she added jokingly.

The corners of Elizabeth's mouth twitched, as if she were trying to smile.

At that instant Pierre yelled, "Stop!"

Jessica looked over and saw that Claudine had crept under the table and secretly tied his feet together with her pink sash. "Come on, you guys," Jessica pleaded.

Claudine was kneeling next to Pierre's chair, fumbling with the sash. "I can't untie it now," she yelled.

Jessica rolled her eyes and started to get up, but her twin stopped her.

"I'll handle it," Elizabeth offered, her voice suddenly firm and steady as she walked over to the table. "Claudine, you go sit next to Jessica. After I untie your brother, I'm going to do your hair."

"Go, Liz!" Jessica cheered, incredibly relieved.

170

Elizabeth gave a smile over her shoulder. Her eyes were still red but no longer brimming with hopelessness. "We don't have all day, Jess. Don't you think it's time you got into your fairy godmother costume?"

Jessica giggled. "She's back, and she's as bossy as ever!" she declared happily.

Kneeling at Pierre's feet, Elizabeth pulled apart the tight knot his sister had tied in the sash. "OK, Miss Cinderella, come here and let me put this around your waist where it belongs," she ordered.

Claudine came bounding over to her. "Is your stomachache all better now?" she asked.

Elizabeth smiled. Jessica's words had stirred her fighting spirit back to life. "My stomach feels fine," she answered. She threaded the sash through the loops around Claudine's dress and tied the ends in a pretty bow. "You're a beautiful Cinderella," she said. "And Pierre is a handsome footman. I'm sure we're going to win the tableau contest."

Claudine and Pierre cheered.

Elizabeth settled them on opposite ends of the couch with a pile of picture books between them and a stern warning to be still.

"Now it's your turn," she said, scooping Manon into her arms. The little girl giggled and hugged Elizabeth's neck.

She dressed Manon in the long gray shift they'd chosen for a stepsister costume, then sat her down at their makeup table. "Mademoiselle Jessica put spots on my nose and made me into a monster," Manon boasted.

"I remember," Elizabeth said as she uncapped a black eyebrow pencil. "And after I put them back on your nose, I'm going to put some on mine."

Elizabeth was brushing dark shadows under Manon's eyes when Jessica returned. "It's my fairy godmother!" Claudine exclaimed.

Jessica executed a graceful pirouette, ending with a deep curtsy.

"You look absolutely beautiful," Elizabeth said.

Jessica took another spin in front of the mirror and smiled at her reflection. "I do, don't I?"

Elizabeth chuckled. "And you're so humble," she teased. She picked up the empty toilet paper roll that was on the table and waved it at Jessica. "Time for your hair appointment, fairy!"

Elizabeth wound her twin's hair around the cardboard cylinder, building it into a sleek, elegant tower. Then, using thick globs of setting gel, she twisted strands of hair around her finger and let them drop along the sides of Jessica's face in delicate, wispy curls.

"That's nice," Elizabeth remarked, stepping back to admire her work. Next she took out Jessica's emerald pendant and secured the chain around the tall chignon with hairpins. Elizabeth carefully arranged the pendant so that the stone draped at the center of Jessica's forehead. "It looks exotic," Elizabeth said.

172

Jessica looked at the effect in the mirror. "Fairy godmothers tend to be very exotic." She jumped to her feet and waved Elizabeth into the chair. "It's your turn now, wicked stepmother," she announced with a mischievous grin.

"I was just getting to that," Elizabeth murmured. The truth was, she hated the idea of appearing before the de Sainte-Maries and all their guests dressed as the wicked stepmother in an ugly mustard-colored dress and with hideous makeup on her face.

Jessica uncapped a green makeup pencil and began outlining Elizabeth's lips. "You're going to be the ugliest-looking woman to have ever set foot in this château," Jessica promised, then added with a giggle, "well, the third ugliest anyway. I don't think you can ever outdo the countess and Antonia, even with your lips painted green."

Elizabeth chuckled weakly. *I wonder what Laurent will think of me when he sees me in the tableau,* she thought. Her heart ached at the memory of his last kiss, but she refused to let herself fall apart again.

Finally they were all ready. The twins rounded up the children. "Remember, when it's our turn, we have to be perfectly still—just like statues," Elizabeth instructed.

"And Pierre, if you tickle Claudine's foot, I'm going to strangle you," Jessica warned. Elizabeth noticed that her pendant had slipped to the side.

"Just a minute, Jess." Elizabeth grabbed a few more hairpins and, pushing back Jessica's lace veil, anchored the chain around her twin's forehead more securely. "There," she said, adjusting the veil around her sister's face. "I think we're finally ready!"

Chapter 12

Laurent followed Prince Nicolas and Princess Catherine into the makeshift theater in the west wing of the château. All the guests stood up and applauded the royal family.

The convertible walls that normally separated the parlor, the music room, and the library had been rolled back to create a single large space. A platform stage with a red velvet curtain had been set up at one end. There was a door behind it that would allow the presenters to get onstage without being seen by the audience. Strains of music resonated from the end of the room, where the world-famous pianist Lirlyna Kyung was performing on Princess Catherine's Steinway grand piano.

Laurent slouched in his front-row seat, a heavy, dull ache in his gut. He kept replaying that morning's horrible scene in the garden in vivid detail . . .

the tears shimmering in Elizabeth's eyes, the sadness in their blue-green depths . . . the trembling of her soft lips. . . . Laurent hated himself for hurting her. He knew it was wrong not to have been honest with her from the start.

Elizabeth had accused Laurent of deceiving her in order to play a cruel joke on her. But it was himself he'd tried to deceive . . . and if there had been a cruel joke played out, it had been on him.

The professional master of ceremonies hired for the occasion stepped up to the front of the room. After he welcomed everyone on behalf of the de Sainte-Marie family, he officially called for the game to begin. Laurent realized he would see Elizabeth soon, and a burst of excited anticipation shot through him. He would have the luxury of being able to gaze at her for the five-minute span of the tableau.

The lights dimmed, leaving only the spotlights that shone on the stage. Then the red velvet curtain parted to reveal the first tableau, which was presented by Antonia and the countess di Rimini.

Standing on wooden boxes, the two of them were dressed in matching silver evening gowns, with diamond tiaras on their heads and more diamonds around their necks, arms, and ankles. The countess was holding up what looked like a gold baton.

"Dazzling," Laurent heard someone remark. *They certainly are* that, he agreed dryly.

The room buzzed with conversation as the

audience tried to guess the tableau. "The Gemini twins," a man called out.

A woman in the back of the room shouted, "The morning star and the evening star."

"Miss Universe and the first-runner-up," someone else tried. Laurent noticed the countess's expression harden slightly at that guess.

More guesses followed, all of them wrong. When the buzzer finally sounded that the tableau's time was up, there was a collective sigh of relief in the room. The master of ceremonies helped the women step down from the boxes. Laurent could see the fury in the countess's eyes.

"A hint, please?" someone in the audience called out.

The countess raised the baton over her head. "This is my thunderbolt," she said crisply.

"Yes, but who are you?" another person blurted. Several people laughed. Antonia pursed her lips in a sullen pout.

"Please put us out of our mystery, dear ladies, and tell what your tableau depicted," the master of ceremonies said with a bow.

"I am Zeus, and my daughter is Hera," the countess said.

The master of ceremonies nodded blankly. "Please continue your explanation," he said.

The countess glared at him with a haughty look. "From the Greek myth," she replied. "Zeus, the god of the sky, and his wife, Hera."

The audience responded with a few drawn-out "Oh's" and a smattering of applause. "That was going to be my very next guess," a man blurted from the back of the room as the curtain closed.

Laurent knew that Elizabeth's tableau was next. His heart pounded against his chest like a drum. *When the curtain opens again, she will be onstage.*

The next few minutes passed torturously slowly. Laurent nervously drummed his fingers on the arms of his chair, then absently traced one of the swirls in the intricately carved design. Finally the second tableau was announced.

The curtain opened, and there she was. "Elizabeth," Laurent breathed. Focusing only on her, he soaked in every detail—the hideous yellow-brown dress she wore . . . her ramrod posture . . . the matronly hat on her head . . . the laced, pointy-toed boots on her feet. . . . Two dark blemishes had been painted on the side of her nose. Dark smudges circled her eyes. Her lips were colored a ghastly shade of reddish green.

She's absolutely fabulous! Laurent thought. The rest of the audience seemed to agree as they responded enthusiastically to the tableau with praising comments and warm laughter.

Does Elizabeth even know how utterly enchanting she looks on the stage? Laurent wondered. But looking deep into her eyes, he could see how miserable she was. She was obviously struggling valiantly to remain in character.

Laurent swallowed against the thickening in his throat. He was incredibly proud of her . . . and so much in love with her that his heart felt as if it might explode any second.

Elizabeth's hand rested on Manon's shoulder. Both of them were snarling across the stage at Claudine, who, as Cinderella, sat primly on a stool with her legs sticking out. Pierre was kneeling in front of her, holding the glass slipper up to her bare foot.

Laurent chuckled, wondering what threats they'd used to keep Pierre from tickling Claudine's foot.

Jessica, the fairy godmother, was standing behind the stool in a light green gown that shimmered under the lights. Her head was covered with a lace veil, and a large green stone pendant adorned her forehead.

Both sisters were beautiful. But Elizabeth's sweetness and generosity made her irresistibly attractive, even in the role of the wicked stepmother.

Laurent felt a sudden tap on his shoulder. He turned and saw that the countess di Rimini had taken the seat right behind his. "Antonia will be out in a minute," she told him pointedly.

Laurent responded with a slight nod and faced forward, his heart sinking. He was bound by duty and honor to follow the plans that had been carefully arranged for him. His feelings for Elizabeth didn't change a thing. *She's not mine . . . and she never will be,* he reminded himself.

The countess tapped his shoulder again and leaned toward him, stirring up a draft of cloying perfume. "How simpleminded and unsophisticated!" she complained in a raspy whisper. "Leave it to the Americans to present a scene from such a common children's story."

Laurent bristled. "I think they're charming," he retorted.

The countess gripped the back of his chair. "Your young siblings are adorable, of course," she amended. "But those au pair girls . . ." She exhaled a sharp sigh of indignation, fanning Laurent's ear with her stale, hot breath.

Laurent clenched his fists and pressed them into the sides of his chair. "I think," he began, disciplining his voice to a low, even tone, "Elizabeth and Jessica Wakefield are two of the most intelligent, creative, resourceful, compassionate, and friendly girls I've ever met."

"Maybe so," the countess returned with a haughty smirk. "But as au pairs—"

"As au pairs," Laurent repeated sharply, cutting her off, "Elizabeth and Jessica are doing an excellent job. More, my brother and sisters adore them." With that he turned around, his face hot with the anger that simmered just beneath the surface.

His stepmother glanced at him just then, and obviously presuming that he and the countess were having a friendly chat, Princess Catherine gave him a broad smile of approval. Laurent sighed wearily.

The countess di Rimini gripped the back of his chair and pressed on, relentless, astonishing Laurent with her stubborn vindictiveness. "*Look* at them," she hissed into his ear. "Those girls are wearing dresses of style and worth—and they *still* manage to present an image of low-class vulgarity and cheap garishness." The countess shuddered dramatically. "That one with the darkened eyes and garish lipstick looks positively frightening."

Laurent realized she was talking about Elizabeth, and his temper snapped. *That's it,* he resolved, primed for battle. He could sense how difficult it was for Elizabeth to maintain her position on that stage, her heart bleeding after having been ripped to shreds that very morning.

By me, Laurent reminded himself. Waves of guilt and remorse crashed over him. He knew with gut certainty that he'd never forgive himself for the pain he'd caused Elizabeth. *But I'm not going to stand by and let her be insulted by this nasty, ignorant snob!*

"And her sister, the *fairy godmother,*" the countess uttered snidely.

Laurent turned around fully and glared at her. "If you dislike the tableau so strongly, then I suggest you leave!"

The countess suddenly blanched. Her jaw dropped, and her eyes blazed with a look of shocked rage. A choking gasp escaped from her open mouth.

Laurent was surprised by her reaction. He hadn't thought his words would pack such a wallop, especially on someone as dense and self-righteous as the countess. Then he realized that she wasn't even looking at him. Her eyes were fixed on something in the *Cinderella* tableau.

Elizabeth silently counted the passing seconds to distract herself as she maintained her pose in the tableau. She'd done the math in her head—there were three hundred seconds in five minutes, and she had more than two hundred seconds left to go. Then the timer would buzz, signaling the end of her torture.

Elizabeth wondered if her evil-stepmother scowl would last that long. Her lips were already twitching with cramps, and the muscles in her neck and jaw felt as if they'd turned to stone. She had an itch behind her left knee, and something sharp was poking her upper back.

Elizabeth felt totally miserable on the inside too. Despair and heartbreak hovered at the edge of her thoughts, threatening her composure. She didn't look into the audience for fear that she might catch a glimpse of Laurent.

Elizabeth knew that without the constant distraction of counting off the seconds, her mind would drift into the danger zone. She would probably fall apart and have to finish the rest of the tableau as a sobbing heap in the middle of the stage.

Elizabeth felt a glimmer of relief when she mentally counted up to two hundred and forty—the tableau would last only one more minute. The itch behind her left knee had spread to include her ankle, her elbow, and a spot just above her lips.

Suddenly Elizabeth heard the countess di Rimini's voice shriek angrily. The children reacted immediately. Manon threw her arms around Elizabeth's legs and hid her face in the stepmother costume. Claudine dropped her foot, Pierre jumped up, and both of them looked to the twins for reassurance.

Elizabeth's heart sank. All their hard work, everything she'd endured . . . it had all been for nothing.

Then she got mad. *That woman has gone too far this time*, she thought.

She and Jessica exchanged meaningful looks. Elizabeth understood that her twin felt the same way. They turned toward the audience and faced the rude heckler together.

The countess was standing close to the stage. "Shameless," she raged, glaring at the twins. Then she whirled around and stormed out of the parlor.

Later that evening Jessica stood in front of the mirror in her bedroom, inspecting her appearance. The lavender silk ball gown had been an inspired choice. It fit her perfectly, as if it had been created especially for her. The full skirt swirled gracefully when she moved. She was wearing long white gloves that covered her arms up to her elbows and gave her an especially sophisticated formal look. The gloves would have covered her new bracelet, so she'd decided to wear it with the pearls around her ankle instead.

Jessica picked up her emerald pendant and held it to her neck. She still hadn't decided whether to wear it to the ball or not. "I think it's beautiful," she declared. But Jacques's words still rang in her ears, mocking her for admiring such a "garish piece of junk."

For several minutes Jessica debated with herself, picking up the stone and putting it back down. *Since when do I let other people dictate my style!* she fumed. She was sick of royal snobs and their superior attitudes. Jacques would soon learn that she wasn't the sort of girl he could push around.

Jessica put the chain around her neck and smiled at her reflection. The pendant shimmered in the light from her lamp. "I'm wearing it tonight, and no one is going to stop me," she declared.

She rotated the clasp to the front to fasten it, then adjusted it so that the pendant draped in a graceful V at the base of her throat. The effect was absolutely stunning. Jessica exhaled a deep, satisfied sigh.

Just then she heard a heavy knock at her door. "Come in, Liz," she responded, presuming it was her twin. Jessica hoped that Elizabeth's spirits had lifted since their disastrous tableau.

But when the door burst open, the countess di Rimini marched into the room, with two armed guards behind her. The witch pointed to Jessica's pendant and shouted, "That's it! The girl is a thief!" The countess raged in English.

Jessica stepped back, stunned. "What!" she exclaimed. "How dare you accuse me!"

One of the guards came forward. "How long have you had that piece of jewelry?" he asked.

"Since my boyfriend gave it to me," she retorted.

"Enough!" the countess bellowed at the guards. "I want her locked up immediately. You can ask your questions later." Her thin lips twisted into a cruel smile. "I'm sure her answers will be much more truthful after she's spent a night in the dungeon."

"No!" Jessica pleaded. "I can explain everything. . . . I didn't steal it. . . ."

Heedless to her cries, the guards grabbed her by her arms and dragged her out of her room.

Chapter 13

"No more jumping on the bed, kids!" Elizabeth ordered, punctuating her words with a loud clap. She and the children were in her room, getting ready for the ball.

"My bow fell off again," Manon complained, holding the pink barrette up to Elizabeth.

"Come here," Elizabeth said with an indulgent smile. She brushed Manon's hair and reattached the bow-shaped barrette. "It would stay there if you'd stop jumping around like a little rabbit."

"I want to dress up like a rabbit next time when we play tableau," Manon immediately declared.

Elizabeth groaned inwardly. *Let's hope there never is a next time,* she thought, recalling the countess's rude behavior during their tableau.

The countess was a one-woman riot starter, stirring up hot tempers wherever she was. Only a few minutes earlier Elizabeth had heard her shrieking in the hall. Totally uninterested, she'd stayed in her room with her door firmly closed. She hadn't felt curious enough to find out what the commotion was about or even to peek out of her room.

Elizabeth turned her attention to her reflection in the mirror. Except for some puffiness around her eyes, she looked fine. She was wearing an elegant gown of white brocade, with a fitted bodice and thin straps over the shoulders.

Elizabeth slipped a pair of silky white gloves over her arms and looked at the effect in the mirror. "Nice!" she exclaimed.

She was surprised to see herself actually smiling. *I'm beautiful,* she thought confidently. *Those witches haven't knocked me down yet—and they never will!* she vowed.

"OK, everyone line up for a group inspection." The children rushed over and squeezed together in front of the mirror, giggling.

Earlier that evening Elizabeth had dreaded having to take charge of the children. But she owed it to Jessica, who had stayed with them at the tableau while Elizabeth had escaped to her room for a long, hard cry.

But now, laughing at their hilarious expressions as they preened in front of the mirror,

Elizabeth realized that the children had helped lighten her gloomy mood. Despite everything that had gone wrong that day, she wasn't filled with dread at the thought of walking into the ball. No matter what anyone said, deep in her heart Elizabeth knew Laurent loved her as much as she loved him. Antonia di Rimini meant nothing to him.

Elizabeth exhaled a deep sigh. Maybe she would even muster up the courage to confront him with the question that burned in her mind—why was he planning to marry a girl he didn't love. . . .

From the corner of her eye Elizabeth noticed Pierre and Claudine exchange mysterious looks. "What's going on?" she asked, glaring at them in the mirror.

"Don't tell her," Pierre insisted.

Elizabeth folded her arms. "I'm waiting. . . ."

"It's a secret," Claudine explained.

Elizabeth pulled Manon away and bent down to her level. "You'll tell me what they're up to, won't you, sweetie?"

"Maybe they want to dress up as bunny rabbits too," Manon offered.

Elizabeth rose to her full height and leaned against the door. She knew Claudine and Pierre were up to no good, and she feared they might be planning to pull a prank at the ball. Elizabeth refused to risk another public humiliation. "No one leaves this room until you tell me the secret," she announced.

Claudine's jaw dropped. "Forever?"

Elizabeth nodded. "You're my prisoners."

Finally Pierre cracked. "We found a place at the beach where there's lots of little crabs. Tomorrow we're going to go there and catch them." He lowered his voice to a whisper. "And then we're going to dump them out in the countess di Rimini's bed."

"We know where she sleeps," Claudine added.

Elizabeth pressed her hand to her mouth to keep herself from bursting out laughing.

"Here she comes!" Pierre gasped.

Elizabeth frowned, wondering what he meant. Then she heard it too: heavy footsteps and the countess's loud voice bellowing out commands and threats. Elizabeth slouched back against her door and crossed her arms. *Doesn't that nasty hag ever take a rest?* she thought.

The commotion grew louder and louder. Suddenly Elizabeth's door was thrown open, knocking her to the floor with its force. She landed heavily on her side, her elbow slamming against the hardwood floor. Elizabeth groaned at the sharp, pinching pain that shot up and down her arm.

Elizabeth lifted her head and turned around, her eyes wide with shock and anger.

The countess was standing over her, snarling like a vicious, rabid dog. Elizabeth almost expected to see foamy saliva spewing all over the woman's fleshy jowls. She was accompanied by two uniformed guards, who came forward and roughly hauled Elizabeth up by her arms.

"What is going on?" Elizabeth demanded as she struggled to loosen her arms out of the guards' tight hold.

The children looked terrified as they huddled together on the small, four-poster bed, sobbing hysterically. The countess approached them. Manon buried her face in the pillow.

"Go away!" Pierre screamed.

Tears pooled in Elizabeth's eyes, blurring her vision. The sound of the children's frightened cries pierced her heart like hot daggers. "Leave the kids alone!" she pleaded.

The witch whirled around, her eyes blazing. "You have no right to hand out orders, young lady."

Elizabeth flinched, as if she'd been slapped across the face. *Why does this person hate me so much?* she wondered.

The countess stepped closer to the children. "Don't be afraid," she cooed in French in a shrill, evil-sounding voice. "Your au pair girls are very bad criminals—they've stolen something very valuable from me. But we're going to lock them up so they can't hurt you."

"What?" Elizabeth gasped, enraged. "That's a lie! We haven't stolen anything from you, and you know it!"

The countess jerked her head around and waved dismissal with her arm. "Take her out of my sight," she commanded the guards. "Her face sickens me."

Elizabeth struggled desperately to get free as the guards dragged her toward the door. The children screamed and begged them not to take her away.

"Go to Anna," Elizabeth shouted to them. "And don't be afraid. This is all a big mistake. I'll be fine, and I'll probably see you later at the ball."

But as the guards led her to the back of the château and down a cold stone staircase, Elizabeth hoped her parting words to the children hadn't been a lie.

Alone in his cottage, Laurent gazed at the fire burning in the hearth. He was scheduled to make his entrance at the ball in twenty minutes. Guests from all over the world had been arriving at the château since the previous evening.

After this evening my days of freedom are over for good, Laurent realized with a sinking feeling in his gut. He braced his elbows on his knees and hung his head. His future seemed to spread out before him like a barren, desolate trail. *If only I had the girl I love at my side . . .* , he thought. He pictured himself and Elizabeth standing together at the ball as everyone cheered their announcement and wished them well. . . .

Laurent squeezed his eyes shut in a feeble attempt to block the image from his mind. It hurt to think about what might have been. But Elizabeth's beautiful face continued to haunt him, as he knew it would for the rest of his life.

Laurent rubbed his hand over his mouth and sat back, staring at the ceiling. The burden of his duty and honor weighed him down like a huge marble slab strapped to his back. And now he'd dragged Elizabeth down too.

A knock at the door caught him by surprise. His heart leaped to his throat. Lately the only person who ever dropped by unexpectedly had been Elizabeth. *Please let it be her,* he hoped as he rushed across the room. He longed to hold her one last time . . . and kiss her sweet lips . . . and hear her say that she loved him. . . .

Laurent's hands trembled as he unlatched the door. But it was his father who stood there. Laurent's heart plummeted with bitter disappointment.

Prince Nicolas walked into the cottage with a purposeful stride, his face drawn into a grim expression. "I have something to tell you." He spoke in French, his voice low and serious. "Sit down, Laurent. This might be difficult for you to hear."

Antonia has broken our engagement? Laurent thought snidely as he returned to the couch.

"The American girls have betrayed our trust," his father told him.

Laurent stiffened. "What do you mean?" he demanded.

Prince Nicolas sat down in the chair across from Laurent and leaned forward. "They've been implicated in the theft of the countess di Rimini's emerald."

"That's ridiculous!" Laurent retorted. "That woman has been out to destroy Elizabeth and Jessica from the moment they arrived. You saw her at the tableau! She was rude and disruptive."

His father shook his head gravely. "That doesn't change the facts, son. Those girls are thieves—and liars. I shudder to think of how we trusted them with the little ones."

"It's simply not true," Laurent argued. "Whatever the countess may have said—"

"The guards found the countess's pendant less than an hour ago," Prince Nicolas told him. "And do you know where?"

Laurent rubbed his knuckle against his lips as he stared at his father. "Where?" he challenged.

"In their quarters," his father replied. "Hanging from a gold chain around one of their necks."

Laurent reeled back, as if he had been socked in the jaw. "I still don't believe it. Elizabeth and Jessica are not thieves!"

His father gave him a sympathetic look. "I know you trusted them. We all did," he admitted. "There's a lesson to be learned from our mistake. The only ones you can trust in this world are people like yourself, people on equal footing who have no need or desire to steal from you."

Laurent's temper flared. "That's ridiculous, Father! It's that kind of nonsense that keeps us locked in the Middle Ages."

Prince Nicolas exhaled wearily. "You can't argue with the evidence. Those girls were caught with the stolen emerald. Isn't that enough to convince you of their guilt?" he questioned. "Or would you prefer to hold your judgment until one of them shows up wearing the di Riminis' diamond necklace?"

"No!" Laurent shouted. But deep in his mind a kernel of doubt existed. "Elizabeth and her sister can't be guilty," he insisted.

"Are you trying to convince me of their innocence?" his father asked pointedly. "Or yourself?"

Laurent clenched his jaw. His father's barb had struck a nerve. "I already know they're innocent," he stated. But even to his ears, his voice sounded slightly weaker.

Elizabeth . . . a thief? Laurent wondered, forcing himself to consider the difficult possibility. He had fallen for her so quickly and completely. Maybe he *was* blinded by his strong feelings. He closed his eyes and groaned to himself. Maybe it was safer to stick to tradition and duty and to forget about love. . . .

Prince Nicolas rose to his feet. "I must return to the château now," he commented, adding,

"you're expected to arrive on time this evening."
He offered his hand to Laurent.

Laurent hesitated. Finally, with a deep sigh, he stood up and shook hands with his father. "I'll be there," he promised as he walked him to the door.

"Never oppose the countess unless you absolutely must," Prince Nicolas warned. "She's an important ally. Likewise, she would prove to be a formidable foe."

Laurent nodded. He knew his father was right. The countess di Rimini wielded power in both social and political circles. But the thought of having her as a mother-in-law turned his stomach.

Curled up in a fetal position on the hard stone floor, Jessica sobbed. The sound echoed in the cavernous dungeon, as if the walls were mocking her cries. She thought of Jacques and her life back in Sweet Valley. "What if I never get out of here?" she wailed. No one who might be able to help her knew where she was. *I don't even know where I am,* she realized.

Her one last hope was Elizabeth. As twins they shared a deep connection and often sensed when the other was in trouble. *Please find me, Elizabeth!* Jessica's mind screamed desperately. *I need you!*

She heard someone coming and jumped to her feet. Standing on tiptoes, she peered through the small barred window in the heavy wooden door. Two burly guards were dragging her sister toward the cell. Jessica's heart sank.

The guards swung open the door of her cell with a loud, metal clang. They thrust Elizabeth to the floor.

"She says to leave them secured," one of the guards reminded the other.

Jessica knew exactly who "she" referred to. *I'd like to choke the living daylights out of that countess,* she fumed. The guards chained Elizabeth and Jessica to the wall with metal cuffs around their wrists and ankles.

"Please don't do this," Elizabeth begged, tears streaming down her face. "You don't understand!"

The guards ignored her. With a heavy clang, they slammed the huge wood and metal door on the twins.

"I don't understand any of this!" Jessica cried. "That pendant they accused me of stealing isn't even valuable." She rubbed her back against the rough surface of the stone wall to scratch an itch. At this point it hardly mattered if she ruined the silk gown.

"You're sure?" Elizabeth asked tearfully.

Jessica nodded. "Jacques told me the stone was fake when he gave it to me on the train. He gave me the pearl bracelet to replace the emerald." She glanced at her ankle and let out an angry groan of disappointment. "It's gone. It must have fallen off when those goons dragged me down here."

Elizabeth smoothed her white gown over her knees. Jessica saw that it was stained and ripped along the hem. "You would have looked beautiful at the ball," Jessica murmured.

"Thanks," Elizabeth replied glumly. "I'll bet this doesn't have anything to do with the jewelry. The countess has it in for me because of my relationship with Laurent. I'm convinced she would stop at nothing to get me out of the way—even if it means framing us for jewel theft and locking us up in this dungeon."

Dragging her chains on the floor, Jessica reached over and patted Elizabeth's hand. "Don't worry. Jacques knows this castle inside out. He'll save us."

Elizabeth sighed wearily. "Laurent does too. The question is—do they know we're down here?"

"Jacques will find us. I'm sure of it," Jessica said. But inside, she wasn't so sure. She'd left him with some very harsh words. *What if he thinks I really don't want to see him anymore and goes away for good?* she worried. A feeling of cold panic moved through Jessica's body, like ice water in her veins. *What if no one ever finds us?*

Elizabeth turned to her with a blank expression. "There's something I don't understand," she said. "If Jacques gave you the bracelet to *replace* the pendant, why did you still have the pendant?"

Jessica cracked a tiny smile. "He wanted me to get rid of it. He claimed it was too junky for me," she explained. "But I refused to go along with him. He even tried to sneak it out of my room a few times." Tears sprang into her eyes as she recalled their many scrimmages over the emerald. "We had so much fun fighting over that emerald," she added wistfully.

Elizabeth narrowed her eyes and shook her head. "Jessica, that doesn't make sense. Why would he have bothered with the emerald if it were a fake?"

Jessica chewed her bottom lip as a disturbing possibility began to take shape in her mind. *Jacques was on the train when the countess screamed about her stolen heirloom,* she remembered. He had given it to her just before he'd gotten off the train.

She thought back to the times she'd spent with Jacques at the château. He'd always made excuses to go to her room, and she'd caught him red-handed several times. Jessica had assumed their heated scrimmages over the pendant had all been a game, a kind of flirting. *Maybe I was wrong. Maybe that emerald was the real—and only—reason for his visits to the Château D'Amour Inconnu.*

Jessica squeezed her eyes shut as pieces of a frightening puzzle fell into place. *Jacques is the thief,* she realized. He's *the one who framed me!*

She didn't want to believe any of it, but the truth was like a wailing scream tearing through her mind, shattering her heart like glass. *Elizabeth and I might be left in this medieval dungeon to die . . . because of Jacques Landeau!*

HAPPILY
EVER AFTER

Written by
Kate William

Created by
FRANCINE PASCAL

BANTAM BOOKS
NEW YORK · TORONTO · LONDON · SYDNEY · AUCKLAND

To Anna Smith

Chapter 1

"This is a nightmare!" Jessica Wakefield moaned. She tossed her blond hair to one side and stifled yet another round of tears that threatened to overflow her eyes. "We were supposed to have the greatest summer ever, and now we may never even see daylight again."

Jessica rubbed her wrist where the iron cuffs chafed her skin. She and her twin, Elizabeth, were chained to a dank and moldy stone wall in the dungeon of the Château d'Amour Inconnu on a remote island in France.

Under most circumstances Jessica would have been happy, considering the way her lavender ball gown fit snugly around her body, showing off her curves. Its fluffy skirt billowed to the floor around her legs, and elbow-length white gloves gave her a sophisticated elegance. But what good was a

1

beautiful gown when no one could see her?

Upstairs the prince and princess de Sainte-Marie were hosting a glittering ball, with music and dancing and champagne. That's where the twins would have been if they hadn't been accused of stealing a valuable jewel.

"Oh, why did this happen?" Jessica wailed.

"Well, it wasn't my idea to come to Europe as an au pair this summer," Elizabeth grumbled. "I wish I'd never left Sweet Valley!" She wrapped her free arm around the fitted bodice of her stunning white ball gown. Her blond hair was arranged in large curls atop her head, with a single strand dramatically framing the right side of her face.

"Me too," Jessica said. It seemed as if they'd been away from their friends and family back in California for years instead of weeks.

Jessica knew she'd bullied Elizabeth into accepting the au pair position, but she had imagined them living like princesses at the château. Instead they had been thrown in the dungeon like criminals. She pounded her fist on the little cot in the cell with sudden vehemence. "I could kill Jacques for giving me that stupid emerald!" she cried in frustration.

Jacques Landeau, supposedly the future duke of Norveaux, was the sexy young Frenchman Jessica had met while they were traveling from Paris to the royal château. He was tall and incredibly handsome, with dark brown hair and almond-shaped, deep brown eyes. He swept her off her feet with his sultry French accent and flowery words, and when he gave her an emerald pendant, she just knew she was in love with him.

Elizabeth shot her a scathing look. "You would have to fall in love with a jewel thief," she said accusingly. "Why didn't you listen when people told you there was no such place as Norveaux?" Her tone turned sarcastic. "Jacques Landeau, the duke of Norveaux. *Please!*"

"You don't know for sure that he stole it!" Jessica insisted. "And besides, I'm not the only one who fell for the wrong guy. Since when do you steal other girls' boyfriends?"

Elizabeth winced, and Jessica smiled triumphantly. Her sister had been more than a little swept off her feet by darkly handsome Laurent de Sainte-Marie, eldest son of the prince and princess. Because Elizabeth and Jessica were responsible for taking care of his younger brother and sisters, Elizabeth and Laurent had been thrown together more than once. Their chance encounters had quickly become planned rendezvous.

Jessica had actually encouraged the relationship all along. After all, her sister deserved an incredible guy like Laurent. Why should a silly little thing like his fiancée get in the way? But now Elizabeth was attacking Jacques, and Jessica wasn't about to sit around and be the only person who felt lousy.

"He said he loved me," Elizabeth said, and Jessica heard the tears in her sister's voice. "I was so sure he

3

was telling the truth. I don't understand how he could tell me that while he was engaged to Antonia."

Antonia and her mother, wicked and snobbish Countess Doloria di Rimini, had traveled with Jessica and Elizabeth on the train from Paris to the château. Both red haired and green eyed, they imperiously ordered everyone around and expected the first and best of whatever was available, whether food or service. From the start they had given the twins nothing but grief, and it was the countess who finally accused them of stealing her emerald pendant.

"I just want to get out of here." Jessica groaned, shivering in the damp. "This cell is so dark and cold!" There was one barred window in the stout wooden door and another window high in the opposite wall, where Jessica could just see stars in the sky. One dim lightbulb hung from the ceiling, giving off only enough light for them to see each other.

"If we do ever get out of here, I never want to leave home again," Elizabeth said, tugging on the chains that bound her to the wall.

Jessica and Elizabeth were identical twins, but their long blond hair and stunning blue-green eyes were practically all they had in common. Jessica was impetuous and a first-class flirt, not above stealing another girl's boyfriend if she wanted him. Elizabeth was a good student and far more serious. Before they left home, she had had a steady boyfriend, Todd Wilkins, and would never even

4

have thought of being with another guy.

At least Todd and Liz broke up before we left, Jessica thought. *Todd's such a drip, and Laurent is so much more exciting. I'm glad I burned the one letter Todd sent her. Elizabeth didn't need the grief!*

Jessica always enjoyed being the more adventurous twin but never hesitated to coax Elizabeth into helping her out when she got herself into trouble with her wild schemes. Sometimes she even thought her sister *liked* to swoop in and save the day.

Only now Jessica's wild nature had landed them in a dungeon, and neither one of them was enjoying it.

"I wish Dad had never even mentioned this stupid au pair job!" Jessica complained, trying to remove some of the blame from herself. She shifted on the hard cot, tucking her left foot under her right leg.

"Just because he mentioned it didn't mean we had to go for it," Elizabeth snapped, tugging at the chains again. The clattering of the metal against the bricks was beginning to grate on Jessica's nerves.

"Why do you keep pulling on those things? Have you suddenly developed some kind of super-human strength?" Jessica asked irritably.

Elizabeth heaved an impatient sigh, as if Jessica had just asked the most ridiculous question in the world. "This château is hundreds of years old. These chains might be rusted enough to pull away," she explained impatiently.

"I never thought of that," Jessica said, and she tugged at hers too. "They feel pretty tight to me."

5

"Yeah, but at least it's something to do. I can't *stand* just *sitting* here," Elizabeth said vehemently.

"But even if we get the chains out of the wall, how do we get the door open?" Jessica demanded.

"One thing at a time," Elizabeth said grimly. She switched her attention to her leg chain, as if she was hoping it might not be as secure.

"I knew being an au pair wasn't the most glamorous job in the world," Jessica said as she bent down to help Elizabeth. "But I never figured we'd end up strapped to a wall like common criminals. We should be waltzing around that ballroom right now, mingling with royalty."

Jessica gave up and plopped back down on the cot, sticking out her bottom lip in an exaggerated pout.

"I think I'm getting somewhere," Elizabeth said. Jessica watched hopefully as Elizabeth was able to wiggle the bolt that held her foot chain back and forth in the wall.

"Wow, Liz, you were right about this old place," Jessica admitted. "If we can just unchain ourselves and get the door open, I promise you Jacques will pay for what he did to us."

"Don't make promises you can't keep," Elizabeth warned. "And don't forget there's a guard outside to get past too."

"The guard . . . ," Jessica said thoughtfully. She could feel an idea beginning to hatch, and she stood up and approached the door. The guard outside was sitting on a wooden chair that he had tilted back against the french wall. He was short, with dark hair, and his uniform was too tight for his paunch. "Why didn't I think of this before?" she wondered out loud.

"Think of what?" Elizabeth asked, still working on her chains.

Jessica whirled around to face Elizabeth. "The guard is a *guy*," she whispered excitedly.

"So?" Elizabeth whispered back. By the light of the dim bulb overhead, Jessica saw understanding light up Elizabeth's face. "You're not serious!"

"Yes, I am. He might be on the old side; and he might speak more French than English, but he's still a guy," she pointed out. "And you know what I can do when I set my mind to it."

Elizabeth shrugged, her hands in the air. "I can't think of a better plan," she admitted. "And doing something is better than doing nothing at all."

Jessica smiled at her twin and turned back to the door. "*Excusez-moi, monsieur,*" she began, smiling through the bars. "*Parlez-vous anglais?*" She hoped that he did indeed speak English, because those two French phrases were practically the only ones she knew really well.

The guard looked up at her, his black eyes flat in the dim light. "Yes, I speak some," he said with a heavy accent.

Jessica cast about in her mind for a good question. "Do you know what time it is?" *Lame*, she thought. But he did look at his watch.

7

"Just after eleven," he said gruffly in his heavily accented English.

"Thank you," she said warmly. Now that she knew he could understand her, Jessica plunged ahead eagerly. "It must be awesome to be a guard in a royal household. Did you have to go through a lot of training?" She hoped that he could see her brilliant smile from behind the bars.

"We are all highly trained," he said, his voice softening a bit. Jessica watched as he stood up and sucked in his gut. *Gotcha!* she thought triumphantly.

Now that she could see his full face, she realized he wasn't bad looking. His eyes were actually brown instead of black, his face was smooth shaven, and his full head of thick black hair showed touches of gray at the temples.

"I can tell," she said. "You look like you're in good shape. Do you have lots of muscles in your arms?" Behind her she heard Elizabeth trying to stifle laughter. "Can I feel them?" She batted her eyelashes and smiled even more, stretching her fingers toward him through the bars.

The guard came a little closer, looked her up and down, and locked eyes with her. Jessica kept her expression as innocent as possible.

"American girls, ha, so forward!" he sneered. "No, you cannot feel them. Sit down and shut up if you don't want to get into more trouble!" He snorted once before sauntering back to his chair, where he sat heavily and pulled out a newspaper to read.

Jessica stamped her foot in frustration. *Just one more thing to hate about this country,* she thought. She slumped down next to Elizabeth and pouted. "This place is awful," she snapped.

She fought back the urge to cry, but what was the point? They were trapped here in the dungeon, alone and shivering, and no one but Elizabeth was going to hear her sobs. Jessica could feel the cold from the hard stone floor seeping through her satin slippers and making her feet ache.

"At least you tried," Elizabeth said with a sigh.

"It's all my fault!" Jessica wailed, giving in to her misery and beginning to weep, the tears rolling down her cheeks. She tasted the salty tears on her lips and sniffed to keep her nose from running. "Jacques seemed so sincere with his talk about moonlight and French nights," she continued. "Oh, why did I believe him? How could I be such an idiot?"

"I hate to say it, Jess, but I tried to warn you Jacques was bad news right from the beginning. If you weren't such a flirt," Elizabeth accused, "he probably wouldn't have given you the emerald in the first place!"

Elizabeth stood up and paced. Of course, the chain that held her to the wall didn't permit her to go more than a few steps in any direction. She wished Jessica would either stop whining or think of something productive to do, something other than trying to seduce the guard. After all, she *had* gotten them into this mess.

9

"I never even wanted to come to this dumb château. Why did I ever let you talk me into it?"

Elizabeth had turned down an exciting summer job at *Flair* magazine, where she would have learned a lot about being a professional writer, just to come here. She hadn't been totally comfortable about the decision in the first place. Then the night before they left Sweet Valley, Jessica's best friend, Lila Fowler, had given them a big going-away bash at her father's mansion, Fowler Crest. It started out as a great party, but Todd had ruined the evening by breaking up with Elizabeth unexpectedly. His rash decision had come as a total shock to her. He had actually said they should be free to see other people during the summer!

Elizabeth wasn't sure if Todd had severed their relationship because he felt hurt that she was going so far away or if he was already interested in someone else. But his words had broken her heart, and she had lashed out at him. Elizabeth winced at the memory. *He was probably dying to find a new girlfriend after that,* she thought. Just imagining Todd with another girl made her want to sob her heart out.

"Well, what about you, Liz?" Jessica said accusingly, breaking through Elizabeth's sad thoughts. "You didn't exactly make the right choice of guys."

Elizabeth sighed. She couldn't begrudge Todd a new relationship after the way she had acted this summer. After just a few meetings with Prince Laurent she had fallen helplessly in love with him.

"You're right, Jess. But you can't deny that Prince Laurent is something special." She tingled at the memory of how she had burst from the château's maze of hedges that first day only to find the stunningly handsome Prince Laurent practicing his fencing. He had taken her breath away!

The muscles in his shoulders and back had rippled at his every movement, his back glistening with sweat in the bright sunshine. Elizabeth had experienced a weird sense of déjà vu. Later she had recalled a dream she had had on the plane. She had dreamed of Laurent even before she met him!

A few days later a sudden storm forced Elizabeth to take shelter in what she thought was a deserted cottage, but it turned out to be Prince Laurent's hideaway. The tall prince captivated Elizabeth, with his warm blue eyes, thick black hair, and noble, chiseled features, as well as his sensitive, caring nature and great sense of humor.

From the moment Elizabeth met Laurent, it seemed as if they'd known each other forever. He tempted her away from her au pair duties for horseback rides and picnic dinners in the moonlight. Even finding out that he was engaged to Antonia di Rimini hadn't managed to extinguish the fire he'd lit in her heart.

"Do you think Prince Laurent will try to get us out of here?" Jessica asked hopefully.

"I hadn't really thought about it," Elizabeth admitted. "But I do believe he loves me. I can't imagine that he would leave us here, if he even knows where we are."

"You're right! Who would tell him?" Jessica whined. "I don't think the de Saint-Maries want him socializing with us in the dungeon while there's a ball going on."

"Probably not," Elizabeth agreed. Her head was pounding from the effort to figure a way out of this dank, creepy dungeon. Her hands were so cold, they were going numb, and she put them under her arms to try to warm them up. "But I bet the countess has told everyone and anyone how she caught the thieves who stole her necklace!"

"I can just hear her now," Jessica sneered. "How can Prince Laurent even think about marrying anyone as disgusting as that Antonia?"

"Laurent is a very dutiful son," Elizabeth said, rushing to his defense. "It's very brave of him to keep with tradition and follow through with his father's wishes." *Even if it's not what he truly wants,* she added silently.

"You mean *stupid,* don't you?" Jessica asked. "No one would ever force me to marry someone I don't love, not even our parents."

Elizabeth couldn't imagine what Laurent's life would be like, married to Antonia. And the horrible countess would be his mother-in-law! What could be worse?

"Stop criticizing Laurent," Elizabeth warned her sister. "After all, it was Jacques who got us into this

12

awful place, but Laurent will be the one to rescue us."

"You don't know that for sure," Jessica pointed out snidely.

"Let's not fight about this," Elizabeth pleaded, suddenly weary of the struggle. She dropped the chains with a loud clang. "Oh, Jess," Elizabeth said with a sigh. "I was right. We never should have come to the Château d'Amour Inconnu!"

Prince Laurent moved through the steps of the waltz automatically and without thought. The music, the decorations, the glittering jewels on the women, all were lost on him. Along one wall of the ballroom, mirrors were hung floor to ceiling, and he watched himself dance with Antonia.

She was wearing a stunning silver ball gown that was cut low in the neck and clung to every curve. Her red hair was dressed with pearls, and a matching necklace adorned her throat. But her scornful expression and uplifted, imperious chin spoiled any beauty her outfit might have loaned her. *How much more beautiful Elizabeth would be in that dress*, Laurent thought.

He couldn't stop thinking about Elizabeth and how it should have been her in his arms instead of Antonia. He couldn't really believe that Elizabeth was guilty of stealing the countess's emerald. At first he'd doubted Elizabeth—he'd fallen in love with her so quickly, and they came from such different worlds. But as the evening wore on, he couldn't stop remembering the sweet, innocent look in Elizabeth's blue-green eyes, from the very first moment she had come to his cottage in the storm. Now he was sure she could never be a thief, and his heart was torn at the thought of his one true love sitting in the dungeon. He needed to get away from this place and these people and find a way to see her!

But one glimpse of his father from across the room reminded him of his duty. He looked down at Antonia's upturned face.

"Are you having a good time?" he asked, not really wanting to know the answer.

Antonia fluttered her eyelashes up at him. Did she have something in her eye? Feeling disgusted, Laurent realized that Antonia's rapid blinking was her idea of a sexy look.

"I've never been so happy in my whole life," Antonia purred. "This is a dream come true, dancing in your arms like this."

"I'm glad," Laurent managed to say, though his voice came out flat and unemotional. All his thoughts were concentrated on Elizabeth. *Is she cold and scared in the dungeon? How can I get her out? I must get away soon to see her!*

Laurent waltzed Antonia past the dais where his parents and the countess were sitting, and he flinched when he saw the pleased expressions on their faces. He quickly averted his eyes.

When he'd learned that his parents had

14

arranged a politically important marriage for him with Antonia di Rimini, he was devastated. He wasn't sure he wanted to get married at all, and he hardly knew Antonia. Of course, the reason that Antonia and her mother had come for this extended visit to the château was so he could get to know her better.

So far, he knew he didn't feel for her what he thought he should feel for his future wife. He certainly didn't love her! In fact, he disliked her, and he positively hated her overbearing mother, the countess.

Then, when Elizabeth Wakefield had entered his life and turned his world upside down, he knew for certain that his destiny didn't lie with Antonia. He had actually dreamed of Elizabeth before he knew she even existed, when he fell asleep in his favorite spot by the pond one afternoon. But when she showed up at his door that stormy night, he felt as if lightning had struck.

After that, Laurent fell in love with Elizabeth without even trying. Every moment they spent together was like being in his dream, and he never wanted to wake up. His parents believed he would do his duty and marry Antonia. But they didn't know that he was desperate to find a way to spend the rest of his life with Elizabeth Wakefield instead. She had captured his heart, and he had no intention of trying to take it back.

"Laurent, you look a thousand miles away," Antonia complained in her shrill voice, cutting into his thoughts. "What are you thinking?"

"I'm sorry if I seem distracted, Antonia," he said, pushing his memories of Elizabeth to the back of his mind for the moment. "I guess I was just daydreaming."

"About me, I hope." She batted her eyelids again, and Laurent fought the urge to laugh at the silly gesture. He wished he could tell her how foolish she looked.

"Hmmm," he murmured noncommittally. "Well, would you like something to drink? It's quite warm in here."

"Yes, it is. Perhaps champagne?" Antonia led Laurent to a corner of the ballroom where they could sit on a narrow love seat and be partially concealed by a potted plant. He almost groaned out loud at the thought of being so isolated and intimate with her. But he did the right thing by waiting until she was seated before bowing slightly and going in search of the champagne.

While Laurent got their drinks, he let his thoughts return to Elizabeth. His heart ached to think of her in the cold, dark cell of the dungeon. He longed to put his arms around her to comfort her. He yearned to place his lips on hers in a long, passionate kiss. How long did he have to put up with Antonia before he could break away and get to Elizabeth?

When he returned to Antonia, she was waving her fan lazily before her face. At the sight of him she smirked and patted the love seat beside her. "Come sit right here, Laurent," she cooed.

"Your champagne, Antonia," he said, handing her a glass. He sat down as far from her as he could, but the love seat wasn't large. At most he could put only a couple of inches between himself and Antonia.

Antonia smiled and sipped at her champagne, and then she started that repulsive eyelash thing again. "Oh, Laurent, let's not rest too long," she said. She pressed her knee against his boldly. "I could dance all night in your arms with no trouble at all!"

"And I yours," he said automatically. Just then, out of the corner of his eye, he noticed the countess bearing down on them, a gleam in her eye. Antonia was almost tolerable, but Laurent was beginning to believe the countess was pure evil.

Laurent stood up respectfully and gave the countess a slight bow. "Countess. I'm sure you and Antonia have a great deal to discuss, and this love seat is certainly too small for three. So if you will excuse me, please?" He bowed again and walked away without waiting for either of them to speak.

As soon as he left them he crossed the ballroom, ignoring anyone who called his name. He was on his way to the dungeon! Even a few stolen moments with his beautiful Elizabeth would be better than the torture of Antonia's company.

Chapter 2

Jessica opened her eyes to almost total darkness. Where was she? Her cheek was up against a cold, hard surface, like a stone. *A stone wall?* She groaned, remembering that she and Elizabeth were still locked in the dungeon. She must have actually cried herself to sleep earlier, after her frustrating attempt to enlist the guard's help had failed.

As she gradually awoke she became aware that Elizabeth was standing at the cell door, peering out the small, barred window. "What are you doing?" Jessica asked groggily.

"It's the kids," Elizabeth hissed back.

Jessica hopped off the cot to join her twin at the window. In the dim light of the bulb that hung outside their chamber she could see that the door between the hallway and the stairs was open. The guard was looking down at something in the doorway, and

Jessica heard Claudine's voice speaking French. "What is she saying?" Jessica asked Elizabeth, leaning close to her ear and whispering.

"She said they want to see us, talk to us," Elizabeth answered. Jessica could see Elizabeth's eyes bright with expectation and new hope. The guard spoke in a flurry of French, and Jessica was about to ask Elizabeth what he said when Pierre's voice piped up.

"Claudine, we must to speak English, like the au pairs tell us," he insisted.

"Yes," Claudine said. "Pierre is right. English. We want to see Mademoiselle Jessica and Elizabeth."

"No. You should not be here," the guard replied in his own halting English. "This is no place for children!"

"Please," Pierre whined. "We only want *un moment* with them!"

The guard began to try to herd them up the stairs with his open arms. "No, no, no," he said.

"Wait," Claudine cried. "A splinter. My finger. It hurts!"

"Mon Dieu!" the guard exclaimed, slapping the palm of his hand to his forehead. "What next?"

"Ooh, it hurts, it hurts!" Claudine cried again, jumping up and down. Manon, the youngest of the three children, began to jump too, giggling.

"Let me get a flashlight," the guard said, "and I'll try to get it out." He half turned away from the children, and Pierre gave him a sudden push into his chair. The guard, caught off-balance, sat down heavily and for a moment was too stunned to react.

Jessica grabbed Elizabeth's arm, and they held their hands to their faces to prevent their laughter from exploding. The kids had come to rescue them! Suddenly Jessica was sorry for ever thinking the kids were a bother. How sweet of them to do this!

While the guard struggled and sputtered and shouted French words that the children probably shouldn't be hearing, Claudine danced around the chair with a rope, wrapping it tightly around the guard so he couldn't move. She sang a little song as she skipped. "La, la, la, la, la . . ."

"I can't believe this," Elizabeth said into Jessica's ear. "They've got him tied up!"

"Les enfants terrible!" the guard screamed until Manon stepped up and shoved a red sock into his mouth. Then he could only moan and glare at them. The kids ignored him. Pierre crouched next to the guard's chair and fiddled with the snap that held the ring of keys to his belt.

"Kids," Elizabeth said, "aren't you going to get into trouble for doing this?"

"Oh, Liz, lay off them, will you? I think it's great what they did. And what do you think their parents are going to do, spank them?" Jessica asked sarcastically. "Would you rather rot in this cell?"

"No," Elizabeth admitted grimly.

Pierre finally got the key ring free, and the kids rushed over to the door. The keys jingled and jangled as Pierre tried first one, then another in the lock. "Where is the key?" he shouted in frustration.

"Let me try," Claudine said, pulling at his arm.

"No!" Pierre shrieked, pulling back. "I will do it!" He returned to trying the keys in the lock one by one while Manon further confused things by jumping up and down and reaching for the keys, crying, "Me! Me!"

Suddenly, with a scrape and a clank, one of the keys turned and the door opened. They were free! The guard just glared at them while Elizabeth hugged Claudine and tried to hug Pierre. Jessica reached down and scooped up Manon in her arms. "You guys are the best!"

After a quick hug Jessica put Manon down and went quickly to check on the guard. Claudine and Pierre had tied the rope tightly, but Jessica gave it one more twist to make sure. "You're not going anywhere for a while," she told the guard with a flippant toss of her head. He glared daggers at her. *Serves him right*, she thought.

Pierre had successfully dodged Elizabeth's embrace and was saying, "Mesdemoiselles Elizabeth, Jessica, you must get away. You must run away from this place. *Alors*, never mind us!"

Jessica knew he was right, but the idea of running away bothered her. It would make them look so guilty. "If we escape, they'll think we were guilty all along," she said to Pierre. "I hate letting the countess gloat over how right

21

she was when she's really totally wrong."

"I know," Elizabeth said glumly. "But who believes us? Even if Prince Laurent stands up for us, he has no way to prove our innocence." She rubbed each wrist painfully and sighed. "The fact is, we were on the train with the countess when the emerald was stolen. And we were in the château when the diamond necklace was stolen. They don't even know that Jacques exists, so they have no other logical suspects."

Jessica scowled, trying desperately to think. Claudine tugged at her arm, and Manon clutched her around the neck.

"I guess you're right," she said finally. "Without Jacques we can't convince anyone of our innocence."

Elizabeth reached out and placed a comforting hand on Jessica's arm.

"Our only choice is to somehow find Jacques, and that means we have to leave," she said in a soothing voice.

"Yes," Pierre agreed, pulling on Elizabeth's hand. "You must to leave."

Elizabeth knelt down in front of the little boy. "Pierre, what you did tonight was very brave. Thank you for freeing us." This time he permitted her to hug him for two seconds before pulling away.

Jessica put Manon on the floor. "I'll never forget you, you little monsters," she said, tears of joy welling in her eyes. She brushed them away impatiently with the back of her hand. "Come on, Liz," she said, heading for the door.

Jessica led the way up the stairs, and they tip-toed along the hallway until they found a door to the outside. Once out in the fresh air they sprinted across the lawn in the direction of the woods.

Elizabeth knew she was more unhappy than Jessica about running away, even though she was sure it was the logical thing to do. All her life she had believed that telling the truth was the only way to go. And for the most part that's what she did, even when the truth was painful or led to her being punished. *But this time it's different,* Elizabeth told herself. *No one will believe the truth until we have proof.*

"Wait, Liz," Jessica said suddenly, pulling Elizabeth's arm to direct her toward a nearby tree. "Where are we going?"

"What?" Elizabeth asked. It was chilly outside, even though it was a summer night. The black sky spread above them, dotted with silver stars, and a breeze gently ruffled the branches of the tree.

"Where are we going? I don't have a clue where Jacques really is. We left all our money back at the château, and we don't know anyone," Jessica said.

"I hadn't thought that far ahead," Elizabeth admitted, leaning against the tree. "It seemed so important just to get out of that cell and find Jacques. We have to figure out where to start."

Suddenly Jessica snapped her fingers. "Jacques must be staying in the town across the river. We can find him if we can just get to town," she said, tossing her blond hair from side to side. "He knows how to get in and out of places without being seen. I know he'll do something to help us, for my sake."

"But Jess, what about the emerald?" Elizabeth asked. "He's the reason we're in this mess in the first place."

"Even more reason for him to help us," Jessica insisted. "Besides, he has some explaining to do about that emerald!"

"But even if he agrees to help us," Elizabeth argued, "I'm sure we can't trust him. There's just something about him. . . ."

Even in the dark Elizabeth could see Jessica's expression change from anxious hope to anger. "All right! If you're so smart, you tell me what we're going to do. What's your big plan?"

With a sinking heart, Elizabeth had to admit the truth. "I don't have a plan," she said quietly. "I guess we don't have any other choice but to try and find Jacques. You're right. He owes us an explanation about the emerald." Elizabeth kept looking around, hoping there were no guards close by. She felt practically naked standing in the darkness outside, wearing a white ball gown. "How far is it to town?" she asked.

"I'm not sure," Jessica admitted. "But if we don't make it tonight, maybe we can flag down a ride in the morning. At least it's some kind of plan."

"OK," Elizabeth said, reluctantly following her twin across the lawn and toward the woods.

At the café at their inn in the middle of town Jacques and his father were having a late supper. "How is the soup, Papa?" Jacques asked, hoping to divert the older man from his favorite subject: Jacques's shortcomings as a thief.

Louis tasted the aromatic soup gently. "Not bad," he said. "But I have had better."

Jacques let his mind drift from his father's voice while he pushed his food automatically into his mouth. He was more than preoccupied with thoughts of Jessica Wakefield, the beautiful American he had met on the train from Paris. They had talked and joked and flirted the entire first night on the train, and he had known right away that she was someone special.

"Jacques . . . Jacques . . . are you awake?" his father was saying insistently. He tapped Jacques's hand with his finger. "I am asking you what you want to eat. The waiter tells us they have just run out of the beef."

Jacques looked up at the waiter, who was waiting with barely concealed impatience, his foot tapping the flagstone terrace, his pencil poised above his pad. "The veal will do," Jacques said quickly, anxious to be rid of the irritated waiter.

"Where is your head tonight, my boy?" his father demanded. "With that little American?"

Jacques felt himself blush red-hot. "No, of course not, Papa," he mumbled, lowering his eyes

25

to his plate. He pushed the salad greens around a bit. *How can I bear to eat?* he thought. *I can't even taste this food when my mind is so full of Jessica.*

Since that fateful train trip the emerald had become a source of anguish for him and the reason he repeatedly went to see Jessica. He'd had to get it back! His father had promised it to one of their "clients."

But the more time he spent with Jessica, the more she came to mean to him, until his heart leapt at the very sight of her. This only confirmed what he had suspected from the start—he had been falling in love.

As Jacques brought another forkful of green salad to his mouth his father launched into another tirade. "I cannot believe you didn't get the emerald. It's the whole reason you went to the château in the first place," he reminded Jacques. "It was a bad risk, and you came back empty-handed!"

"It's not as if I *intended* to come back without it," Jacques said, trying to be reasonable.

"You should have just snatched it away from her," Louis said between spoonfuls of his steaming soup. "Do you think this is some game we're playing here? You meet an American girl, and you forget everything I have taught you?"

"No, Papa," Jacques responded patiently, wishing his father would speak English so people wouldn't understand his shouting. He hated to fight back when his father got like this, which wasn't often. Of course, this was the first time Jacques had failed to recover one of their jewels. "Things just happened," he finished helplessly.

"Things never 'just happen,'" the older man shot back. "You make things happen. If you don't know that by now . . ." Mr. Landeau threw up his hands. "Jacques, you are my only son . . . my only family. I love you very much," he said in a kinder tone. "And I can understand how a pretty face can turn a young man's head. But you must recover that gem. You know it has to go to our 'friend' as payment for my debt."

"You've explained all that to me before, Papa," Jacques said in a strained voice.

"It doesn't hurt to say it again since your head is in the clouds over a girl." Mr. Landeau sighed, and his blue eyes softened. "Jacques, my Jacques, I don't have anything against that little girl. She's quite pretty. I just want the emerald back." He put down his spoon as a signal he was done with the soup, and the waiter immediately moved toward the table to take the bowl away. "Now, let us not spoil our supper over this matter. You know what you have to do."

"Don't forget, Papa, my visit to the château wasn't a total loss," Jacques pointed out desperately. "I did get the diamond necklace."

"Yes, and it is very nice, Jacques. And it did make up somewhat for your recent bad judgment," Mr. Landeau admitted as he leaned back to allow the waiter to take his soup dish away. "But I think I will not let you work anymore until you get the emerald and until you get over that American girl."

The waiter came back with their main course of tender, perfectly cooked veal and potatoes. Although Jacques's appetite wasn't at its best, he could hardly resist such a delicious meal. As he ate he wondered just what he was going to do about Jessica.

I should never have let myself fall for the girl I had to use to hide the jewel, Jacques silently berated himself. *Will she ever forgive me? How can I ever explain it to her?*

Just as Prince Laurent reached the door of the ballroom a reporter stepped in front of him. *"S'il vous plaît,"* the reporter said insistently as he shoved a microphone into Laurent's face. "Will there be an announcement soon about you and the daughter of the countess?" the man asked in French.

Laurent wanted to roll his eyes in frustration, but there were too many cameras pointed in his direction. "I cannot comment right now," he replied. "Please let me go."

The journalists formed a wall at the door to the ballroom, a seemingly unbreakable barrier. Their eager faces and poised pencils filled Laurent with disgust. *Let me out of here!* he wanted to scream.

Just as he was about to shove them aside he felt a hand on his arm. He turned quickly to see a guard at his elbow. "What do you want?" he asked impatiently.

"Your father wishes to speak with you," the man said in a low, respectful tone.

"Not right now," Laurent said, attempting to shake the man's hand from his arm.

"Your Grace, I'm sorry," the man said. "Your father insists."

Laurent looked at the reporters watching him expectantly, then back at the guard, also waiting for him. He felt like a rat trapped in a cage. There was no way he could openly defy his father to go to the dungeon to see Elizabeth. Besides, the reporters might follow him!

"Very well," he said, defeat freezing his heart. He followed the guard over to the dais where his parents sat.

"Laurent," his father said, standing and pulling Laurent toward a corner of the room in order to achieve some degree of privacy. "I noticed you leaving the ball," he commented sternly.

"Just for a moment, Father," Laurent pleaded. "I'm smothering in this place. It's like being in a fishbowl with the reporters and Antonia."

"Son, do not forget your duty," his father warned. "You may not leave this ball."

"Father," Laurent insisted, placing one hand on his father's arm, "I must see Elizabeth . . . only for a moment."

"That is quite simply out of the question," his father said, his eyes growing wider in agitation.

"It would never do for you to abandon Antonia for the sake of that American girl."

"But she must be terrified in the dungeon," Laurent argued. "I would be there for one moment only, just to reassure her, to let her know that she will soon be released. She will be released soon, won't she, Father?"

The question seemed to make his father uncomfortable. "Now is not the time or place to debate this," he informed Laurent. "My decision stands. You may not leave this ballroom until the evening is over."

Laurent's sense of defeat increased, weighing him down with anguish. "Very well, Father," he agreed, knowing that he couldn't go against his father's wishes so openly. The pain was so intense, his heart actually ached in his chest.

"Laurent, we know this is a difficult situation," his father said. "But you must return to Antonia."

"Yes, Father," Laurent replied woodenly. He squared his shoulders and clenched his fists as he walked toward the corner where Antonia still sat with her terrible mother.

Someday, Laurent thought desperately, *I will do whatever I choose, no matter what anyone says or thinks. And somehow Elizabeth will be with me!*

Chapter 3

"Jessica, we're safe now. I have to catch my breath." Elizabeth bent over and placed her hands on her knees for support. They had just entered the woods, and she felt more secure under the blanket of darkness the trees provided.

"OK, but not for more than a minute," her twin warned.

"Any sign of the guards?" Elizabeth asked, taking in great gulps of the cool night air and resting a hand over her wildly beating heart.

"Not that I can see," Jessica answered, glancing around and squinting into the woods.

They had stopped in a small clearing, surrounded by tall, thick trees. The moon had risen, casting a cool white light over the weeds and shrubs of the small field. The clearing was carpeted in soft grass, which felt spongy beneath

Elizabeth's satin shoes. Crickets sang, and somewhere a frog croaked. At any other time Elizabeth would have been soothed by the beauty of the night. But since they'd begun their escape, a concern had been weighing on her mind, and she could no longer deny its urgency.

"Jessica," Elizabeth began, "I know we decided that finding Jacques is the right thing to do, and I agree that he owes you an explanation, but . . . I really need to see Laurent. I can't stand the thought of him thinking I'm . . . *we're* thieves . . . and maybe he could help—"

Jessica cut her off with a swipe of her hand through the air. "Elizabeth, the closer we are to the château, the more chance there is that we'll be recaptured. I just don't think it's worth the risk," she finished.

"How would you feel if a guy you really cared about thought you were a criminal?" Elizabeth was close to tears, and in trying to be quiet, her voice came out harsh and raspy.

Jessica nervously raked her hand through her hair. When she spoke, Elizabeth could feel the desperation in her words. "And how are you going to convince Laurent you're not a thief if we end up back in the dungeon?"

Jessica was angry, but Elizabeth wasn't in the mood to go along with her twin. "Jessica Wakefield, you are the one who badgered me into coming to Europe against my better judgment, right?"

"I know, but—"

"And how many times have I gone along with your schemes in the past?" Elizabeth interrupted.

"A few," Jessica mumbled.

"A few? Let's see, there was the time you stayed out all night and I had to cover for you the entire day because you couldn't drag yourself out of bed," Elizabeth began, ticking off her fingers one by one. "And then there was the time at camp when I had to compete in all your color war events . . . need I go on?"

Jessica held up both hands in a classic defensive posture. "OK, OK, I get the point. Enough with the guilt trip!"

But Elizabeth was warming to her subject and refused to let her twin off easy. "You do this to me all the time! You beg and plead until I do what you want, then when we end up in trouble, you're no help at all! Now I want just one little thing, and you have to go all logical on me! How can you let me down like this?"

"Good grief, Liz," Jessica said, grabbing Elizabeth by the shoulders. "Enough already. So we'll go back and try to see Prince Charming. But if we get caught, so help me, Liz . . ."

Elizabeth was exhausted by her tirade, and she gave Jessica a tired smile. "Thanks, Jess."

Jessica let her go and shrugged. "I had to do something to get you to shut up. I bet every guard on the island heard you," she said grumpily. She

33

grabbed Elizabeth by the wrist, and they started back to the château.

As they trudged across the grass Jessica grumbled under her breath, "We came all this way . . . now we have to go all the way back . . . and for some drippy prince. . . ."

Despite their awful situation, Elizabeth was having trouble keeping her laughter in check. "Oh, Jessica," she finally said. "Nag, nag, nag, all the time."

They broke from the woods and approached the château silently. The ballroom was easy to find. Music filtered across the lawn from the partially opened, tall windows that were blazing with light.

With Jessica close behind, Elizabeth crept to one of the windows and peered inside. All the women wore ball gowns, in every color of the rainbow. Precious jewels glittered on each throat and around every wrist. Some of the ladies carried fans, which they flicked back and forth as they floated around the room. The couples who weren't dancing lined the walls, laughing and talking in a carefree manner. Almost everyone was holding a glass of bubbly champagne.

There were so many people whirling around the dance floor, Elizabeth could barely make out their faces. Then a tall, dark-haired guy twirled past, and Elizabeth gasped. It was Laurent. And he was dancing with Antonia . . . and smiling! How could he? Did he care so little for Elizabeth that he could carry on as if she didn't exist?

What I wouldn't give to trade places with that disgusting Antonia! Elizabeth thought desperately. *That should be me in that gorgeous, fairy-tale dress, dancing in Laurent's arms! And Antonia in the dungeon!* She smiled wryly at the thought of Antonia shivering in the cold darkness of that musty cell.

Antonia was wearing a smug look of triumph on her face that made Elizabeth want to scratch her eyes out. She felt a sob catch in her throat at the frustration of it all. A tear rolled down her cheek.

Jessica abruptly pulled Elizabeth away from the window.

Elizabeth whirled around to face her sister. "Oh, Jess, did you see—"

"Forget about the couple of the century for a minute," Jessica interrupted quietly, squeezing Elizabeth's arm reassuringly. "We have company."

Elizabeth's heart froze as she expected to see a troop of guards coming their way.

Instead she saw the three younger children standing behind Jessica.

"What are you three doing out here?" Elizabeth demanded, glad to have something to focus on besides Laurent and Antonia.

Pierre was scowling. "Mademoiselle Elizabeth, why are you still here?"

Jessica rolled her eyes and jerked her thumb at Elizabeth, her mouth twisted into a smirk.

"Lovesick here had to have one last word with your brother," she said sarcastically in a stage whisper.

Pierre leaned over to the giggling Claudine and whispered a flurry of French into her ear. As his younger sister sped off into the château Pierre bowed to Elizabeth with a flourish of his little hand. "I am not as handsome as my brother, but surely, mademoiselle, you have time for one dance with me," he said gallantly, deepening his voice.

"Oh, no," Jessica moaned. "Are you crazy? Now I know we're going to get caught."

"No, pretty Jessica," Pierre said with a smile that was hauntingly like Laurent's. "You are safe. No one even knows you are out of the cell." He held out his arms to Elizabeth, and she couldn't resist the sweet gesture.

Pierre actually danced well, which Elizabeth should have expected. As the son of European royalty, dancing was part of his education. He whirled her around rather expertly.

Jessica threw up her hands. "The whole world is insane," she said, "but who cares? I guess if you can't beat 'em, join 'em." And with that she picked up little Manon and began to dance too.

The music swelled and subsided, swelled and subsided as they glided through the steps of the dance. Manon was seized with fits of giggles, and Elizabeth saw her little hands gripping Jessica in a stranglehold around her neck. Pierre beamed up at her, seeming much older than six. "You dance so well," he said to Elizabeth.

"Thank you, sir," Elizabeth replied primly. "So do you."

"What about us?" Jessica insisted, dipping Manon so close to the ground, she squealed in delight.

"You two look great together," Elizabeth said, laughing. "You know, Jessica, you should dance with more three-year-olds. It suits you!"

"Thanks a lot," Jessica said in her most sarcastic tone.

Elizabeth suspected that Claudine had been sent to get Laurent, and she hoped the little girl would hurry. Just one last word with her prince was all she wanted, then she didn't care what else happened!

Inside the ballroom no one would have guessed that Laurent had his mind on anything but Antonia. He chafed to go to the dungeon for just a glimpse of Elizabeth, but his ever present sense of duty, as well as the unpleasant confrontation earlier with his father, made him stay and see to Antonia's every need.

But this wasn't an easy thing to do, for she needed so much! More champagne, something to eat, another dance, an introduction to a member of the royal family . . . it was endless! It was a struggle not to wince every time she opened her mouth.

37

They were now moving through a slow dance, and Laurent was stiffly refusing to allow Antonia to press her whole body against his.

"Wasn't it wonderful that the jewel thieves were finally caught?" Antonia asked languidly. "I never rested easy from the moment my mother's heirloom disappeared on the train."

Laurent opened his mouth quickly to respond but then shut it just as fast. He wanted so badly to contradict Antonia. But what was he supposed to say? That he didn't believe the twins were guilty? Based on what? His love for Elizabeth? That would go over well with his fiancée.

"I'm afraid I'm not entirely convinced we have the real thieves," he said quietly. Inside, his heart was aching with longing for Elizabeth, and his mouth went dry every time he thought of her in the dungeon.

Antonia's eyes opened wide, and her lower jaw dropped open in shock. "Laurent, how can you say that?" she insisted. "That horrible, uncultured au pair had the audacity to wear the emerald in public!"

"I have no desire to argue with you, Antonia," Laurent began, straining for patience, "but it hardly seems likely that a thief would display her guilt by wearing the stolen object."

"But Americans are bold and stupid at the same time," Antonia insisted. "I can't believe you're defending them!"

"All I am saying is that no one knows how

Jessica came to have the emerald, and there are many unanswered questions," he said, hoping his firm tone would discourage further comments.

"Well, anyway, they were terrible au pairs, a huge disappointment to your parents." Antonia sniffed, her mouth downturned.

"I cannot speak for my parents," Laurent said stiffly.

"Oh, yes, they ignored the children, they were always late. . . . Americans shouldn't be allowed to take such positions anyway," she stated. "They have such unpleasant notions about equality. Imagine a country with no sense of upper- and lower-class. How gauche!"

Laurent let her voice drift away as he buried himself in his own thoughts. What Antonia had to say was less than important to him. Elizabeth was his only priority. What if she got sick from being locked in that damp old dungeon?

There must be something I can do to help Elizabeth, Laurent thought. *But how can I do anything without hurting my parents and shirking my duty? Why did I have to be born a prince?*

Just then, as Laurent danced Antonia over to the ballroom entrance, one of the journalists took pictures. It reminded Laurent of how publicly he lived his life.

Whenever he rode into town, he watched other boys his age racing to their next class at the university, or walking hand in hand with a girl, or sitting at the café, debating politics with friends. How he envied them!

Tomorrow that picture of Antonia and me dancing will be all over the newspapers, he thought in despair. *Just once I'd like to open my mouth to speak without worrying what words to use or what political position those words put forth. I'd like to go someplace without being followed and photographed!*

"How exciting!" Antonia gushed. She actually stopped dancing and posed beside Laurent, clutching his arm in her hands. She threw back her head and extended one leg to reveal a silver sandal. "How's this?" she asked Laurent.

"Very nice," he said through clenched teeth, hardly able to keep still while the camera flashes blinded him. As soon as the last bulb went off he pressed Antonia to resume the dance so he could blend in with the crowd again.

Laurent's parents smiled at him and Antonia as they glided past the dais. His father was chatting with a foreign ambassador and smiling, but Laurent knew his father disliked the man. *What rubbish!* Laurent thought. *All I want is to be normal, to be free to come and go as I please, to be able to like and dislike whom I will . . . and to be with the girl I love!*

Suddenly he felt a tugging at his coat. He looked down to find Claudine smiling up at him. "What is it, my sweet?" he asked, pulling Antonia away from the stream of dancers and into a secluded corner with Claudine.

Laurent squatted down next to his sister so he was eye to eye with her.

"You must come with me, *mon frère,* now," Claudine whispered in his ear with a secret smile.

Laurent knew instinctively that this had something to do with Elizabeth. He said to Antonia, "There is some emergency with the children, Antonia. Please excuse me for a few moments. I know you will be kind enough to do this."

"Laurent, let me go with you," Antonia whined. "Maybe I can help."

Laurent almost panicked. Was there no way to get her to leave his side? He cast about in his mind for the words to dissuade her. Then a thought came to him, and he had to stop himself from smiling at his ingenuity.

"Antonia, I'm afraid that's not a good idea," he began. "You see, Manon has an upset stomach. I'll spare you the details because you're a lady, but . . . she's made a bit of a mess. The children are afraid to call the servants. If you would like to come along, by all means . . ."

Antonia's long nose wrinkled in distaste. "Perhaps it would be best if you went alone," she said, turning a very faint shade of green.

Laurent heard Claudine giggling behind him as he walked Antonia over to where the countess was standing, talking to friends. Then he followed

41

Claudine. He didn't even turn around when Antonia's whining voice followed him. "Laurent, when will you be back . . . ?"

This time Laurent muscled his way past the reporters in spite of his father's glare. He was going to see Elizabeth!

For the first time in hours Elizabeth actually felt lighthearted. There was no way to resist Pierre's charm; even at six he reminded her of Laurent, and her heart was touched. *This is real,* she thought. *Everything* else *that's happened—the theft, the accusation, the dungeon—is not part of real life.*

Suddenly she felt a hand on her arm and she spun around, expecting to see a guard.

"Oh," she said, clapping her hand over her mouth.

It was Laurent!

Elizabeth flew into his open arms and laid her cheek against his broad chest. Like magic, nothing mattered anymore. Nothing could really go wrong as long as she was in his arms.

If only I could stay here forever, she thought, nestling deeper into his embrace. She felt his hand reach up to stroke her hair gently. His other arm held her tightly around the waist, as if he would never let her go. *I hope he never* does *let me go,* she told herself.

In the arms of a prince, Elizabeth felt like a

fairy-tale princess. It was like stepping into the picture books she had loved as a child. She felt just as graceful, just as beautiful as the heroines she once adored.

But then Elizabeth couldn't help feeling torn. Laurent was engaged to Antonia—he had to marry her. So no matter how much he said he loved Elizabeth, it didn't mean he would change his mind. She pulled away from him and opened her mouth to explain how she felt, but Laurent put one finger on her lips. "No words, my love," he said softly. "This moment there is you and me and no one else in the world."

Elizabeth desperately wanted to believe him, but Antonia loomed large in her mind. Oh, if only she could just stop thinking about everything! All she wanted was to love Laurent, to let her heart rule instead of her head!

Inside the ballroom the orchestra began a new song. Without a word Laurent began to guide Elizabeth into a waltz. She felt like Cinderella, Sleeping Beauty, and Snow White all rolled into one. She willingly followed her prince into the dance, wanting nothing more than to enjoy this fairy-tale moment of swaying in the arms of a real live prince.

The ballroom windows cast a golden light over the perfectly even flagstones of the terrace as they floated along. Laurent locked Elizabeth's eyes with his own, and her heart overflowed with joy. His hands were warm and strong on her waist and around her hand. Her other hand rested on his broad shoulder.

"I love you so much, Elizabeth," Laurent whispered. "You are the most beautiful girl in the world."

"I love you too, Laurent," Elizabeth replied, warmed at the love she saw in his eyes. "No one has ever made me feel the way you do."

"The thought of you sitting in the dungeon . . . ," Laurent said in a pained voice. Elizabeth saw tears glisten in his eyes.

"I've never stolen anything in my life," she said, desperate to make him believe her. She felt her own tears wet on her cheeks.

"I know that," he assured her, squeezing her a little to punctuate his words. "I wish things could be different. . . . I wish Antonia and I—" He broke off suddenly.

If only Elizabeth could forget everything but Laurent and the waltz. But she couldn't do it. She couldn't take another step and pretend that she wasn't devastated by his engagement. "Laurent, it's no use," she said in despair. "I can't do this, knowing that you and Antonia—"

A shriek suddenly pierced the air. "Thieves!" came the countess's shrill, demanding voice.

Elizabeth gasped as Jessica grabbed her by the arm and said hoarsely, "We have to go . . . *now!*" Images flew by Elizabeth's eyes in a blur: the countess and two guards emerging from the doorway onto the terrace, Laurent's heartbroken face, the prince and the princess following the countess. Then Jessica almost yanked her off her feet.

"Get them!" the countess roared behind her. "Release the hounds!"

Elizabeth followed Jessica down the lawn and toward the woods. Her heart skipped a beat when she heard Laurent calling out to her.

"Elizabeth, please come back!"

Before the guards could get organized, Jessica had dragged Elizabeth halfway across the great lawn. Suddenly it seemed as though the woods were miles away. *So far, so far,* Jessica's heart pounded in time with the rhythm of her feet.

What scared Jessica most of all was the sound of the dogs barking. She could just imagine sharp canine teeth sinking into her leg when they caught up with her and Elizabeth. Would the guards let the dogs tear them limb from limb? Jessica risked a glance over her left shoulder as she madly dashed toward the edge of the forest.

The guards were still on the terrace, holding the dogs' leashes, and no one else seemed to be moving. *Thank goodness,* she told herself, turning back around to concentrate on where she was going. She looked over at Elizabeth, who was running beside her, holding up the skirt of her dress to keep from tripping.

Jessica couldn't believe how romantic it had been when Laurent took Elizabeth into his arms. *Why couldn't that have been me?* she thought with a sudden burst of jealousy. There was no doubt in Jessica's mind that Laurent and Elizabeth felt something really strong for each other. *I thought Jacques and I did too,* she moaned to herself.

She concentrated on the line of trees that loomed ahead.

"Almost there," she gasped to Elizabeth, who nodded and kept running.

Finally they reached the edge of the forest, and Jessica risked another look backward. The guards had moved off the terrace and were following, but they weren't running. *They know we can't get too far away on an island!* she thought.

After what seemed like hours of running, Jessica and Elizabeth were in the woods and surrounded by trees. But instead of going faster, they had to go slower. The ground was covered with leaves and fallen twigs, and roots poked through the soil, forcing them to hike their way carefully through the underbrush. Of course, this also gave them a chance to catch their breath, but Jessica was worried that the guards might be closer to them than she thought.

"The last time . . . I looked back . . . ," she began, her chest heaving from fear as much as from the exertion of their speedy flight, "the guards . . . didn't seem to . . . be hurrying."

46

"How far . . . can we go?" Elizabeth asked, breathing heavily. "Sooner or later . . . we'll get to the river . . . and it's not like we can swim it. The drawbridge is heavily guarded at night."

"One thing . . . at a time," Jessica huffed.

As Jessica's heart slowed down and she realized that the guards were nowhere near, she could think more clearly. "Liz, what was *with* you back there? I practically had to *tear* you out of Laurent's arms. I've never seen you so hung up on a guy."

Elizabeth sidestepped a fallen branch and picked delicately across some moss with her satin-slippered feet. "I don't know, Jess. Maybe it's being in France and the fact that he's a prince, or maybe it's because he really does love me," Elizabeth offered. "Our connection is so strong, no matter what his parents want him to do."

Jessica ducked under a low branch and tucked a stray lock of hair behind her ear out of the way. "I admit he's handsome and charming, but it looks like his parents are going to win out on this whole engagement thing."

"But he doesn't care a thing about Antonia," Elizabeth said defensively. "Maybe he's just waiting for the right time to tell his parents how he really feels."

"But it looks as if he's willing to go through with it," Jessica continued, "no matter how much he loves you."

"I know it looks that way," Elizabeth said,

47

desperation in her voice, "but I can't shake the feeling that he's hoping somehow there'll be a way to get out of it."

Jessica couldn't believe how much her twin was counting on Laurent's love for her. "That's just a feeling. And since when do you act only on your feelings?" Jessica had a sudden sense of the world shifting, as though Elizabeth's personality was changing in front of her eyes. What would she do if Elizabeth began to act impulsively? It was an outrageous thought. *Jessica* was the impulsive one!

"I can't ignore how I feel this time," Elizabeth explained. "It's just too strong!"

Jessica stopped for a moment to look around and get her bearings. "Well, Laurent is still a prince, and he will take the throne one day. If you married him, you'd be a princess," Jessica stated. "Do you think you could you handle that?"

"I don't know, Jess. But why are we even talking about this? It's slowing us down," Elizabeth said, fanning her face with her hand. "Never mind about Laurent. Let's just get going. Can you see anyone behind us?"

"No. Maybe we lost them," Jessica said hopefully. "We have to find a way to get to town. The sooner we find Jacques, the sooner we can clear up this mess."

They came to a stream, gurgling between the trees. The sound was somehow strangely comforting in the still of the night. "Now what?" Jessica asked, trying to gauge how far the other side of the stream was.

Elizabeth bent over and stuck her hands in the water, wiping them across her face quickly. "Ooh, that feels good," she said, using the hem of her ball gown to dry it.

Jessica crouched down to do the same. She felt dirty and sweaty. "Well?" she demanded. "Are we going to cross this thing or what?"

"Maybe there are some stepping-stones," Elizabeth suggested, standing and smoothing the front of her ball gown. "Let's look."

They walked upstream a few steps, and Jessica spotted what looked like dry stones sticking up out of the water. "There," she said excitedly, pointing. "Up there it looks like stones. We could try crossing."

"Great, Jess! Let's go," Elizabeth said.

Jessica placed a foot on the first stone, extending her arms to enhance her balance. Then she placed the other foot on the second stone, moved her first foot to the third stone, and half turned to Elizabeth. "This isn't too bad, Liz," she said. "Come on, try it!"

"OK," Elizabeth said tentatively, her foot on the first stone.

"See?" Jessica said. She promptly slid off into the water. "Oh, no! Now on top of everything else my feet are wet!"

"Shhh," warned Elizabeth. "You'll have every

guard on top of us. We can't do anything about your feet right now. You'll just have to live with it."

I hate wet feet! Jessica thought. *But then, hmmm, isn't that what animals do to throw off other animals, walk through water? I can't remember.*

Jessica's thoughts started to spin off in a million directions. *What if we can't find Jacques? And what if he did deliberately steal that emerald? And what if Elizabeth gets all mushy on me again? Oh, why did I ever even think about coming to France?*

Chapter 4

The countess had drawn herself up to her full height and was pacing the prince's study. She had worn white to the ball, and her dress was too formfitting to suit her figure; her jewels too were garish and ostentatious. She turned a hard eye on Laurent and said, "They're nothing but common thieves, young man." The countess leaned her face in much too close to Laurent's, and he could smell her stale breath. "And now they're running away to heaven knows where," she added.

Laurent resisted the impulse to push the countess away from him. His father stood calmly to one side of the massive fireplace while his stepmother reclined in a nearby chair. Their formal attire made them seem more imposing than usual. His father's medals glittered as a sign of military prowess. His stepmother's jewels sparkled in the harsh light of the lamp beside her chair. Their faces were grim.

"I know Elizabeth quite well, Countess," Laurent began quietly. "It's hard to believe that she would steal food if she were starving, let alone a precious gem. There must be some other explanation." He looked at his parents, his eyes pleading for their support.

Laurent's father shook his head, and his voice was firm but sad. "I'm sure your intentions are good, Laurent, but I'm afraid the evidence is rather conclusive," he stated.

The countess huffed, a sound that Laurent couldn't help comparing to a camel's cough. "My dear boy, you are naive, aren't you?" She continued pacing, waving her arms around. "Don't you know anything about American girls? Those two may have sweet faces and pretty blond hair, but underneath they want to get their hooks in you and take you for everything you have."

"Countess . . . ," his stepmother began, but the countess strode up and down the room, ignoring her.

"And by the way," the countess demanded, turning her steely gaze on the prince, "how exactly did they escape? They could not have done it alone. Who helped them?" The countess walked toward Laurent, and he was momentarily afraid she would hit him. "Was it you, perhaps? I saw you trying to leave the ball earlier!"

"Of course not!" Laurent cried in self-defense.

Laurent watched his father close his eyes in fatigue and frustration. "Countess," the older man said in a tired voice, "it was the younger children who somehow managed to disable the guard and free the girls. They are so very young, after all—"

"*What?*" the countess screamed, cutting off the prince. "Your children have been brainwashed by those horrible girls! What will their punishment be?"

"They are my children, and their punishment is none of your concern," Laurent's stepmother answered coolly. Laurent could tell she was appalled by the countess's audacity and was struggling to stay calm.

"They should be whipped at the very least," the countess continued in her loud tone. "Imagine . . . such behavior . . . such . . ."

Laurent's stepmother rose from her chair and glided toward the countess. She took the countess by the arm and said firmly, "Dear Countess . . . Doloria, you must not tax yourself so." The countess refused to budge and dug her heels into the carpet. "We must return to the ballroom," Laurent's stepmother continued. "Our guests will be wondering where we are."

The countess practically jerked her arm away. "Prince Laurent must be made to understand what went on here earlier, and we must discuss the punishment of the younger children," she insisted. "He must accept the fact that the little American girls are nothing but common thieves! You must assure me the younger ones will be spanked until their bottoms are red!"

The princess turned her back on the countess and crossed the room to the window. Laurent was amazed at her ability to remain composed in the face of such insults.

Laurent's father took the countess's other arm. "But now is not the time for these matters, not when we are expected to entertain our guests," he said stiffly. "Do you want the press to get involved in this matter?"

"Of course I wish to avoid a scandal," the countess conceded with a scowl, "but not at the expense of the truth!"

Laurent, mindful that he was obligated to be polite to this horrid woman, clenched his fists at his sides and said in a tight voice, "I don't care about other American girls. I refuse to believe that Elizabeth did anything wrong." He tried to make his voice softer, gentler. "Please, you must not hunt them down like dogs. Let me find them, and then we can reason through this."

The countess laughed. "An American, reasonable? How absurd, my dear boy. All Americans have the intellects of earthworms!" The countess's voice actually became louder, if that was possible. "No, these foolish girls will be thrown back into

54

the dungeon once they are captured."

The thought of Elizabeth going back to that dank, musty, cold cell made Laurent's stomach turn in disgust. He looked at the three adults—the countess with her hard face, his father looking sad but resigned, his stepmother wringing her hands in distress—and he knew he was on his own. These people would never understand what he knew about Elizabeth, that she was sweet and honest and, above all, innocent.

"Laurent," his stepmother said in an anxious voice, "come back to the ball with us now."

"Yes," the countess interjected in her annoying tone. "Antonia is waiting for you."

Laurent's father tried to put an arm around his shoulders, presumably to herd him back into the ballroom, but Laurent sidestepped the embrace.

"Father, you are so anxious for me to be a man," he said grimly. "But I will never be a man if I do not act now. I'm sorry, but I am going to find the twins."

Laurent knew there was only one thing to do. He would take Pardaillan and ride into those woods to look for the girls. He turned away from his parents and the countess and stalked off in the direction of the stables.

If I can reach the twins before anyone else, Laurent thought as he left the château by a side door, *maybe I can sort through this mess and make everything right. I owe Elizabeth that much at least.*

Pardaillan whinnied at the sound of Laurent's boot steps as he entered the stables. Laurent flung off his constricting uniform jacket and hung it on a nail. He loosened and removed his pure silk tie, which had been feeling more and more like a noose as the evening wore on.

He found his saddle and secured it on the horse. "Easy, boy," Laurent said in French, patting the stallion's hindquarters and pulling the cinch tight around his belly. Laurent next inserted the bit into the horse's mouth, pulled the reins over his head to rest on the saddle, and led him outside before mounting him.

"Yes, Pardaillan," he whispered into the stallion's ear as they turned toward the woods, "you and I are going to find my beautiful Elizabeth and rescue her from the wicked countess." Pardaillan neighed in response as he broke into a gallop.

"I just hope I am not too late," Laurent whispered to the night.

The forest had long ago enclosed the twins in its murky depths. But now the moon had slid behind a dark cloud, leaving them in pitch-darkness. Elizabeth couldn't see where she was putting her feet. It was impossible to tell which was the right way to go. It would be disastrous if they emerged from the woods into the waiting arms of the château guards.

Elizabeth could barely make out the figure of her twin, walking a few steps in front of her. Tree branches clutched at their worn and dirty ball gowns, and Elizabeth wasn't sure how much farther she could go. Her shoulders and legs ached, her arms were covered with scratches from the trees and bushes she had stumbled into, and she thought any moment they would hear the dogs barking.

The darkness was a mixed blessing. If Elizabeth couldn't see, then the guards wouldn't be able to see either. And the soft carpet of moss and leaves on the floor of the forest made it possible for Elizabeth and Jessica to move quietly.

Suddenly Elizabeth's foot sank into a deep hole. She went down hard, her ankle twisting painfully to one side. She let out a little yelp and grabbed at her foot.

"Jess, Jess, stop, I twisted my ankle! Ooh, it hurts!" She sat on the damp grass in her ruined ball gown and rubbed her ankle, trying to ease the pain.

Jessica fell to her knees beside her. "Oh, Liz, what are we going to do?" she cried. "Just when I think it can't get any worse! How could you put your foot in a hole?"

Elizabeth groaned in frustration. "I didn't *see* the hole or I wouldn't have stepped into it," she said tersely.

"You should have been more careful," Jessica accused.

"I didn't do it on *purpose!*" Elizabeth insisted. "Jessica, get a grip!"

Jessica sighed. "I didn't mean to blame you," she admitted, "but this is the worst thing that could happen. How will we ever get out of these woods now, with you like that?" Jessica's voice was near hysterical. "I just don't know how much more I can take!"

"Shhh," Elizabeth said quickly. "Don't get crazy on me now. The guards might be near."

Jessica clapped a hand over her mouth, her eyes wide and scared. "Oh, no," she said in a loud stage whisper. "Now that you can't move, they'll find us for sure."

Elizabeth heaved an enormous groan. "I do know I can't go any farther tonight," she said. "If I could see better, maybe then I might risk it. But if I turn this ankle again, it'll probably break."

Jessica hugged herself tightly, rocking back and forth on her knees. "I'm just so tired. Maybe we should stay here till dawn. Then I can go for help."

"I'm so exhausted, I can hardly keep my eyes open," Elizabeth admitted, "but what if there are wild animals in these woods? There's no way we could defend ourselves. We're like sitting ducks if we aren't on the move."

"But we can't see, and now you can't walk. No, we better stay here." Jessica sounded less shaky. "Don't you remember what the camp director said

58

last summer? Wild animals usually go after food, and we don't have any."

"Oh." Elizabeth groaned. "Did you have to mention food? My stomach is growling."

Just then the moon slipped out from behind a cloud and showered a silvery light between the trees. "Yes!" Jessica said excitedly. "Now that I can see better, I'll try to build us some kind of shelter for the night with these fallen branches. What do you think?"

Elizabeth was heartened by the optimism in Jessica's voice and her boundless energy as she started gathering the branches. "You know, Jess, sometimes you drive me crazy, and you did get us into this mess, but I am awfully glad we're sisters," she said warmly.

Jessica laughed. "Thanks, I'm glad I'm not all that bad." She pulled several branches toward an opening between two sturdy tree trunks.

"That's a good spot," Elizabeth said, trying to shift into a more comfortable position. As she watched her sister lean branch after branch against the trees she couldn't help being impressed. "That looks great, Jess."

"What else did you expect from your perfect twin?" Jessica asked with her nose in the air.

"And modest too," Elizabeth quipped.

Jessica laughed in response. "Now I just have to make the bed. . . ."

"Make the bed?" Elizabeth asked doubtfully.

Jessica laughed again as she began to remove rocks and twigs from the area inside the shelter. When she had cleared a space, she stood up and wiped her hands on her tattered dress.

"There, it may not be our clean sheets and feather pillows from home, but it's a safe place to sleep tonight," she said proudly.

"What a day!" Elizabeth sighed, struggling toward the shelter. "I can't ever remember being this tired."

"Here, let me help you." Jessica supported Elizabeth as she crawled into the shelter, then followed her inside. They draped their sad, dirty ball gowns over exposed skin as best they could and snuggled close together for warmth.

Elizabeth closed her eyes and tried to relax.

Maybe I'll wake up back in my bed in Sweet Valley, she thought. *Maybe this really is just a nightmare.*

Jacques knew it was very late, and he was more than ready to sleep after the argument with his father earlier in the evening. But there was an uneasiness in his stomach, a feeling that something terrible was happening somewhere.

He went to the window of his room, pulled back the blue damask curtain, and peered outside. The street was silent and empty. He turned back into his chamber and sat heavily on the neatly made mahogany bed. *What's wrong?*

he wondered. He was answered by another flutter in his stomach.

Jessica! he realized suddenly. *I just know she's in trouble. Somewhere out there, she's in danger.*

But how could he help? His feelings for Jessica were confusing and strong—he wanted to charm her in the easy, carefree French manner he'd learned from his father, but he also wanted to hold her close and promise his undying devotion. Now that was a joke! Someone who lived the way he did, moving around, never putting down roots, couldn't promise undying *friendship,* let alone devotion!

"What spell have you cast on me, Jessica Wakefield?" he asked the empty room, feeling more like a caged animal every minute.

I have to do something. But what? he thought. *Should I try to find her, try to save her from . . . whatever? Or should I just mind my own business and forget about her?*

"She was better off before I came along anyway," he said aloud.

No, if I have charmed Jessica in this short time since we met, then she has charmed me twice as much. I can't just erase her from my mind. He raked his hand through his hair.

"Perhaps if I return to the château, I can find out what is going on. Maybe there is nothing to worry about," he told the bedside lamp. "And I did see a stable down the street that isn't heavily guarded. I'll bet no one would even miss a horse if I 'borrowed' it for a few hours."

Jacques crept out into the night, feeling energized by his decision to act. He stopped just outside the inn to take stock of the town. Only a cat stirred, stalking among the bushes and small trees.

He slipped down the alleyways in his usual stealthy manner, stopping every few steps to make sure no one had detected him. The stable lock was simple to open, the horses too sleepy to be alarmed.

He chose an average-size horse, dark in color so it would blend with the night. Although Jacques worried about being caught and his sense of fear for Jessica hadn't diminished, he didn't move too quickly. He had learned from experience that the faster you tried to do something covert, the more likely it would go wrong.

Not bothering with a saddle, Jacques secured only the bridle on the horse.

"Come on, old girl," he whispered as he pulled on the reins and led the horse from the stable. Once outside, he walked the horse to the nearby mounting block and swung onto her back. Gripping the horse with his thighs, he pulled the reins to the right, aiming for the road out of town.

Of course, he thought as the horse began to move, *if I return to the château, it might be possible to recover the emerald after saving Jessica from whatever danger she's in. And if I do save her, she'll probably be so grateful, she'll part with the emerald without a whimper. Even though I wouldn't mind tussling for it like we did earlier.* He grinned.

At the edge of town another rider on a large white horse came galloping toward him. As they neared each other Jacques recognized Prince Laurent. *What is that pampered young man doing so far from his glittering château? And at this time of night!*

"Hmmm," Jacques said to himself, "I wonder how much money he carries?" Then he rolled his eyes at his own thieving reflex and mentally slapped himself. "I'm supposed to be changing!"

Aha, he suddenly remembered, *Jessica mentioned that her sister had attracted the attention of the prince himself. Perhaps he is doing the same thing I am . . . trying to find the twins. So they are in danger! They must have left the château for the prince to come all this way so late at night. Maybe if I stop to talk with him, I will learn something useful.*

Laurent almost slipped from the saddle in exhaustion when he reached the edge of the town. He felt as if he'd combed every inch of the forest. Now, as a last resort, he was going to look in town. It was just possible that Jessica and Elizabeth had made it this far.

The town was as still as a tomb. Not even a cricket dared to disturb the night's quiet. Pardaillan's hooves sounded unusually sharp and loud as they struck the cobbled streets. Laurent's tired eyes scanned the road even as his brain registered the fact that there was no one to see. *What will I do if they aren't here?* he wondered. *What if I can't find them?*

Then he noticed a young man riding toward him. Laurent reined in Pardaillan and tried to smile. "A bit late for a ride, isn't it?" he called to the rider in French.

"Or early. I could say the same for you, Your Grace." Atop his horse the young man bowed with a flourish of his hand.

"So you know me," Laurent said. "Have we met before?"

"I do not believe so," the young man answered easily. "I know you only from reputation. I am but a poor farmer and have not had the opportunity to mingle with royalty. Until now, of course." A casual smile lit his face.

Laurent bristled at another reminder of his removed social position. There was no reason he shouldn't socialize with such a polite and friendly man.

"Well, I'm glad we've had the opportunity to meet, Mr. . . ." Laurent raised an eyebrow in question.

"Pardon me, Your Grace. I am Jacques Landeau." The young man bowed again briefly.

"It is a pleasure to meet you, Monsieur Landeau," Laurent said, nodding. "Unfortunately I must be going. I hope you will pardon my rudeness."

"But if you will pardon *my* presumption, Your Grace, you appear to be distracted and hurried," he said. "Is there some way I can be of service to you?"

Laurent had never felt so frantic in his life, but he had also never felt so tired. *I have never had a friend to confide in,* he thought, *but I am so full of thoughts and feelings.* And when he looked up, young Jacques Landeau was still giving him that quizzical expression. Did Laurent dare take this stranger into his confidence?

"First I must ask," he said quickly, "are you a journalist? A member of the press?"

"Hardly," Jacques said with a laugh. "I am a farmer, as I told you. If there is anything I can do . . ."

Laurent considered his offer again, considered whether he trusted this young stranger enough to confide in him. It was clear he was getting nowhere by himself. Another pair of eyes and ears would no doubt help the search. He quickly decided that it was worth the risk.

"Two young American girls came to the château this summer as au pairs for my younger brother and sisters," Laurent explained. "The countess who is visiting us has had two pieces of valuable jewelry stolen recently, and one of them was found in the possession of one of the American au pairs."

Laurent knew he sounded hysterical, but he was too tired to care. He wasn't even sure this young man could help, but just putting his fears and thoughts into words made him feel immeasurably better.

"The girls were thrown into the dungeon," he continued, "but somehow they escaped, and I have been searching the woods for them. All night, in fact." He pulled on the reins to steady the agitated Pardaillan, and Jacques's horse sidestepped in response.

In the uncertain light of near dawn Laurent thought Jacques had turned a shade paler, and his eyes seemed to widen slightly.

"There were two American girls on the train when I traveled here," Jacques said. "Let me see, can I remember their names? Blond, very pretty . . ."

Was Laurent imagining the quaver in Jacques's voice? "Their names are Jessica and Elizabeth Wakefield."

Jacques's hand clenched on the reins, and Laurent noticed his thighs tighten around the horse's sides. "I believe Jessica and I spoke briefly on the train," Jacques said slowly. "How can you be sure they did not steal the gem?"

"I have come to know one of them . . . Elizabeth . . . extremely well," Laurent explained. "It is inconceivable to me that she would steal anything. But since the girls are only au pairs and

Americans, no one wants to believe in their innocence."

"And you say they have escaped? Then the guards are after them," Jacques said, turning still paler. "They must be terrified."

"Yes, I am sure they are," Laurent agreed. "That's why I need to find them. I'm sure I can straighten everything out. There must be a logical explanation for Jessica wearing that stolen emerald." He ran a hand over his eyes, which felt as if an entire beach full of sand had taken up residence there.

Dawn was only moments away. Laurent looked up at Jacques and thought, *There is something unusual about this young man and his reaction to my story. He seems much more agitated than a true stranger would be. Is it possible he talked to Jessica for more than a few moments? All the more reason for him to help!*

"If you are willing to help," Laurent began, "I would be very grateful. Two heads are better than one, as the saying goes."

Jacques felt like he was falling over a cliff. *Oh, no! How could this happen? I can't believe I caused Jessica and her sister to be accused of this theft. What am I going to do to help them?*

"Of course I will help you, Your Excellency," Jacques said, trying to stay composed.

"Thank you, my friend. And please call me

Laurent. I hate titles," the prince said, steadying his horse by patting the big stallion's neck and cooing softly. Jacques was surprised by the prince's gesture of familiarity. Maybe royalty wasn't all bad.

"Now that we are a team, what should our first move be?" Laurent asked. Obviously the prince had begun to think of Jacques as an ally, and Jacques decided to encourage that.

"You said you have been searching all night, so you must be very tired," Jacques said. "Return to the château to rest, and I will take over the search." He looked at his watch, which he could now read in the growing dawn light. "I will contact you in three hours whether I find them or not, agreed?"

"I would feel much better if I could come with you. I believe they are still in the woods," Laurent said, stretching upright as if to ease his aching back. "We could each enter from a different side and meet in the middle, fan out from there."

Jacques couldn't permit Laurent to accompany him. If he did find the girls, they would be sure to ask dangerous questions about the emerald and his involvement in the crime. But he also couldn't afford to make the other young man suspicious.

"You look ready to drop from the saddle," he observed. "What would your father and mother do if something happened to you, if you fell asleep and then fell off your horse?"

"It is imperative that I continue searching with

you," Laurent insisted. "With both of us out here it greatly increases our chances of finding them."

Jacques could feel his hands turn clammy on the reins. So the parental concern tack wasn't going to work.

"They might not have continued through the woods," he suggested. "What if they doubled back to the château?"

Laurent's eyes widened in astonishment and understanding. "You are right!" he cried. "They might be there even at this moment, and if I am not present, my parents will surely throw them in the dungeon again!"

"Without a doubt," Jacques agreed eagerly. "With you back at the château and me searching out here, we have both places covered." Jacques sighed in relief. He was on his own again, just the way he liked it. "Three hours and I will call," he told the prince.

"Three hours," Laurent cried as he wheeled his magnificent stallion around and started off in the direction of the château.

Jacques turned his own horse toward the woods, watching Laurent grow smaller and smaller as he galloped away. All the while his mind raced.

My dear, sweet Jessica! First trapped in a dungeon and now desperately fleeing through the woods to escape. And it was cold last night! She might be sick or hurt somewhere in those woods! And all because of me.

Jacques groaned out loud at this new twist. He wanted more than ever to change. He and his father had lived this life of crime for too long, and his father's failing health made it even more necessary for them both to reform their ways. Once he found Jessica and somehow made everything right, he would do whatever it took to make his father give up on crime.

Resolutely Jacques spurred the horse forward and into the woods. *Just hold on a while longer, Jessica,* he pleaded silently. *I'm coming for you.*

Chapter 5

Dawn was tingeing the sky pink when Jessica first opened her eyes. She heard a groan and rolled over to look at Elizabeth.

"Oh, my ankle!" Elizabeth cried with a wince.

"Let me see," Jessica said. She sat up and pushed aside Elizabeth's now filthy white ball gown. The ankle that she had twisted the night before was swollen and ugly red in color. "It looks pretty bad."

"What are we going to do?" Elizabeth asked in what was for her an unusually whiny voice. "I can't walk on this ankle."

Although on the inside Jessica felt like a scared little girl, it wouldn't help either of them if she acted like one. She bit her lip, trying to think what to do.

"Maybe you should stay here and I should go find help," Jessica suggested.

"Great. Just leave me stranded," Elizabeth answered, shifting her position so there was no weight on her ankle.

"Well, what do you want me to do?" Jessica wailed. "How far do you think we can get if I have to support you on my shoulder?"

"I don't know, Jess. But I really think we should stick together. I mean, you can barely speak French. How are you going get help if you can't explain the situation?"

I hate this! Jessica thought. But she had to admit that Elizabeth was right. She wasn't going to get very far on her limited vocabulary.

"So we'll find Jacques in town, like we originally decided," she said in resignation. "We'll just have to go as fast as we can without getting you hurt again. Let's see what I can do about making something for you to lean on."

"That's silly, Jess," Elizabeth said in the same whiny voice, which was beginning to get on Jessica's nerves. "What are you going to use around here to make a crutch?"

"Just you wait and see," Jessica said, still trying to be cheerful. Under her ball gown she was wearing a long slip that would be perfect for binding branches together. She took it off and ripped it into several long strips of material. Then she gathered three thick branches and ripped the smaller twigs off each one.

"What are you doing?" Elizabeth asked, trying

to massage the pain out of her ankle.

"Making something to help you walk, silly," Jessica said firmly.

"Since when did you turn into such a Boy Scout?" Elizabeth asked, sounding slightly amused.

"Never mind," Jessica shot back. Using the strips of her slip, she bound the thick branches together as tightly as she could. She found some soft moss at the base of a tree and bound this to the top with the last strip of material. It was a crude crutch, but it might work. "There," Jessica announced. "How's that for imagination?"

Elizabeth rolled her eyes. "Not bad. Should I applaud?"

"Of course," Jessica said with a toss of her head. "And any donations will be gratefully accepted."

"Come on," Elizabeth grumbled. "Let's find Jacques and get this thing straightened out so I can take a bath and change clothes. I feel totally grungy!"

"Me too," Jessica agreed.

Elizabeth rolled over on the ground to her hands and knees. Then she carefully put her good foot flat. Using a nearby stump for leverage, she managed to stand up. "OK," she said, "here we go!" Holding up her hurt foot, she reached for the crutch, and Jessica handed it to her.

"That's it, Liz," Jessica said encouragingly while Elizabeth positioned the crutch beneath one arm. Then she gripped the crude instrument at its midpoint, moved it forward about a foot, and leaned on it while she swung her good foot forward and onto the ground.

Jessica jumped up and down and clapped. "That's great! It really works!" she cried.

"It might be slow going," Elizabeth warned. "But at least we can get to town sometime today."

"I hope the guards have given up by now. There's no way I could run at this point," Elizabeth commented as she and Jessica began wandering through the woods again.

"We're almost to the town, and we haven't seen any guards since last night, so don't worry about it," Jessica said reassuringly.

Just after dawn they crossed the drawbridge over the river that separated the chateau's land from the town.

"Only a little farther to go!" Elizabeth said, feeling better now that she could see the roofs of the town buildings in the distance.

"I'm so tired and hungry," Jessica moaned when they finally reached the edge of town.

"Try not to think about it," Elizabeth said grimly, holding the edge of her skirt above the ground with one hand while using the makeshift crutch as best she could with the other.

"But I can't even remember the last time we ate," Jessica went on. "And look how disgusting these dresses are!"

"They are pretty bad," Elizabeth admitted, looking down at what was once a beautiful, white, fairy-tale ball gown. It was now just a tattered, dirty rag, and it made her feel filthy. "But we can't do anything about that now. Let's just find Jacques."

"Jacques," Jessica said through clenched teeth. "When I get my hands on him . . ."

"Don't put all the blame on him, Jess," Elizabeth said. "You should have never trusted a stranger in the first place."

Jessica stopped dead in her tracks, and her eyes opened wide. "Well, is that the thanks I get for taking care of you last night?" she asked incredulously. "Building someplace for us to sleep and then making a crutch so you could walk? Hmph!" She turned her back on Elizabeth and folded her arms.

Elizabeth felt suddenly deflated. "I'm sorry, Jess," she conceded. "The last thing we should do is fight with each other. We have enough trouble on our hands."

Jessica turned slowly, and Elizabeth noticed tears in her eyes.

"Apology accepted," she said with a pout. "And don't yell at me anymore. I'm just as upset about this as you are!"

"OK, OK. Anyway, you know I can't stay mad at you for long. Let's go," Elizabeth said, trying to smile.

They limped into town, and Elizabeth tensed, expecting a legion of guards to attack them at any moment. Luckily the coast was clear.

"You have no idea where Jacques is staying?" Elizabeth asked.

"I don't remember the name of the place. In fact, I can't remember whether he even told me or not," Jessica said thoughtfully, chewing on her lower lip. "But how many hotels can there be? Look, you can see the end of the town from here."

The first inn was a quaint building designed like a French château. There was a café with sidewalk tables arranged outside and balconies on each window, which must have given the rooms a great view. For a fleeting moment Elizabeth wished she were a guest here so she could crawl upstairs and right into a nice bubble bath. She followed Jessica inside and found the innkeeper, a short, stout woman in a flowered dress and white apron.

"Do you have a Jacques Landeau staying here?" Jessica asked in English.

The innkeeper just shook her head. "Oh, well, Liz, let's go. . . ."

"Wait," Elizabeth said. She turned to the innkeeper and said in French, "Did you understand? We are looking for a young man named Jacques Landeau. He might be staying here with his father, the duke of Norveaux."

"There is no Landeau registered here," the innkeeper said gruffly in French. Then she laughed roughly. "And who is the duke of Norveaux? There is no such person!"

"Are you sure?" Elizabeth asked, trying to keep the desperation from her voice. She was so tired and hungry, and it felt like they would have to walk miles just to get to the next inn.

The innkeeper shook her head. "Even when you speak our language, you refuse to understand," she told Elizabeth in French. "Look at you in your dirty rags, trying to find a person I've never heard of. Norveaux?" She laughed again. "There is no such place!"

"Now what are we going to do?" Jessica moaned.

Elizabeth took a deep breath. "We can't give up yet," she said hopefully. "There's more than one inn, right? So let's go to the next one."

"Are you sure you can walk, Liz?" Jessica asked, her brow creasing into a frown. "Wouldn't you rather sit here while I check?"

"I'm not letting you out of my sight," Elizabeth warned. "What if the guards got you?"

"They wouldn't get me without a fight," Jessica assured her.

"Heaven help them," Elizabeth said ruefully. "Never mind. We go together or not at all."

"All for one and one for all?" Jessica teased.

"You got it," Elizabeth said, really smiling for the

first time. But inside she was worried. *What if Jacques has left town? How will we ever get out of this mess if he's disappeared?* she wondered to herself.

Jessica turned toward the door and smacked into the person coming in. Elizabeth looked up and gasped.

"Jacques!" she and Jessica both said at the same time.

"Jessica, you're safe!" Jacques cried as he grabbed Jessica by the shoulders and practically lifted her off the ground in a hug. His handsome face reflected both relief and exhaustion. "I can't believe it!" he cried.

Jessica was struggling in his arms. "Let me go, you creep!" she screamed. He immediately obliged, taking a step back.

Jacques's shoulders visibly slumped, as though he had suddenly taken on a heavy burden.

"I'm sorry," he said in a tired voice. "I was just so worried about you." There were dark circles under his eyes, and his mouth was down turned and sad. He looked as though he'd been up all night.

Elizabeth looked at Jacques, then at Jessica, whose feelings were written all over her face. Obviously Jessica still cared about Jacques, but she also looked suspicious.

"Where have you been?" Jessica demanded.

"I've been looking for you," he replied. "I ran into Prince Laurent last night. . . ."

"So you know?" Elizabeth asked harshly. "You

know about all the horror we've endured? How could you do this to us?"

"Please, please . . . ," Jacques said, his hands outstretched. He tried to touch Jessica's arm, but she flung him off.

"I want answers," Jessica began sternly, "and I want them now. Where did you get that emerald?" Jacques firmly took her arm and tried to lead her to a chair in the corner, but Jessica jerked away again.

"Don't touch me!" she said, but her expression softened.

Elizabeth noticed that the innkeeper and another bystander were watching them. "Shhh," she said, "let's not make a scene. Jacques, are you staying at this inn? The innkeeper kept telling us she never heard of you."

Jacques's face turned red. "Um, um . . . ," he said.

"The *truth*, Jacques," Jessica insisted, "if you can figure out how to tell the truth!"

Jacques squared his broad shoulders and said firmly, "My father and I are staying here, but we are not registered under the name Landeau. Jessica, Elizabeth, there is a lot you don't know about me. I'm sorry I tried to deceive you, but my name is not Landeau and I am not a duke's son."

Jessica sucked in her breath sharply and clapped a hand over her mouth. She groped backward, and

Elizabeth grabbed her arm and awkwardly led her to the big, overstuffed chair in front of the lobby fireplace.

"I can't stand it . . . ," Jessica said from behind her hand. "I believed in you!"

Elizabeth's heart went out to her sister as she watched the cold reality of Jacques's words register on Jessica's face.

Jacques swallowed hard. "Please, you must allow me to explain," he said in a shaky voice. "At least hear what I have to say."

Jessica was crying now, the tears making wet tracks down her cheeks. "How could you?" she said over and over. "How could you do this to me?"

Elizabeth wiped one hand across her eyes, struggling not to collapse with fatigue. "Jacques, can you tell us the truth?" she asked. "Will it be the truth? Because we're in a lot of trouble. . . ."

"I know," he said resignedly. "And I want to help."

"All right," Elizabeth said, making the decision for both herself and her sister. Jessica didn't look capable of doing much of anything. "We'll listen."

Laurent tossed and turned for two hours, then gave up trying to sleep. He had never heard from the young man, Jacques Landeau, and he thought that was an ominous sign. Could he still be searching?

He went for a walk in the early morning,

trying to exorcise the demons of the night, but it was no use. He could think of nothing but Elizabeth, lost somewhere, cold and alone. Even the sight of the pond didn't soothe him as it usually did. Instead it brought back memories of the happy times they'd spent there. *Where are you, Elizabeth?* Laurent thought as he gazed into the still blue water.

While he was heading back to the château, contemplating whether or not to start the search again, a guard approached. He handed Laurent a written summons to his parents' private drawing room, where they received close friends and family in a less formal atmosphere. Laurent dreaded this meeting, for he knew they would talk about Elizabeth's alleged crime. He knew the twins' escape didn't look good, but his heart told him Elizabeth was innocent. He somehow had to make his parents understand.

His hands were clammy and his shoulders were tense when he entered the private drawing room. His father was pacing up and down on the elegant Oriental rug before the fireplace, and his stepmother sat on the couch.

At least they looked less threatening than they had the night before. His father wore a simple dark blue business suit, with a crisp-looking immaculate white shirt and maroon silk tie into which he had poked a diamond tie tack. His stepmother had on a beautiful yellow silk dress that flowed around her ankles.

Neither one of them smiled, but at least his stepmother had a look of compassion on her face.

"Good morning, Father, Stepmother," Laurent began.

The prince stopped pacing and looked Laurent up and down. "The au pairs," he began, "are obviously guilty, my son. Why else would they have run away last night? Can you tell me that?"

He stopped, apparently to give Laurent a chance to answer his question, but Laurent said nothing.

"It appears the countess is right about the American girls," the older man went on. "They are nothing but common thieves!" His voice was stern and a frown cut deep into his forehead as he resumed his pacing and stopped once to shuffle some papers on his desk.

Laurent's stepmother delicately cleared her throat. "We understand how you feel, Laurent, how much you wish the countess to be wrong."

"Don't coddle him!" the prince warned as his anger obviously increased. "I will not tolerate any more discussion about the supposed innocence of those thieving young Americans. It is most obvious that the countess has been right all along." He wiped a hand over his face. "I should have known better than to trust an American. I have had many business dealings with them and had come to respect them. But I should have remembered they are still foreigners. I risked our children, no less!"

Laurent forced himself to keep quiet, hoping that his silence would somehow calm his father's rage. He had never seen him quite this angry before, and it was a daunting sight. He fought off the temptation to cringe.

"Yes," his stepmother admitted sadly, "I had grave reservations about the girls even before I met them. Do you remember, my dear?" she asked his father.

"Yes, yes," his father replied. "The age was the thing. Sixteen is quite young to take on such responsibility." He shook his head in dismay.

"That's why we hired both of them rather than one, because of their youth," his stepmother said. "Now I see our mistake. They are too young to be responsible."

Laurent's father nodded. "Yes, dear, you were right all along, it seems. You were wiser than I." He punctuated his remark by flinging both hands up in the air in a gesture of frustration.

Finally it seemed as if Laurent's silence made an impression on his father, for the older man stopped pacing and approached him. Face-to-face with his father, Laurent resisted the urge to lower his eyes.

"Laurent, what have you to say for yourself?" the prince demanded.

"I will never believe that Elizabeth stole that emerald," he began firmly. "She hasn't a dishonest bone in her body."

His father rolled his eyes, but his stepmother

spoke from her seat near the window, more coolly this time.

"It is obvious to us that you have become . . . *attached* to Elizabeth, but the jewel was found in her sister's possession," she insisted. "Surely you have some explanation for that if you are so certain Elizabeth is innocent."

Laurent hung his head and said quietly, "I have no explanation." Laurent would hate himself forever for his next words, knowing how badly they would hurt Elizabeth if she heard them. He knew Jessica meant more to Elizabeth than just about anyone else in the world.

"But please remember, the jewel was found in *Jessica's* possession, not Elizabeth's," he said, immediately feeling guilty. "You can't blame Elizabeth for something Jessica may have done." He fervently hoped Elizabeth would never find out how disloyal he had been.

Now, for the first time, his stepmother was openly and clearly unsympathetic. She sat up straighter in her seat, and her fingers drummed restlessly on the table beside the couch.

"You can't honestly believe Elizabeth would not know," she insisted. "They're right next to each other in those tower rooms. How could she not know her twin sister had something so obviously valuable?" she asked.

"But we never even heard their explanation," Laurent insisted, walking up and down a few steps to relieve his frustration. *How can I get through to them?* he wondered helplessly. "They were just thrown into the dungeon without the opportunity to speak."

His stepmother waved one hand dismissively. "There was no time for them to speak. There was the ball to see to, and we could not afford any negative publicity on such a public occasion," she explained.

His father raked one hand through his hair. "You must learn, Laurent, that scandal is the one thing royalty must avoid." The older man went to his desk, where his pipe rested in an ashtray. He went about the business of filling and lighting his pipe, using tobacco that he carried in a breast pocket and a solid gold lighter from the desktop. Soon the air was filled with the aroma of pipe smoke. Laurent had always found the smell curiously comforting.

"I admit we might have handled it differently," his stepmother continued, "but it's done now. And we would have let them out of the dungeon to explain first thing this morning." She used her right hand to adjust the diamond tennis bracelet on her left wrist. "Unfortunately the fact that they ran away does complicate matters."

"We cannot ignore that fact," his father interjected, brushing some imagined dust off the cuff of his suit jacket and puffing on his pipe. "Nor can we ignore the importance of the countess, who suffered the loss. Do you realize how unpleasant she could make things for all of us?"

The thought of the countess wielding her power against them must have ignited his father's anger once again because he resumed his pacing.

"This is an international incident already! And the countess has threatened to call a press conference and *publicly* accuse the girls if they aren't found soon!" he shouted, pounding on a nearby desktop to punctuate his words.

"Yes, Laurent." His stepmother picked up where his father left off. "And you know how difficult it is to appease the countess. I'm worn out trying to keep her occupied, let alone cope with this situation."

Laurent was dizzy from the constant barrage, though he realized all that his parents said was true. But he just couldn't give up.

"Then at least allow me to find them myself," he pleaded. "They must be terrified, with the dungeon and the dogs and all. Elizabeth will trust me, and then we might get to the real truth."

Laurent's father cleared his throat. "And what about the missing diamond necklace?" he asked more quietly. "That was stolen right here in the château."

Laurent's stomach clenched. "I don't know. But my heart tells me the twins did not steal anything. . . . They are not criminals . . . at least not Elizabeth. I am willing to do whatever it takes to help prove that."

Laurent's father stroked his cheek thoughtfully, apparently considering his son's words. He strolled over to the window to look outside, and for a long time Laurent wondered if he would say anything at all. The smoke from the pipe curled upward from the window in a lazy ribbon.

"All right," he said finally, "I will make a deal with you. I wish to secure our country's future by your marriage to Antonia di Rimini. But it has become obvious to me that you do not wish to marry her." He turned from the window with raised eyebrows, and Laurent nodded uncertainly. "If I can promise that the countess will not prosecute the girls, will you fulfill your duty? Will you marry Antonia?"

Laurent felt as if his father had reached inside him and torn out his heart. He reached for something, anything to lean on, and when he realized there was a chair nearby, he sat down quickly. His knees had turned to jelly, and his head was swimming.

Is this man really my father? he wondered to himself. *How can he suggest such a thing? How can he ask me to make that choice? Doesn't he realize he's making me throw my life away?*

"I don't know what to say, Father," he began, his voice sounding hollow in his ears.

His stepmother stood up and joined the elder prince. She refused to meet Laurent's eyes, and he could see the reddish tinge of a blush in her cheeks.

"I must see to the countess, my dear," she said to his father. "I'm sure I can smooth her ruffled feathers for the time being, until you bring her Laurent's decision." She left the room.

Finally Laurent looked up at his father, who was still standing beside the fireplace. His father's expression was stern and unyielding, and for the first time in his life Laurent came close to disliking his own father.

"How can you be sure the countess will agree to drop the charges against the twins?" he began, desperately hoping there was some other way to help Elizabeth.

"This political alliance means as much to the countess as it does to us," he said in a slow, deliberate manner. "If I can assure her that you will marry Antonia, I'm more than certain she will agree to my terms." The older man reached up to smooth the front of his tie.

Laurent knew his father was right. Even the countess was intelligent enough to have noticed that Laurent was less than interested in Antonia. Letting a couple of teenage girls go back to America with a clean record would probably be trivial compared to risking an international incident. Laurent lowered his head and stared at his clasped hands in his lap.

"Please make up your mind, Laurent," his father persisted. "Agree to this marriage, and Elizabeth is free."

Laurent took a deep breath. He felt trapped, and all he wanted was to run from the château and never look back. There must be someplace in the world where he wouldn't have to face this hopeless decision! His father might as well throw him into the dungeon. Marriage to Antonia would be like prison. *Worse.*

And yet Laurent's heart constricted as he realized he was Elizabeth's only chance. How much did he love her? Enough to throw his life away for her sake? And if he didn't marry Antonia, would he be able to live with what would happen to Elizabeth? There was really only one choice, wasn't there?

"Very well, Father," he said softly. He pressed the palms of his hands down hard on his thighs to keep them from shaking. "I will marry Antonia."

The prince smiled for the first time since Laurent had entered the room. "That's my boy," he said, his relief obvious as he approached Laurent and patted him on the back. "I knew you would do the right thing in the end, son."

Laurent wanted to fling his father's hand away, but he did nothing. He had promised to live a life of misery. A life devoid of love and passion. *But it was surely worth it,* he thought with grim determination. He would do anything in his power to save the only girl he would ever love—Elizabeth Wakefield.

Chapter 6

Once Jessica and her sister were safely behind the closed door of Jacques's shabby room, she whirled on him with fury.

"How could you do this to me?" she demanded. "How could you set me up like this?"

She clenched her fists, and her chest heaved with anger. "What kind of creep are you to talk about love while lying through your teeth about who you are? I want answers . . . *now!*" She wanted to scratch his eyes out, or pull his hair, or . . . *something*, anything to make him feel as much pain as she was suffering.

Jacques kept his eyes lowered while Jessica was screaming. His shoulders were slumped, and he kept his hands very still at his sides. When he finally raised his eyes to her, the pain in them made her almost sorry she had yelled so loud . . . *almost.*

"Jessica—" he began.

"Do you realize everything we've been through?" she continued, steeling herself against the sudden wave of pity she felt for him. "We were in the woods all night! In the cold! With no blankets, no coats, nothing to eat!"

"That, at least, I can fix," Jacques said quietly, picking up the phone.

Jessica felt faint at the thought of food. She could tell Elizabeth was feeling the same way, and her heart thawed a bit at Jacques's immediate thoughtfulness. She wished desperately that there was some logical explanation for everything he had done to them. He was so handsome, and they had shared so many special moments. She couldn't help loving him, even after all that had happened.

Minutes after Jacques called down to the kitchen, the innkeeper brought up a tray of flaky croissants, strawberry jam, and a big pot of strong coffee. Jessica and Elizabeth immediately dug in, each grabbing a pastry while Jacques poured the coffee. The simple act of eating released much of the tension in the air.

"How did you run into Prince Laurent last night?" Elizabeth asked, spreading some jam on a croissant.

Jacques offered a steaming cup to Jessica and began filling another one for Elizabeth.

"I felt that Jessica was in danger," he said. "So I

borrowed a horse and rode out of town to try and see you at the château. I met Prince Laurent coming into town, and he told me what happened."

"You felt that I was in danger?" Jessica asked, her heart leaping at the thought of how strong their connection was. Then she noticed the intent stare her twin had fixed on Jacques.

"Prince Laurent was looking for us?" Elizabeth asked with wonder in her voice.

"Yes. In fact, he was quite worried," Jacques said, smiling for the first time. "He told me he did not believe you were thieves."

Elizabeth sighed, and Jessica saw tears come to her eyes. "Even after all that's happened, he still believes in us!" She wiped at her eyes and placed her half-eaten croissant on a plate.

Jacques didn't touch his food, and Jessica noticed his leg bouncing up and down nervously.

"It is time for me to be honest," he began slowly. He looked down at his hands, clasping and unclasping them. "My real name is Jacques Savant."

He studied their faces for their reaction to his words, then lowered his eyes again.

"Uh, hmmm . . . ," he stuttered. "M-My . . . my father and I are commoners . . . and . . . we make our living . . . as jewel thieves." The last three words came in a rush, then he stood up and went quickly to the window.

Jessica could see how difficult this whole thing

was for Jacques, but she was too shocked to care. She dropped the croissant she was holding and jumped to her feet. "You . . . you . . . creep! You knew all along exactly what you were doing. You set me up deliberately, and now Elizabeth and I are going back to that horrid dungeon!" The traumatic events of the past twenty-four hours caught up with Jessica, and she burst into tears.

"I knew you were a fraud," Elizabeth said angrily.

Jacques turned quickly from the window and grabbed Jessica by the arms.

"Please, Jessica, give me a chance!" His face was very pale as he looked deeply into her eyes.

Jessica struggled and tried to break free, but Jacques was too strong. She wriggled for a moment more and then was still. She felt positively overwhelmed by everything that had happened over the past few days.

"They set dogs on us . . . we ran and ran . . . and Liz hurt her ankle!" The words spilled out of her mouth.

"Oh, Jessica," Jacques said, trying to pull her close. "You will never know how sorry I am."

She jerked herself free and pushed him away as hard as she could. He fell back a few steps, and his stricken look told her how much the rejection hurt him.

"Don't touch me! I don't want you near me after what you did to me!" she screamed.

"I said I was sorry, and I do still love you. At least listen to my story," Jacques pleaded.

Jessica calmed somewhat at the soft, firm strength she heard in his voice. The plea in his warm brown eyes was nearly irresistible, and she sat down next to Elizabeth.

"Well?" she demanded, determined not to make this easy on him.

"When I was very young," Jacques began, taking a seat across from Jessica, "my mother and father and I lived in Paris. My father sold vegetables, and my mother was a seamstress for many rich people." Jacques's eyes turned wistful at the memory.

"Her work was so good, many of them would consult no one else for their fancy ball dresses and suits for afternoon tea. But then," he said, pain turning his voice harsh, "*Maman* got sick, and my father went to her rich clients, convinced that because of her service to them they would willingly help with the expensive medicine she needed."

Jacques sucked in his breath, and Jessica felt her eyes start to fill with tears all over again. He looked so distraught and helpless. She couldn't believe the effect he had on her.

"What happened when your father asked for their help?" Jessica asked in a quiet voice, fearing she already knew the answer.

"No one would help!" he cried bitterly, bringing one hand to his face to cover his eyes. "*Maman* died a slow and painful death, and it changed my father overnight into someone I didn't know, a bitter old man. As they lowered the coffin into the ground *mon père* swore we would never again be poor, no matter what."

This part seemed to be harder for Jacques because he swallowed a few times before continuing.

"So he began to steal," he said haltingly, "first from *Maman's* rich clients, then from others, but always only from rich people—people who he thought had too much."

He took a gulp of his coffee before plunging ahead. "Papa gradually stopped being angry, and stealing became more like a game, especially when I was younger."

"Didn't it bother you that your father was a criminal?" Elizabeth asked.

Jacques shook his head.

"When I was little, I didn't know any better," he answered. "I thought it was all in fun. It was exciting to slip in and out of the big houses. And there were times when we stole so much that we could live like kings on the Riviera."

Jacques sighed and looked up at the ceiling.

"But the years took their toll. Now we live a simple life, stealing only when the money runs out." Jacques glanced at the twins, an expression of desperation on his face. "Please understand. This is the only way of life I've known since my mother passed away."

When neither Jessica nor Elizabeth spoke, Jacques shook his head hard, seemingly impatient with his own explanation.

"My father needed the emerald desperately to repay a debt," he said wearily. "I hoped only to have enough money to find him someplace warm to retire, for his health."

"And you, Jacques?" Elizabeth asked, her voice hard. "Will you keep stealing jewels and framing innocent people?"

"I deserve that," he said contritely, then sighed again. "No, I do not wish to steal anymore. Once my father is settled somewhere, I will work at something, it doesn't matter what, so long as it is an honest living."

Jacques looked down at his hands. He appeared to be trying to make a decision.

"As for now," he said quietly, "I am ready to give myself up so you and your sister can go free, Jessica."

Jessica could no longer contain herself. She flew into Jacques's arms, hugging him close, the tears spilling down her cheeks. Yes, he was a thief, and stealing was wrong. But poor Jacques, growing up without a mother! Poor Mr. Savant, whose wife died because of selfish rich people!

"I'm sorry I was so hard on you, Jacques. How terrible it must have been to lose your mother," she said. Thinking of her own loving parents back in Sweet Valley, Jessica could only begin to imagine his pain.

96

Jessica looked over at Elizabeth and saw tears in her sister's eyes too.

"I'm sorry," Elizabeth began, "but I have to ask. Do you have the diamond necklace?"

Jacques pushed Jessica away gently, and she reluctantly let him go.

"I must get it from my father," he said. "Will you wait here for me?" His loving look wrapped Jessica in warmth as she nodded. She heaved a deep sigh as he left the room, suddenly sure that everything would be all right.

Elizabeth's heart ached as Jacques quietly slipped from the room. She realized how lucky she was to have two parents who loved her and how difficult it would be to do without either one of them. She leaned back in her seat and wiped the tears from her eyes.

"Oh, Liz, isn't there something we can do for Jacques and his father? It's terrible that a sick old man and his young son have to go to prison," Jessica cried.

"Jacques's story is a sad one," Elizabeth admitted, "but they've been stealing for years. How would you feel if he had taken the diamond earrings Grandma gave us?"

"Not too good," Jessica said ruefully. "I'm just afraid they'll get the death penalty or something."

"Law in France is different than in America," Elizabeth said with a smile. "But I really don't think they would execute anybody for stealing. Especially if the stolen article is returned."

"How can you be so sure?" Jessica demanded. "They threw us in the dungeon without even waiting for an explanation!"

"True," Elizabeth replied slowly. "But it has to make a difference to the prince that the jewels are being returned."

Jessica's face brightened. "You may be right," she said. "And maybe you could talk to Prince Laurent, get him to help!"

Elizabeth's heart sank at the mention of Laurent. It eased her mind to know that Laurent believed in her, but that didn't change the fact that he was still engaged to Antonia.

"I'm not sure what Laurent could do," she mumbled.

Jessica instantly put an arm around Elizabeth. "I'm sorry, Liz. I didn't mean to make you feel bad by bringing up Laurent. But at least he doesn't think you're a criminal," she said brightly. "And he did spend the night trying to find you."

"I know," Elizabeth said wearily. "But Jess, he's still going to marry Antonia, no matter how he feels about me!" She felt as if she wanted to cry, but her eyes were all dried out. *It's hopeless even to think about Laurent anymore,* she told herself bitterly. *He's lost to me forever!*

Jessica squeezed her gently.

"It'll all work out, Liz, you'll see," she said

encouragingly. "And if it doesn't, just think of him spending the rest of his life with that witch, Antonia. That's a great punishment for breaking your heart."

Elizabeth had to smile then. "Yeah, I guess you're right. I wouldn't wish Antonia di Rimini on my worst enemy!"

Chapter 7

Jessica took a sip of her now cold coffee and wrinkled her nose.

"What's keeping Jacques?" she wondered out loud.

"I hope he hasn't disappeared on us," Elizabeth said ominously.

Jessica shot her an irritated glare. "Can't you cut him some slack, Liz?"

Just then Jacques burst back into the room.

"My father . . . he is gone! He left this note!"

Jessica could see Jacques's hands were trembling as he handed the note to Elizabeth. She clutched the crumpled paper in her hand, a bewildered look on her face.

"Well, Liz, what does the note say?" Jessica demanded.

She watched while Elizabeth scanned the note

quickly, then went back to the beginning for a more thorough read. Then she began to translate. "I am worried that you are getting soft, my son. I have taken the diamond necklace to satisfy our friends. If they are not repaid, they will surely seek revenge."

Jessica sat back on her chair hard. "Oh, no," she moaned aloud. "This means we have to go back to the château without the necklace. They'll put us back in the dungeon for sure!"

"Calm down," Elizabeth said sternly. "Let's think about this."

But Jessica was too distraught to think.

"Why can't we just get on the train to Paris and never look back?" She jumped up, every fiber of her being screaming to run away. "We have to get out of here!"

"Running away isn't the answer," Elizabeth said. "Besides, where would we run to?"

"Home," Jessica said immediately, her mind racing. "Jacques can go with us. If he came to Sweet Valley, he'd be safe too." *Yes,* she thought, *it's the only way. Jacques can't stay here—they'll put him in jail or maybe even kill him. The only thing left to do is get out of the country as quickly as possible.* Suddenly she noticed Elizabeth's shocked face, her mouth hanging wide open.

"What's wrong, Liz?"

"What are you talking about, Jess? We can't take Jacques back to America with this hanging

101

over our heads!" Elizabeth jumped to her feet and waved her arms in an agitated manner. "The countess is so powerful, she could make Jacques come back, and us too for that matter. It's called *extradition*."

"No one is that powerful, Liz," Jessica sneered. "Besides, I want to go home!"

"Jessica, this isn't some movie here!" Elizabeth cried. "This is real life! And they think we're criminals!"

"All the more reason to leave!" Jessica retorted. "They're convinced, and we can't change their minds."

"We already made it look bad by escaping from the dungeon," Elizabeth went on. "It'll look even worse if we try to leave the country."

Jacques put one arm around Jessica's shoulders and squeezed gently. "Elizabeth is right, Jessica," he soothed. "America is out of the question for me."

"Don't say that!" Jessica cried, jerking away from his arm. "We're all going home! We'll be safe there!" She couldn't believe they didn't see this her way.

"No, Jessica," Jacques went on calmly and firmly. "We are going back to the château, where I will explain everything. Then all will be right again."

Suddenly Jessica understood what Jacques was saying.

"But if you explain everything, that means . . ." She turned wide eyes on him. "Do you want to be put in the dungeon?"

Jacques nodded slightly. His eyes were sad but determined. "There is no other choice," he said.

"But . . . but . . . ," Jessica stammered.

"Calm down," Elizabeth repeated, this time moving close enough to Jessica to take her hand.

"No. I refuse to let Jacques be locked away. We are going back to Sweet Valley." Jessica sat down and crossed her arms over her chest, looking straight ahead. She wasn't going to budge. There was no way she could agree to seeing the one guy she really loved give himself over to a life in prison.

Elizabeth moaned and turned her back on Jessica. Obviously Jessica's sensible sister was going to take a little more convincing. "C'mon, Liz," she exclaimed, standing up again and walking around in excitement. "Can you see Lila's face when I bring home my very own French boyfriend? She'll be positively green!"

And I can show Jacques all the hangouts, Jessica thought, her imagination taking flight. *The beach, the Dairi Burger, school. He can come watch me at cheerleading practice, maybe even take courses at the university.*

You may not know it yet, sister dear, but we are going home, and Jacques is coming with us!

Elizabeth had watched Jessica get tangled up in

her own illusions before, but this was the worst. She knew logic never worked on her sister, but it was the only weapon she had left.

"Jessica," she began, turning around to face her sister's beaming eyes. "It's going to be pretty hard to get to California with no clothes or money."

What a mess! Elizabeth thought, trying to ease her ankle into a more comfortable position. *I'm filthy, injured, and penniless, and to top it off, Jessica's finally lost it.*

Jessica didn't answer, but her determined expression didn't change either.

"Did you hear me, Jess? We have no clothes, no money!" Elizabeth insisted. "The only way out of this is to return to the château."

If we run away now, nothing will ever be the same again, Elizabeth thought. *This horrible summer will hang over the rest of our lives like a dark cloud.*

But Jessica just stared at her stupidly, almost as if Elizabeth were speaking to her in a language she didn't understand.

Elizabeth grabbed Jessica by the arms and shook her a little. "Jessica, look at me, look at yourself!" she said firmly. "We have to go back!"

Jessica's grim expression suddenly drooped, and her eyes cleared in reluctant understanding.

"OK, Liz, you can stop shaking me now," she said in a dull voice. "I guess we have to go back."

Elizabeth heaved a sigh of relief.

"Thank goodness!" she cried. She wasn't really keen on Jacques going to the dungeon, or anyone else for that matter. True, she hadn't entirely trusted him up to now, but no one deserved to be in that cold, dank, musty place. It was like something out of the Middle Ages! And Jacques seemed somehow different, more sincere. There was no more of that phony French moonlight in his voice.

But now Jessica was staring at her unhappily. "I can't believe how insensitive you are, Liz," she said, a sob catching her voice. "Jacques is going to the dungeon, but you don't care one bit. If it were Prince Laurent being sent up the river, you'd be bawling your eyes out right now!"

"We don't know that Jacques is going to the dungeon," Elizabeth insisted. "We won't know anything until we go back to the château."

"That's right," Jacques said. "But there is one thing I *will* promise you, Jessica. Even if I do go to prison, it is not the end for us."

Elizabeth was warmed by Jacques's compassion for her sister's feelings, and she smiled slightly. She was grateful that she wasn't the only logical person in the room. *Maybe I really did misjudge him after all,* she thought. *But I'm still not letting him out of my sight until our names are cleared!*

"Come on," Elizabeth said, hoisting herself to her feet with her makeshift crutch. "We might as well get this over with."

"All right," Jessica said grudgingly. She reached

out a hand and helped Elizabeth get her balance.

Jacques shook his head and smiled sadly. "You must not leave my country in disgrace, Jessica," he pointed out.

Jessica suddenly threw her arms around Jacques's neck.

"I can't believe you're actually going to confess!" she cried. "I don't understand why there isn't some way to prove that we're innocent without having to turn you in!"

Jacques removed himself from Jessica's grasp and smiled at her sadly again. Then he walked over and opened the door, holding it as the twins passed through.

"Everything will be fine, Jess," Elizabeth said as she hobbled into the hallway. Relief coursed through her tired body. She was just glad that they were on their way.

I'm going to get a chance to explain everything to Laurent. No matter what else happens, he'll always know I was innocent.

Prince Laurent lifted his chin slightly so his valet, François, could button the top button of the formal uniform he was wearing to the upcoming press conference. True to his word, he had allowed his father to invite reporters from all over the country so they could be there when he announced his official engagement to Antonia di Rimini.

"If I may say so, sir," François began deferentially,

"you look very fine this morning. This must be a happy day for you." François was a short, stout man in his early forties, with graying hair at his temples and an absolute sense of what to say and do at the perfect time. Laurent had known him all his life.

"Thank you," Laurent replied automatically. "Of course it is." Laurent frowned, sad that he could not confide his real feelings even to his own valet, a man who had known him since birth.

Every piece of clothing he wore was heavily braided in gold, with epaulets and shiny buttons and military medals that he hadn't earned but that his rank allowed him. Never before had the formal court dress weighed him down so. But he knew it was really his spirit that was so heavy.

His future stretched out before him—marrying Antonia, having children, ruling the country—a great dark span of years filled with duty and responsibility. And all without the one thing he most desired, the love of Elizabeth Wakefield.

"Did Miss Antonia like the ring you gave her this morning?" François asked. He was busy brushing and examining Laurent's tuxedo, which he would need for the betrothal celebration that night. Laurent knew that François would make sure his evening clothes were perfect.

"She was . . . appropriately pleased," Laurent said carefully. Actually, when he gave her the ring shortly after breakfast, she had let out an ear-piercing screech. In a split second she had flown out of her

107

chair and practically strangled him with a hug, smearing her garish lipstick all over his cheeks with her kisses.

He could not imagine how she would be able to function as the wife of an international political leader. *At our first state dinner she will probably jump up and down when she shakes hands with some dignitary,* he thought ruefully.

Still, it was better to follow his father's directions in order to free Elizabeth and her sister from the countess's evil designs. At least he would always know that Elizabeth was free to pursue her own dreams.

Laurent waved François away from giving his uniform one last brushing and left his rooms to meet his parents on the large terrace outside. Everything had been set up for the press conference. When he emerged from the château, cameras flashed wildly and microphones were thrust in his face as reporters fired questions at him.

He ignored them all and made his way toward his parents. They were standing to the side of a podium with the Countess di Rimini. His father wore military dress identical to his own, complete with braid and medals. The countess wore a tailored yellow linen suit that barely disguised her bulges. His stepmother was smartly turned out in a flattering two-piece suit in a lovely shade of green. The countess posed herself with an eye to the many cameras that flashed here and there.

"Father, Stepmother, Countess," Laurent greeted them, nodding slightly.

"You look very handsome, Laurent," his stepmother commented.

"Yes, son," his father said approvingly. "We are all awaiting your important announcement."

"I will remain true to my word, Father," he said in a careful tone. It would never do for his heart's pain to come through in his public speaking voice. The countess said nothing, as if daring him to back out.

Antonia waited for Laurent at the podium, dressed in a rather outrageous red suit, cut low across the bosom. She held her head high, nose in the air, plainly triumphant. Occasionally she moved her left hand so the sun could glint off her new ring. *That's hardly an appropriate outfit in which to announce an engagement,* Laurent thought. *Elizabeth would never wear something like that!*

Laurent approached the podium and leaned down slightly toward the microphone.

"May I have your attention, please?" His voice boomed out over the expectant crowd. A chorus of whispers and "Shhhs" greeted his request. He looked back at his parents before beginning, and their pride shone on their faces. He wished he could feel the same about what he was now going to do.

When all was quiet, he began in French. "It is my honor and pleasure to announce today my betrothal to Antonia di Rimini." There were more flashing lights and buzzing comments, and all Laurent could think of was Elizabeth's sweet face, her sea blue eyes, the way she moved in unconscious, graceful gestures.

If anyone looks or acts like a princess, it's Elizabeth, he thought. He couldn't help comparing his lovely, elegant Elizabeth with the shrill, coarse, self-centered Antonia. Then he mentally shook himself in order to be able to answer the reporters' questions, pointing to one persistent woman who had her hand raised.

The reporter opened her mouth to speak but was cut off.

"Look!" someone shouted suddenly, and all heads turned. Stumbling across the lawn, in their dirty, torn ball gowns, blond hair in matted tangles, came Elizabeth and Jessica.

Laurent almost called out to Elizabeth in joy but snapped his mouth shut when he saw someone emerge from the woods behind the twins.

It was Jacques Landeau.

Chapter 8

Elizabeth leaned on Jessica and Jacques as they made their way toward the château. Her heart leapt into her throat when she saw the vast array of reporters and cameramen arranged on the front lawn.

"Oh, no, they must be announcing the theft and identifying us as fugitives!" she exclaimed in panic.

She lost her grip on the crutch, and it clunked to the ground. Jacques quickly scooped it up before she could lose her balance and placed it in her hand.

"Do you think so?" Jessica asked, glancing down at her worn, filthy dress. "I don't want any reporters taking pictures of me in this ratty old ball gown!"

They stopped abruptly when the whole crowd turned in their direction. Elizabeth felt as if the eyes of the entire world were on her, and in a

111

corner of her mind she realized this must be how Laurent felt every day. It was how he lived his life—under a microscope.

Then Elizabeth noticed the Countess di Rimini and Antonia openly smiling, almost puffed out with happiness. *Oh, no,* Elizabeth thought, tears welling in her tired eyes. She scanned Antonia's left hand, and sure enough, a huge diamond engagement ring glittered there in the sunlight.

Antonia looked down her nose at Elizabeth and smiled smugly. She raised her left hand and wiggled the ring finger until Elizabeth was almost blinded by the reflection of the sun off the twinkling diamond.

"What a tasteless witch she is!" Jessica said into Elizabeth's ear. "I bet even Lila would think that ring was too much!"

Elizabeth didn't care what Lila thought. "How could he?" she moaned under her breath. Numbly she looked at Laurent.

Laurent lowered his eyes quickly to stare at his clenched hands, as if he were ashamed to face her, but Elizabeth had already seen the evidence of his broken heart written across his features.

"It makes me sick," she said to Jessica, her pain mingling with outrage that she had so misjudged Laurent. "He's trading his happiness for his duty. Why doesn't he stand up for himself? He's nothing but a coward."

But even as she said the words, Elizabeth knew

they weren't true. It was just the hurt talking. Laurent was a brave and wonderful person. And she knew he loved her. There must be some other reason he had agreed to marry Antonia and leave Elizabeth behind.

But why, Laurent? Elizabeth asked him silently. *What could make you throw away our love?*

Elizabeth slumped a little after her outburst, and Jessica wrapped her arm more tightly around her sister's shoulders. She glanced over Elizabeth's head at Jacques, and he locked eyes with her.

"Take care of Elizabeth, Jessica," Jacques said firmly. "I'll do the rest." Then he started across the lawn.

Elizabeth leaned against her heavily, and without Jacques's support Jessica nearly fell over. It seemed as if Jacques was moving in slow motion, taking one step after another, moving toward the podium, every head turning to follow him.

"Jess, you're hurting me," she heard Elizabeth say. She looked down at where she gripped Elizabeth's arm and saw how tightly her fingers were wrapped around it. She loosened up a little and looked back toward the podium.

Jacques had finally reached the terrace. Jessica wanted to scream as Jacques politely asked Laurent to step away from the podium. *He can't do this, he can't do this!* she thought frantically. *How can I stop him? Should I just run up and shove him aside?*

But Jacques was already speaking in French. "What is he saying?" she asked Elizabeth.

"He's apologizing for the interruption," Elizabeth explained in a low voice. "And he's saying that we never stole anything."

"Yes, yes, I just heard our names!" she said impatiently. "What else?"

"He's admitting he stole the emerald and the diamond necklace. I can't believe it!" Elizabeth continued. "Somehow I didn't think he would go through with his confession."

"I have to go up there," Jessica said. She looked around frantically for something for Elizabeth to sit on. She grabbed one of the chairs from the cluster where the reporters had been sitting and dumped Elizabeth into it.

"Wait here!" she hissed and then sprinted forward as the guards came to claim their prisoner. "Don't hurt him!" she cried desperately in English.

The guards didn't seem to hear her. They grabbed Jacques by each arm and almost pulled him off his feet as they dragged him away from the podium. Jessica looked at the royal family, but the prince and princess were only shaking their heads sadly.

Laurent seemed to be in a state of shock. The countess's expression alternated between triumph and consternation. It seemed to Jessica that she

114

couldn't make up her mind whether to be happy that the real thief had confessed or upset that it hadn't been Jessica and her sister after all.

Jessica knew she would get no help from anyone on that terrace. She followed the guards as best she could, dodging in and out among the reporters and photographers who were stampeding in an attempt to get a statement from Jacques. *Evidently,* Jessica thought, *his confession is even more newsworthy than Prince Laurent's announcement.*

But the guards wouldn't let anyone get near Jacques. They managed to drag him into the château. Jessica knew they would throw him into the dungeon, probably into the same cell Jessica had shared with Elizabeth. Somehow she had to get in there and see him . . . if only to say good-bye!

Jacques knew he would be taken away once he made his announcement, but he had no idea the guards would be so swift or so rough. He just managed to catch Jessica's eye and mouth the words "I love you" before they hauled him to a back entrance of the château. The last thing he saw before they closed the door was a sea of unfamiliar faces . . . the reporters from the press conference who were screaming questions and taking pictures.

The guards dragged him down a long flight of

jagged steps into a dark cellar, where they pushed him into a cold, stone cell and slammed the door shut.

"Dirty thief!" the taller guard spat at him in French before they both disappeared.

Now what? Jacques pulled himself off the floor and sat on the cot. It was lumpy and uncomfortable but better than the floor. The one window in the tiny cell was high on the wall, but by standing on the cot on tiptoes he could just see outside.

It seemed incredible that the sun could still be shining and that a tangy sea breeze could find its way into this dank cell. He wondered what Jessica was doing. Was she worried about him? Would she try to see him?

Everything Jacques had was gone, except for Jessica. At least he hoped he still had Jessica. His father would never come near the château. It was too great a risk. Jacques had no other family or friends. Just Jessica. He hoped she would at least try to visit him.

At least his father was safe. The dungeon was a cold, smelly, damp place, and Jacques figured prison would be no better. His father's health would never withstand being locked up in a cell like this. It was better that Jacques should be locked away. Perhaps there wouldn't be a long sentence. He could still be a relatively young man when he got out.

But who was he kidding? With the countess

involved, he had no reason to hope for leniency. No, he might as well face it. His life was over.

Although he hadn't cried since his mother died years ago, Jacques sat back down on the cot and buried his face in his hands, tears falling between his fingers.

As Laurent watched Jacques being dragged away he felt as if he were dreaming. *None of this is happening,* Laurent thought. *It can't be.*

Now that this Jacques person had come forward, the reason for Laurent's engagement had vanished. The girls were no longer under suspicion of theft, so he had agreed to this idiotic engagement for no reason.

But now the damage was done. The whole world had heard about the betrothal. It would be humiliating for his family and Antonia's if he backed out now. For the sake of propriety he would have to throw his life away.

Elizabeth was still sitting on the chair that Jessica had found for her, and Laurent noticed for the first time that one of her ankles was bound with a bandage. Elizabeth was hurt! More than ever he wished he could gather her in his arms and swear to her his undying devotion.

Her eyes were so sad. Anxious to erase the pain he saw there, Laurent began to move off the terrace in her direction. Elizabeth, however, shook her head ever so slightly. She stood shakily and spoke to a nearby guard, who then began to help her into the château. Now that she was no longer a suspect, the guard seemed only too happy to help. As Laurent watched her limp away, his heart constricted. *This is the worst day of my life,* he thought in despair.

Suddenly a hand grabbed his arm. He looked down into Antonia's upturned, beaming face.

"At long last," she said in a loud, shrill voice, "we're officially engaged!"

Laurent could only nod.

"And we'll have the most beautiful wedding," she went on, apparently unaware of his total revulsion. "The attendants will all be in blue. What do you think of a spring wedding?"

"Fine," he said in a bland voice, wishing he could jerk his arm from her grasp. Her touch made his skin crawl.

"Son," the countess said, embracing him stiffly. "Welcome to our family."

His stepmother embraced him formally, and then his father stepped up. As he too embraced Laurent he said into his ear, "And your Elizabeth is cleared completely, it seems."

"Yes, Father," Laurent said in a tired voice. "So it would seem."

"And our children will be absolutely gorgeous. . . ." Antonia was still gushing at his side, making him cringe.

Laurent patted her hand absently, thinking, *I*

118

have to listen to that voice for the rest of my life. I don't know if I can stand it. Maybe I'll travel, make a lot of state visits and leave her at home with the children. Maybe I'll encourage her to visit her mother frequently . . . without me. Maybe I'll lose my hearing early and never, ever get a hearing aid!

Chapter 9

Jessica raced up the stairs ahead of Elizabeth, anxious to take a shower and change her clothes. She desperately wanted to visit Jacques in the dungeon, but not before she got rid of that tattered, dirty ball gown. And her hair! It was a veritable rat's nest.

As the hot water beat down on her back Jessica put her mind to work on the problem of getting Jacques out of the dungeon. The fact that he freely confessed to the theft of the emerald and the diamond bracelet just had to mean something to the countess and the prince and princess. And what about Jacques's father? He was to blame too.

As Jessica was drying her hair the guard helped Elizabeth into the room.

"That's a good idea," Elizabeth said once the guard was gone. "I could use a shower too."

"Can you manage with your ankle?" Jessica

asked, hoping Elizabeth wouldn't need her help. She didn't want Jacques to languish in the dungeon any longer than necessary before knowing she still cared about him.

Elizabeth smiled wearily. "Planning on a visit to Jacques?"

"How can you tell? Is it that obvious?" Jessica asked almost sheepishly.

"Yep." Elizabeth nodded, lowering herself onto the bed and smiling slightly at the gaurd as he turned to leave. "But I can take my shower without you. I feel so crummy, I won't even notice the pain if I can just get clean."

"Did you talk to Laurent?" Jessica had to ask, even if it hurt Elizabeth to talk about it. It wouldn't be good for her to brood about her feelings alone.

"No," Elizabeth said, and Jessica could tell she was trying hard not to cry. "Antonia was looking pretty possessive, so I decided to just come up here."

"Maybe he won't marry her after all," Jessica offered, but the words sounded lame. "I'm sorry about all this, Liz."

Elizabeth managed a crooked smile. "I'll be all right. But you better get going if you want to see Jacques."

Jessica smiled as she put the last finishing touches on her hair. She tossed it from side to side, admiring the way it billowed in golden waves. Perfect!

"Well, Liz, wish me luck."

"You're not going to try to break him out, are you?" Elizabeth asked in a shocked voice.

"No, I need luck just getting *in*," Jessica explained. "If the guard is the same one we had, it'll be hopeless."

"OK, OK, good luck!" Elizabeth shook her head as Jessica bounced from the room.

Jessica took the back stairs down to the dungeon entrance, not wanting to explain to anyone where she was going. She stared down to where the guard stood at the bottom of the stairs. Jessica let out a sigh of relief when she saw that a different guard was on duty.

This one was younger and more handsome than the first. He had reddish brown hair and an attractive mustache, and his broad shoulders tapered down to a trim waist. He watched her come down the steps, his gray eyes alert but not unfriendly. In fact, when she got to the bottom of the stairs, he actually smiled at her.

"May I please speak to the prisoner?" Jessica asked in her carefully rehearsed French.

"I am not sure that is a good idea," the guard said, but his expression was still friendly and open.

"Oh, please," she said in her most honey sweet voice. "Only for a moment. *Un moment, s'il vous plaît?*" She hoped he thought her French accent was cute enough to grant her request.

"You have no files or skeleton keys, no?" he asked in halting English.

Jessica beamed her best innocent smile at him. "No, sir."

"Then you may see him," the guard said, pointing toward the cell.

She walked down the hallway, shuddering at the memory of having been locked up in the place. The walls dripped damp slime, and the cold came right through the soles of her shoes. When she got to the cell and peered inside, she saw Jacques stretched out on the cot, staring up at the ceiling. He looked so lost and forlorn that her heart ached.

"Jacques?" she asked tentatively.

Jacques jumped from the cot, and his whole face lit up when he saw her.

"I was hoping you would be able to come down to see me," he said. "Did you have trouble getting in here?"

"No," she answered, leaning her hands against the wooden door so she could get closer to the small, barred window. "But Jacques, it broke my heart when they dragged you away! Did they hurt you? Are you all right? Did they say anything about a trial?"

Jacques smiled sadly at her and reached a single finger between the bars to stroke her chin gently.

"There will be no trial, my dear Jessica," he said. "I confessed, so there is no need for a trial.

They will merely sentence me, probably to life in prison."

"Oh, no!" she cried, stricken at the thought of such a harsh sentence. "They can't do that! Surely it counts that you confessed on your own. How can they be so unfair?"

She could feel the tears start at the thought of this young man spending the rest of his days behind bars. That could be sixty years or more!

Jacques sighed. "It is up to the judge, *ma chérie*."

Jessica was suddenly angry. "It's not like you killed someone! You stole some crummy jewelry, and you can just give it back. Doesn't that make a difference?"

"You make it sound so simple, my sweet Jessica," he said ruefully.

Jessica's mind raced as she tried to think of a way to help Jacques. How could she make the prince go easier on him?

"Maybe my sister could talk to Prince Laurent," she offered. "He could beg his father to have mercy on you."

Jacques shook his head. "Jessica, you do not understand. Stealing from the countess, who represents a foreign government, is an international crime," he tried to explain patiently. "The countess would be dishonored before the whole world if she did not pursue a heavy sentence."

Jessica tossed her head defiantly. "The countess! That old cow should be put away herself!"

Jacques reached his fingers through the bars, and Jessica grasped them in her own.

"She might retaliate against this government," he continued. "And no one will take that risk."

"Wait!" Jessica said as another possibility popped into her head. "What about *your* father? If your father gave back the diamond and the emerald and tried to make some kind of deal . . ."

"I will never go to my father!" Jacques cried. Jessica jerked her hand away from his in shock. "I will protect my father to the end of my life," he added more quietly.

"I'm sorry, Jacques," Jessica began, but he cut her off.

"And you must promise never to ask me again to betray my father," he said firmly. "He is the only family I have left. You must swear to keep the truth about my father a secret."

"I swear," Jessica said in a small voice, completely subdued by the force of Jacques's plea.

"You must swear on your sister's life, Jessica," he insisted.

He's so sexy when he's intense like this, Jessica thought, her heart thumping.

"All right, Jacques," she said quietly. "I love you enough to do what you ask. I swear to you on my sister's life that I will not say anything about your father."

Laurent thought the betrothal dinner would

never end. With Antonia clutching his right hand and the countess crowding him on the left, he could hardly even eat.

The executive chef had positively outdone himself, with the first course of baby artichoke hearts in a delicate lemon sauce, a course of grilled fresh salmon, and a main course of tender beef in a flaky pastry crust. The wine flowed freely, and everyone but Laurent was tipsy by the time the meal was halfway over.

Of course, food was the last thing on his mind. All he could think about was the way Elizabeth had turned away from him that afternoon. Even the messages he'd sent up to her room had gone unanswered.

"Oh, Laurent, you have made me the happiest girl in the world," Antonia gushed into his right ear.

"You made the right choice, young man," the countess thundered from his left.

The right choice. The words echoed in Laurent's mind, mocking him. *I haven't made the right choice. I haven't made any choice at all,* he thought. All he wanted was Elizabeth. Instead he had Antonia . . . and his honor. What good was honor when he was destined to be miserable the rest of his life?

Laurent chewed slowly and let his mind wander. *It's true, I don't have to marry Antonia now that Elizabeth is out of danger. What's the worst that can happen if I refuse? My country will suffer scandal. Antonia and her mother will be humiliated. My parents* . . . His heart lurched in his chest at the thought of the reaction his father and stepmother would have if he refused to go through with the wedding.

"Laurent," Antonia whined in his ear, "you're not paying any attention to me at all!"

"I'm sorry, Antonia," he said woodenly. "It's been a long and exhausting day."

"But your father said there would be dancing after dinner," she said petulantly.

Laurent looked into Antonia's eyes, and it hit him like a thunderbolt. *I will not marry this girl,* he thought suddenly. *I don't have to, and I will not.* All that remained was for him to tell his father and stepmother, and that would take all his courage.

All his life Laurent had been a dutiful son. Now he would be defying centuries of tradition for the sake of the most beautiful girl he had ever known. A shiver ran down his spine and his stomach flopped over at the thought. All he had to do was tell his parents, then he would be free to love the only girl who'd ever managed to capture his heart!

Though the coming confrontation filled him with dread, the night no longer seemed so unbearable to Laurent. He was even able to dance with Antonia without too much revulsion, knowing he wouldn't have to spend the rest of his life with her.

When the dancing was finally over, Laurent returned to his rooms to find François waiting patiently.

"I must talk with my parents tonight," he said without preamble. "You may retire if you wish."

"Is anything wrong, sir?" the other man asked, concern in his voice and etched on his face.

Laurent was touched by the valet's reaction. "It is very kind of you to ask, François, but I am fine. There is so much going on, I am feeling distracted," he half lied.

"Very good, sir. If you need anything, please call," François said, bowing slightly and gliding out of the room.

Later, as Laurent went to his parents' private quarters to tell them his decision, he nearly lost his nerve. *What am I doing? How can I go against their wishes? This is my country's future I'm deciding, not just my own!* At the door he almost turned away without knocking. Then Elizabeth's face came to mind, and he lifted his fist and knocked firmly.

His father was relaxing in a chair before a blazing fire in the fireplace, smoking his pipe. He was wearing his favorite emerald-colored smoking jacket with gold trim, and his reading glasses were perched on the end of his nose. He held a sheaf of papers in his hand.

His stepmother was seated directly opposite, in the other chair beside the fireplace. The princess was dressed in a graceful caftan of royal blue silk. She too wore glasses in order to see the tiny decorative stitches she was placing in her linen sampler. He knew her motto was, A true lady never sits idle.

"Father, Stepmother," he said. He took a deep breath, hoping they would someday forgive him. "I will not marry Antonia."

"What?" his father asked sharply. He stood up from his chair and set the papers he had been reading aside. He pulled off his glasses and looked at Laurent, one eye squinting slightly. "What are you saying, Laurent?"

"I will not marry Antonia. . . . I—I cannot marry her. . . . I don't love her. . . ." He hated the way he stammered in the face of his father's anger.

Princess Catherine was frowning. She had remained motionless after Laurent's announcement, but now she calmly set aside her needlework.

"Laurent, I thought you had decided once and for all. How can you humiliate us this way?" she asked sternly.

"Father, we made an agreement," Laurent pushed himself to say. "But now that we know Elizabeth and her sister are innocent of wrongdoing, there is no need for the agreement or the engagement." The simple mention of Elizabeth's name seemed to give him greater strength. "And I find I cannot tolerate the thought of being married to Antonia!"

"Do not raise your voice to me!" his father

thundered. "You are defying me for the sake of that American girl? Do you think we would permit you to marry her?"

"It's not just because of Elizabeth, Father," Laurent tried desperately to explain. "It also has to do with what I want, how I feel about marriage. If I am to live with someone for the rest of my life, I must love her!"

"Love! *Bah!*" The prince slashed the air with his arm. "Love is a fleeting, illusory thing that soon passes. It is the day-to-day companionship, reliance on each other. . . ." He wiped his face with one hand. "You are too young to understand!"

"I am *not* too young to know my own mind," Laurent asserted. "Whether or not I marry Elizabeth is not the point. The point is I don't want to marry Antonia!"

"Oh, how humiliated Antonia and the countess will be!" his stepmother moaned. "I can only imagine how they will retaliate. Did you think of that?"

"It is no use," Laurent said, valiantly pushing forward. "If they do not suffer this little humiliation now, Antonia and I will both be miserable for the rest of our lives. I don't love Antonia, and I don't think I ever could. I don't even *like* her. I'm sure she wouldn't want that kind of relationship any more than I would." Laurent wasn't really sure about that, but it sounded good.

"Love! Love!" his father stormed. "You are obsessed with this romantic notion of marrying for love!"

"It's not just a romantic notion, Father," Laurent insisted. "Millions of people all over the world will marry only for love. I merely want to be one of them!"

"Millions of people . . . ," his father sputtered. "Commoners, all of them! We are the royal family, we make alliances! You cannot afford to give your own wishes any credence!" He paced up and down a few steps. "Why would you want to act like a commoner?"

Laurent knew he wouldn't win in a shouting match with his father, but then a thought came to him that gave him courage. "But Father," Laurent asked in his quietest voice, "didn't you marry for love the second time around?"

His father suddenly stopped and looked at Laurent, a surprised look on his face. There was a thick silence in the room for a moment or two. When the prince spoke again, it was much more quietly under the watchful eyes of the princess.

"Yes, my son," he said reluctantly, "I did."

"And you are happy with my stepmother?" Laurent continued, immediately sensing he had hit on the perfect argument.

"Yes, yes." The prince's shoulders slumped a little, and he sighed. "I am beginning to see your point. Perhaps, Laurent, we have been unfair to you, trying to impose outdated traditions."

Laurent felt his heart soar at his father's words. "Thank you, Father," he acknowledged with a smile.

The older man approached Laurent and put an arm around his shoulders. "I will do what I can to reason with the countess," his father said wearily. "I am sure you know what her reaction will be."

Suddenly the countess burst through the closed door.

"He will not have to wait to see my reaction!" she thundered. "How can you break my daughter's heart like this!"

The prince and princess were momentarily shocked, their mouths hanging open.

"Were you listening at the door?" the prince demanded.

"That's not important!" the countess shrieked. "Don't bother me with ridiculous details!"

Laurent moved forward to intercept the countess. "Please," he began, "it was never my intention—"

"You are a disrespectful young man who needs to be taught a lesson!" she boomed at him.

"Why don't we all calm down?" Princess Catherine pleaded softly. "Let us all be rational and discuss this like adults."

"Discuss!" the countess huffed. "I demand that you force this shameless young man to marry Antonia!"

The prince's face hardened at the countess's words.

"He is neither disrespectful nor shameless, Countess," he said in a tone that said he expected

132

not to be challenged. "Perhaps it is time to accept the modern way of doing some things. We no longer live in the Middle Ages. Perhaps with Laurent we should begin redefining our traditions."

Laurent shot his father a grateful glance. It was the last thing he would have expected, to hear his father defending a point of view so new to him. And yet here he was, acting as if it had been his idea all along!

"Well, I *never!*" the countess cried. "This matter is by no means decided," she shouted over her shoulder as she flounced from the room.

And Laurent was afraid she meant it.

Chapter 10

The next morning Elizabeth sat by the window in her chamber, the sunlight streaming down over her. It was good to feel clean again, and her soft cotton shorts and simple, short-sleeved shirt were infinitely better than the ball gown. Even the memory of that filthy, torn rag was enough to make her shudder.

The warmth of the sun felt good, especially on her sore ankle. The court doctor said it wasn't a bad sprain but that she should rest it as much as possible. That meant Jessica had to do most of the work with the children.

Normally Elizabeth would have been secretly pleased that her sister was being forced to take on some responsibility. It seemed as if every time they started a project together, Elizabeth ended up doing all the work.

But this summer had been different. Elizabeth had shirked her duties more than once in order to spend time with Laurent. On a couple of occasions, when it was her turn to take the kids, Elizabeth hadn't shown up at all. And now she felt incredibly guilty that Jessica had all the responsibility yet again. *Of course,* she thought with a wistful smile, *it's really all Laurent's fault. If he hadn't been so handsome and charming . . .*

"Why did I have to go and think of Laurent?" Elizabeth groaned. Her eyes quickly filled with tears. *I wonder what he's doing this morning. How can he even think about marrying Antonia when he loves me? What good is a tradition that forces you to ruin your life?*

Elizabeth jumped as a soft knock on the door broke into her reverie. She didn't really want to see anyone, but then she heard Pierre's tiny voice. "Mademoiselle Elizabeth, please let me to come in."

"All right, Pierre," she said resignedly, wiping her eyes with the backs of her hands.

Pierre looked very solemn when he entered the room. He walked right over to Elizabeth, threw his little arms around her neck, and hugged her hard.

"I am sorry you are so sad," he whispered in her ear.

Elizabeth was touched by his concern. "That's

very sweet, Pierre," she said, struggling not to cry again. "Thank you." Gazing at Pierre's thick, wavy dark hair and soft brown eyes, Elizabeth could have been looking at Laurent as a child. She felt a sudden sharp pang in her heart. Would she ever see her prince again?

Pierre plopped onto Elizabeth's bed and crossed his legs under him.

"Can I do something to cheer you?" he asked, his small upturned face hopeful.

Elizabeth managed a slight smile. "Sometimes it takes a while for a person to feel better after they are hurt," she tried to explain. "But I'll be fine."

"Are you going to marry my brother?" Pierre asked hopefully.

Elizabeth's heart lurched. His expression was so innocent, she could hardly bear to tell him the truth.

"Laurent is going to marry Antonia," she said delicately.

"But I hate Antonia!" Pierre said vehemently. "I do not want her for my sister!"

Elizabeth wiped fresh tears from the corners of her eyes. "Things don't always work out the way we want, Pierre," she told him sadly.

"I want you!" he said boldly. "You would be a good princess."

"Thank you, Pierre. That's very nice of you," she said simply. She turned to gaze out the window again so he wouldn't see the pain written on her face.

"*Pardonnez-moi.*"

Elizabeth jumped slightly when she heard a voice that made her skin crawl. She looked up to find the countess standing in the open doorway.

"I must speak with you, my dear," the older woman said, entering the room without being asked. Her voice was honey sweet, a tone Elizabeth hadn't thought her capable of using.

The countess was dressed in a stylish black suit with a filmy, bright green silk blouse that actually complemented her hair. For the first time since Elizabeth had seen her on the train weeks ago, the countess seemed subdued and calm. It made Elizabeth suspicious.

"Pierre," Elizabeth said, reaching over to ruffle his hair. "Why don't you so downstairs and play with your sisters? I'll see you later."

"OK," he answered, jumping off the bed. He scrambled quickly out of the room, and Elizabeth knew he was glad for the opportunity to get away from the countess. She wished she were so lucky.

"May I help you?" Elizabeth inquired in her iciest tone of voice. She wished she could stand and look the countess in the eyes. Sitting on her bed, she felt powerless against the awful woman's imposing form.

"I came to apologize for accusing you and

your sister of theft," the countess began.

"Thank you," Elizabeth said shortly, refusing to let down her guard. She didn't believe the apology for a minute. *What can she really want from me?* Elizabeth thought, eyeing the countess warily.

"You must be very happy," the countess went on. "First the charges were dropped against you, and now Laurent has called off his engagement to my daughter."

"H-He . . . he what?" Elizabeth gasped, and her hand flew up to cover her mouth. She nearly jumped up and shouted with joy. Laurent wasn't getting married after all! Suddenly she was overflowing with excitement. Her hands were shaking, and her heart was hammering against her chest. Could it really be true? Had Laurent actually stood up to his parents?

Elizabeth struggled to keep her emotions in check, not wanting the countess to see her so flustered.

The countess looked her up and down, a slight sneer on her face.

"In fact," the countess continued, "after you were absolved, he hardly waited a moment before breaking my daughter's heart."

"What do you mean, 'after I was absolved'?" Elizabeth asked slowly. What did her innocence have to do with Laurent's decision to break with tradition?

"You see," the countess said, peering down her nose at Elizabeth, "he only agreed to marry my Antonia when I promised to drop the charges against you and your sister. Now that you have been proven innocent, he has backed out on his agreement. Laurent seems unable to stay true to his word."

Elizabeth's heart flipped. Laurent had been ready to throw his life away in order to save Elizabeth and her sister. She couldn't believe the sacrifice he had almost made for her! How could she have misjudged him, thinking he had allowed himself to be bullied by tradition? He had only been trying to help her all along. And now he had finally defied his father and taken charge of his life. Elizabeth felt her face flush with pride.

But the countess wouldn't let her stay happy for long. She began to walk around the room, her high heels clicking on the wooden floor.

"You know," she began again, still speaking in a reasonable voice, "this kind of international affront can lead to bad blood between governments. It would be terrible, wouldn't it, to be the cause of an international incident?" she asked pointedly, turning and staring directly into Elizabeth's eyes.

Elizabeth felt her brave front begin to crack as the full implication of the countess's words sank in.

"What kind of incident?" she asked, fighting to keep the fear out of her voice.

"Trade wars, embargoes. There could be all kinds of political implications," the countess answered matter-of-factly.

Elizabeth felt a rising panic take control of her emotions. The severity of the countess's thinly cloaked threat overwhelmed Elizabeth as her thoughts rushed along at lightning speed.

Could something as trivial as one broken engagement really have that kind of effect on the relationship between two countries that had been allies for years? As Elizabeth looked into the countess's smug face she realized that the horrid woman actually meant to act on her threats. *If I had never come to the château, Laurent would have married Antonia and none of this would have happened.* Elizabeth had no doubt that Laurent's love for her had given him the strength to stand up to his father.

If I were to leave, she thought slowly, *maybe Laurent would go through with his agreement with the countess. Maybe he would see that it's the only way to secure the future of his country. But if he does marry Antonia, he will never be happy.* For the first time Elizabeth truly understood the pressure that Laurent had been forced to endure his whole life.

"Naturally," the countess said smoothly, "if Laurent wasn't 'distracted,' he would be happy to marry Antonia and avoid any ugly incidents."

Elizabeth knew that this was the point the countess had been trying to make all along.

"Countess," she said quickly, summoning up her strength. "Your little mission has been accomplished. Now if you'll excuse me, I have some things to attend to." She stood up, hobbled over to the door, and opened it, facing the countess with her chin held high.

The countess flashed a triumphant smile.

"Of course, my dear," she said in that awful, fake voice. She floated out of the room, looking smugly satisfied.

As soon as the countess was gone Elizabeth sprang into action. She had to get out of the château . . . *now*. The only way to prevent the "international incident" that the countess had alluded to was for Elizabeth to disappear. *Laurent will do what's right,* she thought, frantically pulling clothing from her dresser drawers. *As soon as I'm out of the picture, he'll know what he has to do.*

Elizabeth hobbled around her tower room, packing her bags without bothering to fold things neatly the way she usually did. She tossed her T-shirts, shorts, and jeans into her suitcase in one jumbled pile, then dumped her brush, journal, and few cosmetics on top, mashing the whole mess down with the palm of her hand.

Elizabeth somehow got the clasp fastened,

pushed her hair impatiently away from her eyes, and used her new crutch to hop out the door. The suitcase was heavy, and Elizabeth stumbled a few times as she negotiated her way down the narrow staircase. Near the bottom her crutch fell to the floor with a clatter, and Elizabeth had to hop the rest of the way.

A startled young servant stood at the base of the stairs, holding the fallen crutch. Elizabeth reached out and snatched it from the girl, alarming her unintentionally.

"*S'il vous plaît,*" Elizabeth said, trying to keep her voice calm. She hoped her French wouldn't desert her in her agitated state. "I need a car to take me to the train station."

Luckily the servant composed herself quickly. "Of course, mademoiselle," she offered with a smile. "It will only be a moment."

Elizabeth carried her suitcase through the corridors, grateful that she didn't bump into anyone she knew. *I hope Jessica will understand,* Elizabeth thought fervently. She wished there was time to go to the nursery and explain. But she had to get out of there as quickly as possible, before Laurent came to see her and realized she was gone. She left the château by the servants' entrance and waited for the car to come.

Gaston, the same chauffeur who'd picked Elizabeth and Jessica up at the train station when they first arrived, pulled the car around the corner.

He smiled brightly at Elizabeth as he stepped out of the car.

"Leaving us, mademoiselle?" he asked in his excellent English. He popped the trunk and placed her bag inside, then opened the door to the backseat.

"Yes, Gaston. There is . . . an emergency at home," she lied, slipping into the car. "Jessica will be staying to complete our job, but I must go home."

Gaston leaned over and looked at her through the open window as he closed the door behind her. His brow puckered into a frown.

"Does this have to do with that accusation . . . that you and your sister stole some jewels?" he asked carefully.

Elizabeth felt herself blush up to the roots of her hair. "That was all a misunderstanding," she said, wishing he would just get into the car and drive. "They caught the real thief. Didn't you hear?"

"Of course," Gaston replied. "But I would hate for you to leave France because of such a misunderstanding. You might never wish to come back."

He has no idea how right he is, she thought.

"I'll be back someday," she said, willing to say anything to get them on their way. "But right now I really need to get to the train station."

"Good. I am glad. I hope you enjoyed your stay with us, mademoiselle," Gaston said with a smile.

He finally walked around to the driver's side and got in.

"Yes, yes," Elizabeth said impatiently. She hoped he wouldn't want to chat all the way to the train station. Gaston must have sensed her discomfort. He mercifully kept his mouth shut until he pulled up in front of the station.

He carried her bag to the train for her and helped her on board.

"Au revoir, mademoiselle," he said, bowing as she climbed the steps into the car. "Safe trip."

Elizabeth smiled gratefully and thanked him for his help. She found her seat and slumped back against the soft cushions, willing herself to relax. *Sweet Valley, here I come*, she thought grimly.

"Elizabeth, will you marry me?"
No, no.

"Elizabeth, will you be my wife?" Laurent's arm slashed the air in frustration. "Elizabeth, will you do me the honor of becoming my wife?" *Better, but not perfect.* He paced the length of his bedroom, trying to think of the perfect words.

Laurent grew tense as he turned over different approaches in his mind. He began to feel suffocated by his jacket and tie and hastily removed them, flinging them aside. He strode the room in a soft white silk shirt, sleeves turned up at the cuffs, and formfitting black pants. Now that he was comfortable, maybe he could think straight.

This is the most important question I will ever ask in my life, he thought helplessly. *The moment must be absolutely perfect*.

He put a hand on either side of his head as if trying to squeeze the right words from his mind. "Why can't I think?" he asked the empty room.

"Laurent!" Pierre burst into his room, shouting his name. "Laurent, you must stop her, you must stop her!"

"Stop who?" he asked. "What is it, Pierre? What are you saying?"

Pierre took a deep breath. "I listened at the door. The countess, she said mean things to Elizabeth." He stopped to try to catch his breath. "She told Elizabeth the country will be in trouble if you don't marry Antonia. There will be an embar . . . an embarge . . ."

"An embargo?" Laurent asked in disbelief.

Pierre nodded. "That's it. And Elizabeth ran away. Please stop her, Laurent!"

Laurent grabbed his little brother by the arm. Suddenly the whole world seemed upside down.

"Where exactly did she go?" he demanded.

Pierre burst into tears at his brother's stern tone of voice. "To the train station," he sobbed. "I heard her tell the driver to hurry."

"It's all right, Pierre." Laurent took a single moment to hug his little brother. "I'm not mad at you. You did the right thing. Now, tell no one else about this," he insisted. He waited to see Pierre nod before he flew out of the room on his way to the stables.

Laurent waved away the help of one of the grooms and ran into Pardaillan's stall. The horse whinnied and stamped his hooves at the familiar footsteps of his master. "Come along, Pardaillan, we have a job to do," Laurent told the stallion as he slid the saddle onto the horse's back and tightened the girth.

"I can't believe she ran away," he told himself while he adjusted the bridle. Pardaillan snorted and shook his head as if he were feeling as angry and anxious as Laurent. The prince led the horse out into the yard, mounted swiftly, and ground his heels against Pardaillan's flanks.

The horse sprang forward, and the wind caught his mane as he galloped across the lawn toward the woods. Laurent's hair flew in the breeze, and his shirt billowed out around him. He felt the strength of the horse beneath him, the sun warm on his back. He dug his heels in a bit more, urging Pardaillan on.

None of this would have happened if it weren't for that horrid countess! I would give anything to get back at her somehow! he thought wildly.

The woods loomed near, and he slowed Pardaillan just a little. They entered the forest, and the stallion picked his way delicately through the roots and across the fallen branches. They splashed through the stream, and Laurent directed the horse over a stray log.

"Easy, Pardaillan," he said to calm the horse after the jump. The big animal sidestepped and almost tripped over a hidden root, and Laurent leaned down and patted his horse reassuringly. "It's all right," he said into the horse's right ear. "Just keep going—we must keep going!"

He heaved a sigh of relief when he saw the edge of the woods ahead. Laurent ducked a low-lying branch, guided Pardaillan around a hole, and burst from the woods at a full gallop.

I hope I am not too late to stop Elizabeth, he thought frantically. *I just can't be too late!*

Chapter 11

Jessica trudged her way through the morning with the children, counting the hours until their nap time. There was no way she could sneak down to the dungeon to see Jacques again until the kids were asleep. When Pierre went off with his mother that morning, Jessica was more than happy to let him go, but that still left Claudine and Manon.

The midday meal consisted of tomato soup and ham and cheese croissants. Jessica giggled to herself. *These princesses eat almost the same thing as American schoolchildren*, she thought. "Claudine, please don't stick your sandwich in Manon's ear," Jessica reprimanded the five-year-old.

"It is to make her laugh," Claudine said in English. Manon was indeed giggling uncontrollably.

"Just don't do it," Jessica said. "And don't dawdle. It's nearly nap time!"

Manon flung half of her croissant to the floor, and Jessica bent to retrieve it.

"Jessica, Jessica," Manon sang as she took the piece of bread from Jessica's hand and immediately threw it back on the floor.

"Manon!" Jessica wailed. "Please don't do this today!" She grabbed up the discarded food and tossed it in a nearby trash can.

"Let's go. It's time for your nap," Jessica said, ushering the girls away from the table.

"Only one story before you lie down. We'll read more tomorrow," Jessica promised as she herded them into the nursery and their waiting beds. As they crawled under the covers she noticed they looked tired, and she smiled in satisfaction. In a few minutes they would be sound asleep and she would be on her way to see Jacques. She read them their story, waited to make sure they were both asleep, and hurried down the steps to the first floor.

All morning she had been formulating a plan. Now, with a little courage, she was ready to act. It was the only way she could think of to help Jacques. And she had to help him. Even after all that had happened, she still loved him.

Jessica stopped at a large, round table in the middle of the huge entrance hall. A beautiful flower arrangement had been placed in the center. Jessica playfully pulled a rose from the blue china vase.

149

"They'll never miss it," she told herself as she continued on her way. She couldn't wait to see Jacques's face when she gave him the flower.

Finally she reached the dreary corner of the château where a thick wooden door protected the steps leading to the dungeon. She struggled to open the door, marveling at how heavy it was. By the light of a dim bulb she made her way carefully down the uneven, cold stone steps.

At the bottom of the steps Jessica greeted the guard with a smile, thankful that it was the same man who had let her speak to Jacques yesterday. He waved her toward the cell, not even bothering to stand up.

"Jacques?" she called through the bars.

"Jessica! You came yet again!" He stretched his hand through the barred window in the cell door as far as he could reach, and Jessica grasped his fingers in hers. It made her feel sick that she might never again feel his arms around her.

"I have something for you," she said brightly, pushing the bottom end of the rose through the bars. "Since you can't go outside, I brought nature in to you."

He took the rose and sniffed it, his eyes closed in ecstasy. "What a beautiful thing to do, Jessica!" he said. "Thank you."

"I only have a little time," she told him.

Jessica shot a glance at the guard, who was staring blankly at a newspaper. She took a deep breath. It was time to put her plan into action.

"How I wish I could feel your arms around me just once more," Jessica said, raising her voice so she could be sure the guard would hear.

"That would be heaven," Jacques agreed.

"Soon I'll leave for America, and we'll never see each other again!" Jessica wailed dramatically in her best soap opera voice. She noticed the guard looking over at her from the corner of his eye. *I am so good,* she thought.

She smiled slyly at Jacques and then pulled away from the door.

"Jessica," Jacques hissed. "What are you doing?"

Jessica approached the guard slowly.

"Could you do something for me?" she asked in her sweetest, most innocent voice.

"Depends on what it is," the young man said, his eyes suddenly wary.

"It's just . . . ," Jessica began, willing tears to form in her eyes. "It's just that . . ."

The guard waited expectantly.

"It's just that I love him so much!" she wailed, bursting into uncontrollable sobs.

The guard jumped back a little, startled by her sudden outburst.

"I need to feel his arms around me one more time," she cried, reaching out and clutching his shirt. "Please, please let me into the cell. I'm never going to see him again!"

The guard shook his head and removed her hands from his arm.

"That I cannot do, mademoiselle. I would lose my job if someone found out," he told her, his voice firm but kind.

"Oh, but I wouldn't tell anyone," she said, wiping at her eyes. "If you did this for me, I would be so grateful. I would never forget your kindness."

She flashed him a hopeful smile, tears still streaming down her face.

The guard hesitated, obviously wanting to grant her request but still worried about the consequences. For a moment Jessica thought her plan had failed. Then he finally smiled.

"I think you are more French than American, mademoiselle," he said with a shake of his head. "So much passion and emotion in such a little girl."

He got up and chose the correct key from the ring of keys he wore at his belt.

"Thank you," Jessica gushed, impulsively reaching up to kiss the guard lightly on the cheek.

The guard blushed again and touched his cheek. They walked over to Jacques's cell together.

"I will have to lock the door behind you, mademoiselle," he said, turning the key in the lock.

"I understand," Jessica agreed, nearly jumping out of her skin with excitement. In a moment Jacques would be free!

As soon as the cell door was open she threw herself against the guard with all her strength.

152

"Run, Jacques, run!" she screamed.

The guard was so surprised by Jessica's action that he fell to the floor off-balance, and Jessica tumbled on top of him. The guard sprawled and struggled beneath her as Jacques sprinted from the cell down the short hallway and up the dungeon stairs.

"What are you doing?" the guard screamed in French. "Get up now!" Jessica rose slowly, taking her time to give Jacques a better chance.

Jessica smiled to herself at her success, not even minding that the guard was spewing French at her in an angry voice as he tried to get to his feet. When he began to follow Jacques, Jessica stuck out her foot, and the guard went down again with a thud. She skipped to the side to avoid the guard's grasping hand and ran toward the door.

Just as she reached the bottom of the stairs she heard a scuffling noise on the stairway. She looked up to find Jacques, almost suspended off the ground, between two other guards.

"Jacques!" she cried, her hand flying to her throat in shock.

"Sorry, *ma chérie,*" he said sadly. "Thank you for trying."

They dragged Jacques down the stairs, and Jessica reached out to him as they passed. Jacques tried to grab her hand, but the guards yanked him away. They threw Jacques back into the cell and slammed the door the door shut with an eerie thud.

153

Jessica was too shocked to move. Jacques had come so close to freedom.

One of the new guards stomped over to base of the stairs, where Jessica was still standing.

"If I see you down here again," he spat in a guttural voice, bringing his face within inches of hers, "I will lock you up too!"

Jessica fled the dungeon with fresh tears of real pain streaming down her cheeks.

Elizabeth sat on the train, wondering when it would finally get going. She almost believed she could feel her heart actually breaking inside her. She missed Laurent desperately, and knowing she would never set eyes on him again made it that much worse.

The quicker she got to Paris, the quicker she could get on a flight home and put this summer behind her. That was all she wanted now, the comfort of her parents and friends, of her own world.

Jessica will probably kill me for leaving her alone with the kids for the rest of the summer, she thought. Elizabeth's heart ached for her sister too. Jacques was in the dungeon with no hope of being released, and Elizabeth knew that Jessica felt as horrible as she did. How did everything go so wrong?

Nothing has ever hurt this bad, she thought, shifting in her seat as if changing position would ease the pain she felt.

"I'm really never going to see him again," she said to herself, as if saying the words out loud would help her accept the reality they described. *Why is doing the right thing always so unbelievably hard?* she wondered.

The train gave a sudden lurch. *Thank goodness we're on our way,* Elizabeth thought. She turned her head to look out the window at the passing scenery. Suddenly she saw a man on horseback barreling toward the train at top speed. *What kind of idiot would ride a horse up next to a train?* Elizabeth asked herself. *Isn't that kind of dangerous?*

But as the rider came closer, Elizabeth's eyes widened in surprise. She would know those broad shoulders and that thick black hair anywhere.

It was Laurent. And he was guiding Pardaillan next to the moving train!

Elizabeth's heart jumped into her throat, and she wondered if she were dreaming.

No, she thought suddenly. *He's really here! He came! He came for me!*

Elizabeth held her breath at the sight of him, galloping up to the train on Pardaillan. He looked so strong and unbelievably handsome. Elizabeth half stood as her heart pounded up into her ears. Laurent spotted her through the window.

"I love you, Elizabeth!" he shouted. His hair whipped back from his face as he leaned forward in the saddle, trying to pick up speed.

Pardaillan moved forward to the door of the car, and Elizabeth pressed her face against the window so she could see Laurent leap from the saddle and through the door. Her joyful tears left streaks on the glass. She whirled around to see him enter the car, tall and commanding.

"Stop this train at once!" he ordered the conductor.

The other passengers were all talking excitedly in mingled English and French. "It is the prince!" "Prince Laurent has stopped the train!" "He is more handsome than his picture!"

Elizabeth was barely conscious of those snippets of conversation as Laurent strode toward her.

He had never looked so handsome or sexy. His dark hair was ruffled after his wild ride, and the cuffs of his white shirt were rolled up, exposing his strong, tanned arms. He looked more like a prince at that moment than he had in any uniform she had seen him in.

"Laurent," she whispered joyfully. She could hardly believe he was there.

Laurent reached over and swept her up in his arms. He looked deeply into her eyes, and she went dizzy with the intensity. Before she knew what was happening, he was kissing her passionately, and she tightened her arms around him to keep from buckling under the force of her own overwhelming emotion. She had never loved anyone as much as she loved Laurent at that moment.

When they finally drew apart, Elizabeth slowly realized that the people in the car were cheering wildly and waving their arms. Elizabeth felt herself blush furiously at the thought that all these people had watched her and Laurent kissing.

But she couldn't stay embarrassed for long. Nothing mattered as long as she was with Laurent.

He clasped her hands in his.

"Oh, Laurent," she said, almost afraid to look into his blazing blue eyes again.

"You were crazy to leave like this, Elizabeth," Laurent began in mock sternness. "I don't care if it does cause a war; I won't marry Antonia. I can't stand the sight of her. Because of you I know what true love really is. And I refuse to settle for less." Laurent knelt before her, right there in the aisle. "Elizabeth, please marry me."

Elizabeth gasped, hardly daring to believe all he had just said.

"What . . . but . . . ," she stuttered.

Laurent stood up and put his finger gently to her trembling lips.

"Don't answer right away," he said quickly. "Just promise me you'll think about it." Elizabeth could only nod, she was so overwhelmed.

As Laurent took her in his arms again Elizabeth lost control of her emotions. She laughed through tears of joy and buried her face in the front of his soft silk shirt.

Laurent kept one arm securely around

Elizabeth's shoulders as they made their way down the aisle to the door.

"Please have Miss Wakefield's luggage sent to the château at once," he asked the conductor.

"Of course, Your Grace," the conductor answered quickly, saluting.

The passengers were still clapping and cheering as Elizabeth stepped from the train. Outside, a man was holding Pardaillan's bridle.

"Here, Your Grace, I have kept your horse for you," the man said in French.

"Merci beaucoup," Laurent replied. He turned to Elizabeth and effortlessly lifted her onto the front of the saddle. Then he climbed on behind her and wrapped one arm securely around her waist. She leaned back into the embrace, feeling totally secure and blissfully happy. As they rode off toward the château Elizabeth's ears still rang with the cheers of the passengers. She was living the fairy tale; she only hoped it would end happily ever after!

Jessica waited in the darkness of her room, her door slightly ajar, wishing Laurent would finally let Elizabeth go in to bed. She desperately needed to talk to the prince about Jacques, but she didn't want to disturb the happy couple.

They were sharing a lingering kiss in front of the door to the room, and the way Laurent caressed Elizabeth's cheek made Jessica's heart melt.

Good for you, Liz! she thought. Her very own sister had snatched a prince out of the grasp of that horrid Antonia di Rimini.

At least one of us ended up with royalty, she thought. She remembered that when they started this trip, she herself had dreamed of a romance with a handsome noble. She'd even thought she'd snagged herself a future duke when she met Jacques. But she wouldn't change places with Elizabeth. Jacques might not be what she'd thought he was, but that didn't make her love him any less.

At long last Elizabeth opened her door and went into her room. Laurent let out a deep, satisfied sigh and turned to leave.

"Laurent," Jessica hissed from the shadows.

Laurent spun around, his expression startled.

"Who's there?" he asked quickly, then saw her face. "Jessica, why are you hiding?"

Jessica clasped her hands tightly together to keep them from trembling.

"I have to talk to you, but I didn't want to bother you and Elizabeth when . . . well, you know," she said, and gestured toward Elizabeth's closed door.

Laurent smiled slightly and nodded his understanding. "What can I do for you?" he asked.

"I need your help, Laurent," she explained. "Where can we talk privately?"

"This way," he said, and led her down the stairs

of the tower and into a small sitting room. Shelves of leather-bound books lined the walls. It smelled musty, as if it wasn't used very often. But when Laurent lit the lamp, the room immediately became warm and cozy.

"Is this private enough, Jessica?" he asked kindly.

"Oh, yes, thank you," she said, feeling much more hopeful now that Laurent was being so cooperative.

They sat down on soft, comfortable red damask chairs on either side of the big stone fireplace. "Would you like me to have a fire built?" Laurent asked. "These unused rooms can be cold even in the summertime."

"No, thank you," she said, warmed by his kindness. She took a deep breath. "It's about Jacques, Laurent. Is there anything you can do to help him? All he wants is to return the things he stole and try to make an honest living." Jessica tried to keep her emotions under control, knowing hysterics probably wouldn't work on the levelheaded prince.

Laurent leaned forward with real concern in his warm blue eyes. Jessica could understand why Elizabeth had fallen so hard for him; he positively radiated compassion.

"Jessica, in this case my hands are tied," he told her plainly and quietly. "It is bad enough that I caused trouble by refusing to marry the woman my father chose for me. That's enough of an international mess."

"What do you mean, 'international mess'?" Jessica asked. She had been so wrapped up in her concern for Jacques, she had missed the scandal that the countess's threats had caused.

"The countess tried to drive Elizabeth away by making her feel guilty about my decision. She even said there might be a trade war if I don't marry Antonia," he explained.

"But you broke up with her anyway?" Jessica asked, amazed. She hadn't known Elizabeth could have such power over men.

"Yes," Laurent answered wearily. "But my father is an accomplished diplomat. I believe he will find a way to appease the countess."

Laurent raked an impatient hand through his thick, dark hair. "But as for what you ask . . . Jacques's crime was too great. I do not know if my father could fix the present situation if he also refused to prosecute the thief who stole the countess's jewels."

"But he's willing to return them!" Jessica cried. "Do you think she might agree to let him go if she got her crummy jewelry back?"

"I doubt it," Laurent answered, touching her shoulder in sympathy. "She has never been reasonable about anything else."

The tears overflowed her eyes and cascaded down her cheeks, and Jessica made no effort to wipe them away. "I wish I had never even heard of the Château d'Amour Inconnu," she wailed, covering her face with her hands.

"Jessica, please don't cry," Laurent said in a pained voice. "Here, take my handkerchief."

Jessica groped for the soft cloth and held it to her eyes, despair overwhelming her heart.

"Poor Jacques," she said through her tears.

"Jessica," Laurent said decisively, "if I see the opportunity to help Jacques, I will. I promise. There's no telling, of course, if it will be possible. But I give you my solemn oath, on my honor, that I will try."

Jessica smiled at him through her tears.

"Thank you, Laurent!" she said quietly. "Just knowing that you'll try to help makes me feel much better." She sniffled and dabbed at her eyes, wondering if she dared hope that Jacques might after all be set free.

But she could only hope and wait, and that had to be the hardest thing of all.

Chapter 12

Elizabeth sat down in front of the mirror and smoothed a bit of moisturizer over her face. She looked at her lips, still warm from Laurent's kiss. Having Laurent whisk her away from the train like that was the most romantic thing that had ever happened to her. No one had ever made her feel so cherished.

And that proposal! Prince Laurent actually wanted to marry her. She pinched herself for the hundredth time to make sure she wasn't dreaming. What if she said yes? What would it be like to be a real princess?

For a moment Elizabeth let herself daydream about the possibilities. Her picture would appear in every newspaper and magazine in the world. She would attend balls and receptions in honor of her engagement to Laurent. And after the wedding they would travel to different countries all over the world.

"The things I would learn!" she said in awe. "International politics, new languages . . . I would be speaking perfect French in no time."

Elizabeth placed the jar of moisturizer on top of her bureau and walked over to the window. Outside, moonlight bathed the lawn in shimmering silver light. It truly looked like something out of a fairy tale. Would she be spending her future in this wonderful place?

If she agreed to marry Laurent, their years would be divided between Paris and the château. They would spend their summers here, riding and swimming with their children. In time Laurent would assume the throne, and Elizabeth would be at his side, his partner and his love.

Elizabeth could see herself, sitting beside a roaring fire, two little children playing at her feet. One of them might be a darkly handsome little boy, toddling about, grasping at her knee to steady himself. And maybe, playing on the carpet with a baby doll, a blond little girl, singing softly.

The travel would be the best, she thought. *Laurent and I could walk along the banks of the Seine and discuss philosophy and literature. We might even read poetry together!*

She turned away from the window and sat down on her narrow bed, tucking one foot beneath her. *What exactly does a princess do with her days?* she wondered thoughtfully.

"Let's see," she said out loud, organizing her thoughts, "the royal family in England does a lot of charity work and fund-raising."

That would be great, but what about a career? She could hardly pursue a conventional writing career as a princess.

"Of course," she continued out loud, "everything I wrote would sell!" For a moment her heart soared at the thought of such success.

But then a new thought deflated her.

"That would hardly be fulfilling. I want my writing to be published because it's good, not because I'm some kind of celebrity." She leaned back against the headboard and folded her knees up under her chin, hugging them with her arms.

"What am I doing?" she asked herself harshly. She was actually considering accepting Laurent's proposal! It hadn't been long since she believed she and Todd would be together forever.

Suddenly her eye caught sight of the cover of her journal on the desk. She jumped off the bed to retrieve it, then sat in the chair by the window. She flipped through the pages absently, reading little snippets as she went. There were the names of all her friends—Enid, Maria, Winston . . . Todd.

What if she did just go back to Sweet Valley and pick up her life where it left off? What was really left back there anyway? Todd had made his desires perfectly clear. . . . They were free to see other people. Elizabeth couldn't believe it actually still hurt to think about that last night with Todd!

Was it that they had such a history together? Elizabeth and Todd had known each other since they were kids. And Elizabeth couldn't remember a time when she hadn't loved him. *We have had our ups and downs,* she thought. *But no matter what has happened, we always end up together in the end.* Could it ever be the same with Todd again?

If she said yes to Prince Laurent, her relationship with Todd would obviously be over, but what about everyone else? What would her friends and family say if Jessica came home without her? Would they believe that levelheaded, down-to-earth Elizabeth could have her head turned by a prince?

She closed the journal abruptly, put it back in its place on the desk, and flopped into bed. Pulling the covers up to her chin, she stared at the ceiling, her mind unquiet.

The one thing Elizabeth had no doubt about was her own feelings for Laurent. She did love him. But she also found herself longing for Todd and the security of home. Laurent excited her in a way no boy ever had, but Todd was still such a huge part of her life. Elizabeth knew she would never sleep that night.

What am I going to do?

Laurent woke up with a strong white light shining in his eyes. He instinctively put a hand in front of his face.

"Who are you, and what are you doing in my room?" he demanded.

"Shhh," said a strange voice as the light was directed across the room. "I will not harm you."

"How did you get in here? Answer me, or I'll call the guards!" Laurent moved for the lamp on his bedside table and turned it on. An older man with graying hair and soft blue eyes was standing beside his bed, dressed completely in black.

"No need for that, sir," the man said quietly.

"Then tell me who you are!" Laurent thundered. "I can have you thrown into the dungeon for entering this room uninvited in the middle of the night!"

"Sir, I beg you, please keep your voice down. There is no need to alert anyone to my presence here." The older man backed up a step, and Laurent felt better. He got out of bed and tied a robe around his waist. Being on his feet made him feel more in control of the situation.

"Unless you tell me right this instant who you are and what business you have here, the whole château will be alerted," Laurent said in a quieter but no less demanding voice.

"My name is Louis Savant," the man began. "I am the father of Jacques Savant, the young man you have in your dungeon. I am the real thief, sir."

Laurent was surprised but not at all frightened. Now that he had the chance to look the man up and down, he could see that everything about him seemed to be gentle and nonviolent. He stood there so quietly, hands at his sides, shoulders relaxed. The love Louis felt for his son was obvious, shining like a beacon in his eyes.

"Why have you come here?" Laurent asked again, but this time more kindly.

"Will you listen to what I have to say?" the man asked in his cultured French. "I mean, really listen?"

"Of course. Provided what you tell me is the truth," Laurent said, trying to sound firm but fair.

"I am not a liar," Louis protested.

"But you are a jewel thief," Laurent pointed out. "Some people might have a hard time believing your version of any truth."

"Agreed," Louis said. "But I swear to you on my son's life that I will be honest."

Laurent gestured to two chairs in the corner of his room. The older man sat and crossed his legs comfortably. He looked as if he would be at home anywhere from a waterfront tavern to the ballroom of a king. Laurent found himself warming to the older man in spite of himself.

"I am listening," he said to Louis, crossing his own legs and placing his arms on the chair's armrests in a posture of complete attention.

"Many years ago," Louis began, his voice a little

wistful, "I owned a grocery shop in Paris. I sold the finest vegetables in the city. Great chefs would buy from no one else for their fancy restaurants." He began to cough, leaning forward in his chair, his hand cupped before his mouth.

"Would you like some water?" Laurent offered. The cough sounded chronic and quite serious.

Mr. Savant shook his head no, and when the coughing subsided, he continued.

"My wife was a very fine seamstress, and together we made enough to live comfortably. Not extravagantly. We had Jacques and each other, and we wanted nothing more."

Laurent was puzzled. "It's a huge leap from the kind of life you're describing to a life of crime."

"Yes," Mr. Savant said, nodding to emphasize his words. "When Jacques was ten years old, my wife became ill, there was no money for her expensive medicines, and she died. I suppose . . . I suppose a piece of me died with her. There I was, left with Jacques, but I had no more desire to work or even to live."

"I'm sorry your wife died," Laurent said with real sympathy. "But many people lose loved ones. They don't all begin stealing jewels as a result."

Mr. Savant shook his head sadly.

"I was very angry and bitterly hurt," he explained. "You see, I applied to my wife's customers for help paying for the medicine. I would have paid them back in time, but no." His voice turned harsh. "While she was well, they would have no one else make their fancy dresses. But they had no feeling for her when she was helplessly dying."

"We all do things we regret when we are angry or hurt," Laurent admitted. "But why bring Jacques into it? Surely it was unwise to teach a young boy to steal!"

Mr. Savant smiled. "Jacques was a reluctant thief at the best of times. He has been after me for some years to retire."

"I'm still not sure what reason you have for coming here tonight," Laurent said, although he was beginning to suspect one.

"I make no excuses for myself," Mr. Savant said firmly, sitting straighter in his chair. "I made my choices, and now I am willing to pay for my crimes. If you will just release my son, you can take me in his place. My life has nearly run its course. He has all his life before him."

"But why come to me?" Laurent insisted. "It is my father who has the power to release Jacques."

"Your father is a man known for his fairness and generosity," Mr. Savant said carefully. "But he is also a political leader. I don't believe he can extend such mercy without losing his standing in the international community."

Laurent was amused at how well Mr. Savant avoided criticizing his father. He realized he didn't want to see this man rot in prison for the rest of his life. He was too charming and too kind. And if what he said about Jacques was true, he didn't deserve to be locked away either.

Suddenly a thought occurred to him.

If Jacques and his father both disappeared, the countess would be cheated of her revenge. *What a perfect way to pay her back for what she did to Elizabeth!* Laurent thought.

The prince reached out and grasped the older man's hand.

"I understand how great your loss has been and how much your son means to you. If the guard in the dungeon had to leave . . ."

"Yes, Prince Laurent?" Mr. Savant asked eagerly.

"If there happened to be a trespasser, and I told the guard to check the front lawn, that would leave your son unattended," Laurent said in a conspiratorial voice.

"And if Jacques is unguarded, he might escape," Mr. Savant prompted.

"With a little help," Laurent assured him quickly. "There is a spare set of keys on the kitchen wall downstairs. Here," he said, opening a drawer in his desk, "you will need some money to get away." He handed Louis a few bills.

"What an extraordinary young man you are," Mr. Savant said warmly. When Laurent reached out to clasp Louis's hand, he felt something small and jagged press against his fingers. He pulled his hand away to find the diamond necklace resting in his palm.

"You have earned my eternal gratitude," Louis said.

The two men slipped from Laurent's room in silence, ready to put their plan into action.

Jacques thought he was dreaming when he heard someone call his name. He awoke slowly, his eyes struggling to adjust to the pitch-darkness. He heard the scrape of metal on metal and wondered what was going on.

"Hello?" he called softly. Could the guard be coming in here for some reason?

It seemed like only a moment ago that the man had told him it was time to turn out the light and go to sleep. Engulfed by darkness, Jacques had no choice but to lie on the cot and lose himself in his miserable thoughts. But eventually sleep came and with it dreams of Jessica, her shimmering golden hair and startling blue-green eyes, the way she touched his arm when she talked. It hurt so badly to think they would be apart forever.

Now Jacques sat up on the cot and could just make out the figure of a person on the other side of the barred window in the cell door.

"Who's there? What are you doing?" he called softly.

Jacques stood up in his cell. Who was on the other side of that door? Could it be Jessica coming to release him in the dead of night? Or perhaps the guards had been ordered to take him somewhere else. He wished his eyes would adjust to the darkness.

After more scraping the cell door swung open and a voice whispered, "Jacques, are you there?"

Jacques would have known that voice anywhere.

"Papa!" he whispered into the darkness, clasping the older man to his chest. "But how . . . why . . ."

"Shhh, my son. You did not think I would let you rot in this dungeon, did you?" The old man sounded as cheerful as ever, as if they weren't both in danger of going to prison for the rest of their lives.

"How did you find out I was here?" Jacques asked hoarsely. He couldn't help hanging on to his father. He had thought he would never see him again.

"You know I have my ways," the older man replied, patting Jacques's hand, which was on his arm. "At least now I know you have not been harmed. I have been crazed with worry for you!"

"I'm all right, Papa," Jacques answered, tears in his eyes. "Especially now. I thought you were gone forever."

"Jacques, I must tell you something," Louis said, for once sounding very serious. "I vow to you we will never steal again."

"But Papa," Jacques said, "what made you decide this? I have been hoping for years, but—"

"When I learned you were in the dungeon,"

Louis interrupted, "I thought I would die. The thought of you sitting in this cell . . . it changed my mind about everything."

Jacques hugged his father again.

"Oh, Papa, I am so happy," he cried. "We will go somewhere warm, where you will feel better and get completely well again. I will work very hard."

"We both will," Louis said. "We will do this together, son." Louis glanced back nervously at the dungeon door. "Let us go. We dare not delay."

Jacques put a restraining hand on his father's arm.

"Wait. I must leave a note for Jessica. I need to say good-bye."

The older man sighed impatiently. "The American girl again? Why are you so taken with her?"

"I don't know, Papa," Jacques said, equally impatient. "I only know it would be terrible to escape without letting her know I am all right."

"Ah, Jacques," Louis said with a sigh. "You are truly my son to insist on this. Nothing gets in the way of romance."

Jacques rummaged through the desk where the guard sat and found paper and a pencil. He began to scribble a hasty note. His father watched over his shoulder.

"Papa, I can't think with you standing right there," Jacques complained.

"You should say something about the moonlight and her eyes," Louis offered in a dreamy voice.

"Don't worry, Papa," Jacques assured him with a smile. The old man was a hopeless romantic. "I know exactly what to say."

He wrote Jessica's name on the outside of the folded paper and left it on his cot. In a last sentimental moment he kissed the tips of his fingers and touched the paper with them. "Good-bye, beautiful Jessica," he whispered.

At the top of the stairs, with freedom a few steps away, Jacques put his hand on his father's arm.

"Papa, tell me truthfully," he said. "You have not hurt anyone in order to get me out, have you?"

"Your release is the gift of a very kind and compassionate young man," his father explained.

Jacques could think of only one young man who could have done this. Somehow his father had persuaded Prince Laurent to help them escape. Why else would the guard have left his post? How else could his father have obtained a key to his cell?

Jacques's opinion of the prince changed completely. Maybe he wasn't such a spoiled, pampered young man. Maybe there was some substance to him after all. Jacques and his father were now in Laurent's debt. And Jacques silently vowed that someday he would repay the prince's kindness.

Chapter 13

The next morning Jessica thought she would never get her makeup right. She was so distraught over Jacques that she barely slept a wink, and her eyes were puffy and would look terrible if she wasn't careful. She expertly applied the palest blue eye shadow, followed by a few swipes of mascara.

"Perfect!" she said to her reflection, smiling in satisfaction.

She picked up her brush and combed her hair until it gleamed.

I'm not exactly looking forward to fighting past the guards this morning after what happened yesterday, she thought. *But I just have to do it. Jacques needs all my support.*

She stepped backward to admire herself further. She was wearing a stylish white sundress with spaghetti straps that made her blond hair even more brilliant than usual. Low-heeled white sandals completed the outfit, making her look positively angelic.

"Jacques has no one else in the world but me," she said out loud, her heart giving a painful lurch. Jacques's father seemed to have vanished into thin air. Did he even know his son was in the dungeon at the château?

Jessica remembered that the note Jacques's father had left at the inn had mentioned some friends he was meeting. So it was entirely possible he didn't know about Jacques's arrest. But would he risk coming here even if he did?

"Right now it doesn't matter," she told herself. "Until his father shows up, I have to support Jacques. I have to get in to see him."

She left her room resolutely and walked down the tower steps, wondering how she could persuade the guards to let her see Jacques.

She walked quickly through the corridors of the château. The paintings of Laurent's ancestors scowled down on her from the walls, and she stuck out her tongue at one particularly snobbish-looking woman.

Maybe if I pretend to be Elizabeth, they'll let me in! Jessica thought as she hurried along. *Those stupid guards couldn't possibly tell us apart!*

Jessica had begun forming her plan when she halted in surprise. The door to the dungeon steps was standing wide open. She picked down the stairs. There was no guard. What luck!

177

Jessica stepped carefully down the uneven, cold stone steps, wrinkling her nose in distaste at the familiar, musty smell. It couldn't be healthy to stay in this cold, clammy place for very long. Jacques had to get out of here!

When she reached the bottom of the stairs, Jessica realized that the door to Jacques's cell was open as well. *Where is he?* she thought frantically. *Did they take him to some other cell? Or did they take him directly to prison? I should have stayed here all last night!*

There was something on Jacques's abandoned cot, something white and square. A piece of paper. She entered the cell and sat on the cot, snatching up the paper and realizing her name was written on it. With trembling hands Jessica unfolded the note.

Dear Jessica,

I will always love you. For now I must go away, but I promise you we will meet again. Never forget me, for I will never forget the beautiful American who stole my heart the way I used to steal gems.

Jacques

Jessica felt a wave of relief wash over her like the waves from the Pacific Ocean at home. She held the note up against her wildly beating heart, wishing Jacques could know how much she loved him and how happy she was that he had gotten away.

Oh, Jacques, she thought as tears of joy stung her eyes, *please be safe! Maybe someday we can be together again!*

"Mademoiselle Jessica?" a small voice said.

Jessica started and looked up to see Manon in the doorway of the cell.

"Manon, have you been following me?" Jessica demanded.

Manon's only answer was to stretch out her pudgy little arms, imploring Jessica to pick her up. Jessica couldn't help smiling, and she stood and went to the little girl. She lifted Manon into her arms and hugged her, then sat back down on the cot with the child on her lap.

"What are you doing here?" Jessica asked.

Manon shrugged, then said carefully in English, "I do not know."

"I don't know either," Jessica said frankly.

"What is it?" Manon asked, pointing to the paper, which Jessica still held in her hand.

"This?" Jessica said. "Nothing you need to worry about for a long time." Suddenly she felt chilled. This was no place for a small child. "Let's get out of here. It's cold."

Jessica stood and put Manon down. Then she folded the note twice, creasing it very carefully, and shoved it deep into the one pocket in her dress. She would keep the note for the rest of her life as proof that she had known and loved a handsome French thief named Jacques Savant.

179

"What do you intend to do about the escape of that rapscallion jewel thief?" the countess demanded of the prince and princess, flushing an unnaturally dark shade of red. Laurent wondered if she would soon just blow up, like an overheated balloon.

The older prince took a deep breath.

"We are not even sure of his name, let alone where he may have run to," he said in his most diplomatic voice.

"You should have every guard combing the countryside," the countess continued shrilly.

"They have been searching the grounds since the escape was discovered at dawn," the prince said wearily. Laurent could see the countess was beginning to wear on his father.

"Countess," the princess interjected, "you must not worry yourself over these matters. Please allow my husband to take care of the search for the thief and of his ultimate fate, if we find him. You have your jewels back; what more do you wish?"

"I demand justice!" the countess thundered, almost purple with rage. "Don't you think I know how that boy escaped? It was those horrible au pairs. Those American brats!"

Laurent couldn't let the conversation go on this way.

"No, Countess," he interjected, straining to be

polite. "I can assure you Jessica and Elizabeth had nothing to do with the escape."

"Yes," his father said quickly. "We considered they might be tempted to try to help their friend again, so I had a guard stationed outside their rooms all night. They never left the tower."

"I don't believe it," the countess huffed.

For the first time in dealing with her, Laurent's father looked angry.

"Are you saying you doubt my word and that of my son?" The prince began to drum his fingers on a nearby tabletop, a sure sign that he was about to lose his temper.

Laurent couldn't tell whether the countess was insensitive to the warning in his father's voice or simply too angry to care.

"Your son has been stubborn and disobedient, not to mention disrespectful. Why should I believe anything he says? As for you . . ."

Laurent saw his stepmother go pale and his father's face turn the slightest shade of red.

"Countess, I believe that there are matters in Italy that demand your attention," he said, his tone formal and firm. "I am so sorry you will have to cut your visit short, but I understand that duty calls."

"You are asking me to leave the château?" the countess sputtered. "You are throwing me out?"

"Whatever interpretation you choose," Laurent's father continued. "I am certain you will be happier away from my family and away from France."

"Well," the countess said, squaring her shoulders and taking a deep breath. "It is certainly fortunate our royal houses will not be joined."

"I assure you," Laurent's stepmother said with a smile, "the good fortune is entirely ours." Laurent smothered a laugh as the countess flounced from the room. He hugged each of his parents. "Thank you," he said, his spirit light.

The prince and his stepmother smiled at him.

"Go find your beautiful American, Laurent. Be happy," his father said.

Laurent's heart soared with happiness and love as he turned and hurried from the room. It was time to see Elizabeth!

Elizabeth and Laurent walked across the lawn, hand in hand, just before lunch. The sun was warm and comforting, and the salty sea breeze ruffled Elizabeth's hair gently. The perfectly manicured lawn was a soft carpet beneath her feet, and the château shimmered in the distance like a fairy castle. Her ankle felt better after a few days' rest. In fact, she hardly felt any pain at all.

Elizabeth was content, walking with her prince. But she was also nervous about giving him an answer to his proposal, so she tried to keep the conversation as light as possible.

"Jessica came back from her visit this morning and said Jacques was gone," she began. "Did you have something to do with that?"

Laurent's warm blue eyes sparkled with mischief.

"Elizabeth, some secrets are better left as secrets," he said knowingly. She could tell he was at the bottom of Jacques's escape, and she was grateful. Her impression had always been that Laurent was a fine and noble person. Why had she ever doubted him?

"I thought I saw the countess and Antonia leaving the château this morning. Have they returned to Italy?" she asked, hoping desperately that they were out of her hair forever.

"Oh, yes," Laurent replied, laughing. "And you should have seen the state the countess was in."

"She's always in a state about something," Elizabeth said, rolling her eyes. "What was it this time?"

"She accused you and Jessica of helping Jacques to escape," Laurent explained. "And when I stood up for you, she accused me of being a liar. So my father suggested she might be happier in Italy, and she practically exploded!"

"Oh, no," Elizabeth cried, bursting into laughter. "Your father actually threw them out?"

"I think he would say he reminded them of where they actually belong," Laurent said, still grinning.

She sobered a moment later, though, as she considered Laurent's parents. "How do your parents really feel about your decision not to marry Antonia?" Elizabeth asked, genuinely concerned.

"I was surprised at their reaction," Laurent said. "They're making a real effort to understand how I feel. They told me it's time to make a change in our traditions."

"That sounds encouraging," she said. "I always thought your parents were nice. It must be hard to uphold family traditions, sit at the head of a country, and raise a family, all at the same time." She wasn't just talking about Laurent's parents. She was thinking what it would mean if she was faced with that kind of future.

"I've never been sure how they kept it all together," Laurent admitted. "I suppose I never gave it a lot of thought."

They stopped walking when they reached the edge of the pond, which reflected the sunlight and brightened the day even more. The long, wild grasses that grew just at the water's edge bent gently in the breeze. Elizabeth settled on the grass, patting it with her hand.

"Let's sit here," she suggested.

"What a perfect day!" Laurent said, taking a deep breath of the tangy air.

"Do you remember the first time we came here?" she asked. "I thought it must be the most beautiful place on the whole island."

"It is," he said, "and also my favorite spot to daydream. It's where I first saw the beautiful blond girl who later came into my life."

"We have managed to make some wonderful memories, haven't we?" she said. "The dinner on the beach, even the dance the night of the ball . . . I'll remember all of it, always."

As they sat beside the pond in comfortable silence Elizabeth knew the moment of truth was close at hand. She would have to give her answer to Laurent, and part of her was still undecided. The water glistened in the sunlight, rippling ever so slightly. The trees surrounded them on the outer edge of the lawn, like silent sentries. Even the birds' songs seemed to have a hushed quality about them.

Laurent took her hand in his and lifted it to his lips, kissing it ever so gently.

"Elizabeth, we should talk," he whispered against her hand, looking up at her with his beautiful blue eyes shining.

"Yes, I know," she answered quietly.

"Have you considered my proposal?" he asked.

"Yes, very carefully," she said, thinking of the hours she had spent turning the question over and over in her mind. She looked into his eyes and almost changed her mind again. But she couldn't do that and be true to herself.

She took a deep breath and spoke. "Laurent, I truly love you more than anything in this world, and I believe we could be happy together. But I have a whole other life back in Sweet Valley."

"I know that," Laurent said quietly.

"I have family and friends that I care about. My sister is going home soon, and we've hardly ever been separated since the day we were born," she said, feeling the tears just behind her eyes.

"What are you saying, Elizabeth?" Laurent asked, his eyes suddenly clouding over.

Elizabeth took both of his hands into hers and kissed him deeply, with all the love she felt in her heart. When she pulled away, her heart felt heavy.

"I can't marry you, Laurent."

Laurent was crushed by Elizabeth's words. He had been so sure she would say yes!

"But the way we love each other, Elizabeth," he pleaded, "it is for life!"

Tears welled in the corners of her eyes. "I know, I feel that way too, but—"

"No 'buts,'" he said quickly. "I cannot bear the thought of a life without you by my side!"

"Laurent, please," she said, trying to wipe away her tears with her hands. "We're both so young, we have our whole lives ahead of us. Maybe we will end up together, just not right now."

Laurent leaped up from the grass and paced back and forth. "But I want you now!" he cried, not caring how desperate he sounded. "My parents expect me to marry soon, and I won't marry anyone but you!" He jerked his handkerchief from his pocket and handed it to her. It hurt him to see her crying, but he also couldn't bear the thought of life without her.

"Marriage is such a big step," Elizabeth went on, her voice pleading and reasonable. "I can't just rush into it, even loving you the way I do."

"What can I say to persuade you?" he said wildly. "A long engagement? You could go back to Sweet Valley to break it gently to your parents." Elizabeth just shook her head, and Laurent raked a hand through his hair in desperation. "Tell me what I can do to make you say yes."

"Nothing," she said softly. "Please, Laurent, forgive me for hurting you, but I can't say yes, not right now."

Her gentle, quietly spoken words somehow calmed him. She sat there on the grass, dabbing at her eyes with his handkerchief, her shoulders trembling with silent sobs. His heart felt too large for his chest, and there were tears behind his eyes.

"There is nothing to forgive," he said, and his voice was hoarse with unshed tears.

Elizabeth looked up at him, her blue-green eyes watery and yet more beautiful than he had ever seen them.

"Thank you," she whispered.

Laurent sank back onto the grass, feeling more defeated than if he had just fought a great battle.

"I can't force you to marry me," he said in a softer voice. "It's just that I love you so much. I feel for you what I always thought I should feel for the girl I would marry."

"I feel the same way," Elizabeth said, and she

seemed to be recovering herself. She wiped the corners of her eyes one last time, then held the handkerchief in her lap.

Laurent reached up and pushed a strand of her golden hair back in place.

"Thank you," he said, looking deep into her eyes. "To know that you love me as much as I love you is something I will hold in my heart always."

Elizabeth smiled. "Whoever you marry will be a truly lucky girl. You will be a wonderful husband, Laurent," she said, reaching out to hold his hand.

"Someday," he said and took her hand. "Perhaps you are right, we are too young. If my parents allow me to pick my bride, they should also allow me to marry at whatever age I feel ready."

"Good for you," Elizabeth said encouragingly.

"What do you think our future will really be, Elizabeth?"

"Together?" she teased gently. It was good to see her smile, even if it was a rather watery smile.

"Together, apart, tell me what you think," he coaxed. He put his arms around her, and she leaned in against him.

"I want to pursue a writing career, but I'm not sure whether I want to try for newspapers or magazines," she said thoughtfully. "I almost had a summer job working for a magazine before Jessica persuaded me to come here."

"Are you glad she did?" Laurent asked.

"I am now," she admitted, "though I had doubts at the beginning. What about you, Laurent? What do you want your future to be like?"

"I know I'm destined to rule," Laurent began, choosing his words carefully. "The thought sometimes frightens me. I hope my father lives to a very old age so I'll have enough experience when I take the throne."

"It will be challenging," Elizabeth agreed.

"I will have to marry someday to secure the succession. But hopefully my bride will be someone I know and love." He touched her hair gently and turned her chin up so he could look deeply into her eyes. "Maybe in two or three years I will come to see you in your Sweet Valley."

Elizabeth's blue-green eyes sparkled at his words, and she smiled.

"I would like that very much. Anything is possible, Laurent," she said. He was unable to resist her lips, and she returned his kiss with all the passion he had come to expect.

"Yes," he said softly as he pulled away reluctantly, "anything is possible."

Elizabeth flung her arms around Laurent's neck, laughing and crying at the same time. "Oh, Laurent, whatever else happens, you'll always be my knight in shining armor!"

Chapter 14

"I can hardly believe we're on our way home," Elizabeth cried, watching as the scenery got smaller and smaller while the plane climbed through the clouds.

"Neither can I!" Jessica said, wriggling in her seat. She reached into the seat pocket in front of her and pulled out the in-flight magazine. "I can hardly wait to land."

"We have a few hours yet," Elizabeth said wryly.

Just then the flight attendant approached.

"Would either of you girls like a pillow?" she asked, smiling.

"Yes, please," Jessica said, reaching over her sister to accept the tiny pillow. Elizabeth shook her head no, and the flight attendant moved on.

"Maybe that's the job we should try for next summer," Jessica said.

"What job?" Elizabeth asked, her mind still half consumed by the memory of Laurent.

"Flight attendant, silly!" Jessica said, digging her elbow into Elizabeth's ribs. "Earth to Liz! Earth to Liz!"

"OK, OK," Elizabeth said dismissively. "But I don't think being a flight attendant is such a great idea, Jess. Don't you cause enough trouble on the ground?"

"Very funny," Jessica said with a phony pout. "So what do you want to do next summer?"

"Maybe try out that *Flair* job," Elizabeth said distractedly. She was happy to be heading for Sweet Valley, but there was no denying she was leaving a piece of herself behind. She would never forget Laurent—his kindness, his tenderness, and the warmth of his kisses.

"Think of the stories we have to tell everyone. Lila will be positively green when she finds out a prince asked you to marry him!" Jessica said gleefully.

Lila might be Jessica's best friend, but Elizabeth knew her sister enjoyed taking Lila down a peg once in a while. Elizabeth had to admit she enjoyed it too.

"Even the kids turned out to be OK," Elizabeth said, glad she could put away that stupid baby-sitter's guide forever.

"They got us out of the dungeon, didn't they?" Jessica and Elizabeth laughed together at the memory of sitting in the tiny cell in their ball gowns. How unreal it seemed now that they were on their way home!

"And Jacques," Elizabeth said. "Do you think you'll ever see him again?"

Jessica's eyes glazed over slightly. "I don't know," she said in a dreamy voice. "He was so romantic and mysterious and sexy . . . so French!"

Jessica reached down to her bag, stowed beneath the seat in front of her. She opened it, fished around for a moment, then pulled out her hand.

"I still have the pearl bracelet he gave me," she told Elizabeth, displaying it for her.

"It's so pretty," Elizabeth said, reaching out to touch the tiny beads. "But you know it's probably stolen. Why did you keep it?"

Jessica shrugged. "Something to remember him by." She fastened the clasp and shook her wrist, gazing at the bracelet in admiration. "I wonder if Laurent had anything to do with Jacques's escape. You know I asked him for help, right?"

"I thought so," Elizabeth admitted. "But when I asked Laurent, he wouldn't admit to anything. Do you think the prince and princess really meant it when they said they were glad we'd come?"

"Why wouldn't they be glad?" Jessica demanded. "We did a terrific job with those kids and solved the jewel mystery too!"

Elizabeth laughed. "You're right. Did you hear

about the countess when she left the château?"

"No," Jessica said, her eyes gleaming at the thought of gossip, as always.

"Anna told me the countess threatened to bad-mouth the prince and the princess to the press," Elizabeth said in a lowered voice. "When the prince pointed out that the press could easily find ways to be equally unkind to her, she turned purple and sputtered all the way out to the car."

When their fit of giggles over the countess had passed, Elizabeth found her thoughts even more on Sweet Valley.

"I wonder how Todd is doing," she said softly, a pang in her heart. "I love Laurent, but somehow Todd has been there in my heart too. I can't believe he didn't even bother to write."

Jessica winced at Elizabeth's words. It seemed like ages since she had thrown Todd's letter into the fire, and she had hoped the subject would never come up. She would rather be anywhere else at this moment, knowing she should come clean and confess what she had done. Still, it wasn't fair to deceive Elizabeth any longer.

"Liz, I have something to tell you," she began tentatively.

"What?" Elizabeth asked absently.

"I know you're not going to like it," Jessica continued, trying to put off the moment. She pulled at a loose thread on her seat, unraveling the upholstery. "I just hope you won't get too mad."

"What have you done now?" Elizabeth asked slowly.

"Well . . . um . . . actually it's nothing," Jessica said, chickening out. "Never mind. Just forget it."

"Are you kidding?" Elizabeth exclaimed. "You have to tell me now!"

"Um . . . uh . . ." Jessica was so scared, she was momentarily tongue-tied.

"Tell me!" Elizabeth demanded.

"Well, OK, but just remember, if you kill me, your life will be much less exciting," Jessica said, realizing that if Elizabeth got really mad, there wasn't anyplace she could run and hide on the plane. "Boy, I had no idea how hard this would be!"

"Just say it," Elizabeth prompted.

"Promise you won't get mad?" Jessica asked, hoping that Elizabeth would forgive her sometime this decade.

"Jessica," Elizabeth said in an exasperated voice, "you're really beginning to worry me here. What's going on?"

Jessica took a deep breath. "Todd did write," she said quietly. "But I burned the letter." She closed her eyes and hunched her shoulders slightly, waiting for the storm of Elizabeth's anger to hit.

After a moment she opened her eyes to look at her twin. Elizabeth was sitting openmouthed, her eyes widened in disbelief.

"You burned the letter?" she asked as if she didn't understand the words.

Jessica nodded, then took advantage of Elizabeth's shock. "I thought it was the right thing to do. You were so miserable about breaking up with him, and we had the whole summer ahead of us, and then there was Laurent. . . ." She trailed off lamely.

"You burned it," Elizabeth said again. Tears filled her eyes. "How could you do that to me?"

"It's all right, Liz, yell and scream at me if you want," Jessica said quickly, scared by Elizabeth's understated reaction.

"What a terrible thing to do," Elizabeth said, the tears falling freely now. She wiped them away with her hand and sat quietly for a moment, staring blankly at the seat in front of her. Jessica watched her sister in alarm, wondering when she would explode.

"But if you hadn't done it," Elizabeth said finally, slowly, "I might never have allowed myself to fall in love with Laurent."

"And you would have missed being proposed to by a prince!" Jessica said triumphantly. "So I actually did you a favor!"

"Don't get too smug," Elizabeth said warningly, but Jessica could tell she wasn't mad anymore.

She breathed an enormous sigh of relief and settled back in her seat, knowing that once again she had narrowly escaped disaster.

Much later that night Elizabeth and Todd walked along the beach, hand in hand. *This is where I belong,* Elizabeth thought. The familiar beating of the surf warmed her heart as she breathed in the sweet California air.

"I was sick with worry when you didn't write back," Todd was saying. "I was sure I'd made the biggest mistake of my life. I probably should have figured Jessica was at the bottom of it all."

"Hmmm," Elizabeth replied, unwilling to spoil the serenity she felt with too much talk.

"Hey," Todd said, his voice animated, "did you see much of the scandal that happened with the royal family while you were there?"

"Scandal?" Now Elizabeth was all ears. "What scandal?"

"It was all over the news here," Todd went on. "How the prince announced his engagement then canceled the whole thing. And there was some mystery girl no one knows about who the prince wanted to marry, but she turned him down. I can't believe you, with your reporter's instincts, didn't notice all that was going on."

"Oh, there was some excitement just before we left," Elizabeth said, coughing and clearing her throat in an effort not to burst out laughing. *Imagine if he knew that I'm the mystery girl!* she thought. "But you know, we were there to take care of the kids. That didn't leave time for much else," Elizabeth finished, amused at Todd's excitement over the scandal.

"Elizabeth." Todd's tone turned serious. "Can you ever forgive me for the way I acted before you left?"

Elizabeth turned to face him and looked deep into his warm brown eyes. She could see the love he felt for her, but she couldn't forget how devastated she'd been when she left for France.

"I don't know," she said honestly. "It really hurt to think that you might want to date someone else."

"There isn't any other girl in the world for me," he said passionately, clasping both her hands in his. "And I definitely don't want you to date other guys."

"Are you sure, Todd?" Elizabeth desperately wanted him to say yes, but she also wanted him to be honest. If he really didn't feel the same way about her, then she needed to know. She didn't want to be like Antonia, hanging on to a guy even though he didn't want her.

"Yes, Elizabeth, I'm absolutely sure," Todd stated. "Are you?"

She paused for a moment before replying. A memory of Laurent's handsome, chiseled features flitted through her mind. Elizabeth smiled slightly before pushing the image away. Laurent would always have a piece of her heart, but now that she was home, their love seemed as if it had been a dream. Todd's love was real, and he was here now, ready to open his heart to her.

"I'm sure," she answered honestly, smiling up into his handsome face. "All I want in the world is for us to be together." She cuddled closer to him, and he leaned down and kissed her passionately.

When they parted, Elizabeth pulled his arms around her waist and turned to look out at the water, leaning back against his chest. He nuzzled her neck with his lips, and Elizabeth smiled.

Todd is just as much a part of me now as he was before I left, she thought. *Now I'm truly home.*

The living room was silent as Jessica curled up in her favorite chair and stared out the window at the moon. In her hand she clutched the note Jacques had written to her, now worn around the edges from so many readings. She wondered if he was looking up at the same silver globe hanging in the black sky.

Out of the corner of her eye Jessica saw her mother enter the room.

"Are you still sitting here in the dark?" Mrs. Wakefield asked in an amused voice.

"Hmmm?" Jessica said, looking up.

"Never mind," Alice Wakefield said, waving her hand in dismissal and laughing. "Just let us know when you actually come home."

Jessica watched her mother leave. Maybe Jacques was even thinking of her right this instant, just as she was thinking of him.

"Jacques," she whispered into the empty room, "I miss you so much." Jessica shivered, imagining strong arms wrapped around her.

"Someday we'll meet again."

And in her heart she knew it to be true.

SWEET VALLEY HIGH ™

Don't miss any of this summer's fabulous Sweet Valley High Collections!

Double Love Collection
DOUBLE LOVE
SECRETS
PLAYING WITH FIRE

Summer Danger Collection
A STRANGER IN THE HOUSE
A KILLER ON BOARD

Château D'Amour Collection
ONCE UPON A TIME
TO CATCH A THIEF
HAPPILY EVER AFTER

Flair Collection
COVER GIRL
MODEL FLIRT
FASHION VICTIM